BRIAN FLYNN

AND CAULDRON BUBBLE

Brian Flynn was born in 1885 in Leyton, Essex. He won a scholarship to the City Of London School, and from there went into the civil service. In World War I he served as Special Constable on the Home Front, also teaching "Accountancy, Languages, Maths and Elocution to men, women, boys and girls" in the evenings, and acting in his spare time.

It was a seaside family holiday that inspired Brian Flynn to turn his hand to writing in the mid-twenties. Finding most mystery novels of the time "mediocre in the extreme", he decided to compose his own. Edith, the author's wife, encouraged its completion, and after a protracted period finding a publisher, it was eventually released in 1927 by John Hamilton in the UK and Macrae Smith in the U.S. as *The Billiard-Room Mystery*.

The author died in 1958. In all, he wrote and published 57 mysteries, the vast majority featuring the super-sleuth Antony Bathurst.

BRIAN FLYNN

AND CAULDRON BUBBLE

With an introduction
By Steve Barge

DEAN STREET PRESS

Any work of fiction whose language is entirely cleansed of the idioms and expressions of its time would rightly be condemned—by that fact if by no other—as being an unfaithful witness to the world it seeks to portray. Therefore, no apology can be considered necessary for the occasional term or phrase that reflects the era of this book's original publication, even if some may now view such words with unease.
It is hoped that modern readers will approach these passages with an understanding of the historical context, and with the assurance that no malice was intended then, nor is any endorsed now.

INTRODUCTION

"Having once constructed my main plot, I sit down to write and permit the puppets to do their own dancing."

Thus wrote Brian Flynn in an article for Crime Book Magazine. They had awarded *Black Agent* (1949) the Society's Selection for that issue and asked Brian to introduce himself. While Brian had, until recently, been long forgotten as a crime writer, it is unclear how unknown he was when he was writing his fifty-seven mystery novels. From the tone of the article, it would seem that he viewed himself as something of a lesser author—when mentioning *"the distinguished authors who now write detective stories"* and *"the brilliant examples they constantly offer"* he refers to his own "comparative unworthiness for the fire and burden of the competition." However, he ends that section on a positive note:

"The stars have always been the most desired of all goals, so I allow exultation and determination to take the place of that but temporary dismay".

At this stage of his writing career, Brian was writing exclusively for John Long, a publisher that focussed primarily on the library market. His first book, *The Billiard Room Mystery* (1927), was published by John Hamilton, as were the next four, and then he moved to John Long for the rest of his career. (For the sake of accuracy, I feel that I should note that the first John Long book, *The Five Red Fingers* (1929), was actually published before the last Hamilton book, *Invisible Death* (1929).)

A selection of books was published in the US as well, the last of these being *The Case Of The Purple Calf* as *The Ladder Of Death* in 1935. A few other titles were translated into French (*The Case Of Elymas The Sorcerer* (1945) as Bryan Flynn), German (*The Mystery Of The Peacock's Eye* (1928), *The Horn* (1934) and Swedish (*The Case Of The Black Twenty-Two* (1928)). There is, according to a comment by Brian in an article, also a Danish translation, but I am yet to discover any evidence of this.

In the UK, there were some paperback reprints, all by John Long. A few appeared in their Four-Star Thrillers series, and some later titles such as *Such Bright Disguises* (1941), *Reverse the Charges* (1943) and *The Swinging Death* (1949) in the company's Pocket Editions, alongside such authors as Edgar Wallace, John Creasey and Frances Durbridge. By the time of *Men for Pieces* (1949), Brian's books were solely being printed in hardback, destined primarily for library shelves. Of course, this is one reason why copies of his books are particularly hard to find . . .

For those of you who are new to Brian's work, the majority of his output, fifty-three of his books, featuring the gentleman-detective Anthony Bathurst. One other is a children's book, *Tragedy at Trinket*, which can be recommended if you think most schoolboy murder mysteries don't have enough schoolboy cricket in them or vice versa (and features Bathurst's nephew, despite being published by a different company, Nelson). The final three are the Sebastian Stole mysteries, written under the pseudonym Charles Wogan. Stole is the exiled Crown Prince of Calorania, but his exploits only last three books. While the first book is quite distinctive from the Bathurst mysteries, the third one, *Cyanide For A Chorister* (1950), could have easily been one of Anthony's adventures with only minor alterations, and perhaps that is why this one, published between *Men For Pieces* (1950) and *Black Agent* (1951) was the final case for Stole and thereafter Brian focussed exclusively on Bathurst.

Writing exclusively for one sleuth might be seen as problematic, but it is notable how the style of the books varies as the series goes on, which may well be a reflection of the times as well. The country house settings of some of the early titles has long since gone by the time *Men For Pieces* (1949) is published, and there have been some changes to Brian's writing style. While Bathurst's character remains constant, there are far fewer books that are narrated by a third party—all of the five books from *Men For Pieces* (1949) to *The Ring Of Innocent* (1952) are written in the third person. As the series progresses, there are some books that veer away from the whodunit element as well.

A case could be made for the first such deviation from the norm being the inverted mystery *Such Bright Disguises* (1941), but there is still a whodunnit element at the end of the tale. The first of the out-and-out thrillers, however, was *The Grim Maiden* (1944), swiftly followed by *Conspiracy At Angel* (1947) and *Where There Was Smoke* (1951), all of which being tales of a criminal conspiracy where the story is more about the puzzle of what exactly is going on, rather than the identity of the villain of the piece. There are earlier examples of these conspiracy stories—*The Case Of The Purple Calf* (1934) and *They Never Came Back* (1940) for example, but these also have an unmasking at the end of the tale.

This is a reflection, though, of Brian's overall style at this point. The third person focus on primarily Bathurst and occasionally his co-investigators means that the focus of the book is on the investigation. Once Bathurst arrives on the scene, there are few scenes depicting suspects discussing things—we are exclusively seeing what Bathurst sees. One local newspaper review made comparisons to Freeman Wills Crofts, the creator of Inspector French, and this comparison is a reasonable one. Of course, that may not inspire some readers, as Crofts is one of the authors who has been in the past dismissed as "humdrum", thanks in part to Julian Symons' critique, but the Inspector French books are another until-recently-lost highlight of the Golden Age and I do recommend that readers who have dismissed him give him another go. Once you've read all the available Brian Flynn books, of course. After all, an entire narrative spent in Anthony Bathurst's company is no bad thing.

As there were no reprints of the titles from *Men For Pieces* (1949) onwards, we are lucky to be able to bring these five books to you. We have to thank Brian's estate for *Men For Pieces* as in my eight years collecting his work, I have never seen a copy for sale on the second-hand market. I can see why, as it's a really fun mystery, with Bathurst himself all but dismissing a dead body as suicide (he clearly doesn't realise that he's in a detective novel) until the victim's sister spots that the plug from the bath is in the wrong place! That's enough for our hero to dive into a mystery involving stolen and returned money, a plethora of suspects and a genuine surprise at the end. The original cover billed it as "Tense and Exciting" and they are not far from being wrong.

Black Agent (1950)—at this point Brian was clearly using his Big Book Of Quotations to find his titles—has a typically odd set-up for a Bathurst mystery. Barbara Marsden disappeared without trace from a New Year's party in her village. The only trace is spotted a month later when the distinctive yellow dress she was wearing is spotted being used as a costume in a play, only for the woman wearing it to also disappear . . . It's an original (if odd) concept and once the inevitable bodies appear, Brian does a great job of ratcheting up the tension. We also get another appearance of Bathurst's sort-of love interest and one of the earliest examples of a female Scotland Yard officer, Helen Repton.

The aforementioned *Where There Was Smoke* (1951) goes even further with the odd set-up. Donald Finney, a chemist, is offered work by the mysterious Mr Rehoboam, only for Donald's body to be discovered with no obvious cause of death. Questions abound however. Why was his skin discoloured? How did he have a printed note with the local Inspector Stire's name on it? And why was a piece of cooked bacon rind hidden in his belly button? A thriller following Bathurst's investigations—and there are some impressive Sherlockian deductions that Bathurst makes just from the crime scene—and a really fun adventure. Oh, and there's the only creative use of Alphabetti Spaghetti that I've aware of in a mystery novel . . .

Another Macbeth quote provides the title for *And Cauldron Bubble* (1951) although a reader hoping for a witch related mystery may be disappointed. Back to the whodunnits, and this time Bathurst is investigating a disappearance and a murder. Lady Blanchflower and her companion Mrs Whitburn left *The Red Deer* together after dinner, only for Lady Blanchflower to be found strangled and of Mrs Whitburn, there is no trace. And under Lady Blanchflower's body is, for some reason, a man's wig. This is one of the books where we see Bathurst being more fallible. With mostly just his intuition to go on, he follows several dead ends until the truth is revealed. This is similar to the later serial-killer title, *The Seventh Sign*, although we don't see Bathurst sinking to the same levels of frustration and despair here.

The final book in this set of re-releases is *The Ring Of Innocent* (1952) and we kick off with that old chestnut, the overheard conversation. Martin Scudamore overhears a mention of four rings and that if a certain Mr Lovelace interferes, "I'll slit his throat—without the slightest compunction or hesitation". Scudamore mentions it to Helen Repton, who promptly tells Bathurst, they arrive in time to hear Lovelace's dying message—the two words "*innocent*" and "*teaspoon*". It's a good mystery and moves along at a rapid pace, and, most importantly, is probably the title where we get the most insight into the Bathurst-Repton "relationship".

It brings me great delight that we are able to continue to bring the adventures of Brian Flynn back to the masses. I need to thank the many people who have helped along the way to revive Anthony Bathurst, but most importantly the late Rupert Heath, without whom Brian Flynn—and many other authors—would still be naught but a memory.

Steve Barge

PART ONE

THE DEATH OF A KNIGHT

CHAPTER 1

1

The long and distinguished life of Sir Hugo Theodore Stapleton Blanchflower was drawing peacefully to its close. That the end would be entirely tranquil when it came, was assured. All the conditions of his passing had to do with peace and peacefulness.

Sir Hugo was in his ninety-second year and the grand old man, his frame unravaged by disease, was just gently easing his fingers from their clutch on life. And not only the manner—the place of his dying was also embraced by serenity, for Sir Hugo, as a knight of an Order of Chivalry, that of the Grand Star of Africa, had enjoyed, with his wife, Lady Blanchflower, the privilege, by grace and favour, of residence for many years in the cloisters of the castle of Quinster.

The castle itself was occupied at the time this story opens by the fourteenth Duke of Quinster. The apartments that had thus been provided were small, but ample for the needs of Sir Hugo and Lady Blanchflower. The respective rooms were tastefully furnished and had been a comfortable and delightful home for Sir Hugo and Lady Blanchflower in the winter of their lives. The latter, her mind storm-tossed and anxious, sat in the tiny lounge on the evening on which this story opens. A book was in her hands, but her eyes were scarcely ever on its pages and she read from it but seldom. Louisa Elizabeth Bonnammy had been a famous beauty when King Edward the Seventh was Prince of Wales and a prominent figure in society for some years after he came to the throne—until, in fact, she had met and married Hugo Blanchflower. Now, at her age in the early eighties, she held the merited reputation of being a very beautiful old woman. Her white hair was still wavy and her eyes very blue and still magnificent, like two brilliant little lamps in her head.

As she sat in the lounge of her apartments in the castle of Quinster on this evening in late September, there was one dominant thought in her mind. That her husband, Hugo, her very dear husband Hugo, her constant companion for over sixty years, was dying. That his death . . . and the parting which it would mean for her . . . the wrench from which she winced . . . were at the most, but a matter of a few hours distant. For some time now she had endeavoured to prepare herself for this inevitable separation . . . but the preparation had not been easy for her, or her will towards it whole-hearted. Perhaps she had been to blame for this . . . perhaps she had never disciplined herself enough to . . . .

A soft rustle in the room close to her arrested and momentarily diverted her thoughts. It was the nurse from her husband's bedside. The nurse had come into the room and was standing by her chair. Lady Blanchflower searched her face anxiously. She closed the book and held it to her breast. But no question came from her lips.

"Will you please come, my Lady?" said the nurse quietly. "Sir Hugo is asking for you."

Lady Blanchflower put her book on a table and rose to her height—she was tall for a woman and her figure was astonishingly straight considering the number of her years.

"Is it? . . ." she asked uncertainly.

The nurse seemed to understand the entire meaning of the question. "I'm afraid . . . that it may be," she answered. Lady Blanchflower started and quivered—almost as though she had been struck. Then she steadied herself with an effort and slowly followed the nurse out of the lounge and to the bedside of her dying husband.

2

As his wife entered the bedroom, the eyes of Sir Hugo Blanchflower were closed. His right arm lay outside the coverlet. An arm, once strong, now weak with age. Lady Blanchflower looked down at the bed and, as she did so, Sir Hugo's eyes opened and met those of his wife. They seemed to scrutinise . . . to study her . . . with an odd quality of intelligence and superior understanding. As though, almost, Sir Hugo was able to read something on her face that was neither known to her, nor even visible to any other person.

Lady Blanchflower shrank from this strange scrutiny. It seemed uncanny and perhaps not really of this world. "Hugo," she said—but no answer came to her. The great hollow eyes of the dying man flickered at her for a stabbing second—but that was all.

The nurse, quick-footed, moved silently towards his pillow. She bent down to the sick man and Sir Hugo shook his head and opened his lips to speak. The words came slowly and with great difficulty.

"Will you please leave us for a little while? I want . . . to speak . . . to my wife."

The nurse nodded, motioned to Lady Blanchflower, and slid noiselessly from the room. Sir Hugo beckoned to Lady Blanchflower with the fingers of his right hand. "Come . . . my dear."

She went to him and bent down lovingly. "I'm leaving you, my dear," whispered Sir Hugo; "not long now. Leaving you for the last time. Kiss me, Lily darling."

The tears rushed to her eyes at his use of the old love-name. She kissed him softly on the lips. Sir Hugo began to speak again—but the effort became too much for him and for some minutes he lay quite still at the point of exhaustion. His wife stared down at him, distressed and anxious. He was going—there was no doubt about it . . . it was impossible for her to think otherwise. But suddenly the flame of Life flared up again and the grand old man rallied. He made a sign to her that she was quick to understand. But the words that he spoke were feeble and so that she should hear them properly she was forced to place an ear almost to his lips. Sir Hugo was speaking in a last effort. The words dropped from him slowly . . . like drips from a defective tap.

"Something I must tell you, my dear . . . something I've kept from you all these years . . . purposely . . . in case the knowledge upset you . . . but a man should unburden himself on his deathbed . . . confess all he has to confess . . . put your ear closer, my dear . . . and listen . . . because you'll need all your courage . . . " Lady Blanchflower obeyed Sir Hugo's request and she listened to his last words. As it happened he had been only just in time. Then came the final quick quiver of blood, the ashen pallor and the sob of breath that slowly and gradually lessened into silence.

The head of the gallant old man sank for the last time on the pillow. Sir Hugo Theodore Stapleton Blanchflower had answered the call from the Supreme Commander and had been gathered to his fathers!

But his widow's grief at his passing was tinged by another emotion. For her, something like Terror had joined hands with Sorrow . . . as she stood there by the bedside . . . thinking of what she had just been told and gazing down at the dead man whom she had called husband.

PART TWO

THE LIFE OF A LADY

CHAPTER 1

1

It was a Thursday evening during the first week of November, five years after the death of Sir Hugo Blanchflower and the events related. The dining-room of the Red Deer at Quinster, in the county of Downshire, was rather more than comfortably full and indeed much more than usually full. Ordinarily at this time of the year no more than four dining-tables would be occupied on evenings other than Saturday or Sunday. At these ordinary times there would be Mr. and Mrs. Danbury in the right-hand corner by the window; next to them, on the other side of the window, Mr. and Mrs. Grahame and in the centre of the dining-room, Mrs. Whitburn with her inseparable evening companion, Lady Blanchflower.

These six people comprised what John Melville, the proprietor and host of the Red Deer called his 'permanent residents'. Casual diners would normally at this season of the year take up perhaps one additional table, but on this particular evening, there were half a dozen tables in full requisition, and at a seventh sat yet another solitary diner who appeared to be a stranger to all the other occupants of the room.

Bassett, the waiter, gave a quick glance round the company and nonchalantly flicked the corner of one of the tables with his table-napkin. The flick was expert and adroit—the outward and visible sign of Bassett's superb professional aplomb. It was the gesture that usually accompanied the presentation of the wine-list.

On the evening in question, his trained eye took in the fact that the Danburys and the Grahames of his 'regulars' as he termed them, were already seated and expectant, and that several gentlemen were at various other tables—some of whom he immediately recognised as irregular regulars. If that apparent contradiction needs explanation it may be stated that they belonged to the commercial traveller representation and several of them had used the Red Deer for years whenever they were on the road in that particular area. Bassett nodded genially to the man who, by general consent, seemed to be the senior of the party.

"Good evening, Mr. Chester come to see us again, then?"

"That's right," returned Walter Chester with a smile, "just for a couple of days, Bassett. How's everything?"

"Might be worse, sir. Though that seems difficult to believe. Will you leave it to me—for your table—I mean?"

Chester grinned at the waiter. "O.K. Bassett. Do us as well as you can. Most of us have had a pretty thick day. And it's beer in tankards for all my chaps."

Bassett spoke from the side of his mouth. "It *might* be fillet steaks. You never know. I'll see what old Charlie says. Charlie—the monarch of the ruddy kitchen. The cunning old basket. Be seeing you, sir."

Bassett floated away towards his permanent regulars and Chester turned towards the other men at his table. They represented different and widely-varied industries. Chester himself (with the firm since a lad in his 'teens) was Area Supervisor (South-Western) for the Novis Bread Company. Jim Ashdown had been on the road something like thirty-four years for the 'Green Star' Meat Combine. Arthur Stewart had carved himself a comfortable niche on the Sales side of the Derwent Motor Company, and Gavin Crawford, the fourth occupant of the table, was well on the way to the top of the Sales Department ladder in the service of the Rose Petal Soap Associated Companies Ltd.

Walter Chester hinted to them as he turned, as to what Bassett might do for them in food terms with the despot of the Red Deer kitchen. There were murmurs of gratified assent at what he said. Trust Walter Chester to work the oracle if such a thing were at all possible. Walter Chester most certainly knew all his vegetables. Walter Chester's colleagues were of one mind with regard to that!

2

Bassett, smiling and assured, appeared at Chester's table again in due season. The plates he carried on his tray bore ample testimony to the power of his half-promise and the quality of his personal diplomacy. Old Charlie had exuded magnanimity for once in a way and 'done them well'. As Bassett turned to leave the table, Chester spoke.

"Something missing this evening, Bassett. That is to say, to an old hand here like me."

The waiter turned in some surprise. "Missing, Mr. Chester? How do you mean?" Bassett's eyes surveyed the dining-table and its contents.

"No—not here. Nothing of that kind. You don't get me. Centre table." Chester nodded.

Bassett turned quickly as his mind took in Chester's meaning. "Oh— our two ladies! I didn't get you."

As he spoke Bassett's eyes went to the clock on the mantelpiece. "They'll be along, Mr. Chester—don't you worry. They're usually a minute or two behind the rest of the company. Lady Blanchflower's gettin' a bit slow on her pins these days. Not to be wondered at, Mr. Chester. If I'm as well as she is at that age you'll hear no complaints from me. Eighty-seven last March you know."

The waiter bustled off to the lonely stranger whom he had seen beckon to him. Arthur Stewart, the motor-salesman, who had overheard part, at least, of Chester's recent conversation with the waiter, looked up at Chester with a question his lips.

"Isn't there something of a story attached to the two old girls? I seem to fancy I've heard you hint on occasion at something of the kind. Remember, I've been using this place for only the last eighteen months— by no means so well up in its history as you are, Walter."

Chester laughed as he put down his tankard. "Hardly a story, Arthur. Just a sort of interesting touch. You couldn't reasonably call it much more than that. Want to hear it?"

"Tell me," said Stewart simply. "That's what I want you to do."

"Well—it goes back to just over five years ago. I may as well start at the right place—the beginning. In the September of that year . . . "

Chester paused abruptly and looked across the dining-room. There was a stir at the entrance to the dining-room. Stewart saw the waiter cross towards the door.

"Hang up a minute," said Walter Chester to Stewart, "here they are."

3

At that moment there entered the dining-room of the Red Deer, two elderly ladies. And, at the entrance, where they were greeted by Melville, the proprietor of the Red Deer, the noise and chatter which had prevailed at the different tables, suddenly and abruptly died away. The two ladies who had entered accepted the tribute to the manner born. Imperturbable, distinguished, debonair they made their way to the centre table with Bassett as their escort, and as they took their seats the restless hum of the dining-room gradually came into being again.

Lady Blanchflower, still tall and striking despite her advanced age, walked on the arm of her companion, Mrs. Whitburn. The latter was trim and *petite*—the complete antithesis it may be said of Lady Blanchflower, who wore black in accordance with her almost invariable habit. Mrs. Whitburn, on the other hand, was attired in a pleasing shade of dove-grey.

As they passed the table at which Walter Chester sat with his three professional colleagues, he gave Lady Blanchflower his customary smile and semi-bow. For a fleeting second, it appeared that she had not noticed the gesture. Her returning smile, normally so charming, was a little late, but it eventually came and Chester, a trifle relieved, smiled back again. He failed, however, to catch the eye of Laura Whitburn. This occasioned him no surprise as the lady's short-sightedness was well-known to him.

The deferential Bassett stood by the centre table and awaited orders. Mrs. Whitburn's hand took and carefully unfolded her table-napkin.

"I'm sorry, Bassett," she said in a clear voice which was heard by most of the people in the room, "that we're a little late for dinner this evening. You must excuse us. But Lady Blanchflower has a chill . . . and it's a trifle misty out of doors . . . nothing like as bad yet, though, as the radio predicted . . . anyhow, our little journey wasn't quite as simple as it is on most evenings. What is there for us?"

Mrs. Whitburn extended her hand for the menu. Bassett conveyed it to her with the air of a magician dealing with a top secret. Laura Whitburn began to order . . . for herself and then, after the exchange of some little conversation, for her aged companion.

Walter Chester, during the meal that followed, stole more than one glance in the direction of the centre table. It seemed to him, who had known the two ladies for something like a matter of four years, that Time had at long last begun to take its toll of Lady Blanchflower. Eighty-seven last March—eh? Well—it was only to be expected!

4

Arthur Stewart, the Sales representative of the Derwent Motor company, had made several attempts during dinner to induce Chester to finish the story he had been about to tell at the moment the two ladies had entered the dining-room. But on each and every occasion he had made such an attempt, Chester had put him off.

"Wait for it now, Arthur. Wait for it until after dinner. My voice is apt to carry rather—at least so most of my friends tell me and I should hate either of our ladies to hear me discussing her or them. Because I've a particularly warm corner in my old heart for both the old dears. Lady B. is the widow of a man who was by way of being a grand seigneur in his time, and I have the highest possible regard too, for Mrs. Whitburn. You've heard of K. M. R. Whitburn, haven't you?"

Stewart repeated the initials after Chester. "K.M.R.? Seems to ring a bell somewhere. Oh—I know—I've got you. You mean the Kent skipper before the war? Am I right?"

"You are. That's the man. That lady in the grey's his mother. She's nothing like as old as Lady B.—of course. All the same—she's well over seventy. But leave it there until the pipes are going in the lounge after dinner. Then I'll give you the gen."

Stewart grinned almost impishly at the speaker. "You're certainly making me wait for it, Walter."

Chester shook his head. "Not at all. What I'm afraid of is that you're expecting too much and that you'll be frightfully disappointed. There's nothing like a story coming—as I warned you just now. Just a mere—"

Ashdown, from the seat farthest from Chester, leant across the table. "What are you and Arthur in such a huddle about? Nattering at each other like a couple of wenches in a girls' choir! What's more to the point—I'm ordering another round of beer. Are you in?"

"You ought to know by now, Jim," returned Chester, "not to ask ruddy silly questions. Of course we're in." Ashdown laughed and beckoned to the waiter. Bassett slid noiselessly to the table.

5

Chester lit a cigarette from a packet and fanned away the smoke from his eyes. His three companions of the dining-room sat with him in the smoking-lounge. The Danburys and the Grahames had either made tracks for the other lounge or gone out to a cinema, and the 'casual' diners had disposed of themselves elsewhere. Lady Blanchflower and Laura Whitburn were still at dinner. Stewart had taken his seat by the fire and reminded Chester of his promise.

"Come on now, Walter—this is the place and the time—let's have the doings. Somehow or other you've got me much more than normally interested. Let's have it, old man! The Queens of Quinster!"

Chester smiled benevolently at his friend and shook his head—much as he had at dinner in the previous conversation with Stewart.

"I always thought," he said, "and I've always been led to believe, that curiosity was the feminine vice. Now I'm beginning to think differently. But this is the way it goes. Lady Blanchflower is the widow of the late Sir Hugo Blanchflower."

Stewart's mouth rounded with surprise. "What—the distinguished soldier? Of the famous African campaign?"

Chester nodded corroboration. "That was the old boy. Grand old character, I should say from all that I've been told about him. When he put 'em all up his chest was almost covered. Well—he and his wife lived in the cloisters over the way there." Chester half-turned and jerked his head in what he considered was the appropriate direction.

"In the castle—do you mean?" queried Crawford.

"In the castle. In the castle of Quinster. It was a privilege to which I understand Sir Hugo Blanchflower was entitled by reason of his own special brand of knightly order. The Duke of Quinster allowed it, by what is known as grace and favour. Well just over five years ago—when he was well over ninety—Sir Hugo in the natural order of things was gathered to his fathers. Which *should* have meant that Lady B. had to clear out. That is one of the conditions, so I'm told, inseparable from the privilege. Upon the decease of the privileged knight the widow's claim to his residence—should there be a widow—ceases."

"Damned hard luck," said Ashdown, "for an old lady of that age."

"As you say, Jim. Extremely bad luck. Nobody could agree with you more. But there you are—you know how it is with many of these old customs and traditions. When you go into them you often find that there are surprising snags attached to them—things you'd never believe possible if you didn't know all the various ins and outs. Anyhow—in the case that we're talking about—Lady B. didn't take her impending dismissal from the cloisters of Quinster Castle lying down. She put up no end of a fight before she'd haul down her flag. She's a last-ditcher if ever there were one. She saw the Duke of Quinster himself, stated her case, paraded the number of her years, flaunted her late husband's absolutely wizard war record and her own state of loneliness and eventually gained the day. Rumour—and well-foundationed rumour too—has it that an influence was at work on her behalf—actually higher than that of the Duke himself. You can guess whom I mean," concluded Chester significantly.

There were murmurs of surprised interest from his hearers. "By Jove—eh," murmured Crawford, "the old lady's pretty well placed then, if that's the case. Or the old man must have been. I had no idea."

Chester interrupted him. "In the days of Edward the Seventh, of august and revered memory—ahem—Lady Blanchflower was one of *the* recognised beauties who decorated Court circles. She was a Miss Bonnammy. One of the most glamorous debs. of her day. But don't keep chipping in, you chaps, let me finish. Otherwise I shan't finish and Arthur Stewart here will spend a sleepless night. This is how the rest of it goes. Ever since Lady B. gained the day with His Grace the Duke of Quinster with regard to staying on at the castle she has lived alone in her old apartments in the cloisters of Quinster Castle. She manages for herself as best she can with a minimum of help and I understand from what she has told me from time to time that she's one of those fortunate people who are quite happy living alone. Eventually though, the rationing conditions of the war got her down. Food's a pretty grim prospect, you know, these days, for a person with but one ration-book. Many of 'em to my own personal knowledge—grand old people in their respective ways—are half-starved. Their meagre incomes don't allow them to eat out—and well— there you are—that's just one of those things.

"Lady B. however, doesn't belong to that class—financially she's comfortably placed at least—and after a time on her own she began to look round for a place where she could get a decent dinner in the evenings. She told me all this herself a year or two ago now—so I know I'm giving you the authentic gen. Eventually, she thought of this show—the Red Deer. That would be, I suppose, about four years ago."

Chester stopped to make some sort of mental calculation. "Yes—that's right—four years ago in December. Well—at that time there were three couples resident here who were what is usually referred to by John Melville as 'permanents'. The Grahames and the Danburys whom you know—they were dining here this evening—and Mr. and Mrs. Whitburn. Old man Whitburn had been on 'Change, had prospered exceedingly— and had retired. He always said that the life here suited him down to the ground. Told me that frequently. He was near Town—he had the river here—and the Red Deer cuisine has always been tip-top. As all of us here know—none better. He and Mrs. Whitburn liked the theatre, and their weekly Bridge parties—there were Lords and the Oval handy in the summer—and well—there you are—old Whitburn used to say that the Red Deer, from all points of view, was just his cup of tea. I mention these things to let you know that Mrs. Whitburn hasn't always been in the place on her own. Well—as I indicated just now, Lady B. fixed up to come here every evening for dinner. Which is what she's still doing. But for about a year now however she has felt that her age is at last beginning to tell on her, especially, so I understand with regard to her legs. So somewhere about this time last year she made an arrangement with her friend Mrs. Whitburn." Chester paused, to take the cigarette which he noticed Ashdown was offering him. He lit up from the proffered match and then continued his story.

"By this time, Mrs. Whitburn had been widowed—like Lady B. herself—but as most of you probably guess, she's about a dozen years Lady B.'s junior. The arrangement Lady B. made with her with regard to the evening meal was this. Every evening about half an hour before dinner is served here, Mrs. Whitburn just crosses the road and journeys over to the cloisters at Quinster Castle in order to escort Lady Blanchflower over here to dinner. I suppose the distance is about three hundred yards. You saw them arrive together this evening—they were a few minutes late, as you observed. When the time comes after dinner for Lady Blanchflower to think she wishes to return to her own fireside, Mrs. Whitburn will escort her back again. There you are, Arthur, now you know as much as I do. Pour me out some more beer. It's damned dry work—talking."

Stewart smiled and shook his head. "One or two of those concluding remarks of yours sound to me a bit cryptic. When the time comes after dinner for Lady Blanchflower to think—"

Chester cut him *sans* ceremony. "Nothing cryptic about that, I assure you. All I meant was this: sometimes Lady Blanchflower is escorted back to the cloisters directly after she's finished dinner—but on other occasions when she feels like it she'll go into the other lounge and chat with one or two people who may happen to be there. I'm often favoured in that particular respect—I can tell you. It's my belief she took a fancy to me in the early days. But there you are—you can't tell. It's on the cards I suppose that she did nothing of the sort. All the same, she nearly always has a word with me when I'm here, before dinner or after. Unless, of course, she isn't too well. Perhaps she's a bit under the weather this evening. After all eighty-seven's a great age and very few of us are spared to reach it. What do you say, you chaps—shall we have some more bottles of beer in?"

There came a chorus of assent from the others. Chester leant forward and put his finger on the bell. After he had given the order, Ashdown shot a further question at him. "Didn't the Blanchflowers have any family? Or is the old lady entirely alone in the world?"

Chester hesitated a trifle before he replied. The hesitation was all the more noticeable because in Walter Chester, it was a most unusual happening.

"I'm not altogether sure about that," he answered slowly—"you see I've known Lady Blanchflower only in the evening of her life. But I believe there was a son. An only son. How old he would be today I have no idea. Something of a ne'er-do-well, I believe. I certainly recall hearing something of that kind. He went abroad when he was quite a young chap. But I know so little about the circumstances that I can't really say anything."

"Strange that," commented Ashdown with a shake of the head, "a grand old couple like that—and the son of the union turns out a bad hat. I've known it before, though. More than one instance, too. Why do those things happen?"

"Two reasons," contributed Stewart jocularly, "the first—that every child that's born has four grandparents (dead or alive). From which figure you can start multiplying to reach something like the number of the long ancestral line. And if that line isn't studded somewhere with vice of some sort—I should say it's unique! The second reason is eminently simple—it's just the law of cussedness," Stewart concluded with a well-timed shrug of the shoulders.

"Just a minute," contributed Chester judicially, "aren't you by way of contradicting yourself? The first reason that you put forward is based on the influences of heredity—and the second—well it's just no reason at all. You say Nature takes it into her head to go all cussed. The two points don't square up to my way of thinking. They're definitely opposed to each other."

Before Stewart could defend his statements, Crawford had interposed with a question.

"Never mind about that. Let's get down to realities. Because they're something you can't play ducks and drakes with. What happened to old Mr. Whitburn?"

"He died about a couple of years ago. Here in this hotel. But he'd ailed for some time. The war finished him off, I should say. Something internal at the end."

Chester turned the screw-stopper of another bottle of beer and filled the various glasses. "After his death, Mrs. Whitburn decided to stay on here. John Melville, the proprietor was glad to retain her and he makes her as comfortable, I should say, as is humanly possible. With the Grahames and the Danburys, she makes a nice sort of nucleus for him, especially during the winter months when business slacks off. Mrs. Whitburn can still visit the places in Town that used to appeal to her and to her husband. In that way she keeps in touch with old friends and retains many old-established contacts that are, no doubt, pleasing to her. For her years she gets about a good deal. I think she made a very wise decision when she decided to stay on." Chester looked round the circle. "Anybody care for a game of snooker before we hit the hay?"

"Yes," said Ashdown, 'I would. In fact nothing would suit me better."

"Right-o then," replied Chester, "see you chaps for a nightcap round about eleven. Come on, Jim. And I'll bet you a pint I'll blow the living daylights out of you."

"That's on," replied Ashdown.

PART THREE

THE DEATH OF A LADY

CHAPTER 1

1

John Melville, the middle-aged proprietor of the Red Deer at Quinster was at work in his private office on the following morning. He preferred the early hours for his office work by reason of their greater degree of quietude. He had always detested the accountancy side of his business and on the morning in question, nothing was happening with regard to the balancing of his books which would cause him to revise that opinion. He was frowning over a recently discovered miscast which had previously eluded him when there came an unusually quiet tap on his door. A most abnormal happening for this time of the morning. Melville, with his customary geniality called out "come in." Somewhat to his surprise, Bassett, the waiter, entered. Melville looked up from his ledger, the column of which (as usual) he had addled up. It was a most extraordinary occurrence for Bassett of all people to trouble him at this time of the morning! Melville glanced across at the clock on the mantelpiece. Why—it wasn't ten o'clock yet. His frown developed as he spoke to the waiter.

"I don't want to hear about it, Bassett whatever it may be. In other words—won't it wait?"

Instead however of Bassett grinning back at him as he had anticipated, the waiter appeared awkward and anxious. "I'm afraid it won't, sir," he replied, "at least that is to say . . . if what Street says is true." Bassett paused abruptly—still awkward and still anxious.

Melville looked up from his accounts again. His mind seemed far away. It came back tardily to gather up the waiter's words. "Street?" he enquired vaguely.

Bassett became stolid and poker-faced. "Yes, sir. Street sir. That is to say Bella, sir—the chambermaid." Melville's mind had now come back completely from wherever it had been. "What does Bella say, then, that may or may not be true? And that brings you in here to pester me when I'm already being pestered by rows and rows of ruddy figures?"

Bassett swallowed hard twice and crossed the Rubicon. "I wouldn't have bothered you, sir, but for Bella beggin' me to. She explained that if she reported it to Mrs. Barlow, Mrs. Barlow would have come straight to you."

Bassett paused again and took the final fence with a rush. "But the fact is, sir—accordin' to Bella, that Mrs. Whitburn isn't in her room this morning—and what is more important, perhaps, her bed doesn't appear to have been slept in. It's all clean, sir . . . and . . . er . . . undisturbed. They are the facts, sir, which Bella Street, the chambermaid requested me to report to you."

Melville pushed away his account-books, put down his pen and stared hard at Bassett. He stared in this way for some seconds. Then he shook his head slowly and said, "I'm sorry Bassett, but I just don't get it."

2

"Perhaps Mrs. Whitburn's been taken ill. Get hold of Mrs. Barlow," continued Melville, "and we'll go up to the room and have a look. If you ask me, though, the chambermaid's gone daft. Go and fetch Mrs. Barlow."

Bassett said "very good, sir," and went in search of the housekeeper. He knew what a stickler the boss was for the proprieties.

Melville rose from his chair and waited for the others on the threshold of his office. Bassett and Mrs. Barlow didn't keep him waiting long. The latter was certainly not of the normal housekeeper type. On the other hand she was a distinctly attractive *divorcée*—in the late thirties only. Melville wasted neither words nor time.

"Sorry to trouble you, Mrs. Barlow—know how busy you are at this time in the morning. Has Bassett told you what I wanted?"

An attractive light showed in Mrs. Barlow's grey-blue eyes. Melville often saw it. Mrs. Barlow was aware that he often saw it. Mrs. Barlow's knowledge of her vegetables was very sound indeed. "Something about Mrs. Whitburn, isn't it, Mr. Melville? Didn't I hear Bassett say?"

"Yes. Not in her room this morning—and the bed not slept in. That's the chambermaid's story, as relayed to me by Bassett here. Still—I suppose we shall have to have a look and see for ourselves. You and Bassett come upstairs with me—will you? If two heads are better than one, the superiority of three should be immeasurable. No argument necessary there, is there?" He turned to Bassett with a question. "Where's the chambermaid now?"

"Still upstairs, I believe, sir."

"O.K. So she'll be to hand in the event of being needed for anything? That's what I wanted to make sure of. Good. Shall we?" He walked from his doorway and gestured towards the main staircase. As Melville strode along the spacious corridor, Bassett and Mrs. Barlow fell into line behind him.

3

They passed Bella Street, the chambermaid, a few yards from the door of Laura Whitburn's room. Her face suggested that her mind had lost its way years before and was still locked out. The rest of her body appeared to be waiting by predestination for the next celebration in honour of Guido Fawkes, that well-meaning and high-principled Yorkshireman.

When Melville appeared round a bend in the corridor, the chambermaid had opened her mouth as though about to address him. But Melville had promptly gestured her to silence and had passed on with Bassett and Mrs. Barlow to the door of Mrs. Whitburn's room. The door was closed and Melville pushed it open.

His first glance was directed to the bed. There was no doubt that Bella Street's ideas with regard to it not having been slept in were incontestable. Melville looked puzzled. He turned and gave the room a more comprehensive look than he had given it on the occasion of his entrance. Then he spoke quietly to the housekeeper.

"Have a look in the bathroom, Mrs. Barlow, will you please? She may have been taken ill just before she went to bed. You know what I mean," he corrected himself, "it may have come on her when she was preparing for bed."

Mrs. Barlow nodded her understanding and went through to the adjoining bathroom. She was back in the bedroom in a matter of seconds.

"Nobody in there, Mr. Melville. And no sign of any recent occupation. All in order in fact."

Melville sat on a chair and rubbed the ridge of his jaw. There was no doubt that he was apprehensive.

"Can't make it out. Can't make it out at all. Let's try a spot of reconstruction. That's the best thing we can do. When was Mrs. Whitburn last seen?"

Bassett was quick to reply. "At dinner last evening, sir. As usual. She and Lady Blanchflower came in about ten minutes to seven. Five minutes late. It was a bit misty if you remember and it hung 'em up a bit."

Melville nodded to the waiter. "Well—that's all right. How about afterwards? After dinner? At what time did she take Lady Blanchflower back to the castle? Any idea?"

Bassett shook his head. "I wouldn't know, sir. After dinner was over they may have gone into one of the lounges—I couldn't say. But I saw them leave the dining-room soon after eight o'clock."

"We can check that in any case. Mrs. Grahame or Mrs. Danbury will know. One of 'em's bound to have seen her. How did Mrs. Whitburn seem during dinner?"

Bassett hesitated at the question. At last he said, "Well, sir, I did think she was a bit on the lively side. For her."

Melville furrowed his brows. "For her?" he repeated.

"Yes, sir. She was on the quiet side at dinner in the ordinary way, as you know. Lady Blanchflower was the one for the conversation. Last evening they was both rather lively." Bassett stopped but before Melville could make further comment on his statements, he had gone on again. "Another thing, Mr. Melville, she seemed to be a bit . . . well . . . excited . . . at least that was my opinion."

"How do you mean—excited? For heaven's sake, Bassett, don't be so ridiculously vague."

"Well—it's difficult to put into words, sir . . . but she seemed to be watching Lady Blanchflower . . . nearly all through dinner. As though they was sharing some kind of secret. I think they've been like that for about a week—now I come to look back on it. She told me Lady Blanchflower had a chill when they first sat down at table. Perhaps it was on Mrs. Whitburn's mind as you might say and she was trying to keep things cheerful." Melville shook his head as though he were besieged by doubts of all kinds.

"What sort of meal did they have? Anything unusual about it?"

"Nothing, sir." Bassett was emphatic. "Typical, sir. Absolutely typical. No sauces for Lady B. and her customary glass of Amontillado with the soup and half-bottle of Veuve Clicquot '42 to follow."

"H'm. Well—it beats me." Melville sat and thought. Suddenly, he looked up. "Clothes, Bassett? Or perhaps Mrs. Barlow can help us better in that direction? Where did Mrs. Whitburn put her coat after she escorted Lady Blanchflower in? I mean—customarily? I have my own idea with regard to it—I'd like it confirmed."

Mrs. Barlow replied without the slightest hint of hesitation. "She used to hang it on the first peg on the row of pegs in the passage that leads to the billiard-room. She used to go straight there before entering the dining-room. She did *not* bring it up here to this room. Obviously—to have it at hand when she needed it for the return journey when she saw Lady Blanchflower home safely. I've seen it on that peg—the peg I told you—well—scores of times."

Melville nodded corroboration. "That's exactly as I remember it. So that *now* it should be in this room. Mrs. Whitburn used to return from the castle and nine times out of ten, come straight up to her room. More than that—ninety-nine times out of a hundred. Agree with me?"

Bassett said, "I wouldn't know, sir."

Mrs. Barlow nodded in vigorous acquiescence. "I certainly agree, Mr. Melville."

Melville rose from the chair. "In that case, then—let's look in the wardrobe. Can you remember the coat she wore last evening, Mrs. Barlow?"

"I didn't actually see it, Mr. Melville. But for some fortnight now, Mrs. Whitburn's been wearing her fur coat. She would certainly have worn it last evening—on account of the mist."

Melville motioned towards the wardrobe. "See if you can see it, Mrs. Barlow."

The housekeeper went to the wardrobe and opened the door. Melville and Bassett stood behind her. Mrs. Barlow slid occupied dress and coat-hangers along rails.

"It's not here, Mr. Melville," she announced.

"Sure?" he questioned.

"Look for yourself. There's no fur coat in here." Mrs. Barlow stood back.

"True enough," said Melville.

"It would appear to me," said the housekeeper, "that we've hit on the solution of Mrs. Whitburn's absence."

"How come?"

"Why—just this. As I see things now—I don't think there's anything really to worry about. Mrs. Whitburn took Lady Blanchflower back to the cloisters after dinner last evening. Lady Blanchflower was taken ill or something like that before Mrs. Whitburn had time to come away—and Mrs. Whitburn just wasn't able to leave her. She spent the night in Lady Blanchflower's apartments and will come back here later on." Melville's face cleared and even Bassett contrived a degree of cheerfulness.

"Mrs. Barlow," said Melville, "you've taken a load off my mind. Of course! That's almost certainly what's happened. Why didn't I think of it? We'll telephone over to the cloisters immediately and make sure. Now why the heck didn't I think of that perfectly simple explanation?"

As they reached the bottom of the staircase, Mrs. Barlow turned and said, "Shall I 'phone or will you?" Melville looked at his wrist-watch, thought of his unbalanced ledgers and smiled. Then he patted his housekeeper on the shoulder. "You 'phone, Mrs. Barlow. Speak to her as one woman to another."

Mrs. Barlow smiled back at him. The smile was one of the sort that usually paid a dividend (tax deducted at source). "You men," she said kittenishly.

4

Mrs. Barlow went straight to the telephone-box in the receptionist's office at the Red Deer. The blonde receptionist lifted her pen from the paper, her eyebrows from the horizontal, and an undulation of Messrs. Louis and Louis's *'Aroma Souviens-Moi'* came on the wind.

"What is it yew want, Mrs. Barlow? Ecktually, I'm fratefully busy this morning—and if it could possibly hold up until—"

Mrs. Barlow attempted what she considered her withering glance. But on this occasion it withered only at the presentation end. Miss Valerie Skeggs at the reception terminus remained serene and unabashed.

"If you must know," said Mrs. Barlow, "I'm telephoning very specially for Mr. Melville himself. Is your hen-like brain capable of remembering Lady Blanchflower's telephone number. Or am I too, too optimistic?"

The blonde gestured towards a note-book on the table. "Ef yew can read and I knew a cow once who could, you'll find what yew want in there."

Mrs. Barlow smiled sweetly. "The main trouble with this book of yours is the writing. So illiterate. We won't refer to the spelling. For the reason that I am ignorant of Esperanto."

Miss Skeggs tossed her head angrily as the housekeeper flicked the pages of the note-book. Mrs. Barlow began to dial. Each unit of dialling provoked a sniff (crescendo) from la Skeggs. Mrs. Barlow listened intently for the anticipated answer. All she heard and saw was a final and most superior sniff—albeit both obviously and atrociously inbred. By 'Supercilious' out of 'Raised Eyebrow'. It emanated from the territory nearest to Mrs. Barlow's elbow. Mrs. Barlow frowned at the telephone apparatus. She could hear the ringing tone . . . it plugged away . . . monotonously persistent . . . but that was all. In a moment of temporary mental aberration she was heard to murmur, "Lady Blanchflower doesn't answer me."

It was the moment of the Skeggs triumph. Never had she been known to miss an open goal. She raised a hand, examined her nail-varnish and languidly patted her hair. "Who can blame her?" she announced. The syllables dripped in acid.

5

Mrs. Barlow ignored the sulphuric and sought the boss. She found John Melville in his office, as she knew she would. As she entered he looked up at her eagerly.

"O.K.?"

Mrs. Barlow shook her head. But she said nothing. Melville stared at her very much as he had sat and looked at Bassett half an hour previously.

"What do you mean?" he demanded.

Mrs. Barlow found words to explain. "I've been through to Lady Blanchflower's place—but there was no answer. There doesn't seem to be anybody there. It kept ringing, too. The connection was O.K."

Melville looked at the time again. "Perhaps they're late getting up. Can't say it's an inviting sort of morning. And they're old, you know. What do you think yourself?"

Mrs. Barlow shook her head for the second time. "Mrs. Whitburn, in the ordinary way gets up fairly early. I constantly see her up and about before the breakfast gong has gone."

Melville didn't seem entirely convinced by the statement. "Still—that's when she's here. She may have had to nurse Lady B. somewhat, gone to bed well past her usual time . . . and as a consequence . . . overslept herself."

Mrs. Barlow received the suggestion doubtfully. "It means that they're both asleep, doesn't it? Neither of 'em answered my 'phone call."

"Mrs. Whitburn asleep—Lady B under the weather. That's the probable explanation. 'Phone again in half an hour's time. And if I haven't balanced these ruddy accounts by then—"

Melville paused and waved a hand significantly, and Mrs. Barlow, her grey-blue eyes troubled and anxious, floated from his presence.

6

Mrs. Barlow reported back to Melville's office in precisely thirty-four minutes. On this occasion she went straight to her objective. Before Melville could question her, she said curtly: "Still no reply from the cloisters, Mr. Melville. There can't be anybody whatever in Lady Blanchflower's apartments. The 'phone rang without stopping for just on two minutes. I don't know what you think about it—but personally I think it's very funny."

As he took in what his housekeeper had said, Melville's face certainly suggested his agreement. "You mean funny-peculiar?"

"That's the idea. Especially seeing that Mrs. Whitburn doesn't seem to be here either. If she isn't here or there—where is she?"

Melville fingered his chin. "Yes—I'm beginning to think on much the same lines myself. But candidly, Mrs. Barlow, I'm uncertain as to what to do. For the best, I mean."

Mrs. Barlow was silent. She was nobody's fool and she saw Melville's predicament quite clearly.

"You see," he went on, "I shouldn't care to start anything that might—" He paused.

"You mean that you're so much in the dark you don't like—"

"Exactly. We're both of us vague but we see what each other means. There are some things you can't quite put into words." she started.

Mrs. Barlow nodded. "And yet—"

Melville propped his cheek on his left elbow. His hand rubbed his cheek. "It's a blasted worry—that I could very well do without. Especially this morning."

Mrs. Barlow waited. Melville sensed that she disapproved the passive rôle and was favouring some line of action. Perhaps she was right. Perhaps it was the right thing to do.

"Yes," he said, "I think I know what you're thinking. I'll tell you what I'll do. I can't very well interfere in any business of Lady Blanchflower's, but Mrs. Whitburn, in a way, is my pigeon. I have got some right of action as far as she's concerned. If there's no news of her by twelve o'clock—I'll ring the Police."

"Ring 'em now," said Mrs. Barlow, "and take no chances. I've a feeling in my bones she's run into some sort of trouble. Accident of some kind—in my opinion. And delay never got anybody anywhere."

Melville was impressed by the convincing sound of the housekeeper's voice. "Perhaps you're right," he said—"after all." He reached for his telephone. "Stay in here while I'm 'phoning," he said quietly.

CHAPTER 2

1

Melville, as a holder and wielder of Scotch whisky power, was, in the new order, a person of some consequence in the ancient town of Quinster. Men have been elevated to the peerage for doing less than he did. He had rendered service to more than one party. In deference to this citizen-eminence which he possessed, his 'phone-call in connection with Mrs. Whitburn was followed up by the personal call at the Red Deer, of Sergeant Crouch himself within half an hour of the receipt of Melville's message.

With his thumbs in his belt, Crouch looked round the door of Melville's private office and saw that mine host of the Red Deer, was seated at his table.

"Good morning, Mr. Melville. I thought in view of your 'phone message I'd better come along at once."

"Good morning, Sergeant Crouch. Many thanks for the prompt attention."

Melville closed his ledger, rose and shook hands, and then waved Crouch to a chair. The Police-Sergeant removed his helmet and placed it on his knees.

"I've pretty well got the gist of your 'phone message, Mr. Melville. Unless there are any details you've thought of since and which you'd like to add?"

"Don't think so, Sergeant. You see—I'm absolutely in the dark. As I explained to you on the 'phone, the lady was here last evening going about in absolutely normal fashion. This morning—she's not here. And her bed hasn't been slept in. And that's absolutely the sum total of what I can tell you." Melville gestured hopelessly.

Sergeant Crouch produced his note-book. "Just let me get a few of the trimmings first. How old was she?"

"I should think—about seventy-five. That's near enough."

"Full name?"

"Let me see. The initial was 'L'. Er—Laura Whitburn." Melville spelt the surname.

"Been resident here for some years—I think you said?"

"Yes—something like eight or nine I should say without the book."

"Widow—wasn't she?"

"That's right. Her husband died here."

"Any family?"

"Yes. I know of one son. It's conceivable there are others. I'm not sure."

"Don't know the address of the son, I suppose, Mr. Melville?"

"I'm afraid I don't, off hand. But I should imagine you can easily get it."

Crouch made his entries slowly and carefully. "Now to more serious business," he said next. "Who last saw Mrs. Whitburn in this place? Who was that person? Because I'd like a few words with him. Or her," he added.

Melville replied without hesitation. "Bassett, my head waiter, states that Mrs. Whitburn and Lady Blanchflower must have left the dining-room a few minutes after eight o'clock last evening. That is, after they had finished dinner. I can't say with any degree of certainty that Mrs. Whitburn has been seen by anybody since."

Crouch poised his pencil. "Where were the ladies going when the waiter saw them leaving the dining-room?"

"That's another question I can't answer. And, Bassett, my waiter, can't be sure either. They might have been going back to Quinster Castle. I should say that in all probability—they were. I explained to you the arrangement they had, didn't I? About coming here to dinner?"

Crouch nodded and by a prodigious effort contrived to look even blanker than usual.

"The best thing you can do," continued Melville, "is to interview my other residents. They're sure to be in for lunch. That's at one o'clock. They may be able to help you. You may pick up something from one of them. You never know. You must understand that up to the moment I haven't had the opportunity of questioning any of them. When Mrs. Whitburn's absence was reported to me, I talked it over with my housekeeper, Mrs.

Barlow, had a look at Mrs. Whitburn's apartment and eventually . . . and very reluctantly I may as well tell you, after unsuccessfully 'phoning Lady Blanchflower's place . . . decided to get into touch with your people. That's my lot."

For some imperceptible reason, the sergeant brightened considerably. "You've looked at the room, then?"

"Yes. With my housekeeper and Bassett, the waiter I mentioned previously."

"Any disturbance?" Hopefulness was spread thick in the official voice.

"None whatever," returned Melville, "that I could see. I suggest you see the room for yourself? Perhaps you'd like to do that before you start interviewing people."

Crouch rose. "That's a sound suggestion of yours, Mr. Melville. Take me up there now, will you please, and I'll have a look round."

For the second time that morning Melville led the way up the staircase to the apartments of Laura Whitburn.

2

For some minutes Crouch poked round the room. He nodded to the bed. "Tells its own story, doesn't it?"

"Quite," replied Melville, "and makes you think."

Eventually Crouch said: "Nothing much to be gained here—short of a thorough tooth-comb operation. And I'm not ready for that *yet*. Nothing here though, on the surface."

"There *is* perhaps, just one thing I might mention, Sergeant. Before you finish the room."

"What's that, Mr. Melville?"

"In the opinion of both my housekeeper and myself, there's a fur coat of Mrs. Whitburn's missing from the wardrobe there. We're both of us fairly positive the lady was wearing a coat of that sort yesterday evening. Of course—with regard to other articles of clothing, it's just too hopeless for words. Although we can get a full description of what she wore at dinner. The waiter and others who were present could doubtless supply that."

Crouch nodded his agreement and walked to the Whitburn wardrobe. He opened the rather heavy doors and pushed his head inside.

"There's no fur coat in here."

"There certainly isn't. That's what I told you. And we think there should be. Mrs. Barlow will show you where Mrs. Whitburn used to hang it down stairs. Before she entered the dining-room each evening."

Crouch ran his fingers through his hair. "Beats cock-fightin'—doesn't it? Disappearin' like this?"

"It's certainly odd," returned Melville, "to say the least of it."

Crouch turned round and made for the door. "What do we do now?" inquired Melville.

"I'll have a word with those other people of yours. The residents."

"You may have to wait for them. I told you lunch wasn't until one o'clock. Sometimes on a fine day they cut it rather fine, you know."

"Can't be helped, Mr. Melville," replied Crouch doggedly. "I'll wait for them."

The two men made their way downstairs. "Could you sink a beer while you're waiting? Or would it be—"

The sergeant's eyes glistened with a quality that was almost ecstatic. "I wouldn't say 'no', Mr. Melville—and that's a fact."

Melville's finger pressed a bell as Crouch beamed at him.

3

By a quarter past one, Crouch had completed the enquiries he was able to make in the Red Deer and as a result had got exactly nowhere. That is to say he'd seen Mr. and Mrs. Danbury, Mr. and Mrs. Grahame, Bassett the waiter, and Bassett's two waitresses who had been on duty in the dining-room on the previous evening. None of them was able to tell Crouch anything about the missing lady that he didn't already know. From what he was able to gather, the Grahames and the Danburys had left the dining-room earlier than usual in order to visit the Quinster cinema. It was their habit to patronise the cinema whenever there was an attractive picture.

When they got up to go—Mrs. Danbury, when questioned a second time, was absolutely positive about this—Lady Blanchflower and Mrs. Whitburn were still seated at their table in the middle of the dining-room. "Mrs. Whitburn," said Mrs. Danbury, "actually smiled at me as I passed her and I smiled back. The time then would be about ten minutes to eight."

The two waitresses had no help for Crouch whatever. Crouch noted their names—Winifred Cotton and Jean Howard. They were both local girls. They explained that they scarcely ever attended on the Blanchflower table.

"Mr. Bassett always looked after the two ladies himself. Mr. Bassett made a point of doing this. Mr. Bassett has always looked after them."

"Mr. Bassett knows a good thing when he's on one. Thus and thus. Blah—blah—blah." Plenty of commonplace details and conventional trivialities—nothing of any real value to the investigating Sergeant Crouch.

At 1.17 he found Melville again and gave him the gen from the various conversations. Melville listened carefully to what Crouch had to say. When Crouch paused for breath, Melville brushed away the lingering fumes and said:

"There's just one thing, Sergeant. The 'Commercials'. There were several who dined here last evening. One of them may have noticed something which might possibly help us."

Crouch nodded. "That's an idea. Can you give me the names of the people you mean, Mr. Melville? I expect I can get the addresses."

Melville obliged the sergeant. Crouch listed them and tucked away his note-book. "And now for Lady Blanchflower. I'll have a word with her over in the cloisters. She's bound to be up by this time."

Melville accompanied him to the front entrance of the hotel.

"I'll be seeing you, Mr. Melville," said Crouch.

Melville said "thank you". He waved to Crouch as the sergeant stepped off the pavement to cross the road. By this time his worry and anxiety had grown appreciably.

CHAPTER 3

1

C rouch crossed the road quickly to the castle entrance. He passed through the minor gate used for pedestrians and cyclists and had walked a distance of about twenty-five yards when the lodge-keeper, Mark Catterall by name, greeted him. Catterall fancied himself as a humorist and as a purveyor of scintillating wit and lost few chances of jingling the cap and bells.

"Don't tell me 'Is Grace is in arrears with 'is Television payments! Well—well—well—Sergeant Crouch calls at Quinster Castle early on a Friday afternoon in the name of Justice."

Crouch endured him smilingly. "Never mind about Justice. I want to call on Lady Blanchflower. On the right, isn't it?" The lodge-keeper shifted his feet and left his habitat. He came out and ranged himself at the side of Sergeant Crouch. He levelled his right arm.

"See that flight of stone steps on the right there?"

Crouch looked and nodded.

"Go down them. They'll bring you to the deepest dungeon beneath the castle moat. You've 'eard of that, Copper, 'aven't you? In the days of the old Union Jack Library? Well—the old girl's apartments are alongside. In the cloisters. You can't very well miss 'em. There's one o' them monsters sittin' there on a 'oller pedestal lickin' 'is tail just as you turn round. 'E's known I'm told, as a wyvern. Can't say I've got much time for wyverns meself. Especially when they're the size of 'is nibs down there. 'Orrible on a dark night."

Catterall grinned as he turned away. Crouch thanked him and walked along the stone-flagged pathway in the direction of the steps. Crouch descended the stone steps and at once saw the two wyverns. There was one at each end of the great stone balustrade which faced all comers to the castle. He smiled to himself as he thought of Catterall's description of them. But were they wyverns? As he came nearer to them, they seemed part animal—part bird. The tail of each was twisted round the body so that the end of it faced the creature's mouth. Each sat, as it were, on the rear rim of a hollow, stone pedestal, with the clawed feet of the monster gripping the pedestal's respective sides. They were huge, heraldic and horrible.

It may be recorded as surprising that Crouch found himself wondering how long they had been there—these grotesque, stone guardians of the cloisters of the castle of Quinster. And whose had been the mind to conjure them into handiwork? As he rounded the corner by the nearer of the wyverns—that is to say the stone creature that faced him on his own right—Crouch saw but a short distance away the trim grass verge that fronted a rather dainty white front door, tucked trimly away in tranquillity.

Crouch stepped briskly towards it. He saw on the eye level, the neat white board with its beautifully inscribed black letters—"LADY BLANCHFLOWER". By the side of the board was a bell a bell that positively shone and gleamed in the early-November sunshine by reason of the high quality of its polish. Sergeant Crouch squared his official shoulders and put his finger on the shining bell. He planted his feet firmly on the white, trim step and waited for the response.

There was none. Crouch repeated his former activities. He squared his shoulders again and rang the bell again. The second effort, however, was no more successful than the first. There was no answer.

2

Sergeant Crouch stood there with his feet on the step for a matter of seconds, a prey to conflicting emotions. To tell the truth he was undecided as to what to do. For one thing, he wasn't too familiar with the normal habits of Lady Blanchflower. He wasn't completely sure, for instance, that at this particular hour on most days, Lady Blanchflower would be at home. But Mrs. Whitburn was missing from the Red Deer hotel—and now he could get no answer from Lady Blanchflower who was Mrs. Whitburn's friend—these two correlated facts were indisputably causing Sergeant Crouch some degree of anxiety. As he thought things over, his eyes travelled down to the white front door. He saw that it did primary duty as an outer door. His fingers sought the handle instinctively—

it turned easily—and the sergeant found himself standing inside the apartments of Lady Blanchflower. It was all terribly quiet—and perhaps, because of that, rather imposing. There was an air—oh undoubtedly an air! Even Crouch felt it. He knew refinement and elegance when it was his good fortune to encounter them.

The inner door which faced him now was dark-walnut colour. Crouch went forward a pace and knocked on this door. He knocked with a certain humility. As though, almost, the door was marked fragile. But the knock caused no disturbance of the condition of tranquillity—no sound of any kind came from any corner of the apartment.

Crouch's indecision gave way suddenly to stern resolve. Grasping it firmly, he turned the handle of the inner door and entered boldly. Facing him, less than ten yards away, was a small lounge. He could see that—because the door of the room was ajar. Crouch looked round at such doors of the other rooms which were within his orbit of vision. None of these was open. None, indeed, was anything like ajar. Crouch, therefore, looked again towards the little room which faced him and which he had instinctively recognized as the lounge.

As he looked into the room . . . and at the line of the unclosed door, Crouch stiffened with horror and his eyes bulged. For on the carpet, just visible beyond the edge of the opened door, were the tips of the fingers of a human hand. They didn't move . . . these fingers . . . they didn't move at all.

3

Crouch pulled himself together and walked towards the motionless fingers. There was no argument about what he now saw on the carpet in the lounge behind the door. He choked back an involuntary exclamation of horror. On the carpet lay the body of an old woman clad in her underclothes. Crouch knew at once beyond any doubt that he looked at the corpse of Lady Blanchflower.

He knew her well by sight from her frequent usage of the streets and shops of Quinster. Her face was dark—almost black—and much swollen. Her eyeballs were almost bursting from her head and her tongue—badly bitten, in her death agony—protruded over her lower teeth. The upper denture had become displaced and was held, but precariously, between the upper lip and the tongue. Round the old lady's neck was a silk stocking—twisted tight.

Crouch gave a quick, sharp glance round the lounge, saw the telephone on the window ledge and moved quickly to it. His hands trembled as he lifted the receiver from its cradle.

4

The police authorities at Quinster have a high reputation. A high reputation which is deservedly so. Many years' efficiency have contributed to its nurture.

When their Sergeant Crouch telephoned to the Quinster police-station from the lounge of the late Lady Blanchflower, nobody who was in any way concerned or responsible, lost any time. Action, in all its forms, was prompt and decisive. Crouch himself, Inspector Guthrie, Doctor Manners, plus all the modern auxiliary and ancillary attachments to the investigation of crime, had done their stuff before half-past three.

The main points—indeed the only points of real importance which emerged from the aggregate of their respective findings were these. Doctor Manners, the Divisional-Surgeon, asserted that Lady Blanchflower had been strangled by the silk stocking that was so prominently featured and had been dead, in his opinion, anything between twelve and twenty-four hours. She was extremely old, he added, her powers of resistance to assault of the nature indicated were considerably enfeebled, and she had succumbed very quickly to the murderous attack made upon her.

"In other words," concluded Doctor Manners gravely, "a robust child could very easily have killed her in the manner that has been employed."

The second point that emerged from the various investigations was connected with the finger-print department. There were two distinct sets of prints in many places of the late Lady Blanchflower's lounge. The 'dabs' expert who wielded the insufflator hinted optimistically that he certainly thought something valuable *might* have been left behind in this particular direction. "I'm better off," he stated, "than I am usually."

The third feature of interest which raised itself belonged to an entirely different category. On the carpet, underneath the dead body of Lady Blanchflower, was discovered a crumpled, grey wig. When Sergeant Crouch and Inspector Guthrie examined it—they saw to their surprise that it was a man's wig. A wig as would be worn by a low comedian who desired an appearance of more years than were his by nature.

"What on earth," said Inspector Guthrie to Sergeant Crouch, "can a wig of this kind be doing under the dead body of Lady Blanchflower?"

He held the wig on high so that the sergeant could see it better. Crouch shook his head.

"I wouldn't know," he replied. "Unless it belongs to the murderer."

As he spoke, the reason that had brought him to the cloisters came back to his mind. The discovery of Lady Blanchflower's body had driven it summarily away. What would John Melville at the Red Deer be thinking now?

"I say—Inspector," said the sergeant, "what about Mrs. Whitburn? The lady that's missing? Do you think there's a chance she's been rubbed out—as well? In one of the other rooms?"

Inspector Guthrie stared at his subordinate. "Be your age, Crouch. All the other rooms are empty. Bone dry—my dear chap. You don't imagine I neglected to look at them, do you? Show a little 'common'."

Crouch licked his lips at the reproof. Why hadn't he kept his big mouth shut? This murder of Lady Blanchflower descending upon him so suddenly had taken him far beyond his depth and it would be some time before he got back to normal.

"Where is Mrs. Whitburn, then?" The question was almost stammered.

"That, Sergeant Crouch," returned Guthrie, "becomes yet another problem for our professional attention. Who killed Lady Blanchflower— and where is her friend and companion, Mrs. Whitburn?"

Crouch nodded. "Yes—you're quite right, sir. I see your point. Sort of movin' in high Society—aren't we?"

"Speak for yourself, Sergeant," snapped back the inspector.

CHAPTER 4

1

The death, or let it be said, perhaps, the murder of Lady Blanchflower, affected the various people of Quinster in strangely different ways. To Sergeant Crouch it gave a sense of intense official importance more so than at any previous time in his career.

In the case of Inspector Guthrie it brought about an acute inflammation of personal ambition. He had been in Quinster now for more years than he cared to remember and he found this stubborn fact the reverse of pleasing. Maybe his big chance, tardy though in coming, *had* arrived at long last! For ambition, when it takes firm hold of a man's mind can creep as well as soar. Vaulting ambition can o'er leap itself—but there are other and less violent kinds—of such had been Guthrie's.

To John Melville, mine host of the Red Deer, the news of the discovery of Lady Blanchflower's body, brought mingled feelings of horror and alarm. Time after time, he would sit in his office and mentally finger the links of this altogether abominable chain. For, to him, it always seemed after the manner of a chain. As he looked closely at the events one by one there was the clear concatenation of circumstance with each link clearly defined.

First it had been Bella Street seeing Mrs. Whitburn's empty bedroom—then Bella Street had gone to Bassett, his waiter. Bassett had listened to Bella and had reported to him. He had got into touch with Mrs. Barlow and after that with Crouch—and then Crouch, looking primarily for the vanished Mrs. Whitburn, had come all unexpectedly upon the corpse of Lady Blanchflower. And when he reached that particular stage in his mental meandering, John Melville would pull himself up—and his thoughts would switch dully and mechanically to Mrs. Whitburn again. He dreaded to think what the next few days might very well bring.

Would the body of Mrs. Whitburn be discovered anywhere? If it should be—and she were dead—it would be a stroke of ill-fortune he could very well do without.

A gloom, naturally, hung over the best hotel in Quinster and over its proprietor. And it affected the residents thereof. Mr. and Mrs. Grahame and Mr. and Mrs. Danbury—all four of them—seemed stunned and bewildered at the tragedy which had come so close to them. Their dining-tables on the evenings that followed were strangely quiet. Frank Danbury, perhaps, made the most courageous effort to rend the sombre blanket that had descended—but it cannot be said, with any degree of truth that he was successful. The effort fizzled out like the dampest of squibs.

Walter Chester and his professional colleagues had left the hotel on the Friday morning—to return in the evening to their respective homes and houses for the approaching week-end—and were all well away from Quinster and its boundaries before that particular moment of time came when Bella Street couldn't find Mrs. Whitburn. The diner who had graced his table in solitude had left by Friday midday.

But the murder of Lady Blanchflower had perhaps its fiercest impact upon yet another person—who up to the moment in this story has been no more than merely mentioned. Allusion is made to His Grace, Henry Erskine Conyngham Annesley Fitzcuthbert, the fourteenth Duke of Quinster. For it must be recorded that at the time when Sergeant Crouch made his dreadful discovery in the cloister apartments, the flag was flying over the battlements of Quinster Castle. This proud, wind-tossed flag was the sign to the world in general and the good folk of Quinster in particular that His Grace was in residence.

2

It is recorded too, with something like regret that the appearance, the stature and the intelligence of Henry Fitzcuthbert were all in inverse proportion to his rank and high estate. His face was pale with fat blubbery cheeks and wide creases. The eyes were invariably clouded with self-reproach—they were watery-blue in colour and unusually protuberant—and at times an expression would spring into them like that of a cornered rat. The only thing that he could ever remember was that he forgot everything. His hair was of no particular shade and the one aristocratic feature his face held was his nose. It was high-bridged and most obviously patrician—the Fitzcuthbert nose for all the world to see and recognise—and thirteen dukes of Quinster had exhibited it to the world before Henry Erskine etcetera.

At ten o'clock on the morning of the Friday, when Lady Blanchflower was destined to be found dead in her apartments, the fourteenth Duke of Quinster was still asleep. The morning was unusually chilly even for early November and the autumn sunshine was streaming through the windows of the castle in some strength before His Grace awoke under the influence of its benison. He seldom knew whether he was glad to awaken from the bondage of sleep. The dawn of a new day invariably brought him problems which he would much rather have been without, sometimes acute, sometimes painful. Vague doubts, personal anxieties, gnawing worries, from which, in the haven of sleep, he had temporarily escaped, lost no time at all in returning to him with the daylight. And they were all such a damned nuisance!

The Duke for a time lay scrupulously still. He made a habit of doing this. Waking up wasn't so bad—if you remembered to lie absolutely still directly it happened. He had noticed that any sort of early physical movement tended to set him thinking more keenly. He always did his best to avoid the exercise of thought—far better to let his mind wander vaguely and half-heartedly over the problem that had happened to turn up in a groping, short-sighted, impersonal kind of way. On the morning in question the fourth day of November, Henry Erskine listened, half unconsciously, for any sounds of his Duchess—in her nearby apartments. There were none—and then faintly through the castle windows, came the familiar everyday sounds of the outside living, the noise of cars and lorries and the occasional edge of a shout or cry.

The Duke began to loosen himself from his lethargy. He propped himself on a patrician elbow—and rang a bell. Some half-dreaming instinct moving within him, stirred him to the rather pleasant consciousness that if he communicated in this way with his valet, there would be brought to him, morning tea, three very sweet biscuits of the sort he so strongly favoured and several editions of several morning newspapers. Also—that while he drank the tea, nibbled the biscuits and read what his Duchess rather irreverently termed the 'Horse page' of each of the papers, Simmons, his valet, would run his bath-water and mix it for him in those agreeable proportions which betoken the touch of the master.

For some seconds His Grace lay on his back gazing at the ceiling of his bedroom in Quinster Castle. Until, in fact, the door of the bedroom opened to admit Simmons and what Simmons brought.

"Er . . . put it down there . . . Simmons," ordered His Grace, "and . . . er . . . hand me the *Sporting Life* . . . will you?"

3

The Duke of Quinster continued to pass that Friday entirely uneventfully—until just before the time for his afternoon tea. To be precise—until exactly four minutes to four. At that moment, he was exceedingly surprised at the entrance into the Woodcote lounge of the castle, of his personal secretary, by name James Grandison. The Duke's surprise showed itself first of all in a ducal frown. What on earth was Grandison thinking of by such an intrusion? The morning was the time for business, not now.

Grandison coughed deferentially as he advanced towards Henry Erskine Etcetera Fitzcuthbert. Grandison, who had come down from Cambridge, the possessor of a brilliant record of scholarship, was a short, rather stout young man with a round, clean-shaven face and large, dark, intelligent eyes. His brown hair was inclined to run riot on his head and a considerable amount of it normally precipitated itself over the cliff of his forehead. As he advanced, he lost his cough and spoke nervously and apologetically.

"I'm frightfully sorry, sir" (this mode of address was in accordance with the Duke of Quinster's personal wish), "but can I speak to you in private for a moment?"

Before Henry Fitzcuthbert could reply, Grandison had gone on. "I assure you, sir, I wouldn't bother you here and now were it not a matter of supreme importance."

More hair came over the cliff as a result of Grandison's agitation. The Duke had the sense, for once, to see that his secretary meant every word that he said. He turned to the Duchess, who had just awakened from her post-luncheon nap.

"You will excuse me, my dear Beatrix—but Grandison here seems very disturbed about something. He wishes to talk to me for a moment." Then, rising, he addressed Grandison.

"We will go into the library, Grandison, for whatever it is you want. I always feel that it's the appropriate apartment for any matter of more than ordinary importance. I rather fancy that both my father and my grandfather had a similar idea. Come with me at once, will you?"

Grandison bowed to the Duchess and followed his high-born employer into the library of Quinster Castle. Waiting until the Duke was seated, Grandison deliberately went across and closed the library door before speaking.

"My dear Grandison," said the Duke, "what a marvellous conspirator you would make to be sure! You closed that door to the manner born! 'Pon my soul, I can almost smell gunpowder."

Grandison smiled but shook his head uneasily—restlessly almost as though a persistent insect were tormenting him. "I'm sorry, sir, to break it to you like this and at such an inconvenient time—but something particularly terrible has happened. In the castle. Or—that is to say . . . practically in the castle."

The Duke was conscious of a terrific shock. "In the castle?" he repeated blankly; "what on earth are you talking about, Grandison?"

"Lady Blanchflower has been killed, sir. Murdered. In . . . er . . . the most dreadful circumstances. In the cloisters! The police have just telephoned to the castle. It isn't very long, it appears, since they discovered the body."

The Duke's face went ashen and his eyes took on their habitual look of self-reproach. "Lady Blanchflower? Murdered? Dear, dear—how very terrible! My dear Grandison—nobody seems safe these days. Not even the very best people. Or rather—perhaps the best people. Burglars, I suppose? Broke in during the night?"

Grandison shook his head again. "I don't know, sir. The police didn't get as far as that. I took the telephone message and then I felt I had to inform you immediately, sir."

"Quite right, Grandison. You did the right thing. Not a word, though, to the Duchess—yet awhile. Bad news can always keep—that is to say . . . er . . . from some points of view. And the Duchess hasn't had her tea yet."

Henry Fitzcuthbert glared into space as he modified his statement. Then he turned again, almost petulantly, to his secretary.

"How was the old gel killed? Shot—or bashed on the head with the usual blunt instrument?"

"Neither, sir. At least—so I am informed."

The Duke of Quinster contrived to look like an infuriated fish. "Neither? What d'ye mean, Grandison? How else could she have been killed? There are no other ways—are there—when you're in your own quarters, I mean?" .

"Apparently, sir," Grandison swallowed hard

"What d'ye mean, man—apparently?"

"According to the police information, sir, as I had it from them, sir, Lady Blanchflower was strangled. By a stocking, sir, knotted round her throat."

The Duke was silent. This last item of Grandison information seemed to prove too much for him. When he recovered himself, he stared at his secretary with a glassy eye, and said, "Grandison *this is an outrage!* Besides being a foul and dastardly murder—it's an abominable outrage. In the cloisters of Quinster Castle! With me in residence at the time. Me—the fourteenth Duke of Quinster! Why—it might have been the Duchess. The stocking points to such a possibility."

The Duke paused at the thought before adding somewhat moodily, "but of course, it wasn't."

He rose from the chair in which he had been seated. "I'm not sitting down under this, Grandison. No—I'm not enduring this in any shape or form. Whoever perpetrated this dastardly crime has me to deal with. Go to the telephone as soon as you possibly can—and get me the Chief Constable."

"Very good, sir," replied the secretary.

"Among other things," added His Grace, "I shall give the Chief Constable a piece of my mind. And not one of the best pieces either."

"I quite agree, sir," said James Grandison.

"Er . . . what's that?" demanded the Duke. But the door had closed upon the private secretary.

4

"The Chief Constable, sir," said Grandison. The fourteenth Duke of Quinster took the telephone-receiver from the hand of his secretary.

"Is that you, Nightingale?" The Duke waited for the reply. "It is? Do you know, Nightingale, I never 'phone you without thinkin' what a damn silly name that is for the Chief Constable of a county. And that's a solemn fact. What? Yes—this is Quinster this end. I thought you knew that already. And I'm goin' to tell you something, Nightingale—what's that? You know? You've just heard about it? Well I suppose that's very possible. Taking all the circumstances into consideration. But what I want to know is this. What are you damn well doin' about it? Lily Blanchflower was a fine old gel—she crossed swords with me more than once—but that's all over and forgotten. When a time like this comes, you can afford to let bygones be begones. She was a fine old gel—as I said. One of the very best. Salt of the earth. And you for one, Nightingale, ought to be damn well ashamed that she's gone down the way she has. It's a damn blot on your official escutcheon. Strictly speakin' to my way of thinkin' it calls for nothing less than your resignation. Oh yes it does. And there's no damned argument about it." The Duke paused. Brigadier-General Sir George Garnett Nightingale, K.C.B., D.S.O., had gone into action at the other end. The Fitzcuthbert Adam's apple—no trifling affair even in repose—moved convulsively as the Duke listened. What he heard left him in no doubt that Sir George meant business. Strict business!

For at least five years now, Sir George had kept his constabulary very much on the run and he wasn't missing an affair like a murder in Quinster Castle under any circumstances. Whatever his shortcomings, the Duke had sense enough to see that very clearly before the Chief Constable had fired more than half a dozen sentences. Cunningly, Henry Erskine Fitzcuthbert inserted a sentence of his own long before Sir George had come to his own storming finish.

In its effect upon the Chief Constable, the sentence might have been packed with dynamite. It checked the spate of words which flowed from the mouth of the Chief Constable as summarily and effectively as the arched back and spitting mouth of a cat will halt the headlong progress of a boisterous terrier whose mother hasn't told him everything.

"What was that you said . . . er . . . my Lord Duke?" asked Sir George in a suddenly changed voice.

"You heard," replied the Duke, with an entirely unconscious use of the modern idiom . . . and then continued . . . "I shouldn't adopt such a measure, of course, as I outlined to you, unless I considered myself *forced*. But you can quite see, Sir George. you can see for yourself . . . well . . . I am sure you can."

The Duke grasped the telephone-receiver almost lovingly and a look of ineffable cunning spread itself over the ducal face as he waited for the reply. The Chief Constable came again.

"And in the event of my . . . er . . . acceding to your request . . . and falling in with your suggestion generally . . . I could then rely on your full support?"

The Duke purred into the mouthpiece. "Absolutely, my dear Sir George, you can rely on me absolutely. And that would apply, too, to that other . . . er . . . future matter. The one that you . . . er . . . touched on a few moments ago. Entirely, my dear Sir George. You need have no doubts on that score. I give you my word. My full support!"

"In that case, then, my Lord Duke . . . I'll communicate with Scotland Yard at once. I'll inform them I've been in communication with you and I'll give them your message."

"Thank you, Sir George. In that case then (to use your own words) I'll expect you at the castle . . . and them perhaps . . . some time this evening. I felt sure you would see things in their right light directly they were placed in front of you. Good-bye . . . until some time this evening."

The Duke rubbed the telephone-receiver under his chin, leered with an almost malevolent satisfaction at the success his craft had won for him, replaced the receiver in its cradle with the gesture of a conqueror and turned to the silent Grandison at his side.

"Thank you, Grandison. You've heard what the arrangements are. Just as though I was going to allow *any* damned local policeman to take a case of this importance. Let him stick to his *hoi polloi*. What do they take me for! Lil Blanchflower was one of the very best. I'll say she was. And I'll damn well see she has the best now that she's dead and gone! Nothin' less than Scotland Yard itself for Lil Blanchflower!"

PART FOUR

MURDER WITHOUT MOTIVE

CHAPTER 1

1

In the living-room of his flat, Anthony Lotherington Bathurst sat and smoked and stared into the red heart of a fire of logs. It was the evening of Friday, the 4th of November. He had finished an extraordinarily good dinner about a quarter of an hour previously and the quick-fingered, neat-handed Emily had already 'cleared away'. His legs were extended towards the fire to their full length, and his head was half-huddled on his chest. In this fashion he sat and smoked and stared.

After a time his hand dropped to the side of the arm-chair, to pick up a copy of the *Evening Standard*. He had just remembered he hadn't read Hylton Cleaver on tomorrow's Rugger games in London. As his hand clasped the fallen newspaper, the telephone rang at his side. Anthony twisted himself from the arm-chair and picked up the receiver.

"Bathurst speaking." Almost immediately his face changed He knew that the caller was Chief Det. Inspector Andrew MacMorran speaking from the Yard.

"What's *your* trouble, Andrew?" he asked flippantly.

The reply he received surprised him exceedingly. He listened to the Yard inspector for some time. "When?" eventually asked Anthony.

"If it's convenient," said MacMorran at the other end . . . "almost at once . . . afraid it's imperative. I'll pick you up on the way. What's the time now?"

Anthony glanced at his wrist-watch.

"7.38."

"Within seven minutes then—at your place. That suit you?"

"I haven't said so," grinned Anthony.

"Make up your mind. If I'm to be at your place when I said."

"O.K., Andrew. I might have known you'd persuade me. The case sounds on the attractive side, though, I'll say that for it. What sort of night is it?"

"Bit of a mist here. Not too bad, though, Probably fog in other places but we may miss it. Be seeing you." MacMorran hung up and Anthony, some seconds later, slid his arms into his big-sleeved overcoat.

2

The blue limousine from the Yard entered the outskirts of Quinster Castle at almost exactly half-past eight. It entered through the main gates and ran down the carriage-way until it came to the lodge. Catterall, the lodge-keeper passed it through after due ceremonial and told MacMorran that a local police-constable was waiting some little distance away to direct him further.

When MacMorran caught sight of the uniformed figure in the headlights, he stopped the car. He and Anthony alighted. MacMorran pointed significantly to two big cars parked close at hand, beckoned to the constable, made himself known and was conducted with Anthony to the white front door of the apartments of the late Lady Blanchflower. The lights were on in the various rooms and Inspector Guthrie met them but a few inches distance from the front door.

"Hallo, sir," said Guthrie. "I've been expecting you. Glad you're here."

The two men shook hands. They were not exactly strangers to each other. They had met more than once at special police conferences during the war years presided over by the Commissioner.

"Thank you, Inspector Guthrie," said MacMorran, "this is Mr. Anthony Bathurst."

Guthrie's hand went out again. "Inspector Guthrie," explained MacMorran.

"And pleased to meet you, sir," said Guthrie to Anthony.

"Nice of you, Inspector." Anthony smiled.

"Take us along with you, will you?" said MacMorran.

"Not far to go," said Guthrie, "that's one advantage. In the lounge. That's the room you can see just in front of you. The light's on in there and in all the other rooms."

"I understood," said MacMorran, "that the Chief Constable would be here. I was informed to that effect on the telephone."

Guthrie smiled what Anthony thought was a rather enigmatic smile. "Well he is—and he isn't. Actually—at the moment—he's in the castle. The Duke sent for him. We're moving in unusually high places."

"I see." MacMorran moved towards the lounge. "Like that, is it? I take it he'll be back?"

"I should imagine so," returned Inspector Guthrie.

3

Anthony and Andrew MacMorran entered the little lounge behind Inspector Guthrie. "Save for the removal of the body," said the last-named, "everything is just as it was when the crime was discovered. Nothing has been touched. Nothing whatever. You can see the chalk lines which I had filled in for you."

MacMorran looked at the white outline. "Fingers towards the door—eh?"

"That's right. And this is the stocking that did the trick." Guthrie took a silk stocking from his overcoat pocket.

MacMorran handled it with interest and passed it over to Anthony. "No disturbance—to speak of?" asked the Yard inspector.

"Little or none. And as far as can be ascertained—nothing has been stolen."

"Who discovered the body?"

"A sergeant attached to Quinster. By name—Sergeant Crouch."

"What brought him here?"

"A missing woman. But strangely enough—not the woman that's dead."

"Say that again, please," said Anthony.

Guthrie smiled and told of the missing Mrs. Whitburn and the telephone call Crouch had taken at Quinster from Melville of the Red Deer. Anthony listened to the details with keen attention.

"So you see," concluded Guthrie, "looking for one—he ran across t'other. Sometimes that's the way it goes. You never know in our game."

Anthony nodded, and then with one of his whimsicalities said, "Looking for a 'white', he ran across a 'blanche'. Strange coincidence there—if you notice it."

Guthrie looked very much as though he hadn't and wouldn't.

"In the eighties, wasn't she?" asked MacMorran.

"Yes. Eighty-seven, I believe. Wouldn't take a rare lot to kill her."

"No. I couldn't agree more," MacMorran grunted. "What's your idea of the business, then?" He seated himself on the divan. "Tell me, Inspector, what you think of things. I'd like to hear. You've more or less got your fingers on the pulse—I'm a stranger."

Guthrie brushed his top lip with the back of his hand. "I fancy it's a simple case of house-breaking and that Lady Blanchflower, after she returned from the Red Deer with her friend, Mrs. Whitburn, surprised and disturbed the intruder."

MacMorran was about to interrupt when Guthrie checked him with an upraised hand.

"Just a minute, sir, before you say anything. There's something which I should explain to you. Something you should know which had to do with the two ladies we're worrying about this evening. The one that's dead and the one that's missing. I should have told you before, probably, but it slipped me. Anyhow—I'll tell you now—before we go any farther. It'll give you a better picture of things."

Guthrie narrated, with some attention to detail, the habitual evening dinner journeys of the late Lady Blanchflower and Mrs. Whitburn to and from the dining-room of the Red Deer. Again Anthony listened to the local inspector with the keenest attention. He was about to break in, similarly to MacMorran of a few moments ago, when the local inspector checked him as he had checked MacMorran.

"Before you tear my theory to pieces, Mr. Bathurst, there's one *other* piece of information with regard to the crime itself which you haven't yet had."

He crossed to a small coal-cabinet in a corner by the fireside and took something off the top. Guthrie brought the article over to MacMorran and placed it in his hands.

"This wig was found crumpled up under the body of Lady Blanchflower. And, quite frankly—it's got me beat. Interesting—what?"

MacMorran stared at the wig in utter surprise. "Goodness gracious," he said, "extraordinary! A man's wig."

Anthony came over and looked at the wig as MacMorran held it in his hands. If his interest in the case had been keen before, it had now been multiplied tenfold.

"It's a man's wig," announced MacMorran again, "no doubt about that."

"It's a perruquier's wig, too," said Anthony, "of excellent quality and really high-class manufacture."

Guthrie and MacMorran looked a trifle perplexed. Guthrie began to put a question.

"It's not exactly my line of country, Mr. Bathurst—but wouldn't all wigs, as it were—"

Anthony saw his point and anticipated his final question. "I'll tell you what I mean exactly when I say it's a perruquier's wig. It's a wig that does not belong to, has not been made for, and is not habitually worn by, one particular person. Do you get my point?"

"Who would wear it, then?" demanded Guthrie.

"In the ordinary way—members of a cast taking part in a theatrical performance. Probably amateur. This wig has been hired, I should say, from a firm of perruquier's. It should be a fairly simple matter to trace it."

Guthrie wrinkled his brows. "What makes you so certain of that?"

Anthony pointed to the join in the front. "Have a look here, Inspector, all along the join. See anything?"

Guthrie held up the wig to the electric light. "Yes," he said, "there's a faint colouring. Pinkish."

"That's the idea," returned Anthony. "What you can see is the remains of grease-paint. Looks like that hardy old warhorse 'three and a half'."

He tossed the wig back to MacMorran. "Been used fairly recently in a dramatic performance. That absolutely sticks out. As opposed to a wig made specifically to the order of one particular person. All the same—I can't for the life of me see what it's doing here. Especially beneath the dead body of Lady Blanchflower." There was a silence—and then, almost abruptly, as it were—Anthony addressed himself to Inspector Guthrie.

"Tell me, Inspector—your house-breaker theory! I'm interested. How do you tie it up—against this masculine wig effort?" The inspector smiled. "I've been waiting for that, Mr. Bathurst. Because I was pretty certain it was coming. But in spite of this wig—I feel confident that Lady Blanchflower must have been killed by a housebreaker she disturbed. You'll find there'll be some other explanation about the wig."

"You mean he was already here—when she arrived back after dinner? From the Red Deer?"

"Yes. He probably heard Lady Blanchflower come in and hid somewhere."

"But wasn't Mrs. Whitburn with Lady Blanchflower when they returned after dinner. Wouldn't they be together? Didn't I understand that to be the case?"

"She probably accompanied the old lady as far as the front door. No farther. That's my theory."

"You realise that Mrs. Whitburn herself is missing?" A shadow passed over Guthrie's face.

"Yes—I realise that. I think that will prove to be but temporary. She'll turn up somewhere. She must. There may be half a dozen excellent and quite commonplace reasons to account for her absence today—unknown, of course, to us."

Anthony pursed his lips. "But what explanation can there be for the presence of this man's wig. It's an incongruity—surely?"

Before Guthrie could frame a reply, there came in interruption. A man's voice was heard—not so very far away. Guthrie listened carefully and then turned to the door of the lounge.

"Excuse me, sir," he said to MacMorran, "but I rather fancy I can hear the Chief Constable. He's evidently finished at the castle. If you don't mind I'll tell him you're here."

As Guthrie made his way out, Anthony shook his head slowly at Andrew MacMorran.

4

Brigadier-General Sir George Garnett Nightingale, K.C.B., D.S.O. was doubly annoyed. In the first place he was annoyed with himself for allowing the fourteenth Duke of Quinster to outsmart him over the matter of the Yard's intervention in the Blanchflower murder; and secondly, he was annoyed with the Duke for having the craft to carry it out with such success. Also—his recent interview with the Duke had done nothing to allay that annoyance. Rather had it been increased. All the time he had been in the Duke's company he had been conscious of a feeling that His Grace was crowing inwardly at what he had accomplished. No—not crowing—that wasn't the word—gloating!

In addition to these feelings, the Chief Constable had a nasty uneasy suspicion floating round at the back of his mind that the latest of the Fitzcuthberts was a cunning twister and that the odds were that he himself had made an extremely bad bargain. The fact that he had made it for the sake of his wife and his wife's social ambitions was beside the matter. He himself was convinced that he had bartered something very important to him—for a mess of dotage.

Each time he reflected on this, his annoyance grew and waxed fat. When Guthrie brought him in to MacMorran and Anthony in the lounge of the late Lady Blanchflower, his asperity was at its peak. He was a heavily-built man with burly, restless shoulders. He had but little hair—what he had was white—and his skin was ruddy tanned by Eastern suns and wrinkled and lined by years of both malevolent and benevolent tyranny. His eyebrows bristled and beneath them, little 'piggy' blue eyes looked out fiercely at most things.

Guthrie, who knew the Chief Constable very well indeed, thank you, was quick to anticipate the direction of the official wind and made the necessary introduction.

"This, sir, is Chief Det. Inspector MacMorran from New Scotland Yard."

Sir George glared at MacMorran with all the friendliness of a hungry stoat. "I don't really know why I sent to your people. I don't really! Acted rather rashly, I'm afraid. And may live to regret it. Still now you're here—you're here—and that's that."

He turned his glare on Anthony. "Who are you?"

"Bathurst," said Anthony.

"Bathurst? I don't think I—"

MacMorran dropped an eyelid for Anthony's benefit. "Major Farrell-Knox . . . er . . . Assistant Commissioner at the 'Yard' . . . suggested that Mr. Bathurst should accompany me."

Sir George grunted but the grunt was not cordial. "I see. Does he hold your hand—or do you hold his?"

"That's just about the size of it," returned MacMorran.

"What is? Which is it?"

"Both. Neither. Each." MacMorran's face was flat and unruffled as he delivered his verbal discourtesy.

Sir George fumbled mentally for more ammunition. A sudden flash lightened his darkness.

"Bathurst? I think I'm beginning to understand. Are you the Anthony Bathurst that messes round with—"

Anthony cut into the question with a smile. "Guilty, sir. The messing round is admitted. And now that we all know each other everything's fine and dandy. Perhaps Chief, if you'll put one or two rather important points to the Chief Constable . . . "

MacMorran took the cue instantaneously. "There is one thing, Sir George. Before we go any further with the investigation. This Mrs. Whitburn who is missing. Is there any news of her yet?"

"At the present moment," replied the Chief Constable pompously, "Mrs. Whitburn is still missing."

"Thank you, Sir George. That rather conflicts with Inspector Guthrie's idea. Now there are two or three points I'd like your valuable opinion on, before I proceed in various other directions. You have certain knowledges that I haven't."

"What are they? Let's have them. And as quickly as you can—if you don't mind. I'm due back at Headworth after this room's been sealed."

As Andrew MacMorran began to present points, Anthony decided to wander round the apartment.

CHAPTER 2

1

At nine o'clock on the following morning, which was Saturday, Anthony and MacMorran breakfasted at a small baker's shop, about two miles up-river from Quinster and in the direction of Lawne. The name of the village which Anthony had spotted as the car entered it, was Queen's Fulton. The journey back to town late on the previous night and the return to Quinster in the morning had been accomplished during an aggregated period of nine hours, in which each man had contrived some few hours' sleep in MacMorran's room at the Yard.

"Puffed wheat," ordered Anthony, as they sat at a little marble-topped table, "hot rolls—bacon and egg, pot of tea—for two. Is such a breakfast possible in Queen's Fulton?" The rosy-cheeked, broad-beamed woman in attendance smiled and replied: "We'll see what can be done, sir. Queen's Fulton ain't exactly the back of beyond."

The little shop at which MacMorran had stopped, was within a hundred yards of the tow-path, but the race for the Ladies' Plate, alas, was a matter of eight months distant.

"While we're in here," said MacMorran dourly, "let's do a bit of sortin' out."

"I guessed that was the idea. And I'll tell you what I think we ought to do."

"What's that?"

"Ignore the missing woman for the time being. Unless we're convinced by the trend of events that we can't."

"You mean—concentrate entirely on the murder?"

The stout woman came back and said, "That'll be all right, sir. Everything as you wanted, sir. In a few minutes."

Anthony's grey eyes smiled his gratitude. "Oh—thank you. Thank you very much. Hear that good news, Andrew?"

MacMorran nodded. "Continuing from where we were," said Anthony, "we haven't the least idea as to *why* Lady Blanchflower was killed. At all events—that goes for me. I take it you agree with me?"

"All the time. But we should pick up something from the enquiries we shall make today. I've asked Guthrie to keep going with the routine stuff. Damn it all—we *should* dig up something somewhere."

The rosy-cheeked woman brought the breakfast and it was some little time before Anthony spoke again. When he did he said, "What's the actual programme today, then, Andrew?"

MacMorran said, "I thought something on these lines: Red Deer first of all—then anywhere or anybody that would appear to be indicated from what we get at the hotel."

MacMorran poured himself out a fresh cup of tea. "Well—what do you think yourself?"

"One person we absolutely must see is that lodge-keeper chap. At Quinster Castle. That's where I thought Guthrie's theory ran out of juice. Whoever killed Lady Blanchflower must have slipped past 'the afore-mentioned lodge-keeper' in some way or another. No argy-bargy about that, Andrew."

"Unless," replied Andrew slowly, "unless—it was this missing woman, Whitburn. That would satisfy your point re the lodge-keeper."

Anthony considered MacMorran's suggestion.

"Well?" queried the professional.

"Maybe you've got something there. Just can't say at this juncture. No data. Bar a dead woman, a missing woman, a silk stocking and a scratch wig. No psychologies turned over yet." Anthony concluded with a shrug of the shoulders.

MacMorran looked at his watch. "If you're O.K.," he said, "I'd like to be moving as soon as we can. Can you catch that woman's eye?"

"Right-o, Andrew. Red Deer?"

"Yes," said MacMorran. "Red Deer."

"Did you arrange to meet Guthrie there?"

"Gave him the option. Made it clear that he could please himself. Somehow—I think he'll give it a miss."

2

Arrived at the Red Deer, MacMorran took statements from John Melville, Mrs. Barlow, Bella Street, Bassett, Valerie Skeggs, Frank Danbury, Maureen Danbury, Edith Grahame and Stephen Grahame with due deference, of course, to Judges' rules.

The hotel proprietor, who was, naturally, the first person to be seen, explained the dining arrangements of the two ladies chiefly concerned with the tragedy, and then outlined to MacMorran the various incidents that had led up to his telephoning the police at Quinster and getting in touch there with Sergeant Crouch. MacMorran noted the details of the information.

"And now a few questions, Mr. Melville—if you don't mind. Just to give us some little assistance and a clearer view of things. When Lady Blanchflower and Mrs. Whitburn came in to dinner on Thursday evening—did you actually see them enter? That is to say when they came from the castle?"

"Yes. I saw them. I actually saw them come down the street. Mrs. Whitburn was holding Lady Blanchflower's arm—helping."

MacMorran looked up. "Did I understand you to say 'down' the street, Mr. Melville?"

"Yes."

"I don't quite get that. Wouldn't it be across the street, coming from Quinster Castle?"

Melville smiled at MacMorran's nicety. "Oh—I'm sorry. I see what you mean. I'll explain."

"Thank you. I'd be glad if you would."

"We have an entrance to this place in River Street. A side-entrance. Perhaps you didn't notice it when you came in just now, but the hotel stands on the corner of River street and Castle Street. Actually—our side-entrance is directly opposite to one of the entrances to the railway-station. All you have to do to get to the booking-office is to cross River Street. Not more than half a dozen paces. When Lady Blanchflower and Mrs. Whitburn came from the castle they used to cross the main road, come down River Street and into the hotel by the side-entrance. I think I could say that was their invariable habit. They went back to the castle the same way. On Thursday evening, I happened to be close to the River Street entrance when they came down the side turning. Later on, I greeted them at the entrance to the dining-room. Is that clear, Inspector?"

"Admirably, Mr. Melville."

Anthony intervened at this stage. "Just one point, there, Mr. Melville before we proceed, if you don't mind. You said that Mrs. Whitburn was holding Lady Blanchflower's arm. Then I think you said—an amplification, doubtless—'helping her'. I take it there was nothing unusual with regard to this?"

"No. I don't think so. I really don't. Lady Blanchflower has been getting a little feeble these last months. It was quite a natural gesture for Mrs. Whitburn to give her some . . . er . . . physical support on their regular journeys to and from the castle."

"Quite. Just what one would expect. Thank you, Mr. Melville. O.K., Andrew . . . "

MacMorran proceeded: "As far as you know . . . and were able to see . . . everything on Thursday in connection with the two ladies . . . was entirely normal . . . would you say?"

"I saw nothing in any way abnormal, Inspector."

"You have no suggestion of any kind to put forward . . . that might shed some light on this most distressing affair?"

"None whatever, sir. I am absolutely bewildered by the extraordinary turn of events. I had the highest possible regard and respect for both ladies. Last Thursday was a black day for me and my hotel—I can tell you that, gentlemen. The blackest in my humble career, because there's no knowing the repercussions it may have on my business."

There was no doubt that Melville meant every word that he had said. Anthony saw that clearly. MacMorran rubbed his top lip.

"If it's convenient to you, then Mr. Melville, I'll have just a word or two with your housekeeper. Mrs. Barlow, isn't it?"

"Mrs. Barlow—that's right, Inspector. Shall I send for her to come in here? Or would you rather—?"

"Don't bother. She's got a room, I suppose, that's more or less her own? You can direct us there."

"Of course." Melville gave the desired information and indication. "Down that corridor"—he pointed—"first right—you'll find Mrs. Barlow in her room on the left. Or you should."

"Thank you," returned MacMorran. He and Anthony made their way down the corridor.

3

Whatever may have been MacMorran's feelings, Anthony was distinctly surprised when he saw Mrs. Barlow for the first time. The lady, however, was *not* surprised at Anthony's surprise, which she was quick to recognise—not having lived thirty-eight years minus experience.

Unfortunately, however, she had little to offer—that is to say—in the shape of information concerning the principal ladies of the drama. All that she was able to tell MacMorran was entirely on the lines of Melville's information—concerning the normal habits of the two ladies and their last visit to the Red Deer on the previous Thursday evening. Her attractive eyes were eloquent as she spoke. MacMorran noted what she said.

"Mr. Melville sent for you yesterday morning—is that it?"

"Yes. On a report from one of the chambermaids—Bella Street it was—that Mrs. Whitburn was missing from her room. At that time, of course, we had no idea that anything had happened to Lady Blanchflower."

MacMorran nodded. "Quite. I fully understand that."

"Mrs. Barlow," said Anthony, "tell me, if you can. Did you see the two ladies yourself at any time on the Thursday evening? Actually on the Red Deer premises here?"

The housekeeper turned on him one of her brightest and best smiles. "No; I did not actually see either of the two ladies in here on Thursday. But there's really nothing in that. I just didn't happen to be near the dining-room at the precise moment when they came in." The smile was maintained—almost tantalizingly.

"Thank you, Mrs. Barlow," returned Anthony.

MacMorran came to his final question. "You know of nothing, I presume, Mrs. Barlow—that would, assist us in any way to account for this dreadful occurrence. This callous murder of Lady Blanchflower? You haven't observed anything that—"

Mrs. Barlow's denial came immediately. She shook her head with emphasis. "Oh no—nothing. Nothing at all. There hasn't been anything so far as this hotel is concerned. It's just a terrible shock to me in fact I can't believe it's true—even now. To think that anybody should murder a lady like Lady Blanchflower—it's just too awful for words. One just can't contemplate such a thing."

MacMorran nodded. "It is, indeed, everything you say. Well—thank you for your help, Mrs. Barlow. Would it be possible for me to see that chambermaid you mentioned? The name's Bella Street, I think."

"Certainly. Shall I fetch her? Ask her to come in here?"

MacMorran glanced down at what was obviously an internal telephone. "Yes—ask her to come along, will you please?"

Mrs. Barlow flushed—just a little. It was a becoming flush and earned Anthony's full approval.

"If you wish it," replied the housekeeper. Her voice held just the suspicion of a frosty edge. Mrs. Barlow raised the receiver.

4

Anthony knew that they could have skipped Bella and suffered no loss, directly the chambermaid made her appearance.

Her natural dumbness was multiplied a thousandfold by the unusual circumstances in which she now found herself. Inarticulate in her brightest moments, she now approximated for all that MacMorran could extract from her, a Christmas walnut that by cunning positioning on the dish, survives the Yuletide feast and comes up for judgment when the fat has left the land somewhere about Shrove Tuesday.

MacMorran put his questions to the girl and progressed backwards as it were. Anthony formed the opinion that Mrs. Barlow, knowing her Bella, was enjoying the proceedings from the background with an impious delight.

"O.K.," said MacMorran, after five fruitless minutes with the chambermaid; "you can go."

"Where to, sir?" enquired Bella.

"Anywhere," replied MacMorran, "as long as it's far enough."

"Yes, sir," returned Bella; "thank you, sir."

After a somewhat unfortunate collision with the door-edge of the housekeeper's room, Bella, breathless and staring-eyed, scrambled herself out and away.

"I'm afraid," said Mrs. Barlow, rather demurely, "that Bella is merely a good chambermaid. Perhaps I should have told you."

"I'm more than afraid," responded the inspector, "and I'll also take your word as to the quality."

He gave a quick glance round the housekeeper's room. After a slight pause, he added, "Thank you, Mrs. Barlow—I don't think we need trouble you any further. For the present—at least."

Mrs. Barlow heaved a sigh of relief at the words. MacMorran signalled to Anthony, who received a flashing smile from the lady upon his exit. It may have been intended as a reward. On the other hand—it may not.

"What did you think of that?" asked MacMorran.

Anthony grinned at the question. "Extremely smart line in housekeepers, Andrew. If your question was intended to take that direction. The eyes most certainly had it."

"If you ask me—a fast hussy if ever there was one."

Anthony shook his head with mock solemnity. "I was afraid you'd think on those lines. It's that Calvinistic upbringing of yours. I fear, my dear Andrew, that you'll never altogether shake it off."

MacMorran swore. "Calvinistic—my ruddy foot."

Anthony was just able to catch the words.

5

"Bassett next?" queried Anthony.

"Yes; I think so. I'll see Melville, I think. The waiter may not be on duty. Come back with me to Melville's office."

"Bassett?" echoed Melville, when MacMorran projected his request. "Yes—he's here. As a matter of fact I told him yesterday to come along and hold himself in readiness in case he was required for anything. I guessed somebody would want a word with him."

"Get him, will you?"

MacMorran's tone bordered on curtness. It was clear to Anthony that the inspector was still chafing under the *casus* Bella. Melville turned and pressed a bell.

"You'll find Bassett a most reliable chap," he volunteered—"he's been with me a long time—and I tell you straight—I shouldn't like to lose him. I should find it an extremely difficult matter to replace him."

MacMorran made no reply to this effusion. His urge now was severely practical and he waited for the arrival of Bassett with grim lips. When the waiter put in an appearance, Anthony saw a man whom he judged to be about forty-five years of age. He was tall, thin, clean-shaven and rather melancholy looking. Anthony thought as a considered judgment, that Bassett looked more melancholy, indeed, than any man he had ever seen. The waiter had a long, narrow face, with dark, brooding eyes and spiky brown hair. One of his eyes—the left—had a slight but almost incessant twitch.

As Bassett entered Melville's room on this Saturday morning he was nervous, annoyed and—strange to say—dejected. He hated the police, the law, inquests, trials, coroners and even anything but remotely connected with the legal process. In fact, he often boasted when he was off duty, that if he were ever served with a juror's notice he'd see the whole boiling lot in hell before he'd comply with it. When he was questioned as to what procedure he would employ to achieve this torrid end, Ted Bassett would become delightfully vague and evasive, wave an unsteady hand and, if possible, adroitly change the subject. When Melville had told him the day before that "it was a job for the police", Bassett's habitual bitterness in that particular relationship took complete possession of him and it was dominant in his mind when he faced MacMorran and Anthony. Melville arranged chairs and MacMorran gestured Bassett into one of them. It was the chair, by the way, that looked the most uncomfortable, and it is to be regretted, had been deliberately selected by MacMorran for that reason. The inspector wasted no time in preamble, but went straight to the point at once.

"You were on duty, I understand, in the dining-room on Thursday evening? I merely want to ask you just a question or so—that's all. I think perhaps you may be able to help me." The lugubrious-looking Bassett nodded. His thoughts immediately became rebellious. The usual soft ruddy soap—to begin with! Their old game—the cunning baskets!

"That's right," he answered, "I was on duty all right."

"While you were there—you saw Lady Blanchflower and Mrs. Whitburn come in?"

"Yes. That's right. I saw them come in all right. The Guv'nor met 'em at the door of the dining-room. Then, when they was ready, I escorted 'em to their table. That was my usual custom with them. I started it years ago—dunno why exactly—and I stuck to it. Used to do it every evenin'. I fancy the old girl liked it. Lady Blanchflower, I mean. You know—suited her! Bit o' pomp and ceremony. Like what she'd been used to. Took her back, I expect to the days when she was somebody. She was a good 'un—old Lady B. Quite the grand dayme—you know. Home, James—and don't spare the hosses! Always thanked me when I pulled her chair out from the table as though I'd given her a million. 'Thank you, Bassett.' Just like that. No more. 'Thank you, Bassett.' No Blah. No ruddy B.B.C."

Anthony watched MacMorran's face. "Did she say anything to you—besides thanking you?" MacMorran peered closely at the waiter as he put the question. Bassett was on his guard again. Through sheer force of habit. Cunning baskets! What were they after now?

"During the dinner—do you mean?" he asked.

"That's what I did mean."

Bassett's dark eyes brooded into thought. "Nothing that stands out," he replied eventually, "just the normal . . . requests . . . as you might say. And questions . . . as to what was in the nose-bag."

"In the what? Oh—I see—yes—I get you."

"No," continued Bassett, "the only real remark . . . so . . . to speak . . . what you could reasonably call a remark . . . came from old Mrs. Whitburn. I mean—not about the dinner."

"Oh and what was that?"

"Well—there wasn't much in it—just an ordinary sort of remark . . . they was a bit on the late side—that was all. A few minutes after their usual time. Mrs. Whitburn sort of apologised for keepin' us waitin'."

"Am I to understand that they actually *were* late on Thursday? Was it a fact?"

Bassett nodded. "Yes—oh yes. Just a minute or two. Nothing to get 'ot and bothered about."

Anthony cut in before either MacMorran or Bassett could speak.

"Mr. Bassett," he said quietly, "I find myself rather more than merely interested in what you've just told us."

Bassett looked up sharply. This was it! Something cunning coming! The tall bloke was a ruddy twister all right. Of course the perishin' leopard can't change his spots. Everybody knew that. But Anthony went on.

"Was this late arrival in the dining-room an unusual occurrence?"

'Not so bad,' thought Bassett. 'Yet.' "Oh yes—definitely," he said. "Most punctual the two ladies was. Practically always. Wouldn't be late—not once in three months. I mean not more than a minute or so. It's a question of breedin'—that—like good manners—you've either got it or you 'aven't—and both the ladies we're discussin'—'ad it."

Anthony nodded at Bassett's reply and then another idea came to him almost instantaneously.

"Did they by any chance, give a reason to account for their comparative lateness?"

For a moment the waiter's guard was down. He forgot—even though the forgetfulness was short-lived, one at least of the menaces of his years. Anthony's latest question had set his mind going and brought a memory back to him. "Yes," he said sharply—"they did—and that's a fact. Or rather Mrs. Whitburn did. It's come back to me. She mentioned two reasons. The first was the weather. It 'ad come over a bit misty. You get a rare lot o' mist in Quinster. So near the river—you see. And the second was that Lady Blanchflower had caught a bit of a chill. Then I rather fancy Mrs. Whitburn said something about the radio to the other old girl—but she spoke on the soft side and I didn't properly catch it as I was on the half-turn."

"Something about the radio?"

"Yes. I 'eard the word 'radio'—I feel certain. But I didn't catch no more than that."

"Something to do with the radio programme?"

Bassett shook his head . . . what persistent ruddy perishers these busys always were! Can never take no for an answer. "I can't say. I told you I didn't hear properly what Mrs. Whitburn said."

Anthony saw clearly that he would get no further. He handed Bassett back to MacMorran. "O.K., Andrew. Go ahead—and thanks for the break."

MacMorran went ahead. "Would you say, Mr. Bassett, that both ladies were entirely normal during dinner?"

Bassett almost grimaced. "That's the second time I've been asked that question. Or almost! The Guv'nor here asked me that in the early stages when we first knew about Mrs. Whitburn. And the answer's 'yes'. Definitely 'yes'. The wines were all O.K.—I mean by that they 'ad what they customarily 'ad—and I should assert without the slightest 'esitation at all, that both ladies 'ad a real good dinner—which they thoroughly enjoyed. I did 'em well—and they did themselves well."

Bassett sat back and primly folded his hands. Then he began to rub one side of his face.

"If anything," he continued, "givin' my opinion for what it's worth and I've given a lot of thought to it since the death of Lady Blanchflower—they was in rather *high* spirits."

"What do you mean exactly by that?" countered Anthony.

Bassett thought for a moment or two before he replied. "What I meant was high spirits for them."

Anthony thought that he understood what Bassett meant. "Just a minute. Do you mean that the two ladies were in better spirits than was usually the case? Despite the mist and despite Lady Blanchflower's chill?"

Bassett nodded. "That's the idea—that's just what I did mean. They'd been like that for about a week. Perhaps a bit longer. The same sort of thing that in younger people you might describe as on top of the world. I'd noticed it—the same thing I mean—one evening about a week previously. Last Thursday wasn't the beginning of it."

"As high as that eh? Definitely pleased at something—or with themselves? Is that the idea?"

"That's it," said Bassett; "that's just what I did mean—and what I thought on Thursday evening. If you'd prefer the word—'excited'."

MacMorran judged it prudent to put in a spoke. "Can you suggest any reason for their unusually high spirits? That you'd noticed the previous week as well? Did you get any glimmer of what might have caused them?" like that."

"No—nothing

Melville, who had been listening intently, turned to MacMorran. "May I put in a word here?"

"Certainly."

"Thank you." Melville addressed himself to Bassett. "I don't think you mentioned this 'high spirits' business to me, Bassett? When I was running round looking for Mrs. Whitburn? Or at any rate not as strongly as you've just featured it. Why was that, may I ask?"

Bassett shrugged his shoulders. "The words just didn't come into my mind, Guv'nor. But I think I used the word 'excited'. The questions I've just been asked sort of suggested it to me. I'm sorry but that's all there is to it."

"All right," said Melville rather huffily, Anthony thought. "Carry on, Inspector. That's all I wanted to say. But I do like to get things straight."

"Same here," said MacMorran, and then to Bassett, "thank you, Mr. Bassett. That will be all for now. If I should require anything more from you—I'll let you know."

Bassett rose awkwardly and made his exit. His lips seemed to be moving as he went out. The words were framed . . . cunning baskets. They always were, they always had been—and they always ruddy well would be!

6

If Mrs. Barlow had been somewhat surprising and Bella Street definitely disappointing, the blonde receptionist Valerie Skeggs, certainly caused MacMorran to sit up and take rather more than ordinary notice.

The incredible inarticulateness of the chambermaid was levelled up, from an 'averaging' standpoint by the superb and almost torrential eloquence that flowed from the highly-coloured lips of la Skeggs. But actually, from a strict sense of 'values', the receptionist contributed very little. To an acute observer, the main fact which emerged from the spate of spoken Skeggs was that she was intensely flattered by MacMorran's reference to her which from her own point of view had been entirely unexpected.

But she had seen Lady Blanchflower come in on the Thursday evening. But *not* Mrs. Whitburn. Miss Skeggs's seat in her office commanded just a part of the approach to the dining-room which the two ladies had to take if they entered the hotel from the River Street entrance and in the event of her looking up at what she herself described as the "ebsolewtly psaychological moment", it was possible for her to see people on their way to the dining-room.

On the Thursday evening in question she *had* looked up in this way and she *had* seen Lady Blanchflower as she walked along. But *not* Mrs. Whitburn. Mrs. Whitburn was certainly not holding the other lady's arm at *that* moment. Also, she had heard the sound of Mr. Melville's voice coming from somewhere near the dining-room door. She *thought* that he was greeting Lady Blanchflower as he greeted her every evening. But of course that was merely supposition on her part and one mustn't place *too* much relayance on mere supposition, must one?

When MacMorran asked her why she thought she hadn't seen Mrs. Whitburn—Miss Skeggs was eminently reasonable. Her opinion was, she said, that in all probability, Mrs. Whitburn had been a few paces in advance of Lady Blanchflower and had passed out of the Skeggs orbit a second or so before the Skeggs looked up. MacMorran nodded his appreciation of the Skeggs explanation.

He thanked the receptionist for her information, scanty though it may have been. Miss Skeggs returned to her reception records.

For some minutes following the departure of Anthony and the inspector, she continued to preen herself. As the preening process went on, she permitted herself the fervent hope that the "gentlemen from Scotland Yard" would get well stuck in to Mrs. Barlow and would very thoroughly put that unmentionable in her place.

7

"I'm afraid you won't be able to see Mr. and Mrs. Grahame until nearer midday," said Melville a few minutes later, "but the Danburys are available immediately. Perhaps you'd like to interview them in the small lounge? Would that be suitable?"

"Thank you, Mr. Melville. That should suit us very well."

MacMorran gestured. "Lead the way in there—will you?"

The Danburys, already advised doubtless by Melville, were waiting for them in the small lounge. Frank Danbury was a little tubby man, somewhere in the middle sixties. He had a dark, clean-shaven face with muddy, semi-saurian eyes. But despite their unattractive colour (according to Anthony's taste) they were alert and quick-moving. Danbury was a Londoner—an East-ender with all the pert glibness and shrewd humour generally associated with his type. A successful builder, he had made enough money out of the development of estates, to retire at a comparatively early stage in life and able to enjoy most of its good things. He prided himself upon being a man of the world with that best of all gifts (in his opinion)—an unfailing sense of humour. Anthony recognised him at once for what he was—in Anthony's own assessment— the life and death of the party.

Maureen Danbury, his wife, was of superior texture altogether. She was tall and slim with blue eyes, rather high cheek-bones, with a flush of colour on each and a rather attractive spot of similar colour which tinged each cheek. A few years younger, perhaps, than her husband, she still retained a quite reasonable claim to good looks and even better figure. That she had married Danbury for his money and corresponding social advancement, Anthony hadn't the slightest doubt.

Neither of the Danburys however, had anything to add to what the inspector and Anthony already knew.

"As it happened," said Maureen Danbury, "we all went out on Thursday evening as soon as dinner was over. By all—I mean my husband and me—and Mr. and Mrs. Grahame. We all went to the Rivoli—that's the big cinema in Bridge Street. It's rather a habit of ours on Thursday evenings if there's anything like a decent flick showing. So you see, the last we saw of the two ladies—they were still at their table in the dining-room. They hadn't finished dinner."

"I understand," said MacMorran.

"As a matter of fact," Mrs. Danbury continued. "I've already said what I'm saying to you now, to the other inspector who came along yesterday. Inspector Guthrie, isn't it."

"Yes. From Quinster—that's quite right."

Anthony thought that Maureen Danbury held possibilities it would be criminal on his part not to explore.

"Tell me, Mrs. Danbury," he said, "you knew both Lady Blanchflower and Mrs. Whitburn very well. You've lived close to them for a considerable period of time and were able to observe them closely—give me a picture of each of them—do you mind? As you yourself knew them and saw them. I'm certain I should find such pictures extremely valuable."

Maureen Danbury's intelligent features registered pleasure at Anthony's request. Her husband exhibited similar feelings. He was of the type who liked his marriage-partner to be generally admired and delighted in consequence to bask in this condition of reflected glory.

"As a matter of fact—you couldn't have asked anybody better," he remarked encouragingly to Anthony. "My wife's an adept at that sort of thing."

He turned to the woman at his side.

"Go on, my dear. Do your stuff."

"Well," began Maureen Danbury, "supposing I take Lady. Blanchflower first. She was the senior of the two. A really wonderful old lady, and absolutely right out of the very top drawer. Always the aristocrat. Always and everywhere. A trifle hot-tempered—but it didn't last long and ninety-nine times out of a hundred you knew just where you were with her. She was reliable, kind, gracious, courteous . . . and well— how can I put it? You always knew she was *authentic*. The absolutely genuine article. The real thing—nothing shoddy or second-rate about her. Her knowledge of the world—and men and women was immense—she was well-read, widely travelled, and for her age, her mental equipment and grip of almost everything that matters was really amazing."

Mrs. Danbury stopped—and glanced at her husband. "How am I doing, Frank?"

"You're doin' fine, my dear. One hundred per cent . . . I'll say. Lady Blanchflower to a 'T'."

Anthony smiled his thanks. "Now—Mrs. Whitburn."

"Well—Mrs. Whitburn was different. Very different. Naturally! Very charming—upper middle-class, can I say? Nothing like the high society background which belonged to Lady Blanchflower—but all the same—

very charming—and very lady-like. She was a dear little soul, really. And everybody liked her. I could almost say—loved her. Delightfully inconsequential, short-sighted, forgetful—with funny little whims and fancies but all the time retaining an almost irresistible charm. Terribly absent-minded—you know what I mean."

Mrs. Danbury's laugh tinkled through the room. "This sort of thing. She'd put the cat in the oven and the apple-pie outside the back door. Do you get me? Oh—I've thought of something that touches on that— she was all the things I've said, except when she played Bridge. I must mention this—because I regard it as terribly important. Then—she became a very different person believe me. All the forgetfulness and all the absent-mindedness that were hers normally, disappeared like magic. It was really—well it bordered on the incredible. You had to see it and know it—to believe it properly. All the everyday failures of memory became wiped out, as it were, by a great sponge with fifty-two pieces. The charming lady who forgot names . . . and telephone numbers . . . and even what day it was . . . even appointments sometimes . . . and ordinary commonplace matters of that kind . . . played Bridge like a . . . like a brigand! Remembered every card in the pack, knew where it was and watched the fall of every card with the eyes of a predatory hawk. Funny—wasn't it? Don't you think so?"

"No—o," said Anthony—"not altogether—I've known people in my time with somewhat similar characteristics. But please proceed, Mrs. Danbury. I find your pen-portrait extraordinarily interesting. Your husband was right. I hung my hat on the right peg."

Maureen Danbury flushed with pleasure at Anthony's tribute. Her husband would have joined her but for the stern decree of Nature.

"Well," she proceeded, "I feel that there *is* something else I should mention now that I'm so well launched on the subject. And that's this. I don't want you to get an entirely erroneous impression of the two ladies together . . . I mean of Lady Blanchflower and Mrs. Whitburn when they were *with* one another . . . that is to say—in each other's company. I'm afraid you may do, from what I've already told you. But please don't for one minute think that Mrs. Whitburn ever played a sort of second fiddle to Lady Blanchflower. Because she most certainly didn't! Oh, no! Far from it, indeed. She was quiet and fluttery and light and airy . . . all those things . . . but she was much more a foil to Lady Blanchflower than anything in the nature of a second fiddle. You can take that from me, Mr. Bathurst—absolutely! Mrs. Whitburn held her own all right.

Lady Blanchflower was the great lady all the time—I know that full well and I've made it clear to you—you couldn't live here in the Red Deer, as Frank and I have, and not know it—but little Mrs. Whitburn in her quiet little butterfly way, kept her middle-class end up ninety-nine times out of a hundred."

"Good for her," commented Anthony. "You've done splendidly, Mrs. Danbury, and helped us no end. Just one more question—if you don't mind. Can either you or your husband here account for the two ladies being in unusually high spirits at dinner last Thursday evening? Or even for a few days before Thursday?"

Maureen Danbury shook her head slowly and then looked enquiringly at her husband

"High spirits? Unusually so? No—I really can't. I don't think, either, that I really noticed it. At the same time, I don't think I looked their way very often. Did you, Frank?"

Danbury replied with emphasis. "No—my love. That I certainly did not."

"No," repeated the lady, "I certainly can't explain anything like that. Incidentally, who says that they were?"

"We've had reliable information to that effect, Mrs. Danbury," said MacMorran; "but let it pass. It may be that—" The inspector was interrupted by a tap at the door of the lounge. It was John Melville.

"I'm sorry," he apologised as he entered, "but here are Mr. and Mrs. Grahame. May they come in? Also—for your information, Inspector Guthrie and the Chief Constable have arrived."

"Thank you," returned MacMorran. "I'll have just a moment or so with the Grahames and then I'll join Guthrie and his Guv'nor. They can wait for once."

"I'll tell them," said Melville. As he stepped back from the door he called out: "Mr. and Mrs. Grahame! Come in, will you?"

8

Melville made the necessary introductions before quietly effacing himself. Anthony began to take immediate stock of the couple who had just entered.

Stephen Grahame was a retired baker and confectioner, and an East-ender like Frank Danbury. He had leapt to financial eminence in an East-end suburb of London during the War of 1914-18 when his chain of half a dozen shops had coined money in half a dozen contiguous districts. The beginnings of his success had been in several highly lucrative deals in flour which certain fortuitous circumstances had enabled him to transact. When the Second Great War came in 1939, Stephen had 'got out' and his business was now carried on by his son.

Of Quaker stock and the son of a pious Bible-reading father, Stephen had found flaws in the Quaker doctrine and way of life. His health, however, since his retirement, had deteriorated sadly mainly owing to his constant desire to drink the health of almost everybody else and certainly of everybody who came near enough to him to hear the convivial suggestion. His daily and nightly contributions to the coffers of the Red Deer at Quinster were noble and magnificent, and more than once his most able and remarkably efficient wife, Edith, had been heard to remark to a friend in confidence, semi-humorously and at the same time semi-bitterly, "that Stephen had 'bought' the Red Deer many times over."

He was heavy and fleshy with a quirk of humour which puckered his face but his manner of speech, at most times of the day and evening, betrayed a recent and lingeringly-affectionate association with alcohol.

"Of course," he said on his first introduction to Anthony, following on that to Inspector MacMorran, "I know you! You're the fellow that . . . er . . . I know your wife . . . why bless my heart and soul . . . where was it now . . . I'm absolutely positive I know you . . . you were down at . . . where the devil's the place . . . at the hotel there . . . you were staying there when the wife and I . . . damn it all—it was one late summer . . . we'd been to Switzerland before that."

Anthony judged it time to cut into the forest of words. "I'm afraid not, Mr. Grahame. Somebody else. You're mistaking me for another person. Actually, I've never been there."

"Oh—in that case," returned Grahame with a shrug of the shoulders, "it couldn't have been you—could it? That settles it. You must have been there at another time when I wasn't there, when I didn't see you and naturally didn't recognise you. That accounts for my little lapse of memory. Ah well—none of us is infallible."

His eyes smiled and his mouth quirked noticeably. Anthony wasn't sure whether he was going to like or dislike him. All the time this superb conversational effort had been in flight his wife had watched him with a mingled air of supreme resignation and maternal solicitude.

Edith Grahame, like her husband, somewhere round the 'sixty-mark', was of middle-height, with raven hair and kindly pleasant, almost twinkling eyes. Her nose was slightly retroussé and full of character, and for the second time that morning Anthony found himself looking at a middle-aged woman who still possessed a good measure of attractiveness and charm. Had he known then, at their first meeting, that Edith Grahame had been the brains behind and the steady prop of her wayward husband ever since she had propelled him to the altar, he might have questioned her to greater length than he did.

Summing up briefly, however, MacMorran elicited the fact that the story which the Grahames had to tell, tallied identically and absolutely with that which the Danburys had already told. Which, seeing they had spent the whole of the fateful evening in each other's company, was but a natural occurrence and entirely to be expected. As MacMorran noted one or two of the more important particulars, Anthony found time to question the two couples in his company in a general and desultory sort of way.

"Can any of you help us on any of these points?" he asked. "One or two of them may sound strange when you hear them perhaps, but I assure you, they aren't being asked in any frivolous mood."

He waited a moment for the individual reactions. Grahame grinned half foolishly, half knowingly, and his mouth quirked to its invariable habit. Edith Grahame's alert eyes lost their kindliness suddenly and became eager and expectant. Mrs. Danbury's intelligent features shadowed a little and her tinges of colour intensified as her husband achieved a certain somewhat bird-like pomposity. Anthony then put the first of his general questions.

"Did either Lady Blanchflower or Mrs. Whitburn at any time wear a wig? To your knowledge?"

Each of the four faces registered something like astonishment.

After a few seconds Mrs. Danbury slowly shook her head. "If either of them did, it would come as a great surprise to me. Certainly I never noticed anything about either of them to suggest such a thing. I don't know what Edith thinks. What do you say, Edith?"

She turned to Mrs. Grahame with an impulsive gesture as she made her appeal. "Do you agree with me, Edith?"

"Oh yes," replied Mrs. Grahame, "my answer would be 'no'. I'm in exactly the same position as you say you are. No suspicion of that kind has ever occurred to me."

Danbury was equally strong in denial. "Never dreamt of such a thing," he said emphatically.

Anthony looked towards the silent Stephen Grahame. "And you, Mr. Grahame? Anything to add to what's already been said?"

Grahame spread out his hands. "My dear chap! Now I ask you! A bit of York ham perhaps, or a nice middle-cut of Scotch salmon . . . well over the odds . . . I might be able to manage that for you if you gave me the tip in time . . . I've a number of good friends who can usually oblige me . . . they know how to charge, of course . . . but women and wigs! Now, my dear fellow—what do you take me for? They're just not my line of country at all. All the same . . . it's a damned funny coincidence—I had an old uncle used to wear a toupee—but he kept canaries."

"Thank you. Perhaps I understand. Now—another question—even more surprising, perhaps, than its predecessor. Has any one of you any suggestions to make to the inspector here or to me, as to where Mrs. Whitburn might be? You all knew her infinitely better than anybody in all probability—whereas the inspector and I have never set eyes on her."

There ensued a complete silence. "Must I answer?" asked Maureen Danbury with a quick glance at Anthony.

"Of course not. There's no compulsion in any way. But if you *do* have any—"

Before he could finish, Mrs. Danbury had gone on—rather impetuously. "Perhaps it's wrong of me to say it. But I think she's dead, too. I don't think there's any doubt about it."

"You mean—murdered?"

"Certainly—whoever killed Lady Blanchflower, killed Mrs. Whitburn, too. That's how it appeals to me."

"I see. And the body?"

Maureen Danbury shrugged her shoulders vaguely. "In the river. Hidden away somewhere. Anywhere."

Anthony nodded gravely as MacMorran came back to the conversation. The latter challenged the other members of the circle.

"What about you others? Ladies and gentlemen? Do you agree with Mrs. Danbury?"

Grahame wagged his head saying nothing. Danbury puffed out his cheeks and said, "I reckon my missus isn't far out. I'd trust her to put her finger on the right spot."

Edith Grahame thought for a little while and then remarked quietly, "I really don't know what to think. If Maureen's idea's the right one—it would be just too awful for words. But, frankly, I can't make any other suggestion."

MacMorran nodded grimly. "Thank you." He turned to Anthony. "Any more questions you want to ask these ladies and gentlemen. Because if there aren't—"

"One, perhaps." Anthony faced Mrs. Danbury. "Mrs. Danbury," he said, "*why* do you think these two ladies have been murdered?"

Maureen Danbury looked puzzled at the question.

"I'm sorry," said Anthony again. "I see your difficulty. I should have said, 'For what reason do you think these two ladies have been murdered'. What I'm after is motive. Can you suggest one to me?"

The lady looked surprisingly startled. "Well," she said, "I'm very much in the dark—naturally—but surely it must have been robbery—mustn't it? That's what occurred to me directly I heard the dreadful news. Is there any other reason?"

"You can't suggest any other—you, who knew them both so well?"

"I certainly cannot."

"Thank you again." Anthony gestured to MacMorran. "O.K., Andrew."

MacMorran moved to the door. "My thanks as well—to all," he said gruffly. He beckoned to Anthony. "Better see Guthrie now. To say nothing of the Big Noise. We don't want him singing in Berkeley Square."

CHAPTER 3

1

"Ah, there you are," boomed Sir George Nightingale. "Thought you were never coming. Better tell you what Inspector Guthrie's put in hand. You tell the tale yourself, Guthrie."

"Well, sir," said the Quinster inspector, "there's not a whisper of the missing lady from any quarter whatever. That is to say from the local standpoint. I've had half a dozen men on routine enquiries at the usual places in the town—and they've picked up just nothing at all. Not a sausage. So we think, the Chief Constable and myself, that we'd better concentrate on finding a dead body—instead of continuing to look for a living woman. How do you feel with regard to that, sir?"

MacMorran nodded. "I'm afraid I agree. But I don't see it makes a lot of difference—except to the lady herself. What measures are you proposing to take?"

"The river. That first of all. We must drag it in the likely places. Following the river, waste ground. Plantations. Anywhere where there's thick undergrowth."

"O.K.," replied MacMorran; "and what about the two main clues—the wig and the stocking that strangled Lady Blanchflower?"

"The first we'll try to trace—the second's a different proposition, I'm afraid. Must be thousands just like it. To say nothing of the fact that I should say it belonged to the old lady herself."

MacMorran nodded. "What about Mrs. Whitburn's room? Here? I know it's impossible to do everything at once—but all the same, I think we should examine it without further delay. It may lead us to something."

"I couldn't agree more," came the rather strident voice of Sir George Nightingale.

"Tell Melville, then," motioned MacMorran, "tell him we'd like to go up to Mrs. Whitburn's room at once." Guthrie slipped away to find the proprietor.

2

Mrs. Whitburn's room at the Red Deer proved to be very much as Anthony had anticipated. It was spacious, with a connecting bathroom. Besides the bed there were clothes-cabinet, dressing-table, large wardrobe, small writing-table with telephone, two small chairs and a large extremely comfortable-looking basket-chair.

Sir George fussed round the room in the manner of a large tom-cat, as MacMorran and Guthrie got to work on the preliminaries. A tom-cat, however, which had been well house-trained. MacMorran tried the drawer of the escritoire but found it locked. "H'm," muttered Guthrie: "key's somewhere about. Must be. In here possibly."

He tried the drawers of the dressing-table, one by one. The third drawer disclosed a smallish key-ring with seven keys attached. The keys were all small. Guthrie tried them in turn on the drawer of the escritoire.

While the local inspector was getting to work, Anthony walked over for a closer look at things. Eventually Guthrie's fingers found and used the right key and he pulled open the drawer. Anthony looked with interest and curiosity as the drawer slid open. He was remembering what Maureen Danbury had said with regard to the missing woman. He was not unduly disappointed at what he saw.

The drawer, on the whole, was in an untidy state. Not littered—nothing like that—that would be too strong an expression—but the contents were jumbled rather and any attempt at order was conspicuous by its absence. Anthony saw a writing-pad, many loose items of stationery, envelopes and postcards, an identity-card, a fountain-pen, a cheque-book and in one corner of the drawer, an assortment of what looked like miscellaneous papers.

MacMorran bent down and took out this little heap for examination. Anthony saw then, that in the main, they were receipted bills. Anthony caught sight of one or two names on the billheads as MacMorran turned them over in his fingers. He saw 'Harrods' several times, with an occasional 'Selfridges', 'D. H. Evans' and 'Liberty's'. Suddenly he heard a sharp exclamation from the Yard inspector.

MacMorran handed one of the bills to Guthrie. "Something there, Inspector Guthrie, for the grey matter to work on. Have a look at it."

Guthrie took the bill and frowned at what he saw. Then he looked up and began to shake his head slowly. The Chief Constable came bounding from the bathroom where he had used the mirror on several occasions and from divers angles for the purpose of self-profile inspection.

"Hallo," he boomed, "found something. Good work! What is it?"

Anthony listened for the disclosure that was obviously due. "It's a receipted account, sir," said Inspector Guthrie, "in the amount of £20. Described as a deposit paid on two wigs hired for a dramatic performance of *Caste* to take place at the Thespian Hall, Quinster, on Wednesday the 9th of November. One of the wigs is described as 'Eccles', and the other 'Marquise'. Hire account for articles to follow—balance of deposit returnable on surrender of articles hired."

"Good God," exclaimed Sir George Nightingale (inappropriately) and then "who's it made out to" (ungrammatically).

"Mrs. Laura Whitburn, Hon. Secretary, Quinster Dramatic Club, at Red Deer Hotel, Castle Street, Quinster, Downshire."

Anthony extended his hand. "May I glance at that, Inspector," he remarked quietly.

3

Guthrie handed over the account. It was made out on an official invoice of 'Isaac Fleury, Perruquier, Wig-maker and Costumier, Long Acre, London, W.C.2.' As Guthrie had just informed the Chief Constable, the invoice had been rendered to Mrs. Laura Whitburn, Red Deer Hotel, Castle Street, Quinster, Downshire. The remaining details were also in accordance with Guthrie's statement to Sir George. In the middle of the account, was affixed a twopenny receipt stamp across which had been written in thin spidery writing the words:

"Received by cheque £20 (Twenty pounds) as Deposit Fee for and on behalf of Isaac Fleury. L. Saranita, Cashier. Nov. Ist."

Anthony handed the invoice to the Chief Constable, realizing with a sudden tremor of amusement, that that worthy had not yet been privileged to see it. It may well be that Anthony's gesture was well-timed, as Sir George was heard to mutter under his breath as he took the account.

"What do you make of it?" asked MacMorran of Anthony.

Anthony shook his head. "At the moment, Andrew—just nothing. But, of course, there's one comfort (from our point of view), wherever it leads to—it must always lead back to Isaac Fleury, of Long Acre, Perruquier and Costumier. And there's another point, Andrew—where's the other wig?"

"Extraordinary business," boomed Sir George, "why is a wig that's been ordered for a play-actin' set-out, found under a murdered woman's body? Doesn't make rhyme or reason as far as I can see. What's your opinion, MacMorran?"

"Much the same as yours, sir," replied MacMorran dourly. Guthrie took the articles from the drawer of the escritoire as MacMorran sorted out the remainder of his assortment. The identity-card was that of Mrs. Whitburn herself. Guthrie continued to do his job of collection. The rest of MacMorran's heap of papers, superficially, was ordinary and entirely commonplace—receipted bills in most cases for all the various types of everyday necessary wearing apparel. Anthony motioned to Guthrie.

"I fancy I spotted a cheque-book, Inspector. On the right-hand side of the drawer there. Fish it out, will you?"

"That's quite right. Here it is."

Guthrie showed the book in question. "Check the cheque," said Anthony rather impishly.

For the moment, Guthrie seemed at a partial loss. Anthony nodded towards the account at which the Chief Constable was still staring with something very much akin to fascination. "That account over there. Paid by cheque—if we can believe Loretta Saranita."

"Loretta? How do you—"

Anthony cut him. "Lulu, then. Or possibly even Leonardo. Have it any way you like, Inspector."

Light penetrated to the Guthrie mental attic. "Oh—I get you. Yes we'll have a look. Should be here, of course."

Guthrie opened the cheque-book on the writing-desk as the others crowded round him. The search for the Fleury cheque proved to be short and sharp. The last-used counterfoil but one was made out in the following terms:

"October 20th. I. Fleury. £20."

"There it is," said Guthrie, "there it is—all right. That's the payment. All in order and above-board. Mrs. Whitburn ordered those wigs—no doubt about it."

MacMorran took the cheque-book and flicked over the rest of the used counterfoils. The cheque-book which had been issued by the Quinster branch of the Southern and Home Counties Bank had gone into use, according to the date on the first stub, on August 26th and fifteen cheques had been used. Three of them had been drawn in favour of 'J. Melville', one to 'self' for one hundred pounds, one to 'Page Ingram and Co.', three to 'Harrods', three to 'Selfridges', three to 'D. H. Evans' and one to 'I. Fleury'.

"Monthly payments to the hotel here, three of 'em in all, which would be for August, September and October, and the rest seem more or less O.K. One to herself, and nine for monthly shopping accounts. Hallo—what have we here? Something that isn't an account?"

A tiny slip of paper had been inserted between two of the used counterfoils.

"Same writing as the cheque-counterfoils," said MacMorran, "which means presumably, Mrs. Whitburn herself. Let's see what this says."

MacMorran began to read aloud. Anthony listened intently for the words that were to come.

"I must write it down before I forget. Lily says 'Come quickly—Mistress away'. What a perfectly *awful* telegram they would make, to be sure! Fancy having to wire it to anybody. P.S. Must tell K. as soon as possible."

Sir George Nightingale began to clear his throat. Anthony braced himself instinctively and prepared for the worst. "I attach little or no important to any of that," protested the Chief Constable, "just a domestic note—and no more. And probably of a most trivial nature. Slipped itself between the leaves of the cheque-book as a matter of luck—not judgment. Nine times out of ten would have been thrown away." There was an appreciable period of silence after he had spoken. Sir George noticed this and came again.

"Well—don't you chaps agree with me? Say so—if you don't."

"I'm inclined to, sir," replied Inspector Guthrie. MacMorran took no notice of Sir George's last question . . . his thoughts had travelled into opposite directions. Anthony, however, in an attempt to evade the issue, addressed a question to Guthrie.

"Have you done anything yet, Inspector—in the matter of the relations of these two ladies? Any of them been informed—or even sent for?"

Guthrie looked at Sir George Nightingale. "In the late Lady Blanchflower's case," said the Chief Constable, "near relations living anything like close at hand, seem few and far between. But I understand there may be a son somewhere abroad. Enquiries are being made in that direction. But I'm afraid it may take a day or two. With regard to Mrs. Whitburn there's nothing like the same difficulty. Her son is a figure more or less in the public eye."

At that moment, Anthony clicked. "Not K. M. R. Whitburn, the old Kent skipper?"

"Precisely," returned the Chief Constable stiffly. "I should say he's pretty certain to be here some time this morning from what I heard last night."

"Ten to one," said Anthony, "he's the 'K' referred to in that postcript. 'Must tell K.' The dutiful mother thinking of her son."

"It may be so. On the other hand—it may not. When he arrives the matter can easily be put to the test."

"Mr. Bathurst," MacMorran preceded his address with a loud cough. "I'd like your opinion . . . before we go any further . . . with regard to this slip of paper that we found in the chequebook. How does it strike you?"

"What—Lily says', do you mean?" Anthony shrugged his shoulders. "May I look at it?"

Sir George Nightingale into whose hands it had eventually arrived, handed the slip over. Anthony took the Whitburn cheque-book and examined it carefully by the side of the paper.

"Same handwriting, Andrew—as you said. Beyond that—I have no opinion—at the moment that is. Find myself rather puzzled by the confusion."

Sir George heard the final word and repeated it. "Confusion—did you say?"

"Yes, Sir George—confusion. Certainly—confusion."

"Where's the . . . er . . . confusion, may I ask? I fail to understand."

The Chief Constable reached for the slip of paper and examined it again fiercely and belligerently. Anthony dropped an eyelid in MacMorran's direction. He happened to be on Sir George's blind side.

"Confusion of numbers, Sir George—surely?" He added, "Why should singulars suddenly become plurals? That's the point which eludes me."

Sir George growled unintelligibly and went under. "Yes. Tricky point that—I agree. Especially if 'mistress' applies to Mrs. Whitburn herself. As you say—there's Lady Blanchflower to be considered as well. Er . . . quite so."

Guthrie came back from further activities in the room and spoke to MacMorran.

"I don't know there's much else of any account. Everything appears quite normal. Clothes everywhere, of course. In the big wardrobe and the clothes-cabinet. Just as one would expect.'

He stood by the bed for a moment and scratched his head. "Dashed if I know what to—" Then he broke off abruptly and addressed himself to MacMorran. "What do *you* make of it, sir?" MacMorran looked glum at Guthrie's question. In answering he employed an old and time-honoured artifice. He asked Guthrie a question in return.

"You changed your ideas? With regard to the interrupted thief?"

Guthrie was silent for a time under the shaft. Then he said, "It's this disappearance that's worrying me. Where is this Mrs. Whitburn? What on earth can be the reason behind the disappearance of a woman of her age and social standing? Unless—"

"Unless what?" questioned the Chief Constable.

"Unless she's guilty—had a brainstorm or something and run amok in some unpredictable fashion." MacMorran shook his head but said nothing.

"There's the other possibility, you know," said Anthony quietly, "the one that none of us must overlook."

"You mean?" said Sir George.

"That she's dead herself."

"Murdered—do you mean—like Lady Blanchflower?"

"As far as I can see, sir," returned Anthony, "it looks very much like it."

He turned to MacMorran. "Get Melville to come up, Andrew, will you? I fancy it's on the cards he can help us."

"Melville?"

"Yes. In the matter of such things as wigs and the Quinster Dramatic Club."

CHAPTER 4

1

Melville scanned their faces anxiously as he entered the room that had been Laura Whitburn's. He positively hated anything of this kind. He had led an easy and comfortable life for some years now, and he wanted it to continue. His glances finished up on the face of the Chief Constable.

"Sit down, Melville, will you? Chief Det. Inspector MacMorran thinks that you can probably give us some assistance with regard to one or two matters."

"Anything within my power, sir," returned Melville.

"Good man," replied Sir George. "He'll ask you a few questions, then."

The hotel proprietor took one of the small chairs and sat the reverse way to normal, resting his hands on the bar at the back. In this manner he faced MacMorran.

"Do you happen to know anything about the Quinster Dramatic Club, Mr. Melville?"

A puzzled look flitted over Melville's face as he shook his head. "I'm afraid I don't," he replied.

"I take it there is such a club?"

Melville looked rather nonplussed. "Well—you may think it strange, sir—seeing I've been here just on ten years—but I don't even know that—for certain. May I ask *why* you're enquiring?"

"Let that wait for a moment. We can come back to it later. Where's the Thespian Hall?"

Melville looked even more bewildered. "The what Hall, Inspector? What was the word?"

"The Thespian Hall, Mr. Melville? The Thespian Hall, Quinster."

Again Melville shook his head slowly. It was clear that the sense of bewilderment had not yet left him. "I'm afraid you've got me there, Inspector. If I tell you the truth—I've never heard of the place. And that's a solemn fact."

MacMorrow frowned. "Do you mean that there's no such Hall in existence?"

"No," replied Melville with a sudden sharp insistence. "Please don't get me wrong. I *don't* mean that. I wouldn't say that for a moment. I don't go out overmuch—my business doesn't allow me to—and new places can spring up—and old places can have their names changed to more modern and grander ones. All I'm saying, sir, is that *I* don't know this place you're enquiring about. What was the name of it, now? The Thessar—"

"Thespian. Thespian Hall. Well if you don't know it—you don't—and that's all there is to it."

MacMorran turned—looking rather blankly towards Anthony. Before the latter could speak, Sir George Nightingale butted in. "Ring up the Town Hall, man! Tell them it's the Chief Constable who's enquiring. Get through to the Rating department. They'll tell you where the place is—quick enough."

"Good idea," said Anthony.

Sir George tossed up his head—looking immensely pleased with himself. MacMorran looked at Guthrie and gestured towards the telephone.

"You 'phone, will you, Inspector Guthrie? You probably know the number."

"I do," replied Guthrie picking up the receiver from its cradle, "but I'm dashed if I know this 'Thespian Hall'—any more than Mr. Melville does. Personally I've never heard of the ruddy place."

2

Guthrie made quick communication with the Town Hall. He submitted the preliminary announcement of the enquiry in accordance with Sir George's recent instructions. Then the onlookers in the room saw that he was listening to what was coming from the other end.

"Yes that's the idea," said Guthrie, "the Thespian Hall. The Thespian Hall, Quinster. Used, presumably for such things as Dramatic entertainments. What's that? Thank you very much I'll hang on."

He half-turned to the others and spoke from the side of his mouth. "That was a Junior Clerk—or something like it. He's passing the enquiry to a superior. I should have thought . . . hallo who's that . . . yes, that's right . . . very many thanks."

Guthrie stopped talking and began to listen again. Suddenly the others heard him say . . . "Thank you . . . but don't go for half a second, if you don't mind," and then he turned back to them with a puzzled shake of the head and his hand over the mouthpiece of the receiver . . . "no such place as the Thespian Hall is rated in Quinster . . . the Rating people have never heard of it. Where do we go from there?"

Anthony held out his hand, in a quick impulse, for the telephone-receiver. Guthrie surrendered it to him as though he were glad to part company with it.

"Are you the Rating Department?" asked Anthony . . . "thank you . . . would you kindly transfer this call to the Lettings section of the Town Clerk's Dept? Yes . . . yes . . . that's so . . . for the Chief Constable, Sir George Nightingale."

There came a wait of some seconds. Anthony began to speak again. "Is that the Lettings section of the Town Clerk's Department? Or does the Treasurer deal with lettings? What? Yes—yes—that's right. The Chief Constable. What Sir George would like to know is this: Is there any portion of the Town Hall at Quinster or the Municipal offices let for Dramatic entertainments? Yes? I see. Two halls. Two! What would the names of those Halls be? The Major Hall and the Minor Hall? I see. Thank you very much. Yes—I understand that. Now, while I'm on the line, can you tell me if there's an Amateur Dramatic Club or Society operating in Quinster itself, or in the neighbourhood of Quinster, known as the 'Quinster Dramatic Club'?" There was a pause as Anthony's question sank home and as Anthony waited for the reply to come back. The interval extended to half a minute. Then Anthony began to speak again.

"I see. Thank you once again. Oh yes—naturally—I understand that. As far as you know—none—and certainly never any lettings of the Town Hall that you can remember to a club of that name. The 'Quinster Players' you say—yes—I'll remember it—Miss Norah Joyce, Hon. Secretary— yes—I'll take the address as well—Number seventeen Queen's Fulton Road—thank you very much—the Chief Constable is extremely obliged to you."

Anthony replaced the receiver and moved from the writing-table.

"Well, gentlemen—doubtless you heard most of what was said to me. As far as the authorities at the Town Hall know, there's no such club as the 'Quinster Dramatic Club'. It has similar qualities, you see, to the Thespian Hall. Qualities of nonexistence—if such a thing be possible."

"Where the hell are we?" asked MacMorran; "the farther we go—the deeper we seem to be embedded. I'm hanged if I can see a ray of light anywhere. If there's no Dramatic performance—what on earth did Mrs. Whitburn order those wigs for? And where's wig number two? If we knew that—we might—" He broke off, seemingly lost in thought. The Chief Constable looked at his watch.

"I'm afraid I must leave you to it, Guthrie. I've an appointment in town at two o'clock this afternoon. A most important appointment indeed. 'Phone me at my house at ten o'clock tonight. Without fail. Good morning, gentlemen—you must excuse me."

Sir George bustled out puffing and blowing. MacMorran nodded permission to Melville to accompany him. The hotel proprietor took the hint with pleasure and Anthony was left in the room with the two professionals.

"What have we got?" said MacMorran. "Let's see—it's not a bad moment to take stock of what I'll describe as the Whitburn findings. A bill from a perruquier for two wigs (one of which we've never seen)—the counterfoil of the cheque used in payment of the wigs bill—and a scrawled sort of recorded note in the wrong place, asking somebody to come somewhere quickly because the mistress was away! H'm—personally I'm absolutely in the dark."

Guthrie remained silent. "Meanwhile," continued MacMorran, "where *is* Mrs. Whitburn?"

Anthony looked up from the chair he had taken. "That's what we must establish as quickly as possible, Andrew. Until we've cleared that particular pocket of air we're groping in the dark. I say—Inspector Guthrie—something I've been going to ask you—I take it you've seen the lodge-keeper chap at the entrance to Quinster Castle?"

"I have seen him—yes. I didn't find him much good. From my point of view. I certainly didn't get anything out of him that was worth much."

Anthony looked at his wrist-watch. "I think I'll pop over and have a word with him while it's in my mind. I shall just about have time before lunch. O.K. with you, Andrew?"

"All right," replied MacMorran; "see you in the dining-room, then, at one-thirty."

"Without fail, Andrew," returned Anthony. He waved to the two inspectors and made his way downstairs.

3

Anthony walked quickly down the heavily-carpeted staircase, turned by the reception-room which housed Valerie Skeggs and made tracks for the hotel exit which according to what Melville had already told him was in River Street. He found the door without difficulty and then, instead of turning right to the High Street, he turned left and continued down River Street. He had an idea he'd like to see what the rear of the Red Deer looked like while the opportunity presented itself.

As he had anticipated, it was possible to turn into the back premises of the hotel a few yards farther down River Street. Anthony took the turn and found himself in the yard and among the many and rambling out-houses of the Red Deer. It was a well-cobbled yard with long, low-lying kitchens, sculleries, and the like. At intervals were small trees set in quaintly-shaped tubs against the walls. One or two of the tubs were in process of being repainted—so Anthony judged from the sight of a paintbrush on a bench and the smell of wet paint which seemed to pervade everywhere.

As Anthony took stock in this fashion, a brewer's dray drove down River Street and stopped outside the yard entrance. A burly man hoisted himself from the driving-seat, raised a beer-crate to his shoulder and moved resolutely in Anthony's direction. Anthony walked to the far end of the Red Deer premises, passing a 'Men's' convenience and what looked to him like the remains of an ancient horse-trough.

Before he turned again to retrace his steps, he heard voices. When he eventually did turn, he saw that a young fellow in overalls had returned to wield a paintbrush on the tree-tub that had been previously engaging his artistic attention and was now in conversation with the representative of the brewer.

Anthony retraced his steps and came back to River Street. From where he now stood he could see the river with its shabby-looking promenade and occasional landing-stage and Quinster Bridge away in the distance. Anthony turned his back on the river and made for Castle Street.

Outside the entrance to the railway-station in River Street, that is to say, almost exactly opposite to the side entrance of the Red Deer, were several groups of children with various grotesque figures sprawled or tied on old perambulators, push-chairs and similar forms of transport. As Anthony came abreast of them, a girl broke from the group and ran towards him brandishing a collecting-box. Anthony realised with something of a shock as he rendered tribute, that the date was November the fifth—up to that moment he had completely forgotten the fact.

As he moved towards Castle Street, Quinster Castle, and its lodge-keeper—he smiled to himself ruefully—no fireworks for him that evening! No Golden Rain or Roman Candle—not even the scintillating turn of a Catherine Wheel!

4

Anthony crossed Castle Street and faced immediately the main entrance to Quinster Castle. He passed through the small gate, on the left of the main roadway that leads to the castle itself, and proceeded along the paved walk towards the lodge and the lodge-keeper. To the best of his recollection, the distance wasn't much more than the length of a cricket-pitch—and it gave him a certain satisfaction to find that his recollection was accurate.

Catterall, the lodge-keeper, stepped from his covered place of vantage and waited for him. His attitude was not devoid of truculence.

"What might your business be?" demanded Catterall.

"It might be big-game hunting—but it's not. You're slipping, my man. It's time you pulled yourself together." Catterall, the humorist, was somewhat taken aback at this unexpected greeting.

"Just a minute. What's the idea?"

Anthony flicked his official card at him. Catterall read and understood—via memory.

"Your pardon, me lord," said Catterall with heavy-handed humour; "but it was passing dark the time before and I didn't see your face properly when your car came in. From 'enceforth, me lord, I am your Lordship's—"

"Skip all that," said Anthony curtly, "and just answer a few questions. Then we may get on a lot better."

"Yes, sir," returned a sobered Catterall. "At your service."

"I'll just come inside your place if you don't mind," said Anthony; "we can talk more comfortably in there than out here."

"Certainly, sir. Step in 'ere will you."

At the same time, Catterall pointed to a heavy-looking wooden chair with arm-rests. "Sit down there, sir, and make yourself comfortable."

"Thank you. Going back to last Thursday evening, Catterall—did you see the late Lady Blanchflower and Mrs. Whitburn leave the castle when they went out to dinner?"

"No, sir. I did not. Not last Thursday. But there's nothing in that. For one thing it was too perishin' misty—visibility was pretty rough in this quarter last Thursday I can tell you—we're too near the river at this time of the year to miss whatever fog's goin'—and for another, Lady Blanchflower 'ad a 'abit of slippin' along the carriageway if there was no traffic about, and not using the path in the ordinary way. When she did that, I wouldn't always notice her go by. She may 'ave done that last Thursday evening."

"I see. Now what about the return journey? Did you see the ladies come back from the Red Deer? Or either of them?"

"No, sir. Once again the answer's in the negative. Neither of the ladies. But there's another point there, sir, if you'll pardon my saying so. I'd better explain it to you."

Anthony was curious. "How do you mean—another point?"

"I'll tell you, sir. I go off duty at 8 p.m. at this time of the year—nobody relieves me. But the main gates—they're used for vehicular traffic—are left open till ten o'clock. Then they're shut by one of the castle staff—you can't always tell who—because they take it in turns for the evenin' duty. So you see, sir, that if either of the two ladies came back from the Deer after eight o'clock—I shouldn't ha' seen 'er. In all probability I was indoors 'avin' my little bit o' supper."

Anthony was silent. This information which Catterall was giving him was by way of being a disappointment. "So that anybody can get inside the precincts of the castle after 8 p.m.?"

"Well, sir—the gate's closed—but that's really only as far as appearances go. Anybody could get in. Not into the castle itself of course. Just a little way, as you might say. But you'd be surprised, sir—there's practically nothin' doin' in the shape of traffic—any kind of traffic I mean—after about four o'clock in the afternoon. Scarcely a 'uman soul ever comes near. The place is dead, as you might say. Unless, of course, there's a big do on inside the castle itself. Then things are very different. When the Duke's daughter come of age, for example, there was a 'uge ball—all the countryside was present—anybody what *was* anybody—the real *hoi polloi* as you might say—then there was comin's and goin's all night. No off duty for me—on that occasion."

Anthony repressed his smile just in time. "I presume that these arrangements you've outlined to me are by the Duke of Quinster's orders?"

"Naturally, sir. Who else? After all, it's 'is ruddy castle."

"I'm afraid then," said Anthony, "that it comes to this. Whichever way we look at it. Sometime on Thursday evening or during the night Thursday—Friday, somebody entered the precincts of Quinster Castle, got as far as the cloisters and murdered one of the occupants of the cloister-apartments. That is to say, this person walked in without any difficulty, did the job and walked out. He either slipped by you in the prevailing mist or waited until later, when the coast was reasonably clear. Any remarks on that, Catterall?"

Mark Catterall fingered his chin. "It do look like that, sir—I admit. But what can you do about it? You can't stop fog just when you'd like—and no more you can't 'ave an armed guard round the place, night and day, just because the place is a castle."

"No—I suppose you can't—when you get to rock-bottom."

Catterall began to expand under enthusiasm for his theme. "Plenty of people come as far as this, you know, sir. That's to say up as far as the lodge. I think it's mostly done out o' curiosity—if you know what I mean. That's my opinion. Take this morning now. Seein' as 'ow it's November the fifth, I'd 'ad no less than three kids wheelin' perishin' guys in wooden boxes—they nip in out o' sheer curiosity to see what the place is like. Another thing—come out here, sir. I'll show you something."

Catterall stepped into the open and Anthony followed him. "That's what attracts and sort o' fascinates them. Them wyverns up there—the famous Quinster wyverns—see the old baskets sittin' perched up there? See the cruel look on their perishin' faces? Some of the people'll gaze at 'em proper open-mouthed."

Catterall pointed towards the two stone wyverns with an almost dramatic gesture. As he looked at the figures, Anthony thought he could understand why many people stared at them. There undoubtedly was a fascination about them. They were both eerie and cruel—steeped with the malice and menace so often mixed with mythology. He glanced down at his wrist-watch. Would he gain anything by questioning Catterall further? He thought it highly problematical. He had found out what he had wanted.

"So it comes to this, Caterall—you can't tell me, if or when the two ladies got back after dinner on Thursday evening—and you've no check whatever on anything that happened at the gates here after eight o'clock that evening. To say nothing of the mist in the early stages and the fog later. That's the position, isn't it—more or less?"

Catterall fingered his chin again. "Yes, sir—that's about it." Anthony's eyes endeavoured to meet the lodge-keeper's but failed to do so. It seemed to Anthony that Catterall for some reason or other was evading the direct gaze.

"In that case, then," continued Anthony, "I'll say good morning to you. Thanks for the information."

"You off, sir?"

Anthony nodded.

"There's one little thing I'd like to say—before we part company. Did you get the Duke's permission to question me? He's my employer, you know."

Anthony wondered what was really behind this last remark. "No," he answered. "I'm afraid I didn't. But don't worry with regard to that. If there's any explaining to be done—leave that to me."

Catterall shook his head. "I wasn't thinking of myself," he said sturdily, "I was thinking of you."

"That's kind of you," said Anthony.

"That's all very well—but you don't know the Duke," went on the lodge-keeper, "and I do. And it's my bread and butter working for him. Likely as not—when he hears all that's goin' on—he'll get on his 'ind legs. And when the Duke gets on his 'ind legs—"

Anthony never heard the dire consequences that were wont to follow the ducal prance. The time was too close to his lunch appointment with MacMorran.

"Don't worry, Catterall," he said curtly. "I'll bear up"and he turned on his heel.

CHAPTER 5

1

Anthony found a newcomer engaged with MacMorran upon his return to the Red Deer. The inspector went quickly to the introduction.

"This is Mr. Kenneth Whitburn," he said, "only son of Mrs. Whitburn. Mr. Anthony Bathurst." Anthony at once recognised the tall figure of the pre-war Kent county captain. The tall athletic body, the sloping shoulders, the large, dark eyes and the dark, wavy hair had all been featured in the Sporting Press for a good many years. Anthony shook hands.

"I've ordered lunch for three," said MacMorran. "Mr. Whitburn is joining us. Table for three booked. Shall we go in now?"

"That will suit me," said Kenneth Whitburn in a deep, wholly pleasant voice. "I started off pretty early this morning so you can guess I can do with lunch."

"Come far?" said Anthony.

"Just the other side of Maidstone. And as I expect you know even better than I do—Saturday travelling on the road is never particularly thrilling these days."

The three men entered the dining-room. There was no sign of Bassett, so MacMorran signalled to one of the waitresses on duty. The Grahames and the Danburys were at their customary table but at the moment they were the only other diners present.

When the waitress had taken their respective orders, Anthony said: "Well, Mr. Whitburn—this is an unpleasant business. Anything to suggest to us? If you have—it will be enthusiastically received, I can assure you. For at the present moment, Inspector MacMorran and I are absolutely groping in something like impenetrable darkness."

Whitburn's face was heavy with care and anxiety as he answered. "To say that I'm shocked beyond belief would be putting things only mildly. My mother was an extremely able . . . and . . . in many directions . . . a most efficient woman. This disappearance that's been so suddenly thrown at me, is absolutely inexplicable. And when I think of the attendant circumstances—this terrible affair of Lady Blanchflower—well I can find nothing to say at all."

There was a silence as the waitress arrived with service. "Nothing?" queried Anthony eventually.

"Nothing," replied Kenneth Whitburn with unmistakable emphasis. "Absolutely nothing."

"Surely," persisted Anthony, "you can make one suggestion. Even though it may be incredibly painful to you?"

Whitburn looked at him fixedly. His face was still furrowed with thought and worn with worry.

"You mean," he said at length, his voice unsteady with emotion, "that my mother is . . . dead?"

Anthony nodded gravely. "I think you should prepare yourself . . . for that unhappy probability. Believe me—if I could justifiably hold out hope to you, I shouldn't hesitate to do so. But—"

Anthony shrugged his shoulders significantly. Whitburn was silent.

"Come," said MacMorran, "we don't know for certain. We may get news of the lady at any moment."

Whitburn found words awkwardly and almost haltingly. "Do you mean, Bathurst, that my poor mother has met with a death similar to Lady Blanchflower's?"

"I fear so," said Anthony, gravely; "and my fear is intense."

Whitburn half pushed away his plate. "But the whole idea's so utterly preposterous! It's incredible! Who would murder an innocent soul like my mother? Who—I say? And if you can rake up the 'Who', then again I say '*why*' should she be so murdered? There's no sense in it—no rhyme or reason—there's no *motive*! Surely people don't roam about the earth committing crimes that are completely motiveless?"

He stopped for breath. "With my very deepest sympathy," replied Anthony, "all I can say is that such things *have* happened."

"Yes so they may have—but when they do, surely it implies a homicidal maniac? It's the only possible solution—and you can't tell me that homicidal maniacs are let loose of a night in a place like the cloisters of Quinster Castle."

"That, alas—we don't know. The inspector and I must dig and delve—everywhere—to reach the truth behind these crimes. And in the inevitable process, who knows what soil we may be compelled to turn over and disturb?"

Anthony paused and then tangented. "Tell me of Lady Blanchflower. Anything—everything you may know of her."

Whitburn drank beer slowly and looked semi-apologetic. "It will be mainly second-hand, I'm afraid—anything you get from me. Relayed to me by my mother. Do you think that's—"

"You must have met her, though—surely?"

Whitburn nodded. "Oh—yes. Twice, I think. No—three times. Once here and once in town—the other occasion was at Canterbury. Ladies' Day. My mother brought her over."

MacMorran looked puzzled at Kenneth Whitburn's statement. "Ladies' Day? I thought that was at Epsom," he butted in.

"That's another one, Andrew," said Anthony.

MacMorran grumbled. "Never knew there were two," he muttered.

"Impressions, Mr. Whitburn—please?" asked Anthony.

"Of Lady Blanchflower? Oh, one of the best, undoubtedly. The genuine article. Top drawer and all that. No getting away from the fact."

"Your mother and she were great friends, would you say?"

Whitburn hesitated before replying. "No—o. Friends—yes. Most certainly friends. But I'm sure you'll understand me—Lady Blanchflower was *always* Lady Blanchflower—and my mother similarly always had to realise the fact. It was one of those *static* things."

"A great gulf fixed—eh?"

"Oh—no. Don't get an exaggerated view because I said that. Not a great gulf—decidedly not that. For instance—they were on Christian name terms. Shall we say—just one clear and very well-defined stratum of separation? Do you get me?"

"I think so. Well, then, remembering your own words in relation to your mother, why should anybody strangle Lady Blanchflower? Can you give me anything there?"

Whitburn placed his knife and fork carefully across his plate. "Why—surely—robbery, wasn't it? I haven't had time yet to assimilate all the details of the affair, but reading between the lines, I imagined that was the police idea. Am I barking up the wrong tree?"

"As far as we can tell at this juncture," said MacMorran, "nothing of any consequence or value has been stolen from Lady Blanchflower. It was on that account I surr-mise, that Mr. Bathurst asked you the question he did."

As he listened to the inspector, Kenneth Whitburn's face took on another and even graver anxiety. It was clear that MacMorran's last statement had shocked him severely. "Is that a fact?" he asked slowly.

As the waitress brought the sweets to the table, Anthony watched him closely.

"That is," replied MacMorran.

"Look here," said Whitburn, almost desperately, "I'd like you chaps to be open and above-board with me before we go any farther. What have you got wrapped up? Are you trying to tell me—nicely and comfortably—with as little shock to my nerves as possible—that my mother has done herself in after strangling Lady Blanchflower? Is that the scintillating idea?"

There was an edge to his voice which offended Anthony's ear. Anthony left MacMorran to answer Whitburn's question.

"Well, Mr. Whitburn—as you've just observed—there's no good pur-r-pose ser-rved by beating about the bush—let us say we are extremely worried with regard to several aspects of the affair and that the continued absence of Mrs. Whitburn is intensifying that worry."

"Great Scott," said Kenneth Whitburn, "of all the fantastic—why man—if you only knew—"

Anthony essayed a timely intervention. "Perhaps, Mr. Whitburn, I can clarify matters here—not much—just a little —shall we say? Anyhow—I'll do my best."

Whitburn turned to him. He seemed inordinately curious to hear what Anthony was about to say.

"I wish you would," he said. "I can assure you of my eternal gratitude . . . so far—I've received nothing but shocks since I've been here."

2

"Cigarette?" invited Anthony.

Whitburn took one from the proffered case. "Thanks."

"Cigarette, Andrew?"

"No, thanks. I'll have a pipe. I'd rather." MacMorran patted his pocket and felt for his pipe.

"I'm afraid it's going to be yet another question for you to answer," said Anthony; "but there's this about it, too. It's a perfectly simple question. Have you had any recent communication from your mother?"

"None," said Whitburn decisively and without the slightest hesitation, "none whatever. That is, if your interpretation of recent is anything like mine."

"Well—within the last month, say?"

"No," replied Whitburn again; "none at all. The last time I heard from her was early September. I was down at Hastings for the Festival week—and she wrote to me while I was there. That's how I'm able to fix it so definitely."

"A quite ordinary letter—I presume? Nothing to help us in relation to this business?"

"Nothing at all. Just an ordinary, newsy, chatty, conventional letter. And written by a person who was undoubtedly in the best of spirits."

Anthony turned to MacMorran. "You can go on from there Andrew—if you don't mind."

MacMorran nodded his understanding. From his pocketbook he took the paper which had been discovered between the cheque-book counterfoils in Mrs. Whitburn's writing-table drawer.

"Listen to this, Mr. Whitburn, will you please? I think it will be of interest to you. This is one of the few things we have managed to come across." MacMorran read it aloud:

"I must write it down before I forget. Lily says 'Come quickly—mistress away'. What a perfectly *awful* telegram they would make to be sure! Fancy having to wire it to anybody. P.S.—Must tell K. as soon as possible."

As MacMorran read the words, Kenneth Whitburn's brow furrowed in bewilderment.

"May I glance at that?" he asked quietly. "Do you mind?"

MacMorran handed him the paper without hesitation. "Can you confirm the handwriting, Mr. Whitburn? Is it your mother's?"

Whitburn nodded with certainty. "This is my mother's fist all right. You can take that as confirmed. Not a doubt about it. But what's it all about—I haven't the foggiest idea," Whitburn concluded with a decisive shake of the head.

"You see what the postscript says?"

"Yes. You mean the 'K.'. I thought you were probably banking on that. You have naturally taken it to refer to me. It may have referred to me—but whatever it was all about—she *didn't* tell me! She may have intended to—but she didn't."

For the first time since their meeting, Anthony saw Kenneth Whitburn smile. It was a sad reminiscent smile. A smile that looked deliberately into the past—as though he was realizing for the first time that he wouldn't see his mother alive again and that certain fragrant memories of her were all that remained to him for all the days of his life. From the next words which Whitburn uttered, Anthony knew that this idea was right.

"But don't think," said Whitburn, "that there's anything strange in that. I'm afraid that's Mother all over. She probably forgot all about it a mere five minutes after writing it down and never thought another blind word about it. I can assure you, gentlemen, that whatever it was she felt she must 'tell K.', didn't get any farther than the feeling."

"That was typical of her? To do a thing like that? To forget so quickly?" Anthony's questions were quick and sharp. But no more so than Whitburn's answers.

"Absolutely. She had a whimsical, flibbertigibbet, inconsequential, tangenting kind of brain that darted without the slightest provocation in divers directions. Unusually efficient in some directions, totally unreliable in others. That just about sums her up."

Anthony nodded. It seemed to him that Whitburn was telling the truth. His delineation of his mother showed exactly the same pattern and revealed precisely the same traits as that of Maureen Danbury. MacMorran took the piece of paper back from Whitburn, folded it carefully, and replaced it in his pocketbook.

"Now there's something else I'd like to ask you, Mr. Whitburn, before we go any farther. Something concerning which you may be able to help us. For what purpose do you think, would your mother be hiring wigs?"

There was a silence lasting some seconds after MacMorran had propounded the question.

3

"Wigs?" repeated Kenneth Whitburn incredulously, to break the silence.

"Wigs," re-affirmed MacMorran, "same as for where the hair is short. Up here." He gestured towards his head.

"I haven't the slightest idea," said Whitburn. "They certainly wouldn't be for herself—my mother had a very fine head of hair. Really remarkable considering her age. How do you know she ordered them—and where did she order them from?"

"Because I've seen the account rendered for them—made out to your mother—and also the counterfoil of her cheque in payment. Drawn by her on her own current banking account. They came from a firm named Isaac Fleury of Long Acre, London."

Whitburn knitted his brows in perplexity. "Bought—or hired?"

"Hired. That was plain on the firm's account. There was a deposite paid on them—part returnable."

"Search me," said Whitburn, almost with resignation. "I haven't the vaguest idea."

"There is just this possibility, of course," proceeded MacMorran, "that your mother was interested in a theatrical performance of some kind. Does that assist you at all?"

"In what way do you mean exactly?"

"Well—couldn't she have been a member of a local Dramatic Club say with a performance of some play or the other on the horizon?"

"She could have been," said Whitburn promptly, "but she wasn't. So that idea's soon disposed of. It's miles wide of the mark."

"Sure of that?" asked MacMorran, dangerously quietly.

"As sure as one can be sure of anything in this world. My mother was well over seventy. Well over the age for activities of the kind you suggest."

MacMorran answered a little impatiently. "So she may have been— I'm not denyin' it. There can be other interests in an amateur dramatic society—besides the actual acting. What about the executive offices? Stage manager-r, secr-retary, treasurer, member of the committee—they have to be filled, don't they?"

"I expect so," returned Whitburn imperturbably; "but I still say 'no'. I still say nothing doing as far as my mother was concerned. The only interest she ever had in that kind of thing was an occasional visit to a West-End show. When the Guv'nor was alive, they'd go pretty frequently—since his death her visits have been nothing like so frequent. Naturally so, I suppose, in the circumstances."

Whitburn concluded with an emphatic shake of the head. "No— Mother's one really terrific and abiding interest was Bridge. She went to Town at least once every week to play Bridge. She used to play at her Club. She was absolutely mad keen on the game—and a pretty hot player, too. I'll say she was."

Before MacMorran could reply Anthony had interposed. "Where did she play, Mr. Whitburn? When she went to Town for that purpose? What was the name of this Club?"

"The Muliera Club—just off Piccadilly. Ben Trovato Street. She's been a member there for years."

Anthony nodded. "Yes—I know the locality. Thank you, Mr. Whitburn."

MacMorran, chafing at the bit, had further recourse to his pocket-book. With infinite care in the manipulation of papers, he produced the account of "Isaac Fleury, Perruquier, Wig-Maker and Costumier".

"All very interesting, Mr. Whitburn, what you say with regard to your mother's interests . . . and . . . er . . . non-interests and if I may say so, the rather contemptuous manner in which you were pleased to dismiss certain suggestions of mine . . . perhaps you'd care to listen to this."

MacMorran unfolded the Fleury account with the same infinite care and cleared his throat. Anthony thought that Whitburn looked a little startled.

"This is an account," said MacMorran, "as I mentioned to you before, from Isaac Fleury, Perruquier, Wig-Maker and Costumier, Long Acre, London, W.C.2. It was found in a drawer of your mother's writing-table. It is rendered in this form. 'To Mrs. Laura Whitburn, Hon. Secretary, Quinster Dramatic Club, Red Deer Hotel, Quinster, Downshire. It is properly and correctly receipted in the sum of twenty pounds. In respect of deposit paid on two wigs hired for Dramatic performance of *Caste* at the Thespian Hall, Quinster, on Wednesday, November 9th. Hire account to follow—balance of deposit returnable on surrender of articles hired.' There is also a description of the two wigs hired."

MacMorran lowered the account from which he had been reading. "Now, Mr. Whitburn—having heard that—you'll have somewhat less difficulty in understanding the pur-rport of my recent questions to you."

Whitburn extended his hand to the inspector. "May I glance at that, please?"

MacMorran handed over the account. Whitburn scrutinised the perruquier's commercial effort. Then he handed it back. "I'm sunk," he said, quietly; "utterly and completely sunk. Sunk without trace. I can no more explain this than fly. There's some dark and deep mystery here, Inspector. I'm thankful the investigation is in your hands and not in the hands of the local people."

MacMorran looked grimmer than ever. "There's more to come, I'm afraid, Mr. Whitburn. That won't make the mystery lighter or less deep. We've made enquiries here in Quinster—and we've been here a matter of hours only, remember—and we've been informed by people who should know these things that there's no such building in Quinster as the Thespian Hall and no such body as the Quinster Dramatic Club. What do you think of that?" To Anthony's surprise, Kenneth Whitburn took the inspector's question with complete aplomb.

"Well," he said with the utmost composure, "I'm not surprised. Those facts that you've just told me merely serve to confirm what I've been saying to you myself. This dramatic club business is all plain unadulterated hooey. My mother had nothing to do with it—or with anything like it. All the time I've been here, I've insisted that she hadn't. It's a frame-up—in some way or the other."

"If it's a 'frame-up' as you suggest," said Anthony, "there's at least one thing about it—it can easily be tested—and either verified or falsified."

"How do you mean? How can you do that?"

Anthony gestured towards the perruquier's account which was still in MacMorran's hand.

"The account, Mr. Whitburn. All we have to do to authenticate it is to contact the vendor and hear what he has to say about it. If you prefer it—the man hired from the firm of Isaac Fleury itself. Their 'yes' or their 'no' will be conclusive."

"That's true," said Whitburn, his face brightening a little. "Of course— why not do it at once?"

"Unhappily," said Anthony, "it's Saturday and Saturday afternoon at that. Ten to one the place is closed until Monday morning. And to get Isaac Fleury on his own private line—even if it were possible—might be extremely difficult and equally disappointing. Ten to one again he himself is totally ignorant of the transaction."

As Anthony spoke, he glanced up and saw Inspector Guthrie at the door of the dining-room.

"There's Guthrie, Andrew," he said quietly; "he may have news for us. We'd better see him."

MacMorran beckoned Guthrie to come over. Guthrie came in and crossed to the inspector. MacMorran introduced Kenneth Whitburn. The two men shook hands.

4

"I hope you have some good news for me, Inspector," said Whitburn. His tone was anxious and edged with strain and his face now was white, worn and worried. Guthrie took the vacant seat at the table.

"Before you start to talk," said MacMorran, "have you had your lunch? Because if you haven't—you'd better make sure of—"

Guthrie waved away the invitation. "Thank you, Chief—I've had it. Or I've had as much as I intend to have at the moment. So please don't bother."

He turned to Kenneth Whitburn. "In reply to you, Mr. Whitburn—I regret to say that I have no news at all."

"None?"

"None whatever."

"That's bad," said MacMorran, "that's very bad."

"I've had men at work all round the vicinity," said Guthrie. He paused, and then continued; "Actually, the Chief Constable has drafted a hundred extra men on the job. The river, all waste land, fields, ditches, empty houses, the few blitzed habitations that we have here in the district, have all been thoroughly combed—the process in fact, is still going on. So far, however, there is no trace or sign of the missing lady."

"That's bad," repeated MacMorran, "that's very bad."

"In addition to all that," continued Inspector Guthrie, "a systematic enquiry is going on at all railway-stations, bus and coach stations, taxi-cab ranks and motor-garages in the near vicinity. Again—there is no news of Mrs. Whitburn."

Guthrie paused.

"But hang it all," cried Kenneth Whitburn, "she can't have vanished into thin air. Whatever that overworked phrase may or may not mean. She must be *somewhere*—either alive or dead."

Guthrie nodded. "I agree with you, sir. But it's that 'somewhere', that we haven't yet caught up with. I can assure you it hasn't been for lack of trying."

"I don't doubt that, Inspector. I don't doubt that for a moment. Please don't think that I'm finding fault. It's all so mystifying."

"Well," said MacMorran to Guthrie, "you can only keep on with what you're doing. It means time and patience, but it'll get us there in the end. I've had similar troubles to this before now. Days and days of fruitless search—until you felt you'd never get anywhere. And then, just as you thought you'd reached your limit—something turned up. That's how it'll go in this case."

As MacMorran concluded his sentence, Guthrie rose from his chair. "Well—that's how it is, Mr. Whitburn. You've heard what the Chief Inspector says. Just keep on going—and you keep on hoping. If anything does turn up in the course of the next few hours, I'll be sure and let you know at once." Guthrie paused—but then went on again: "You'll be here for some time, I take it?"

Kenneth Whitburn nodded. "Certainly over the week-end. After that—well it just depends on what happens to turn up. If nothing has transpired by say, Monday morning, I shall have to review the position. I can't say at the moment—it just depends how things go."

"Very good, sir. I'll make a note of that. Just like to know where you'll be and where I can find you, should you be required in a hurry."

Guthrie touched his hat to MacMorran with the merest flick and made his departure. For some few seconds after Guthrie had gone there was silence at the table. It was broken at last by Anthony Bathurst.

"Mr. Whitburn," he said, "nobody is more aware than I that while there's life there's always hope. I would be the last person in the world to take that hope from you. At the same time, I feel that I must strongly advise you to prepare for the worst. Guthrie's recent statement has made me even more convinced than before."

Whitburn's eyes met Anthony's fairly and squarely. "As bad as that— you really think?"

"I fear so."

"I see." Whitburn sat silent again. Suddenly he rose and left the table. "You'll excuse me, gentlemen—I'll see you again, of course."

5

Just before six o'clock that evening Anthony stood with MacMorran at the River Street entrance to the Red Deer. No further news had been received from Guthrie. The night was black-dark with every indication of a sharp frost to come. For a Saturday evening, it seemed to Anthony to be almost unnaturally quiet and still.

"Andrew, my lad," he said, "there's a breathless 'ush in the close tonight. Notice what I mean?"

"Ay," said MacMorran, "I've noticed it myself, it's so damned quiet it makes me think something's going to happen before very long. *Too* quiet to my way of thinking."

The words had scarcely left his lips when there came the sound of a loud report and a nearby long-drawn-out "swis . . . s . . . s . . . h". A fiery rocket soared high above the town, broke, cascaded into fire-fragments and fell, and within the space of a few seconds, the quiet of Quinster gave way to the many and varied fearsome noises inseparable from the time-honoured commemoration and celebration of the 'Fifth'.

CHAPTER 6

1

It had turned nine o'clock that evening before Guthrie showed up again. MacMorran met him directly he heard that the Quinster inspector was on the premises and took him into the small lounge which was completely empty when MacMorran stuck his head round the door.

"Come in here, Inspector," he said, "we can talk quietly in here and Melville can arrange for us that we shan't be disturbed. Mr. Bathurst is taking a walk round the town. He's attracted, so he tells me, by such goings on as bonfires and the burning of effigies. They certainly seem to be strongly featured down this part of the world."

"Always have been," replied Guthrie; "something like the Lewes bonfire boys." Guthrie pulled a small table towards him and the fire and took a seat by it.

"First of all, Chief Inspector," he said, "I may as well get this off my chest to begin with—the position is just as it was—there's still no news of the vanished lady. I took reports from my chaps as late as seven thirty—not a sign or sound. I thought you'd like to know that before I start with this other stuff."

MacMorran nodded. "O.K., Inspector. It's bad—but I more or less expected it. Now what's this other stuff you've got?"

"First of all—this." Guthrie laid a silk stocking on the table in front of MacMorran. "That's the stocking that was used on Lady Blanchflower. Notice the quality?"

MacMorran ran it through his fingers. "Superfine—I should say."

Guthrie nodded. "I should say, from what I've been told," he replied, "somewhere round thirty-five bob the pair. That's according to an expert in the rag trade. Not a penny less he says. If anything—might well be a bit more."

"I can well believe it," said MacMorran; "real luxury there and no mistake."

"Right," said Guthrie; "now look at these." Guthrie put ten more stockings on the table—five pairs. "Have a 'dekko' at these, will you, Chief?"

MacMorran did. "Any comments?" asked Guthrie rather anxiously.

"Same quality as Exhibit A," said MacMorran; "not a doubt about it."

"I agree. Same quality exactly. Well—the point is this: those five pairs you see there came from one of Mrs. Whitburn's drawers. Upstairs. I've had another look round the clothing generally."

"In other words," began MacMorran.

Guthrie finished for him. "In other words, Chief, Lady Blanchflower was strangled by a silk stocking belonging to Mrs. Whitburn. And notice the accumulation of evidence that's coming along."

MacMorran whistled. "What are we to make of it?" demanded Guthrie.

There was no immediate reply. MacMorran drummed on the table with his fingers. "What do you want me to make of it? What I think you do?"

Guthrie shrugged his shoulders expressively.

"What you're asking me to believe, Inspector Guthrie," continued MacMorran, "borders on the fantastic."

"In our game, Chief, isn't the fantastic always a possibility? It's continually turning up."

"Also," went on MacMorran from where he had left off, "you're not exactly consistent yourself—are you? Your opinions change rather quickly."

Guthrie shrugged his shoulders again. "I admit that. And I expected to be told so. But I think I'm justified in changing my mind," he said, "taking things as they now are. And, if I may be permitted to say so—it isn't always a sign of weakness—to change your mind."

"No—not always. Only sometimes. Still—arguing won't get us anywhere. Anything else for me while we're at it?"

Guthrie produced a sheet of paper. "Yes—the 'dabs' report. There were two distinct sets of finger-prints in Lady Blanchflower's lounge. There's no doubt that they're Lady Blanchflower's own and Mrs. Whitburn's. We've checked on the latter—with similar evidence over here—and well—I'm told there's no doubt about it. Same mixture, you see, Chief, as before. Notice that?"

MacMorran thought over what Guthrie had said. "What help did Lady Blanchflower have? In her apartments—I mean?"

"She did her own cooking—which wasn't a great deal—so I'm told—and generally kept things tidy. For cleaning, one of the women cleaners from the castle went to her twice a week."

"I see. What days did she go—do you know?"

"Part of Tuesday and Saturday morning."

"H'm! Well—go on. I can see you're bursting to."

Guthrie flushed. "Well—Chief—since you've asked me—I'll say this. I *have* changed my views. It's my considered opinion now that if Mrs. Whitburn were here in this hotel—and not missing—there'd be ample justification for an arrest."

MacMorran grimaced—he had stuck his neck out and received the due reward of the stick.

"Consider," proceeded Guthrie, "she was the last person seen with the deceased—that's so, isn't it?"

"As far as we know. Nothing much in it, though."

"She ordered and paid for the wig found under deceased's body and ordered it under false and completely 'phoney' conditions and circumstances. Are they facts?"

"Circumstantial only," growled MacMorran, "until they're thoroughly investigated and looked into."

"Her finger-prints are all over the lounge where the body was found."

"All over?" queried MacMorran.

"Well—there's a fair number of them. Is that so?"

"You say so. But that's an entirely natural and normal matter—seeing that she was a constant visitor to Lady Blanchflower's."

"All right. Have that your own way. I won't press it. What about the next point?"

"Depends what it is."

Guthrie pointed triumphantly to the stocking. "This stocking."

MacMorran looked down at it. "What's your answer to that, Chief?" cried Guthrie.

MacMorran pointed to the remaining stockings; "the upper ten. Where did you get those, Inspector?"

"From a drawer in Mrs. Whitburn's room. I told you as much just now."

MacMorran nodded with satisfaction. "Well then—what was there to prevent the murderer acquiring his in the same way? Can you tell me?"

Guthrie stared at him incredulously. "But he wasn't here, man, he was over in Lady Blanchflower's apartments. He wasn't in the Red Deer! That is to say if there was a 'he'—which frankly I don't admit for a single instant."

MacMorran altered his tone and his tactics. "Before I commit myself, Inspector, I shall require to know a great deal more about the case. But the murderer may have been here *and* at Lady Blanchflower's—at different times. Maybe though, you've got something. Time alone can tell."

Guthrie was dogged and persistent. "All the same, Chief, say what you like and argue as you will—if Mrs. Whitburn were here in this hotel at this moment, you'd—"

MacMorran broke in impatiently. "But she's *not*, Inspector. And that's the vital point! It upsets your position entirely. Surely your intelligence can grasp that? She's not here—and she can't be found. That's the point the whole case pivots on." As he spoke, there came a succession of sharp reports from outside. MacMorran walked to the window and pulled aside the curtain. The flicker of high, red flames could be seen in at least half a dozen directions. Guthrie joined him.

"That big one," he said, "that you can see over there, is the big bonfire on Quinster Heath. It's been building for weeks. It's the biggest they've ever built. The kids are having the time of their lives this evening."

2

During the time that MacMorran was engaged with Guthrie, Anthony, as MacMorran had stated, was amusing himself with a stroll round Quinster and its adjacent parts. The bonfires that he could see reflected in so many places were giving the town an eerie and almost unearthly aspect and atmosphere. And Anthony had fallen for them. For another thing, he had dined reasonably well at the Red Deer and had felt when the meal was finished that a walk would do him a vast amount of good. Leaving the hotel by the River Street exit, he turned right into Castle Street, walked past the castle and its entrance gates and then, with a sense of gregariousness (unusual perhaps for him), joined the crowds making their way to the giant bonfire due to be burned very shortly on Quinster Heath. Anthony was somewhat surprised at the volume and nature of the crowd which jostled him. Tonight was evidently a red-letter night in the annals of Quinster. Another matter which occasioned him a considerable amount of surprise, was the number of people, chiefly it must be admitted, adolescent, that was wheeling, pushing or trundling various types of 'Guys' towards the conflagration that was about to come. There were grotesque figures in old push-carts, slumped on hand-barrows, sprawled in amateurishly-contrived boxes on home-made wheels and several, too, of a larger sort, carried on carts. More than once, too, he observed effigies of the notorious Guido lying across the front of motor-bicycles. 'The lady may not be for burning,' thought Anthony whimsically, 'but the old lad is—without a doubt.'

As he walked towards the heath, Anthony looked at his wristwatch. It wanted a few minutes to eight o'clock. As he came nearer to the site of the pyre, the crowds with him grew thicker and he could see that not only was the borough of Quinster contributing generously to the crowd, but the outlying villages as well. Away in the distance he heard the clock of a church, in all probability, chime the hour of eight. And, synchronously, there came a succession of loud explosions, followed by a quick uprising of many rockets which soared exultantly, hit the sky, burst into flaming, flickering fairy-like fragments and fell in a shower of scintillation. Then, not so very far away, there came to his ears what must be the roar of the crowd. The crowd round the bonfire. The bonfire that had at last taken the flame for which it had been built and for which it had weeks-waited.

'Yes,' said Anthony to himself, 'the Quinster bonfire's alight—hundred to one on it. I wouldn't have missed this for all the tea in China.'

3

Suddenly and perhaps somewhat surprisingly to a person unfamiliar with the surroundings and general topography of the place, Anthony and the crowd with him, turned a corner—and there in front of them saw Quinster Heath.

An enormous bonfire, thirty feet high, thick with branch and brushwood, packed tight with dry bough and dead bramble, was beginning to burn fiercely and furiously in the middle of the waste. Hundreds of people danced and careered round it and every now and then, a group of people, venturing as near to the fire as was physically possible, would take their own constructed effigy from its peculiar vehicle of transport and heave it, to the accompaniment of loud shouts, into the flames. Judging by what Anthony was able to see and the conversation which went on around him, this procedure was definitely a Quinster custom, handed down traditionally through the years and over many Quinster generations.

Anthony walked round the heath so that he could observe the master bonfire from each of its four sides. As the evening wore on, the villagers began to sing the Quinster bonfire song. The words were unfamiliar to him, but there were occasional lines which could be dimly associated with the familiar doggerel of the Gunpowder Plot. Anthony calculated that no fewer than fifty effigies had already been hurled into the burning mass while he had been there.

Just as he was contemplating his return to the hotel, an incident occurred which in his special circumstances held rather more than an ordinary interest for him. He saw a man wheeling something in the direction of the bonfire which resembled in shape and size, a coalman's trolley. On the trolley, lay an enormous 'Guy', certainly one of the largest Anthony had seen that evening. The man was accompanied by three children—all in their 'teens probably—two lads and a girl. Laughing and shouting at the top of their voices, the four of them lifted the absurdly-apparelled figure from the trolley, hoisted it shoulder-high between them and tossed it on the flaming mass.

Momentarily, the flames brightened perceptibly as they licked at their fresh prey. When the man of the party turned away from them, Anthony caught sight of his face and he knew at once, not only that he had seen the man before, but also the man's identity. It was Mark Catterall, the lodge-keeper at Quinster Castle whom he had interrogated earlier in the day.

Anthony edged himself nearer to the Catterall group with deliberate intent. The bigger lad of the two was now holding the coalman's trolley and Anthony had no doubt from his likeness to the elder man that he was Catterall's son. Probably with another brother and sister. For the second time that evening, Anthony looked at his wrist-watch. It was past nine. Time had gone quickly with a vengeance. He had been round the bonfire for almost an hour. He decided to make his way back to the hotel.

Well, he thought as he turned back, you certainly live and learn. From this time onward, he would always associate bonfires and all fifth of November celebrations with the ancient borough of Quinster in the county of Downshire.

As he eventually turned again out of Castle Street into River Street, the same thought came to him as had assailed his brain on the outward journey. 'The Lady's not for Burning,' re-quoted Anthony; 'but the old lad. . .' and then stopped dead in his tracks just outside the entrance to the Red Deer. A grim fancy had been born in his brain. A fancy which caused him to catch his breath. That the lady *had* been for burning after all!

CHAPTER 7

1

Once inside the hotel, Anthony walked straight to the small lounge. He wanted MacMorran as soon as he could get hold of him. To his intense satisfaction, MacMorran was there, standing at the window with Inspector Guthrie. Better still, thought Anthony—both of 'em—two birds with one stone. Wonder what they'll say when I start theorizing.

MacMorran turned on his heel as Anthony entered. "Some bonfire," he said; "seen it? Don't know that I've ever seen a bigger from a window that is."

"You should have been with me, Andrew," said Anthony, "you'd have seen it better, then. I've been close to it. I walked as far as Quinster Heath. That's the place to see it properly."

"No doubt about that," corroborated Guthrie.

"And I wasn't the only one," continued Anthony. "My plan of spending the evening was shared by several hundreds of others."

"I'll bet it was," said Guthrie again. "November the Fifth's a biggish night in this district. During the War years, it slumped a bit, naturally, but this year they've got it pretty well back to normal."

"Well—it was certainly a sight," said Anthony; "it surprised me. I wasn't prepared for anything on that scale. On the whole—I'm glad the maggot bit me and I went. I wouldn't have missed it for worlds."

Guthrie grinned. "I expect you are. Something to remember—eh?"

"No doubt about that, Inspector."

Guthrie turned to MacMorran. "Well—I think I'll be saying good night to you two gentlemen. Expect me early in the morning. Who knows?

There may be some news." Guthrie shook hands with MacMorran and started towards Anthony. "Good night to you, Mr. Bathurst. No point in my staying here any longer."

Anthony shook his head. "Just a minute, Inspector. I don't want to delay you unnecessarily but I've got something to say. It may be important. At any rate, I'm glad I found you here with the Chief. Get a chair will you, and draw it up to the fire. We're all quiet here—we'll have a little conference." Guthrie looked surprised and even a trifle annoyed at Anthony's intervention, but he collared a chair and came up between Anthony and MacMorran.

"Now what's it all about?" he demanded.

"It's just this," said Anthony. "I've been thinking hard concerning this mysterious disappearance of Mrs. Whitburn. Last seen on Thursday evening. On the way, evidently, to Lady Blanchflower's. Time—well—we'll say half-past eight. That may not be absolutely accurate—but it's not far out—for our purpose it will be near enough. Thursday evening, Inspector! And this is Saturday evening. Over forty-eight hours have elapsed and search how we will, we haven't yet struck anything like a trail."

"The world's a big place," interrupted Guthrie.

"I won't deny that for a moment," returned Anthony. "It wouldn't, however, be *my* reason for the lady's disappearance."

"No?"

"No, Inspector. I haven't the slightest doubt in my own mind that Mrs. Whitburn has disappeared because she was murdered. And murdered by the same person that killed Lady Blanchflower. I've held that opinion almost since I came down here."

There was a silence after Anthony had spoken—a silence broken only by the ticking of the clock on the mantelpiece.

2

It was Andrew MacMorran who eventually broke that silence. "Not the slightest doubt—eh? That statement leaves no margin, you know. Not an inch."

"I admit all that, Andrew. And I still stick to what I said."

"In that case, then," interposed Guthrie, "where's the body?"

"That, I concede, is the problem. It is a problem, though, which may disappear at any moment. I could answer 'in any of a thousand places' which so far your boys have failed to find."

Guthrie shrugged his shoulders at the reply. "That's all very well, Mr. Bathurst. But true only as far as it goes. Which, I submit, isn't so very far. The murderer hadn't unlimited scope. To suggest that he had, would be neither feasible nor logical. There are the factors of time and place. In other words, if there is a body, which you assert so strongly, my reply to you is that it must be somewhere reasonably close at hand."

"That's fair. I'll concede that willingly. And I'll go on from there. If the body's been hidden somewhere since Thursday evening, when the crimes were committed, sooner or later the murderer is faced with the inevitable problem of disposal. The murderer's bugbear since Cain. He has either already been faced with it—or he will be."

Guthrie nodded. "I accept that. There's no argument needed with regard to that."

"Right," Anthony paused. When he began to speak again, he spoke much more slowly. "As I watched the Quinster bonfire this evening, I couldn't fail to notice what appeared to me to be yet another Quinster tradition—custom if you prefer the word." Anthony looked round at Guthrie and saw that the inspector was staring at him fixedly.

"I refer," said Anthony, "to the extremely popular practice of adding the effigies popularly termed 'Guys' to the burning pile. This evening I've watched any number of these grotesque figures tossed or heaved to the flames. In short, Inspector Guthrie, I found myself on my return journey to this hotel, seriously contemplating what I regard as a most interesting . . . almost intriguing . . . possibility."

Guthrie stared at him wonderingly and then interrupted him with sharp insistence. "You don't seriously mean . . . " he broke off with his obvious question still unasked.

"I do," said Anthony quietly and ominously.

"Good God," said Guthrie.

MacMorran came in grimly.

"Amplify—will you? It's a wee bit borderin' on the fantastic—but—"

"Well," proceeded Anthony, "I can assure you that all sorts of weirdly dressed dummies, scarecrows and effigies and the like have been conveyed this evening by divers means of transport to commit an inverted form of 'suttee' on the Quinster bonfire. Men, women, girls and boys have all taken part in this procedure. It occurred to me that the murderer of Lady Blanchflower and also (if you'll pardon me) of Mrs. Whitburn, faced with the disposal of the latter's body, might have found the monster bonfire a highly convenient proposition for his grim purpose. Not only convenient—intensely simple into the bargain. There you are, gentlemen, you may laugh at it but I present it to you as a serious suggestion."

Anthony took a cigarette from his case and lit it. MacMorran rose from his chair and walked to the window. For the second time that evening, he pulled aside the curtain. The flames of the Quinster bonfire were still burning in the distance—red and menacing. Guthrie, still seated, was shaking his head.

"I can't take that—oh no—I can't accept that for a moment," Anthony heard him say.

MacMorran turned and came away from the window. "There's one thing," he declared, "Mr. Bathurst's theory—fantastic though it may appear to be—can easily be tested."

Guthrie nodded agreement. "Of course."

"We'll test it then—as soon as it's practicable. Will you note that, Inspector—please?"

Guthrie rose with a somewhat ill-grace. "It means more—"

"More men—you were going to say?"

"Of course. To say nothing of certain expert assistance. Absolutely necessary."

"The Yard'll do that for you, Inspector," said MacMorran. "I'll make the necessary arrangements immediately."

3

Anthony, MacMorran and Guthrie watched the men at work on the still smouldering remains of the giant Quinster bonfire. They worked with long-handled appliances of the rake variety alternated with large flail-like rotating brooms.

Anthony watched them and their different procedures rather anxiously. MacMorran looked on with an appearance of grim brooding. Guthrie's expression was frankly and evidently also—unashamedly cynical. He shrugged his mental shoulders. MacMorran had issued instructions to all the men engaged that a special look out must be maintained for anything in the nature of false teeth, bone buttons, pieces of hard metal and buckles—in short anything that possibly might have resisted or partly resisted inflammability from the consuming flames of the fire. As time went on, Anthony's anxiety increased and Guthrie's look of cynicism developed in direct proportion. At one o'clock, MacMorran looked at his watch and announced his intention of returning to the hotel for lunch.

"Coming with me?" he said to Anthony, "you may as well—the job's in good hands. There's no point in us staying here all the time. And you know all about the watched pot."

After a second's hesitation, Anthony nodded. "Right-o, Andrew, may as well, I suppose. Looks to me as though my hunch has let me down. To say nothing of you. I'm sorry. Shouldn't have let my imagination run ahead too fast."

MacMorran shook his head. "You never know. The job's not through yet. I'll tell Guthrie we're going. Better do so, I suppose.

MacMorran moved along to the edge of the debris where Guthrie was standing. "Don't know what you're doing for lunch, Inspector—but we're popping back to the Red Deer. We'll probably come back here later on."

"Very good," rejoined Guthrie; "looks very much as though we've wasted our time. And time, too, that could have been better spent. That's the worst of these wild-cat schemes. They seldom get you anywhere. By the way—I've just had three more reports from the station. Re the missing woman. Nothing at all! Not a glimmer anywhere."

"All the more reason, then," replied MacMorran, "why we should look here. O.K. I'll be seein' you." MacMorran turned on his heel and rejoined Anthony.

"Cock-a-hoop?" grinned the latter.

MacMorran nodded affirmation. "You've said it. Wild-cat scheme, etc., etc. We shall have the Chief Constable blowin' his cheeks out before long. I hope it keeps fine for him. I wonder he wasn't here this morning."

"H'm," said Anthony; "pity. Bad job about him."

4

Anthony and MacMorran finished their lunch and the latter lost no time in getting his pipe going. From the depths of a comfortable arm-chair in the small lounge (now practically reserved for them through the good offices of Melville), he looked up at Anthony.

"What's crawling over you? Aren't you sitting down for a wee while? Can't you rest?"

"That hadn't been my intention, Andrew. I was—"

"Feeling the call of the burnt bonfire, I suppose? Can't you possess your immortal soul in patience for half an hour? Man—you're getting rattled in your old age. The fact causes me sur-rprise."

Anthony grinned. "What do I say to that? Sorry, sir? Well—I'm not going to. If you want to know, I'm still rather worried. I never cared overmuch for the personal 'boob' that finds a repercussion on other people. I like as few of them on my escutcheon as possible."

MacMorran chuckled over his pipe. "Do you know why that is, my boy? If you don't, I'll be telling you. That's vanity. Sheer unadulterated vanity. Nothing more and nothing less. But never mind, laddie. You'll grow out of it."

Anthony smiled. "You may be right, Andrew. All the same—*all* the personal prides and vanities aren't to be condemned. Some of 'em are commendably right and highly proper. And I've a definite fancy that the particular one of mine which I just mentioned belongs to that class. Still—let it pass. Being severely practical, Andrew, how long do you intend to park your carcase in that arm-chair?"

"I'm havin' half an hour's ease and comfort. I told you I was. Haven't you ever been told what to do after your Sabbath dinner? And don't tell me that was lunch."

MacMorran stretched out a leg for further comfort. "Besides," he continued, "Guthrie's down there. Everything's going on. 'Tisn't as though the job was at a standstill. Take that armchair on the other side of the fire and relax."

Anthony made no reply. He walked to the window and looked out. Through that same window through which MacMorran had watched the bonfires' flames on the previous evening.

MacMorran settled more cosily in his chair and closed his eyes. Anthony turned and looked at him philosophically. Half an hour! He accepted the inevitable and felt in his pocket for his cigarettes. As his fingers closed round them he heard a voice in the corridor outside and recognised it as Inspector Guthrie's. So the Quinster inspector had come back. What did that mean?

5

Anthony walked to the door of the small lounge and opened it. He saw Guthrie's back and called out.

"We're in here, Inspector. I presume you want to see us." Guthrie turned and came towards him. There was a strange, bewildered sort of look on his face. He looks dazed, thought Anthony, as Guthrie came to close quarters.

"Good afternoon, Mr. Bathurst," said Guthrie. "Do I understand that the Chief-Inspector—'

"He's in here," cut in Anthony; "come in and shut the door."

Guthrie slipped into the lounge quietly as Anthony had invited him and carefully closed the door.

"Good afternoon, Inspector," said MacMorran from his armchair, "in five minutes' time we should have been on the way to you. Anyhow, you've forestalled us. I hope you've saved us the trouble. So Mr. Bathurst's hunch had something after all—eh? Is that what you've come to tell us?"

Guthrie's face registered annoyance at the two questions. Before he could reply, MacMorran said again: "That's more or less what you've come to tell us, isn't it?"

"Oh—no," said Guthrie, "not at all. Far from it—in actual fact. There is no sign whatever of anything in the nature of a body having been consigned to that bonfire. None at all. We've found absolutely nothing to indicate such a thing. Which I understand was what Mr. Bathurst anticipated. In other words, Mr. Bathurst's hunch in that particular respect can be written off as a complete failure. You may as well know that before I go any farther."

Guthrie paused. MacMorran, however, waited for him to go on. He seemed to sense something. As with Anthony, there was something about Guthrie that mystified him.

"No," said Guthrie, picking up the threads of the conversation, "as I said—there are no traces of any kind which might lead one to deduce the presence of a human body. So that it's pretty conclusive that Mr. Bathurst's theory goes by the board."

"I see," returned MacMorran, "and you came to tell us that?"

Guthrie's tone changed somewhat. "Er . . . not exactly. We have found something, however, in the bonfire ash, that in view of what we already know must be considered as important."

"Something? What do you mean?"

"Perhaps I should have said the remains of something."

Anthony ranged himself quickly at Guthrie's side. His anxiety and desire for self-flagellation had vanished under the warm sun of the latter's latest information. "What have you found, Inspector?" he said. "Come on! Out with it."

Guthrie's hand slid to his overcoat-pocket. He was almost smiling.

"This," he said (still rather grudgingly—Anthony thought), "was found on the very edge of the remains of the bonfire—right at the rear of it as you might say. As you see-it's only been partly burned."

Guthrie held up the find for their inspection. It was the remains of a wig!

6

MacMorran took the wig, or what was left of it, from Guthrie. "Good God," he said, "how on earth did this piece of wig—these few strands and wisps of burnt hair—miss the burning? Miraculous!"

Anthony came over and looked at the object in MacMorran's hand. "I think I can tell you how that happened," he said quietly. "When the flames began to get a real hold, parts of the bonfire fell in—caved in, if you like—and that wig which was held up somewhere within the pile, fell to the ground. It fell where it was eventually found—right at the very edge and in that way escaped the fiercest flames. You know what it is, of course?"

Guthrie said: "What it is? I don't know that I—"

"I can tell you," declared MacMorran; "it sticks out a mile—it's the second wig of the Fleury invoice. For the bogus performance of the bogus play at the bogus Hall next Wednesday. Though what the heck it's doing on the Quinster bonfire, God alone knows!"

Anthony remained silent. He appeared to be lost in thought. It seemed to him that the pattern of the case was taking on an added craziness.

MacMorran felt a small piece of the silvery white hair that had been merely singed. "It's a woman's. Different from Wig Number One."

"That's right," said Anthony, "that's the 'Marquise's' wig. The devotee of Froissart. The wigs were ordered for 'Eccles' and 'the Marquise'—don't you remember? This is hers."

MacMorran shook his head as an indication of an inclination to something like despair.

"I remember—but I don't get it. I don't get any of it. And we're *still* left saying to ourselves: Where's Mrs. Whitburn? Dead or alive?"

"Makes you wonder," said Guthrie meaningly. "She ordered the wigs. Nobody else did."

Anthony shook his head. "I don't know. As I see things we're definitely making progress. That remnant of wig there in the Chief-Inspector's hand spells progress for us in capital letters."

"How do you mean?" queried Guthrie.

"Well—to me it's a plain proposition that it was placed on the bonfire by the person who murdered Lady Blanchflower. Don't you agree, Inspector Guthrie?"

"If I do I must still point out that we're just where we were. Looking for Mrs. Whitburn."

"And her murderer," said Anthony gravely. As he spoke, there came a soft tap on the door. MacMorran looked up.

"See who that is, if you don't mind," he said to Guthrie.

CHAPTER 8

1

Guthrie went to the door and opened it. The man outside was Kenneth Whitburn.

"May I come in?" he asked.

"Well," said Guthrie.

Before he could complete anything like a sentence, MacMorran had called out: "Come in, Mr. Whitburn. I can quite understand your wanting a word with us. You've been very patient. Come and sit down."

Whitburn came into the lounge and found a vacant chair. "Thank you. You can guess why I came along. Melville told me he fancied you were in here. Some sort of conference. Is there any news?"

"I'm afraid there is no news of your mother, Mr. Whitburn," replied MacMorran. "Inspector Guthrie has heard nothing at all. And if you can, you must still try to regard no news as good news."

"I'm afraid that's much easier said than done. Time's getting on so. Approximately three days now—you know."

Whitburn looked pale and distressed. MacMorran glanced across the lounge at Anthony. The glance held enquiry. Anthony responded to it with a slight inclination of the head.

MacMorran said: "When I said just now there was no news, Mr. Whitburn, I was referring . . . er . . . very definitely to news of your mother herself. Actually, we *have* managed to pick up something since we last saw you . . . something . . . er . . . rather extraordinary."

Whitburn looked afraid of whatever might be coming next. MacMorran went on:

"You remember my discussing with you that perruquier's account which had been rendered to your mother?"

Whitburn nodded. "Naturally I do."

"You recollect, too, I told you she'd paid a hiring charge for the two wigs described on the account? Paid it by cheque?"

"Yes, of course, I remember all those things."

"Well—now—I'll tell you something else. Something I didn't tell you previously. I kept it from you purposely—out of sympathy for you and with your feelings. Underneath Lady Blanchflower's dead body was a crumpled wig answering to the description of one of the two wigs listed by the perruquier on the account made out to your mother. Isaac Fleury of Long Acre."

There was a tense silence. Whitburn frowned. "I'm frightfully sorry and all that—but as I said to you before—I don't get any of this. It's just utterly crazy and absurd. That is to say as far as it concerns any possible connection with my mother."

"Well," said MacMorran, "I can understand your saying that and making those points—but as a matter of fact I haven't quite finished yet. There's more to come."

Whitburn began to shake his head—as though his condition of absolute bewilderment were beginning to master him completely.

"This afternoon," continued MacMorran, "the second wig of the Fleury account has turned up. And in a most extraordinary place at that. And where do you think it's been found?"

"Tell me the worst," said Kenneth Whitburn unemotionally. "After what I've already heard, I'm prepared to believe almost anything."

2

MacMorran made a sign to Guthrie. The inspector interpreted it correctly.

"Take a look at this," said MacMorran. He dangled the remnants of the burnt wig in front of Kenneth Whitburn. "Good lord," said the latter, "where on earth's it been? Somebody been trying to burn it?"

"Yes," said MacMorran, "you've holed in one. Somebody has been trying to burn it. And but for the hundredth chance represented by the ingenuity of Mr. Bathurst here, he or she would have succeeded. Where do you think this was discovered, Mr. Whitburn?"

"In the fire somewhere, I suppose? Don't tell me I'm wrong or I shall begin to think I'm as crackers as the case is generally."

"Well," replied MacMorran, "you're right—and yet you're wrong. I'll tell you. Not so much in *the* fire as in *a* fire! This sorry-looking affair which was once a wig was found this afternoon amongst the refuse and ashes of the big Quinster bonfire which was set on fire last evening, November the fifth. No doubt you saw something of it yourself?"

Whitburn shook his head. "No. I didn't go out at all last night. I was feeling rather all in and spent most of the time in my room. But tell me I don't think I quite understand—who happened to find that in the bonfire ashes?"

"The police, Mr. Whitburn."

Whitburn shook his head again. "I'm afraid I still don't follow. How did the police come to be there? At the remains of a bonfire?"

"They were looking for—" MacMorran halted abruptly. "Information," he added.

Whitburn eyed him oddly. "I think I understand," he said slowly. "Yes . . . I think I begin to understand." Then he looked at MacMorran again and said steadily. "You found nothing else, I take it? You're not holding anything back from me?"

"No," said MacMorran gravely, "up to the moment we have found nothing else."

"You thought you might? God—what a—"

"No—o," answered MacMorran. "I wouldn't go as far as to say that. Rather that it's just part and parcel of our job to test anything and everything."

Whitburn put his head in his hands. Anthony felt intensely sympathetic towards him.

"Mr. Whitburn," he said.

Kenneth Whitburn looked up.

"Yes?"

"Have you by any chance thought any more of that note your mother made? The one that she might have been intending to tell you about?"

Whitburn shook his head. "I'm afraid I haven't. Tell me what it was again—do you mind?"

"Lily says 'come quickly—mistress away'. That was the note proper."

"Yes. That was it. I remember it now. What was it you wanted to ask me?"

"Simply as to whether you were any nearer to its possible explanation? Whether you'd thought it over? That was all. I was curious."

"No. I hadn't thought about it—but it conveys nothing whatever to me. I should say it was just something between my mother and the late Lady Blanchflower. It wouldn't have been anything terrifically important."

"Something just ordinary—commonplace—do you mean?"

"Yes. I think so, don't you?"

"Most decidedly not," said Anthony, with an emphatic shake of the head; "all my reasoning tells me just the opposite. That it was the reverse of the ordinary and the commonplace. Consider the terms of reference yourself. Take your mother's first note—'I must write it down before I forget.' Why? Why should she need to do that—if it were conventional and ordinary? Why take the trouble to preserve and place on record the absolutely commonplace?"

Whitburn began to nod his head. "Why—of course. You're right undoubtedly you are. I'm afraid up to now I hadn't looked at it seriously enough. But now I see your point."

Anthony went on. "Another indication that your mother regarded the matter as of some consequence is the postcript. 'Must tell K. as soon as possible.' There you have recorded again not only the compulsion to tell you (assuming that you are the 'K.' referred to—and I think we are entirely justified in assuming that) but also that the information must be conveyed to you *without any delay*."

"Yes—I can see you're right, now. But the words as they have been written down make no sense to me. No sense at all. Candidly—they mean less than nothing. That's why I didn't bother myself with them."

"H'm," said Anthony, "pity. I was hoping that you might have been able to find an association somewhere which would have helped us."

Whitburn was apologetic. "Sorry and all that. But the whole thing's an absolute enigma to me. I can see its importance—you've shown me that and I realise that one just can't argue about it but *where* the importance is, well frankly I can't see! The words are absolutely simple and . . . er . . . entirely everyday aren't they? Somebody is requested to come quickly because the mistress (whoever that may be) is away. No—I'm sorry but I can't give you any help at all. I still think it was something between my mother and Lady Blanchflower."

Whitburn concluded his remarks by shaking his head again. Then he returned to MacMorran.

"I'm sorry, too, Inspector, if I interrupted anything when I came in just now. My excuse for the intrusion must be that I was impatient for news. I'm sure you understand. I won't hinder you any more now—later on in the evening—perhaps. Surely, *somebody* will find out something before very much longer."

"That's all right, Mr. Whitburn," said MacMorran, "I understand perfectly and, as you say, there must be news of some sort sooner or later. And when it does come, we'll hope it's of the right kind."

CHAPTER 9

1

Somewhere in the region of five o'clock, Anthony went up to his room. If he had been worried and anxious before, he was doubly so now. As he saw things at this point the more time that elapsed before the pattern of the crimes became clear and distinct to him, the more time it meant for the killer to cover up. Nothing was as obvious to him as that. Lady Blanchflower had died and Mrs. Whitburn had disappeared on the previous Thursday evening. Very nearly seventy-two hours ago.

As Anthony traced the lines of the crimes—this meant one thing and one thing only. It was possible, of course, that he might be mistaken—but he didn't think so. The killer meant suspicion to fall on the lady who was missing. Anthony felt absolutely certain with regard to that. And *as long as she remained missing*, that suspicion would rest. More than that. The suspicion would grow and become intensified.

Anthony began to pace the room—silently and steadily. As he paced, he concentrated on his problem. The more keenly he concentrated, the more certain he became that his theories were sound and correct. The murderer was playing for time. The police couldn't possibly blind themselves altogether to the clues that pointed so unmistakably in the direction of Laura Whitburn. Clues that were increasing numerically and accumulating in force. Anthony began to consider them—one by one.

First of all, there was the disappearance itself. Which invariably and inevitably must turn the searchlight of suspicion on to the person who disappears. Secondly, Mrs. Whitburn was the last person with whom Lady Blanchflower was last seen alive. The searchlight, having found its range and lighted up the object, now becomes more or less fixed. Thirdly, the incidence of the wigs. One found under Lady Blanchflower's body—the other in the refuse of the bonfire. Both ordered, it would seem, by the missing Mrs. Whitburn, invoiced to her and paid for by her. In addition to these details, ordered by her for a mythical dramatic performance in a non-existent hall by a non-existent club.

The searchlight is well trained on Mrs. Whitburn now. She can't very well escape from it. There is more to come, however.

The silk stocking used to strangle Lady Blanchflower is almost certainly one that belonged to the missing woman—and the searchlight becomes a blinding glare! Yes, Anthony saw the pattern of this side of the crime only too clearly . . . for he was positive that Mrs. Whitburn had died when Lady Blanchflower died . . . just before or just after. Which conclusion brought him to this. That the murderer had hidden Mrs. Whitburn's body somewhere in a most cunning fashion. With the hope, very probably that it might be days . . . weeks or even months before it was found . . . if it were found even then.

Anthony continued to pace the room. The problem was a difficult one. What places were there within reasonable distance of Quinster Castle where a body could remain hidden for a length of time? The castle itself? Somewhere *in* the castle? Anthony shrugged his shoulders at the colossal difficulty his general question presented. There was another condition, too. There was always the probability of swift-travelling motor-transport to be considered. A murderer can move many miles in a comparatively short time in a car.

Anthony walked to the window of his room and looked out. It was a dark night. Far too dark to look for anything—with any real hope of finding it. Which meant that nothing more of any consequence could be attempted until Monday morning. Anthony chafed at this last hold-up in the long line of delays. From Thursday evening until the following Monday morning is a longish time and Anthony knew full well that every day counted—in more ways than one. Every twenty-four hours that passed gave an additional advantage to the killer. If it went on much longer—

Anthony thought again of the Quinster bonfire. What a pity his hunch had played him false! But hunches often turned out like that. That was the worst of them. All the same—you had to play 'em when you got 'em!

2

As he entered the breakfast-room on Monday morning, Anthony almost collided with Kenneth Whitburn. "I'm going up to town this morning," said the latter. "I can't very well avoid it—but I've been on the 'phone and made arrangements to come back this evening—if it's at all possible. In fact, I might be able to get back even earlier than that. I feel I should be here, on the spot, while this present feeling of uncertainty exists. Would you be good enough to tell Inspector MacMorran? I tried to find him—but evidently he hasn't come down yet. He can pass it on to Guthrie."

"Certainly," said Anthony. "I'll convey your message to him with pleasure. *And* see you again this evening, I hope."

"That's very charming of you," said Whitburn. "Many thanks." He waved to Anthony as he went by way of the revolving-door.

When MacMorran did eventually put in an appearance at the breakfast-table, Anthony passed on Whitburn's message. "Coming back, is he?" commented MacMorran. "I don't know that it's altogether good for him hanging about here. The suspense must be pretty terrible. He'd be better doing his work. If he's got any to do. Guthrie been along yet?"

"Haven't seen him. But we could scarcely expect to. It's early hours yet."

"He's trying the other river this morning—did you know?"

"The other river?"

"Yes—the tributary to the Quinn. Joins it just above Queen's Fulton."

"What's the name of it?"

MacMorran furrowed his brow at the question. "Blest if I can remember. Guthrie did tell me. Good lord—my memory gets worse and worse—blow me if it doesn't."

"Ah, well—doesn't matter—it's not frightfully important."

MacMorran's face cleared suddenly. "I've got it. The Parrack. It's the largest of the Quinn tributaries. That was something else Guthrie told me. Guthrie thinks Mrs. W. may have got as far as Queen's Fulton—or been taken as far. It's an idea—and he's doing quite right to test it."

Anthony made no reply. He seemed to be staring fixedly at the coffee-pot. MacMorran came at him again.

"Don't you agree with me?"

Anthony came back. "Eh—what's that, Andrew?"

MacMorran repeated himself.

"No," said Anthony.

"No? Why not?"

"By 'no' I meant that I don't think Inspector Guthrie or any other of the Guthrie clan will find the body of our missing Mrs. Whitburn in the waters of the Parrack—the largest tributary of the Quinn."

MacMorran hastened to Guthrie's defence. He pointed out with some care and assiduity that Mr. Bathurst himself had not found the missing lady in the smouldering remains of the Quinster bonfire. Anthony said frankly that he had no quarrel with the justice of MacMorran's indictment. MacMorran said that was all right as far as it went. He also intimated that he always welcomed *constructive* opinions and would continue to do so. Anthony intimated in turn that he was much the same.

"Are you joining Guthrie at Queen's Fulton?" he asked.

MacMorran shook his head. "No. I'm leaving all that routine stuff to him. Let him get on with it. No—I want to see Melville this morning. I want the names and addresses of all the people who stayed in this hotel on the Thursday night. For instance, I know there were some 'commercials' here. Slept here, I mean."

MacMorran poured himself out a second cup of coffee and helped himself to sugar. "What are you doing this morning? Anything special?"

Anthony nodded. "Yes. I'm going over Lady Blanchflower's place again. I've formed the opinion that we haven't looked at it enough. I've no hunches this time, but I may run into something. On the other hand—I may not. Who knows?"

"O.K. When I've finished with Melville—I'll come along and join you there. I shouldn't be too long over my job."

"Good man." Anthony pushed back his chair. "I'll be seeing you then, Andrew."

"That's O.K. As I said—as soon as I'm clear with Melville."

3

After his conversation with MacMorran, Anthony wasted no time. For the reason that he had a definite plan in view. He left the Red Deer by the River Street exit without waiting to see what Guthrie had to say upon arrival. After all, he argued to himself, whatever Guthrie had to say or to report could well wait until Anthony's own return to the Red Deer at midday.

Anthony crossed into Castle Street and over to Quinster Castle, entered by the pedestrian's way, and walked straight through to the lodge where Mark Catterall had already commenced his daily duties. On this occasion, Catterall recognised him at once. He touched the peak of his cap as Anthony drew abreast of him.

"Good morning to you, sir. Shan't make a mistake this time. And what can I do for you this morning? Or is it the Duke himself you'll be wantin' to see?"

At no time, however, did the Catterall levity appeal to Anthony and on the morning in question it jarred rather sickeningly.

"Good morning, Catterall," he said. "I can manage, thank you, without bothering you. Got over your week-end festivities?"

"My what?"

"Week-end festivities," repeated Anthony.

"Afraid them things don't come my way. The old purse-strings are a bit on the tight side these days. But you don't want me to tell you that much."

Anthony looked at him squarely in the eyes. "What about bonfires? Don't tell me you didn't take part in the show on Saturday evening."

Catterall made no direct answer to Anthony's question. "Call that festivities? Cor—stone the crows—what *are* we coming to? You'll be callin' a pint of wallop a goblet o' nectar next. *Everybody* goes to the Quinster bonfire on the 'fifth'—that's to say, everybody in Quinster and the surrounding district. We're all born and bred to it. But that's not sayin' I went on Saturday. I might 'ave 'ad something a great deal better to do. Or on the other 'and—I might not."

Anthony judged it prudent to say no more. It was always as well to keep a card or two up your sleeve. He presented Catterall with something like half a hand-wave and passed on towards the wyverns on their pedestals and the place where the late Lady Blanchflower had spent the last years of her eventful life.

He made for the flight of stone steps on the right, walking along the stone-flagged pathway. No sign of the wyverns yet—he had thought from memory that there would have been. Descending the stone steps, however, he saw them—one at each end of the heavy stone balustrade.

Before Anthony stepped on to the grass verge which fronted the late Lady Blanchflower's apartments, a fancy took him to look closer at the nearer wyvern. Instead, therefore, of turning the corner which led to the cloisters, he walked straight to the great pedestal on his right so that he could take stock of at least one of the famous Quinster wyverns. Anthony was amused by its ugliness, although it reminded him strongly of a human contact he had once made—something to do with a local council somewhere of which, however, he could remember no further details. He looked with interest at the clawed feet of the wyvern which gripped the sides of the pedestals, and philosophised.

"Pity you can't talk, old chap—you might spill something frightfully important one of these days. Even to a detailed description of Lady Blanchflower's murderer."

Anthony grinned confidentially at the wyvern but the stone creature refused to co-operate. He surveyed Anthony with equanimity so Anthony accepted the stony inevitable, saluted him appropriately and stepped towards the green grass and the white front door through which he had already passed once.

The name was still there—'LADY BLANCHFLOWER'. Anthony read it—just as Crouch had read it the morning after Lady Blanchflower had died. He glanced at the bell—and suddenly, materializing as it were from nowhere, two uniformed constables appeared. Anthony produced his card, suitably inscribed by the Commissioner of Police, Sir Austin Kemble.

"You want to go in, I suppose, sir?" said the elder constable.

"That was the idea,' returned Anthony, "unless the seals—"

The constable anticipated the question. "They were removed this morning, sir. By orders of the Chief Constable."

4

"Come this way, sir," said the constable; "as a matter of fact I've got a door open at the back. That's the one me and my mate are using. We find it more convenient."

"Thank you," said Anthony, "that's very nice of you." He followed the constable round to the back of the Blanchflower apartment. The constable pushed open a small back door, painted dark green, and Anthony entered. The constable closed the door behind him.

The rooms were much as he had remembered them from the experience of his first visit with Andrew MacMorran. The lounge where Lady Blanchflower had died, the dainty bedroom, the spotlessly clean little kitchen, the elegant dining-room—'living-room' would be, perhaps the better word—were all to the pattern, shape and size of his recollection.

Anthony stood at the door of each of the rooms and took a meticulously careful mental photograph of each of them one by one. Judging by what he saw, it would have been a comparatively simple matter for the murderer to have gained access to the apartments. Anthony supposed that living as it were in the lee of Quinster Castle, Lady Blanchflower had felt serenely safe from marauders with but little need to bolt and bar her modest little home.

Anthony went into each room and looked round it. Not in any sense, however, of *searching* for anything. He was taking a series of mental photographs. The one thing that was concerning him at the moment was the disposal of Mrs. Whitburn's body and that was the sole problem upon which he was now concentrating. *Where* had she been killed? Could he answer that question with any degree of certainty? The chances were, he had begun to think, that she had been killed somewhere here in Lady Blanchflower's apartments. And again—the chances were that the two crimes had been committed almost synchronously.

Now he was standing virtually where the murder had stood—metaphorically red-handed almost—where could the body of Mrs. Whitburn have been hidden? Easily—smoothly —quietly—but yet effectively. Effectively too, for something in the nature of a lengthy period. That was the problem which Anthony had come to consider. The *rooms* of Lady Blanchflower, Anthony considered, could be definitely ruled out. Anthony decided, therefore, to have a closer look at the rear of the apartments. As he made his way out, one of the constables was still standing at the back door. When he stepped into the 'garden' that had been Lady Blanchflower's, Anthony saw at once that he was in part of the grounds of Quinster Castle.

There was nothing in the shape of fence or wall to indicate definitely the actual garden space which had been attached to the Blanchflower apartments. Sir Hugo, in his lifetime had enjoyed 'part' of the grounds of Quinster Castle. That had been the extent of his privilege. And a delightful little corner, too, thought Anthony, as he stood there and surveyed it. It didn't take him long to determine the line of demarcation as decided by the head gardener of the castle himself. The line had been made most artistically by a semi-circle or crescent of standard rose-trees. Where these trees finished, there was a charming little arbour and beyond the arbour, a small rustic gate which opened to the grounds of the castle proper. The Blanchflower garden was trim and dainty—the grass beautifully tended and the paths and byways almost immaculate.

Anthony walked along the rose-tree crescent, passed into the arbour and came to the little gate. It was of the type that you push so far away from you before bringing it back towards you to give you space for entrance. Anthony pushed, and pulled back and stood in the grounds proper of Quinster Castle. This area, evidently, was mainly used as a vegetable garden. Anthony saw that clearly and at once. Much of the ground had already been limed for sweetening and a small tractor was at work on a large stretch of soil not more than a hundred yards distant from the Blanchflower gate. The Duke of Quinster or his head gardener was a believer, evidently, in natural rather than the more chemical fertilisers, for a large heap of manure steamed and smoked under an unusually bright November sun.

Anthony continued to walk on and saw ultimately that in addition to the driver of the tractor, three gardeners were at work in various parts of the Quinster grounds on that particular morning. One burnt heaps of rubbish, another cut dead wood from trees whilst the third man was pricking one of the large paths. But everything was clear and easily visible and the ground was open—and Anthony felt rather despondent as he looked across at it that he had made no progress at all in the real matter that had brought him here. Nothing at which he looked suggested even remotely that it might conceal the body of Mrs. Whitburn.

He began to retrace his steps towards the gate, the arbour and the rose-tree crescent. His thoughts were restive and uncontrolled and his mind disturbed. Try as he would, he was unable to make any headway— and then, very suddenly, he stopped dead on the grass path down which he had been walking. And he had stopped for an excellent reason!

5

There was something lying down there in the grass which had caught his eyes. Something which had shimmered . . . yes that was the word . . . something which had shimmered and glinted under a stray shaft of sunshine.

Anthony went carefully on his knees, and his fingers, in a twinkle of time, began to separate with the most delicate care, the green blades of grass. He felt sure that the object which had caught his eye, tricked by the sun, was unusually small—and on that account he must run no risk of losing it. His patience and care were quickly rewarded and his fingers closed on a small gold ear-stud.

Anthony rose from his kneeling position and stood erect. It might not be, of course . . . so ran his thoughts . . . but on the other hand, it very well might! He made a quick scrutiny of the ear-stud and dropped it into his ticket-pocket. There were two questions concerning it that needed to be answered—before it assumed more interesting proportions. Had the ear-stud belonged to Mrs. Whitburn? That was priority question. If so, had she by any chance dropped it in circumstances entirely unconnected with her death or with her disappearance?

No sooner had Anthony contemplated these two questions than a third climbed alertly into his brain. Had the ear-stud been the property of the late Lady Blanchflower? Anthony turned himself round deliberately and looked back at the Duke of Quinster's grounds that he had just left. What met his eye brought him again but scant encouragement. All that entered his circle of vision was open country. There were no tree-belts, no plantations. There were no ditches—there were no streams. A grave-digger—or one of his kind, would be the sole solution to the problem of body-disposal in country such as this. Then why the ear-stud—assuming that it were Mrs. Whitburn's—secondly why the ear-stud on that particular grass path where he had discovered it?

As he passed through the little rustic gate and the arbour and reached the crescent of the rose-trees, he saw Andrew MacMorran standing with the two uniformed constables.

6

As Anthony approached, MacMorran swung away from the men with him and advanced towards Anthony. "You're early," said Anthony; "didn't expect to see you here for another hour at least. Did you see Melville all right?"

"Ay. I did that. He was very co-operative."

"Did you get what you wanted?"

"Ay—more or less. Condensin' it as much as possible, we seemed to be concerned with no more than five people. Four 'commercials' and one casual guest. That's the lot. The 'commercials' are all absolutely vouched for by Melville himself, that is to say—as far as he can reasonably go, of course—and the stranger, J. H. Lilley by name—paid his account and left the hotel early on the Friday morning. I feel that we might take a closer look at him. It might pay dividends. There's an address in the Visitors' Book. I'll see about it."

Anthony nodded. "I agree."

MacMorran said: "What about you? Any more hunches?" A second or so elapsed before Anthony replied. When he did, the form of the answer rather surprised the inspector. "Come for a short stroll with me, Andrew—will you? I'd value your opinion on at least two questions that are causing me a certain amount of misgiving."

He conducted MacMorran along the way he had recently travelled himself. The inspector saw the tractor at work, the three gardeners on their respective jobs and all the outward and visible signs of the Duke of Quinster's kitchen-garden.

"Now we'll walk back," said Anthony, "and we'll go by way of that path in front of us. I've a penchant for that particular path, Andrew."

"What's the big idea?" grunted MacMorran.

"Keep going for a few moments," returned Anthony, "and then I'll tell you something."

MacMorran preceded Anthony along the path. So they walked for a few paces until Anthony cried, "Stop there, where you are, Andrew."

MacMorran halted in his tracks and turned round. "What's the game? Going to shove me in a ruddy circus?"

Anthony ranged himself at MacMorran's side. "A few minutes ago, Andrew, I walked along this path as you and I have just walked along it. As I reached this particular spot where I asked you to pull up, I noticed something shimmering in the grass. I went on my haunches, Andrew, sorted out the grass very carefully, and picked the object up."

"What was it?" demanded MacMorran.

"This," replied Anthony. He fished in his pocket and produced the gold ear-stud. He then dropped it into the palm of MacMorran's hand.

"Beyond the article which you now hold, Andrew—I have nothing to report."

MacMorran looked grim and unyielding. "What do you think of it," he asked.

"Ah," said Anthony, "that is the point. What good shall we do by theorizing? How far shall we get? I can't think. I mustn't. But, as an investigator, I can cherish the fervent hope that that ear-stud belonged to Mrs. Whitburn. If that fervent hope be also sound, then the grace of God may lead us to her—via that same golden stud."

MacMorran shook his head doubtfully. "You don't know that it was Mrs. Whitburn's. It may well belong to Lady Blanchflower. I mean 'have belonged to her'. That seems to me just as probable as the other."

"I quite agree, Andrew. We must take our bearings on it at once. Get the ear-stud identified."

"And there is also," went on MacMorran, "a third possibility which I fear I must point out to you. That it belonged to neither of the ladies."

"It's a possibility, of course, but I don't fancy so. One of the two, I say, with the odds on the missing Mrs. Whitburn."

MacMorran partly demurred. "Not heavy odds. I can't admit that."

"Two to one, at least," argued Anthony; "and that's not such a dusty price with only two running. Which despite your timely warning, is all *I* can visualise."

MacMorran and Anthony walked back to the abode that had been the late Lady Blanchflower's. MacMorran scratched his cheek as he walked.

"What was it doing down in the grass there? That's the problem we must solve."

"Dropped there, Andrew. Dropped inadvertently. I'm giving you my opinion now. Dropped either by the owner of the ear-stud or by the person who murdered her."

MacMorran made an impatient noise with his tongue. "We're still looking for a body! Aren't you forgetting that?"

"Forgetting it? How can I, Andrew? I was looking for that body when I spotted that ear-stud. I'm still darned well looking for it."

MacMorran waved to one of the uniformed constables as he and Anthony made for the grass verge and the nearer wyvern. Anthony turned suddenly and faced the entrance to the castle. "Grand looking place, Andrew—yes?"

"I suppose it is. But it's a bit outmoded these days. That's how it appears to me."

"You could hide a body in there, Andrew, as easy as kiss your hand. I'd lay odds cheerfully on that."

"I expect you would. I wouldn't call it a risky bet myself."

"Ever met His Grace, Andrew? The fourteenth Duke of Quinster?"

"Can't say that I have. Why?"

"I wonder what sort of bloke he is. I'd like to get a slant on him. All I can remember of him is that his horses are trained at Beckhampton."

"Why? What's all this about? Why the sudden interest in the aristocracy?"

"Oh—nothing much, Andrew. Just a slice of Bathurst curiosity in eruption this morning."

"Not another hunch?"

"I don't know. It might even be that."

"You come along with me back to the Red Deer," said MacMorran, "and we'll see about this gold ear-stud."

CHAPTER 10

1

"Who first?" said Anthony, as he and MacMorran entered the hotel.

MacMorran considered the question. "One of the two women we saw on Saturday with their husbands. Either Mrs. Grahame or Mrs. Danbury. Always ask a woman what another woman was wearing. A man never knows. He always says, 'Oh—a sort of a—black sort of a,' that's been my experience ever since I was a copper on the beat. The same remarks apply to jewellery."

"Mrs. Danbury, I think," said Anthony after reflection, "in my opinion she's the better bet of the two. What's the time now? Twenty to one. Just about right. Couldn't be better. Lunch in the offing. She's probably in. Get hold of her, Andrew—and bring her into our lounge. Don't be too long. I'll be waiting in there for you."

Anthony made his way into the small lounge, poked the fire into a blaze, put some more coal on it—also two large logs and settled down in the arm-chair to wait for MacMorran and Maureen Danbury. He balanced the ear-stud which MacMorran had handed back to him in the palm of his hand. He was a little excited and a trifle anxious to boot. Since his *faux pas* with Guthrie in the matter of the Quinster bonfire, this anxiety had grown rather than diminished—and it had become an anxiety that he should justify himself. In short, this case was getting on Anthony's nerves—more perhaps, than any previous investigation he had undertaken.

MacMorran wasn't long finding the lady he wanted and Anthony was distinctly relieved when the door of the small lounge opened and the inspector entered with Maureen Danbury. Anthony rose to greet her and waved her to a chair. "I've told Mrs. Danbury," said MacMorran, "that we want her help with regard to something. And she's been very charming about it. Have you got it handy?"

Anthony produced the gold ear-stud. "Have a look at this, Mrs. Danbury will you, please? Look carefully before you commit yourself definitely. What we want to know is this. First of all—have you ever seen it before? And then, if you think you have tell us whom, in your opinion, it belonged to."

Maureen Danbury took the ear-stud and looked at it closely. Without a second's hesitation she answered: "Oh yes—this is most familiar to me. I know it well. I've seen it—well—dozens of times. But I can't tell you whom it belonged to."

Anthony and MacMorran stared at her with some amazement. "I don't quite follow," said Anthony slowly; "would you mind explaining?"

Maureen Danbury smiled at him. "It was a bit enigmatic—wasn't it? But when I explain, you'll soon see why I spoke as I did. In fact I couldn't really say anything else. That ear-stud you showed me belonged to one of two people—either to the late Lady Blanchflower—or to—er Laura Whitburn."

Anthony nodded. "I see. Go on explaining—will you?"

"Well it was like this. There's nothing mysterious about it. Originally, Lady Blanchflower had two pairs of gold ear-studs like this—and she gave one of the pairs to Laura Whitburn—principally I think, because Mrs. Whitburn admired them so. See? That's why it's absolutely impossible for me to say whether this stud was hers or one of those she gave to Mrs. Whitburn. Of course you could find out—"

Anthony cut in before she could complete her sentence. "By going through the stuff Lady Blanchflower has left behind. In jewel-cases, etc. Yes—that's the natural solution. Thank you very much, Mrs. Danbury, for your help. Very charming of you."

He swung round in his chair to MacMorran.

"Extraordinary feature of this case, Andrew! Nothing about it ever comes clean. There's always an 'if' or 'but' or a ridiculous complication. And complications, even though they may be petty, always mean a certain amount of wasted time." He looked at his watch. "Just about time for lunch. Thank you again for your help, Mrs. Danbury. We're very much indebted to you."

2

Anthony and MacMorran sat alone. "What do you think?" enquired the latter. "Lady Blanchflower's jewel-case? As soon as we can get to it?"

"Depends where it is, Andrew. I'd like as little delay as possible. Jewel-cases have an alarming habit of being somewhere else than where you expect to find them. We shall have to see."

Anthony finished his sentence by shaking his head despondently. "It's this Whitburn business we've got to solve. That's the end of the business that matters most. Until we've done that we're just running round in circles—chasing our own darned tails. When I picked up that ear-stud this morning at the back of the Blanchflower place, I felt that I'd got somewhere at last. But when I went and took a look at the adjoining country to try to work out something definite and tangible—I had another think. The only point to my mind is did the murderer carry the body"

Anthony stopped abruptly and looked into space. "Andrew," he said softly—and then paused again—his fingers playing absently round the top of his glass..

"What's the trouble now?" said MacMorran.

"Andrew," began Anthony again. "At last I believe I'm on to something. Good God!".

He pushed his chair back from the table. His fingers still toyed with the glass. The far-away look his face had held had gone completely—it had been superseded by the glow and tenseness of anticipated action.

"Can you get Guthrie?" he asked.

"Of course. At the station. Why?"

"Why? I'll tell you why, Andrew. I've got another job of work for him. Get Guthrie to meet us at Lady Blanchflower's place at—let's see—what's the time now" Anthony looked at his watch; "at three o'clock sharp. Not a minute later, tell him. Tell him also to bring a couple of hefty blokes with him. And . . . er . . . "

Anthony paused. MacMorran was looking puzzled at the shape things were taking.

"And . . . er . . . what?" he asked.

"If you get an acid spurt of sarcasm from our genial friend, the inspector—deal with it in your own inimitable fashion. You know where the 'phone is, don't you."

"O—yes—I know where the 'phone is," said MacMorran. "I also know the most comfortable way to carry the can back. It's mainly a question of practice."

"Good for you, Andrew," grinned Anthony.

MacMorran left his seat and made for the door and the telephone. As he closed the door behind him, Anthony took a deep breath.

"If I'm wrong this time," he said to himself, "it'll take a lot of living down."

3

Anthony walked with MacMorran from the Red Deer to the cloisters. Catterall, when they passed him into the castle grounds, was unable to resist a quip.

"Let me know when the 'Big Five' are expected and I'll 'ave the red carpet put down. Or else roll out the barrel. That'd loosen their tongues—I bet."

When Anthony and MacMorran reached the Blanchflower front door, the former saw with pleasure that Inspector Guthrie had already arrived.

"Good afternoon, Inspector Guthrie," said MacMorran, "thank you for coming along so promptly. I wasn't too certain you'd be here yet. I was afraid you mightn't have got my message till later. No news of any kind, I suppose?"

Guthrie shook his head. "None at all. Bar this business, of course."

"H'm. Pity. I was hoping something might have turned up by this time."

Guthrie's reply was indirect. "What is it this time? More fun and games?"

"Well—for one thing, Mr. Bathurst wants a word with you. He and I have made an important discovery." Guthrie's eyes searched MacMorran's face for further information. MacMorran beckoned to Anthony.

"Just indicate to the inspector what you want done."

Anthony, anxious again, spoke to Guthrie. "I'm a great believer, Inspector, in the application of trial and error. The experience of a mistake in the past may well lead to a success in the future. In one respect we're all three in the same boat. Our problem is to find either a missing woman or that missing woman's body."

"You mean that body that wasn't on the bonfire? Is that the idea?"

Guthrie's words were barbed but the tone of the voice was pleasant.

Anthony smiled back at him.

"That's the one, Inspector. And with that, you've brought me to the point. This afternoon we're going to have another shot at finding it. Where are those two men of yours?"

"Round at the back with the uniformed men. Waiting for orders."

"Let's go and find them," said Anthony, "they don't know it, but it's their cue for entrance."

4

Some moments later, the five men moved away from the back of the little dwelling-place, Anthony leading. "We go along by that semi-circle or crescent of rose-trees, through that arbour at the end and then follow on through the push-gate."

Anthony spoke quietly and the others followed him as he had directed. The five of them pushed their way, one by one, through the wooden gate.

"Do you know where we are now, Inspector?" asked Anthony of Guthrie.

"Certainly," came the swift rejoinder. "Been in here before—many a time—in the grounds of Quinster Castle. In the agricultural portion thereof. The Duke grows a rare lot of stuff in this kitchen-garden of his. If there's a couple of ha'pennies to be made in any way—you can bet your life he'll make 'em. Whether it's from swedes or selling-platers."

"Quite right, Inspector. As you say we're in the grounds of Quinster Castle itself." Anthony paused—to continue almost immediately: "Get your two chaps, Inspector, to scrounge a brace of gardening forks from somewhere. Look—there's a gardener working over yonder—he'll give 'em the tip where to find a couple, no doubt."

The two plain-clothes men looked at Guthrie, who nodded confirmation of Anthony's order. The men set off at a quickish walking-pace. Guthrie turned to Anthony and remarked mordantly:

"Don't tell me they've got to dig up the grounds of Quinster Castle and call out 'Alas! poor Yorick,' at inappropriate moments. That would be just about the last straw."

Anthony grinned. "Feeling a pain in the back—eh? Come, come, Inspector—you're no camel. Trial and error. Where would any one of us be without it?"

Guthrie seemed about to reply again—but he changed his mind and checked himself. Anthony took a side-glance at MacMorran. He saw clearly that the Yard inspector himself was on the business end of several gross of tenter-hooks. None of the three men spoke again until Guthrie's minions returned with the gardening forks.

Anthony looked at the two men and said, "Thank you. Now will you all please come this way."

5

The man working the tractor was much nearer the little wooden gate than when Anthony had watched him at work before lunch. Two of the other gardeners also were in reasonably intimate proximity. The gardener, however, who had been pricking the path, was not now in sight. Guthrie indicated one of the burnt rubbish-heaps.

"More bodies eh? Not so big this time. No bodies there."

"No—no bodies there, Inspector," said Anthony; "too much on the surface."

"Going far?" inquired Guthrie with a dash of cynicism.

"No, Inspector. The rendezvous is already in sight."

Guthrie took a comprehensive look round as he walked on. "Dashed if I can see anything."

"Surely," replied Anthony, "you can see something! Don't tell me the horizon's so bare as all that."

Guthrie took a second look. "Well—stagger me—as I said—if you can tell me that there's any—"

Anthony took a couple of paces forwards and closured him. "This great heap of dung, Inspector! I find it difficult to rid my mind of a belief that it contains the body of Mrs. Whitburn. Get your two chaps to fork the stuff back—do you mind? It may take them some little time but they won't find it tough going, I assure you."

Guthrie heard his words and stared at him in amazement. "Good lord—you don't mean—"

Anthony dropped his tone of raillery and spoke gravely. "I do, Inspector—I do indeed."

Guthrie signalled to the plain-clothes men. "Have a go at this manure-heap, you chaps—will you? You heard what Mr. Bathurst said."

6

The men with the forks stepped forward. Each man spat on the palms of his hands. The heap was large and Anthony saw the question which each man was almost certainly asking himself.

"Attack it from this side," he said, "a person carrying a body to this heap by the route I imagine it came, would travel by the shortest and quickest route. It's worth a shot that way to begin with anyhow."

In the meantime, MacMorran and Guthrie themselves had approached more closely to the big dung-heap. The pronged forks got to work quickly and Anthony's coolness which had suddenly come to him, began to leave him just as suddenly. Surely he hadn't made a second boob! The smoking manure made little resistance to the forks—and any lingering doubt which Anthony may have harboured was quickly dispelled. From where he was standing he heard MacMorran give vent to a sharp exclamation and he saw Guthrie start forward suddenly with a look of horror on his face. Anthony himself moved forward with the others.

When the two plain-clothes men stopped working and put their forks on one side . . . Anthony saw them bend down . . . then he himself caught sight of a dress. It was black. He knew how the body of Lady Blanchflower had been clad . . . Then he saw the two men stoop for the second time.

CHAPTER 11

1

The body of Mrs. Whitburn (fully-dressed) was identified by her son, Kenneth Whitburn, just before five o'clock that same afternoon. It seemed to Anthony that he bore the shock of his mother's tragic death with admirable fortitude and the most commendable dignity.

"I think," he said to Anthony, "that in a way, I'm actually relieved. I felt this morning when I was in the train going to town, that *anything* almost would be preferable to that awful condition of agonizing suspense. Four days of that were just about getting me on the floor. I doubt whether I could have stood much more of it."

Anthony agreed, and added his sympathy and condolence. The cause of the ill-fated lady's death was exactly similar to that of Lady Blanchflower's strangulation. A silk stocking no doubt had been knotted tightly round the throat. There was rather more bruising, however, in the case of Mrs. Whitburn's death than there had been in Lady Blanchflower's. Doctor Manners told MacMorran at the P.M. when the Yard inspector raised the point that this fact was due to Mrs. Whitburn having died 'harder'. The murderer had been compelled to exert more force and a greater degree of pressure and pull. To Anthony's purely professional satisfaction, the dead lady's right ear held an ear-stud exactly similar to the stud he had picked up in the grass path at the back of Lady Blanchflower's apartments, whereas Mrs. Whitburn's left ear held no stud.

Guthrie had listened quietly to Anthony's explanation of his success with a kind of tranquil interest. And, in justice to the Quinster inspector, it must be recorded that he had been neither slow nor grudging in his congratulations.

At six o'clock that evening, MacMorran decided on a conference. From what he told Anthony, the Chief Constable would be present.

"When's it for, Andrew?" said Anthony.

"Eight-thirty this evening."

"Where?"

"In Guthrie's room at Quinster Police-station. I'd like you to come along."

"O.K., Andrew—if you really want me."

2

"Now, gentlemen," said Guthrie, "sit down and make yourselves comfortable." He looked at his watch. "I'm expecting the Chief Constable in about a quarter of an hour's time. He 'phoned me some little time ago that he was on his way. I don't know whether the Chief Inspector would like to make any suggestions before Sir George arrives—or whether he'd rather hold everything until the Chief Constable comes and make one job of it. What are your wishes in that respect, Chief?"

"I'll wait," said MacMorran, "as you've just pointed out—if I start now it'll probably mean going over the same ground again."

Guthrie nodded. "I expected you to say that. Oh—by the way—I hadn't mentioned it—but I believe Sir George won't be . . . er . . . alone."

MacMorran frowned. Then his brows went into a question. "Not alone? What precisely do you mean, Inspector?"

Guthrie seemed a trifle ill at ease. "I rather fancy from what the Chief Constable said on the 'phone that he may be accompanied here by a . . . er . . . distinguished visitor." Guthrie paused and coughed. "I refer to His Grace the Duke of Quinster."

MacMorran's frown became out-size and his eyes hard. "But surely such a procedure's highly irregular? I don't think in all my experience I can recall anything like a precedent."

Guthrie shrugged his shoulders at the criticism. "Sir George likes to be in the Duke's good books. That, I think, is the real reason behind it. And if . . . as I imagine *may* have happened . . . the Duke expressed a strong desire to be present . . . after all—we must look at it in a commonsense way—the two murders have taken place inside his own castle grounds . . . well . . . Sir George feels, I understand, that His Grace *has* a position."

Anthony nodded before MacMorran could reply. "That's very true, Inspector. The murders did take place very near to His Grace and His Grace's ancestral home. I couldn't agree with you more."

"That may be so," said MacMorran, "and that's all very well—but I tell you frankly, Inspector Guthrie, I don't like it. To my mind it's absolutely irregular. I've been in the Force more years than I care to remember—many more years—and I don't think—"

Guthrie interrupted him. "I can assure you, Chief—I'm in no way responsible for what is happening. No more than you yourself are. You'll have to argue it out, if you feel you must—with the Chief Constable himself."

"That'll get me a long way—I've had similar arguments—or partly similar in the past."

"Well—it won't be your funeral, Chief. It'll be Sir George's. Any rap that may be coming along will be for him to take."

MacMorran shrugged his shoulders. "That's so, I suppose. But it doesn't make me like the idea any more—I tell you that."

Guthrie nodded and then stood up listening. "I think I heard the car," he declared; "they've come on from the castle." MacMorran looked at Anthony and muttered something definitely unparliamentary.

3

Sir George Nightingale bustled in with the fourteenth Duke of Quinster a few paces behind him. He introduced His Grace to the others and then proceeded to make certain remarks and explanations.

Anthony took the opportunity to have a good look at Henry Erskine Conyngham Annesley Fitzcuthbert. He saw the fat cheeks and the bulging water-blue eyes, the high-bridged nose and the alarmingly imposing Adam's apple. The Duke took the seat nearest to the Chief Constable and as he seated himself he was heard to say:

"Most distressing! Most distressing! Most ghastly business I ever heard of. What the world is coming to these days—I really don't know."

Guthrie looked across at MacMorran. The latter nodded. Guthrie opened the conference.

"Chief Det. Inspector MacMorran has called this conference," he said, "in view of the . . . er . . . new turn the case has taken this afternoon. So I'll ask him to . . . er . . . just put his views to us . . . as a start-off, as it were."

Guthrie then addressed himself directly to the Chief Constable. "I take it, sir, that you have no objection to the adoption of that procedure?"

Sir George blew out his cheeks. "I'm ready to hear what he has to say . . . and at the same time, Guthrie, I'd like to congratulate you on your findings of this afternoon. Very smart piece of work on your part, very smart indeed. Proves conclusively what I've always argued and maintained, that we, here in Quinster, can hold our own with Scotland Yard practically nine times out of ten."

MacMorran's face was suggestive of the spectrum but Anthony managed to catch his eye and drop an eyelid (his own). The Chief Constable found one of his best and worst smiles.

"Now, Chief-Inspector MacMorran, I'm sure we're all attention and waiting to hear what you have to say to us." MacMorran made a herculean effort but there was no reciprocal smile for the Chief Constable.

"Well, gentlemen," he said, "those of us who are present at this conference officially know what happened this afternoon and how the case now stands. The discovery of Mrs. Whitburn's body, with the cause of death similar to that in the case of Lady Blanchflower, gives the crime a somewhat changed aspect and certainly raises new issues for the police authorities. The main trouble, from our point of view, is still as it was—motive. Up to the moment, we've hit on nothing which we can regard as at all satisfactory in that direction. It was missing when it was a case of Lady Blanchflower only—but now that we've a dead and murdered Mrs. Whitburn on our hands in addition to the first lady, the absence of any known motive becomes even more puzzling. I felt in these circumstances, therefore, that we should get together this evening and have a chat. Now, as a start off—I'd like your views—if you wouldn't mind, Sir George."

Before the Chief Constable could reply, the Duke hooded his eyes and raised a ducal finger.

"My dear sir," he said to MacMorran; "if you please—consider for one moment! The night has a thousand eyes. There are two women dead—and you say there is no motive! My very dear sir—two women—two—why it stands to reason—there must be a thousand motives. Can any sane person doubt it? Years ago a man wrote a play. He called it *Two Sins and a Woman*. When it was filmed, they saved space and called it *Three Sins*."

MacMorran bore the infliction stoically. "Permit me to point out, Your Grace, my words were 'known motive' or one that we could reasonably attach to the crimes. Until we find the motive and are in a position to act on what we find, that thousand of yours might just as well be non-existent."

The Duke made a reply which was inaudible.

MacMorrran turned to the Chief Constable. "Sir George?"

"H'm. Yes," replied the Chief Constable, "well now—since my opinions have been invited—this death of Mrs. Whitburn certainly has . . . er . . . put the fat in the fire. I certainly agree—to that extent. And it appears to me that this second lady was murdered because she was the unwilling . . . er . . . witness to the *first* murder. In my opinion—that's the one and only connection between the . . . er . . . two crimes."

Sir George fussed about and wiped his forehead with a large silk handkerchief.

"Thank you, sir." MacMorran turned to Guthrie. "Now you, Inspector Guthrie. I'd like to hear any new views you may have."

Guthrie paused for a moment before replying. "Well," he said at length. "I'm rather inclined to my original idea again. That the motive behind the crimes is burglary. Mrs. Whitburn was just unlucky. She happened to be with Lady Blanchflower when they surprised the thief. He thought the place was entirely empty of people—and suddenly found it wasn't. Both women were in his way—and they had it. In that way the crime becomes just commonplace."

MacMorran was about to speak when Guthrie checked him with his uplifted hand.

"I think I know what you're going to say, Chief. That, as far as we know, nothing of any value was stolen from Lady Blanchflower. But if you'll pardon my saying so—that's only as far as we know. Who knows what's absent from the place that was there before the murders were committed? I suggest the only person would be Lady Blanchflower herself and only Lady Blanchflower. She might have possessed in her apartment something of extraordinary value. The existence of which was known to but few people. Wasn't she a close friend of King Edward the Seventh? Why—to me—that's far the most likely proposition of any. In other words, Chief—putting things in a nutshell, I've more or less come back to my first opinion."

Guthrie sat back—a trifle flushed. Before anybody could speak, Henry Fitzcuthbert came in again.

"Very sound. Ve-ry sound indeed. Old Teddy—God bless his memory—thought no end of Lil Blanchflower—I can vouch for that.

And he was as good a judge of a filly as was ever known. I've heard the thirteenth Duke of Quinster assert that on innumerable occasions. It's not unlikely that dear old Teddy dropped Lil Blanchflower—or Lil Bonnammy as she was in those days—something of er . . . great value . . . in token of his . . . er . . . friendship. And one or two bright boys attached to one of these new 'professions' may have known of it. Very sound idea indeed."

"Thank you, your Grace," said MacMorran rather acidly, "and thank you, too, Inspector Guthrie." MacMorran paused for a second and ran his hand along the ridge of his jaw. "Before I comment," he continued, "before I comment on anything that has been so far said—I'd like to hear what Mr. Bathurst has to say."

All eyes were turned to Anthony.

"Well, your Grace and gentlemen," he said, "I may as well come to the point at once and say flatly that I do *not* agree with Inspector Guthrie. In the sense that the crimes were committed because Lady Blanchflower and Mrs. Whitburn, returning to the former's apartments, surprised a thief. Or even surprised the murderer. You'll get the implication of that last remark if you think things out. I don't fancy that anything of that kind took place. No, gentlemen, I think the murder of at least one of these ladies was deliberately planned, plotted and, of course, premeditated."

"What makes you so positive of that?" demanded Guthrie.

"The method of killing," replied Anthony; "a thief taken by surprise in the manner that you outlined and suggested doesn't use one of a pair of silk stockings. And a stocking too, which to all evidence, had once belonged to one of the murdered ladies herself."

Guthrie was hard put to it to conceal his annoyance. He shifted his ground a little, perhaps, and said, "I'm not so sure. We haven't anything like all the facts. There's so much that we don't know. And after all—"

It was at this juncture that Sir George came back to the discussion. He turned to Anthony.

"You said one thing, Mr. Bathurst, that . . . er . . . interested me considerably. And not only interested me—rather amazed me."

"What was that, sir?"

"You said, 'the murder of at least *one* of these two ladies was a deliberately-planned affair.' And to my ear, you rather . . . er . . . stressed . . . emphasised the word 'one'. May I inquire to which of the two ladies you were making reference?"

Anthony was silent for a time under the question. He would have preferred that the question had not been asked. When he did reply, he said, "You're quite right, sir. I did point the word 'one' and your ear didn't deceive you. But, quite frankly, I don't know that I *can* answer that last question of yours. As to which of the ladies, I meant."

"Why not, my dear chap?"

"Because I'm by no means sure, sir. Yet. In a couple of days' time, perhaps, I may be sure. Then I may be in a position to answer your question.' "

Sir George looked puzzled. "But surely—you made such a positive remark, you know—with regard to the premeditation and all that you must have certain—"

Anthony bore the fusillade good-humouredly and smilingly interrupted. "Very well, sir. If I *must* make a choice to satisfy you I'll nominate Lady Blanchflower as what we'll term first murderee. But please don't ask me to go a step farther than that at the moment."

"I should have thought," said Henry Fitzcuthbert sententiously, "that there was little doubt about it. Everything about the . . . er . . . outrage suggests to me that Lil Blanchflower must have been the . . . er . . . how shall I put it . . . the primary . . . er . . . target. The . . . er . . . main quarry of the . . . er . . pursuer."

Anthony cut in quickly. "Permit me, your Grace—but how do you arrive at that opinion? What do you base it on, may I ask? I'd be most interested to hear."

The Duke regarded Anthony with a bland and condescending benevolence. "My dear sir . . . ask yourself . . . the matter to me is an absurdly simple one . . . where did the murders take place? The answer is obvious. A criminal who intends to murder Mrs. Jones doesn't go to Mrs. Smith's house to do it. I take no pride in that statement. Because it's a most elementary piece of reasoning."

The Duke's tone had been suave. Anthony's, in immediate reply, was even more so. "I take it, your Grace, your line of reasoning is this. The murderer goes to Mrs. Smith's in order to murder Mrs. Smith. Conversely, if he desire to remove Mrs. Jones from the land of the living, he goes to the house of Mrs. Jones. Is that your point?"

The Duke purred with gratification. "Exactly, my dear sir—that is just what I intended to convey. I'm delighted that I've been able to show you the light."

"The round isn't over yet, your Grace—the bell hasn't gone. Let us take a step or two further. Pursuing your line of argument, the murderer moves in that manner because he knows he'll find the victim on the victim's premises. Is that so?"

"Indubitably," returned the Duke.

"Thank you. Now you have the very reason why I'm in doubt as to which lady was what I'll describe as the 'authentic' victim. Because as I see things—the murderer may well have known that *both the ladies would have been in the Blanchflower apartments at that particular time when he called there.*"

The Duke manufactured an extraordinary noise.

MacMorran rushed in to eliminate the general embarrassment. "If that is so," he remarked, "if Mr. Bathurst's theory of the crime is the correct one, it's clear that in looking for the murderer, we must look for a person, thoroughly acquainted with the two ladies. Conversant with their regular and habitual movements and customs."

"Now, Andrew," said Anthony, "you have said something! You've removed the words from my trembling tongue."

Guthrie, however, shrugged his shoulders. "I should say then, Chief, that you've still put a tough task in front of us. The people in Quinster alone who knew the dining habits of Lady Blanchflower and Mrs. Whitburn would almost certainly number hundreds. Each lady was a well-known local personality."

"Even allowing for the truth of that," countered MacMorran, "it still narrows the circle somewhat. There are thousands that didn't. Couldn't have done."

Guthrie rose from his chair and proceeded with a great deal of noise to put coal on the fire. Sir George looked sycophantically at the Duke of Quinster.

"As far as I'm concerned, your Grace, and with your consent, I think this would be an excellent moment to adjourn our conference. We've all ventilated . . . our . . . er views and opinions . . . and . . . er . . . we've reached certain conclusions which is an excellent thing from all points of view. We are not all, perhaps, in complete agreement . . . but there . . . that's quite an ordinary condition . . . and . . . er . . . eminently understandable . . . people seldom are in . . . er . . . entire harmony . . . it's not to be expected that they will be. We'll leave the case in the competent hands of Inspector Guthrie . . . and . . . er . . . Chief Det. Inspector MacMorran from Scotland Yard in whom I have absolute confidence. In addition to that I shall be at hand to proffer not only my advice but also the general benefit of my long experience. Personally, I've little doubt that an arrest will be made within the course of the next few days. I am more than confident."

The Duke of Quinster, in reply, to the Chief Constable produced one of his more guttural, but less homely, noises. Sir George stood up solemnly.

"The conference is adjourned," he declared.

As the meeting broke up, Anthony distinctly heard profanity balancing precariously on the edge of MacMorran's breath. Profanity with a strong Scots accent!

CHAPTER 12

1

Anthony sat in his room at the Red Deer and reflected. He felt that it was urgently essential he should concentrate on the particular problem which he had previously outlined to Henry Fitzcuthbert, the fourteenth Duke of Quinster.

Lady Blanchflower or Laura Whitburn? Which of the two ladies had raised the lust of murder in the killer's heart? What he had said to the Duke had been by no means a *façon de parler* on his part. There had been no exaggeration whatever in any one of his statements. He found himself absolutely unable to make up his mind as to which was the authentic victim and which the victim *de convenance*. Again—the much-vexed question of motive! Was it obscure, sinister, bizarre, with its genesis foundationed in the years that had gone, or was it on the other hand, simple, ordinary, commonplace, with its origin but new and of but recent, and perhaps trivial, occurrence?

Anthony began to pace the room. To probe hard for the elusive microbe of motive. Why do men kill? He must move along the hard-trodden path of elimination. Why do men kill? More particularly—why do they kill women? Or again—why do women kill women? That was a possibility not entirely to be ruled out.

Anthony ran through the ancient gallery of murder motives. Hatred, revenge, and then anger, jealousy, cupidity, fear. There wasn't much else that wouldn't fall for natural inclusion somewhere in one of those six main compartments. Was there some dark secret, way back in the romantic life of Lady Blanchflower that had caught up with her in the evening of her days? Or, similarly, was there a shadow in the early days of Laura Whitburn which in these last few days had been illuminated by death?

On the whole the scale tipped down, Anthony thought, on the side of Lady Blanchflower. If that were so, and his mental inclination correct, it would mean days of delving and possibly long periods of probing. Anthony began to collect for further examination the clues that already cluttered the crimes. Such as they were. The wigs. Extraordinary! Bewildering! Even fantastic. One, a man's—found beneath Lady Blanchflower's body and the other—a woman's—thrown to the bonfire for burning and destruction. Each wig fitted for a character in Tom Robertson's *Caste*. *But both paid for by Mrs. Whitburn*. Why in the name of conscience? Why? It was crazy . . . distorted . . . in this instance, two things which were equal to the same thing, *weren't* equal to one another.

Whichever way he looked at the matter, Anthony was brought to a dead stop by the fact of the conditions of that Fleury cheque. That Mrs. Whitburn had drawn it on her own current account seemed to be indisputable. That she *had* done so appeared to argue one of two things. She had either carried out the entire Fleury transaction of her own volition or at the instigation or under the influence of a second person. Proceeding from there, that second person, if indeed there had been a second person, must have been somebody in whom she placed the most implicit confidence. Proceeding still further, a person in all probability with whom she was on the most intimate terms.

Anthony began to think hard. Stay a moment—though! He had never seen the actual Fleury cheque. All he had seen had been the stub of the appropriate counterfoil. It would not be an impossibility for the counterfoil and its presumably appropriate cheque counterpart to differ. Yes—quite a simple matter that. And if—Anthony thought he saw a ray of light here and began to rub his hands. If Mrs. Whitburn, under a strong influence, could have been persuaded to—

It was at that precise moment that the jolt came. The cheque *must* have been made out in accordance with the details on the counterfoil. The bill had been duly receipted by the payee. And not only receipted by the payee—a narration had actually been added in similar terms—"paid by cheque".

Anthony ceased his room-pacing and sat on the edge of the bed. This was getting worse and worse. Had there been a cheque substitution? The scale of probability seemed to be rising again to tip down *this* time on the side of Laura Whitburn. Yes—he had much to do he could see that more plainly than ever—much to investigate.

Then his thoughts tangented again. To the small slip that had been discovered tucked away in Mrs. Whitburn's chequebook. Once again his mind ran over those few, conventional commonplace words. "I must write it down before I forget. Lily says 'come quickly—mistress away'. Must tell K. as soon as possible."

Anthony repeated the words to himself, three or even four times. The operative word seemed to him to be "mistress". What mistress or from another possible, though perhaps unlikely, angle, *whose* mistress? "Lily says." That is to say Lady Blanchflower says. To whom? Presumably to Mrs. Whitburn herself, But who in the name of thumping thunder could be reasonably regarded as Lady Blanchflower's mistress?

Anthony shook his head. He was getting absolutely nowhere. Equally who could be Mrs. Whitburn's mistress? Anthony cudgelled his brains. He could find but two moderately justifiable answers to his pair of questions. The Duchess of Quinster *might* be termed the mistress of Quinster Castle by Lady Blanchflower, a tenant of the Duke's, and Mrs. Melville (if there were such a lady—Anthony had no idea whether one existed) *might* be regarded as the "mistress" of the Red Deer Hotel.

Anthony juggled with the two ladies' names and tossed them about from one mental hand to another. He fancied, when he had finished his juggling act, that neither of them really satisfied him that she was the person concerning whom Lil Blanchflower had spoken to Laura Whitburn. In that case then—where was he? Almost in the place where he had started—with alarmingly little progress made.

His eyes caught the telephone on the table at the bedside. That was an idea. He could soon settle one of the questions. Anthony rang "Service". The answer was immediate. "May I speak to Mrs. Melville—please? This is Room 17 speaking—although you doubtless know that."

"Mrs. who?" came back to him.

"Mrs. Melville," repeated Anthony.

"Mrs. Melville? There's no Mrs. Melville here, sir. Mrs. Barlow is the housekeeper and most things to do with the comfort of the hotel are referred to her. Shall I tell her you want her? Actually, she isn't here at the moment."

"I'll wait," replied Anthony. "I'll see her when I come downstairs. Sorry to have troubled you."

He replaced the receiver in the cradle. 'Another stumer,' he said to himself, 'I'm doing well—I must say.'

2

Anthony handed his professional visiting-card to the first cashier on the counter at the Quinster branch of the Southern and Home Counties Bank. The cashier levered a somewhat ancient face above an enormous and equally ancient starched wing-collar. He then blinked after the manner of a venerable owl and looked at the card through a pair of thin-stemmed horn-rimmed glasses (National Health Service variety). When he spoke to Anthony his voice was thin and reedy.

"What can I do for you?"

"Take me to the manager of the bank if you don't mind," replied Anthony, "and tell him—also if you don't mind—that the matter upon which I wish to see him, is extremely urgent. Thank you in anticipation."

The cashier regarded Anthony with a singularly unfriendly glance. All the malevolence engendered by long years of banking service was in it. It flickered over Anthony's face like a fanned flame. It caused him to feel as though he had one foot and another four toes firmly planted in the Slough of Despond known as Carey Street. The cashier looked again at the card. The look was long, lingering and lugubrious. Then he looked again at Anthony.

"The manager, please," said the latter in a species of soft menacing hiss.

The cashier grunted, glared, glowered and then holding the card moved slowly away from the counter. His neck was firmly held in place by his amazing collar. Anthony waited in patience for his return. Eventually the cashier came back to him. He had shed none of his personal charm, naught of his fragrance and nothing of his sweet reasonableness.

"This way," he said sepulchrally. Anthony followed him in a sort of parallel route. The cashier, winning by a short head, lifted a counter flap, joined Anthony on the clients' side of the counter and pushed open a door. Anthony, by a superb body-swerve, sidled in behind him.

"Mr. Bullwinkle," Anthony heard him say, "here's the man that wants to see you."

"Thank you, Mr. Arscott," said an unseen Mr. Bullwinkle. "Show him in, will you please?"

"He's in already," said Anthony gaily, "and thank you once again, Mr. Arscott."

The manager stood up when he heard Anthony's voice. "Good morning, Mr. Bathurst," he said genially.

3

"Good morning," returned Anthony—"you saw my card?"

"I saw your card."

"In the matter of Laura Whitburn, deceased. You've heard the news, no doubt?"

"I have. Dreadful business! Very charming lady. Very charming indeed. With a kind word for everybody. To think that she should have come to such a dreadful end. Dear me—it only shows one, doesn't it? One never knows, does one?" He shook his head—as a conveyance of sympathy. The winkle, Anthony thought, had superseded the bull.

"I've not come here," he said, "to make anything like exhaustive enquiries. But I'd like to examine a cheque which the deceased lady recently drew on this bank. Actually," continued Anthony, "it happened to be—I believe—almost the last cheque she ever drew. The date of drawing was October the twentieth, the name of the payee was 'I. Fleury', and the amount of the cheque was twenty pounds."

Mr. Bullwinkle half-rose from his chair. "Of course," he said, "there's just this point to be considered, the cheque may not have been cleared yet, you know. Let me see—what date was it drawn, did you say?"

"October the 20th," replied Anthony "and from what I know I'm fairly confident that you'll find it has."

"We'll enquire," said Mr. Bullwinkle suavely.

He turned his head sharply and Anthony saw the creases on his fat neck. Mr. Bullwinkle raised his telephone-receiver and cleared his voice for action. The winkle had gone—the bull was back.

"Oh—is that you, Miss Simpson—bring me in the Passbook sheets of the late Mrs. Whitburn. I want them made up—if it's necessary to do so—made up-to-date, I mean with all the appropriate cancelled cheques. Yes please—at once. Or as soon as possible. Put everything else you're doing on one side."

"Thank you," said Anthony, quietly. While he waited for the telephone conversation to finish, an idea came to him.

"Perhaps you can tell me," he remarked to the manager, "was the late Lady Blanchflower's account here?"

"Er . . . no," answered Mr. Bullwinkle with a somewhat sorrowful pomposity, "er . . . no. I should have liked to have had it, of course. I should have liked that very much . . . but . . . er . . . I presume Lady Blanchflower didn't quite . . . er see her way . . . you know the way things go, I'm sure. I fancy that she banked with one of the better known 'private' banks. Very sad—all of it! Great character—Lady Blanchflower. Respected and looked up to by everybody in Quinster. One of the real old vintage aristocracy. I'm afraid there are very few of us left. Very sad indeed."

Anthony treated him to a searching scrutiny. Not bad—that last one.

"Of course," recommenced the manager—but whatever he had been about to say was cut short by the opening of the door and the entry of Miss Simpson.

"Ah—there you are, Miss Simpson. You've done that—eh? Thank you. Put the sheets and the cheques down there, will you? That's right—just down there in front of me. Thank you. You have made it up, of course?"

"Just as you said, Mr. Bullwinkle. All the cancelled cheques you have there."

"Thank you, Miss Simpson."

Miss Simpson made her way to the connecting-door where she stopped and turned. "Mr. Arscott said I was to tell you that Baron Tompkins is here and wants to see you."

"Well he can't," snapped Bullwinkle; "tell him I'm engaged on very special business. Baron Tompkins! Blast Baron Tompkins! You don't need to be a Piddington to know what *he* wants!"

4

"Now, Mr. Bathurst—let's have a look at this little bag of tricks on my table. Let's see now—where are we? Ah—not too many cheques I see."

The manager turned over the cancelled cheques. "Melville, Harrods, Selfridges, Melville, self, Evans, Harrods, Selfridges, Page Ingram and Co., Harrods, Evans, Fleury. Fleury's the last one cashed. Actually cleared on the 5th inst. Dated October 20th for Twenty pounds—as you said. Endorsed 'I. Fleury'. There you are, Mr. Bathurst—there's your cheque you wish to inspect. And if I may say so—prompt service."

Mr. Bullwinkle passed the cheque to Anthony with a gesture that bordered on magnificence. Anthony checked the vital details. The cheque was entirely in order, agreeing with the counterfoil stub in the Whitburn cheque-book in every particular. Anthony scrutinised it and handed it back to the bank manager.

"Thank you, Mr. Bullwinkle, I've seen all I want to see.' Mr. Bullwinkle looked across at him questioningly. "No trouble? Everything as it should be?"

Anthony smiled at the questions. "No trouble. Everything in order."

"Congratulations. Relieved your mind, I suppose?"

Anthony shook his head. "No. I can't really say that. The reverse, in fact. Actually I'd rather it had gone the other way. My bark has been strong and steady but it has been disturbing the wrong foliage."

"Bad luck. Perhaps it'll change before you know where you are. It does sometimes, you know."

Anthony rose from his chair. "Yes—that's the way it goes. There are always the up and downs. And we have to take them as they come." He held out his hand to Bullwinkle. "Thank you again, sir. I won't take up any more of your valuable time."

Mr. Bullwinkle shook hands cordially and started to make for the outer door.

"Don't bother," said Anthony. "I'll see myself off the premises. And . . . er . . . by the way . . . give my very kindest regards to your Mr. Arscott and my thanks for his attention—I'd love to meet him again. He reminded me of the first time I saw a giraffe."

5

'Blank Number Two,' communed Anthony with himself, as he stood on the pavement outside the Quinster bank. Nothing wrong with the Fleury account at all—eh? All pukka and aboveboard. Mrs. Whitburn had ordered the wigs and Mrs. Whitburn had drawn a cheque on her personal account to pay for them. In God's name—why? Once again Anthony castigated his brain to find anything like a reason which might be considered as even semi-satisfactory for such a procedure. A mythical dramatic performance at an equally mythical hall—but the wigs were authentic and so was the cheque. Why?

There seemed only one reasonable conclusion to which he could come. That his feet were being deliberately tangled in false trails. Once again his age-old problem presented itself to him. He must sift the wheat from the chaff—winnow the latter into the furnace of oblivion—separate the false clues from the true, and then finally concentrate on what was left.

Anthony, as he walked towards the Red Deer, thought hard and long. That he was faced with a diabolically cunning killer, he had little doubt. He found himself at the corner of River Street and as he realised where he was, his mind leapt, as it had so often in the past, to a sudden decision. Instead of crossing the street and returning to the hotel, he turned sharp right to the railway-station. Isaac Fleury! He would go to the Fleury establishment in London without further delay. Fleury, the man who had made the wigs, the man who had hired them out to Mrs. Whitburn, the man into whose banking-account her cheque had been paid, might have an interesting story to tell.

Anthony walked briskly to the booking-office and said, "First-class return, Paddington—please."

CHAPTER 13

1

A light, but very chilling mist was swirling as Anthony turned into Long Acre, a mist that was already showing sinister signs of becoming an authentic fog long before the hour of midnight. He located Fleury's establishment without difficulty. Across the window ran the words in letters which formed a species of half-moon, "Isaac Fleury, Perruquier, Wig-maker and Costumier. Established 1851."

Anthony pushed open the door and entered an establishment which was spacious and beautifully neat and tidy. The glass cases of the counter which showed sticks of grease-paint and many gadgets of the perruquier's art, were scrupulously clean and several wigs propped up on small-size pedestals had an exquisite finish about them which it did not need a connoisseur to recognise and approve.

A prim, braided-haired, thin-nosed, sweet-mouthed, white-faced girl behind the left-hand counter looked in Anthony's direction as he entered.

"Yes, sir," she invited him as he advanced towards her. Anthony tucked away the immediate thought that she was probably Austrian or something closely akin—there was something in her accent which prompted the opinion.

"I'd like, if it's at all possible," said Anthony, "to have a word with Mr. Fleury himself if he's available."

The girl looked a trifle doubtful at the request. "Is it an urgent matter?" Her tones were quiet, competent and cultured.

"Yes," replied Anthony, "I'm afraid we might call it even that. Is he . . . er . . . on the premises?"

The girl turned and looked at a clock above her head. "Yes. I think he is. He was a little while ago. What name is it . . . shall I say?"

Anthony handed her his card. When the superscription thereon had been read and understood, the girl showed a pink flush on each cheek which certainly enhanced her looks. "If you wait, please, I will tell him."

"Thank you," returned Anthony with a smile.

2

The sweet-mouthed girl was back almost before Anthony had had time to take full stock of his surroundings. She was accompanied by a short, stout old man with a pink, almost cherubic face, big, round, old-fashioned glasses and grey-white fuzzy hair round the temples that seemed however, to stand in straightish upright bristles over the better part of his head. Anthony saw at once that the official card which had passed between them had caused him serious disquiet.

"I do not understand this at all," he said. "I am Isaac Fleury. But I do not understand what it is that you can want of me."

The accent here was unmistakable. Anthony would have banked chiefly on Vienna—or somewhere desperately close to that once delightful city. He sought at once to put the old man at his ease.

"No need for anxiety, Mr. Fleury," said Anthony. He felt constrained to ameliorate the ancient apprehension as quickly as he knew how.

The old man needed reassurance. "But if I could speak to you in private for a few minutes," continued Anthony, "I'd be very much obliged."

Fleury brightened at Anthony's words. Much of his anxiety slid from him as a cloak will from shapely shoulders.

"Of course! Of course! There will be no difficulty about that." He began to wag his old head as though affirming to himself the truth of the statement he had just made. "Will you be pleased to come this way, sir? And we'll see what we can do for you."

Anthony followed him down the length of the shop, feeling something like a man lighted to his room by a deferential candle-carrying man-servant who would have graced the middle ages. Fleury opened a black-looking door and ushered Anthony into a small, squarish, comfortable-looking room. It appeared to be half-office and half work-room. With the greater accent, perhaps, on the latter.

There was a desk, strewn with papers, and there was a long narrow table rather more in the shape of a counter, which bore much indication of Fleury's recent work as a wig-maker.

There was an ordinary looking chair by the desk and, in addition, a chair of the old-fashioned basket-type. Fleury took the latter and indicated with a courtly gesture that the other was Anthony's for the taking. Anthony accepted the invitation and sat down in the plain chair. Isaac Fleury smiled at him.

"Now, sir," he said punctiliously, "will you be good enough to explain to me exactly what it is that I can do for you." The exotic accent became even more pronounced.

"Thank you, Mr. Fleury. On Tuesday, the Ist of November last, you received a cheque drawn on the Southern and Home Counties Bank, Quinster Branch, in the amount of £20." The old man produced a pencil and carefully noted the amount on a pad in front of him. Anthony continued.

"It was drawn by a Mrs. Laura Whitburn, residing at that time at the Red Deer hotel, Quinster."

More note-taking by Isaac Fleury. Anthony waited for him and then went on again.

"The payment thus described was in the nature of the normal deposit which you require against the hire of two wigs. They were each, presumably, needed for an amateur performance of Tom Robertson's *Caste* in the town of Quinster. One wig was for the character of 'Eccles'— the other for the 'Marquise de St. Maur'."

Fleury made more notes on his pad before nodding his confirmation. "That would be in order. As you remark—that is our system of business. It has been so for years now. The deposit ensures one against the loss of any of my wigs. When the wigs are returned to me—when the club or society has done with them—I return the deposit amount less, of course, my charges for the hiring. You see—my wigs are valuable."

Anthony nodded. "That is what I understood you to say, Mr. Fleury. But let me proceed. The more interesting features of my enquiry are to follow."

Fleury looked up into Anthony's face. It was evident that some, at least, of his earlier apprehension had returned to him. "Your receipt, Mr. Fleury, which went to Mrs. Whitburn in the natural sequence of events, was given by one of your staff, by the name of 'L. Saranita'. That is the signature over the revenue stamp."

"That is so. That would be Lucia, my assistant—whom you saw at the counter a few moments ago."

"Good. Now the position is this, Mr. Fleury. Mrs. Whitburn, a matter of two days after Miss Saranita signed that receipt acting on your behalf, died under the most unusual and tragic circumstances. To put it bluntly, Mr. Fleury, your customer of the 1st of November—Mrs. Whitburn—was murdered. Strangled by one of her own silk stockings."

Fleury by now was ashen pale. "But I have read of it," he exclaimed in tones of sheer anguish. "I have read of it in my newspapers. During the last few days. Without having the least idea that the dead lady had ever transacted business with me. Little did I dream of an occurrence so terrible."

His tones now were those of the undoubted foreigner. "You took no part yourself in the negotiations with the late Mrs. Whitburn for the hire of your two wigs?"

Fleury spread out his hands in emphatic denial. "Ach—none at all. But there is nothing unusual about that. Such things as that are common— they are constantly happening. That is why I have Lucia."

"Well, then," said Anthony, "may I have a word with your officer or representative—that dealt with the matter?"

"But certainly," declared Isaac Fleury, "of course. That would be Lucia again. Miss Saranita. I should call her my right-hand man . . . if she were what she isn't. You understand me! She is absolutely wonderful and has my implicit confidence—I can leave almost anything to her to do for me and she never—what is it that you English people say . . . she never puts me down. But I will call her in here at once and we will find out what we can."

Isaac Fleury rose and opened the door of his room. "Lucia," Anthony heard him call. After a wait of a few seconds Anthony could hear the murmur of voices. Old man Fleury's was easily distinguishable.

"Will you please ask Valentine to take over in the shop for a little while . . . and then will you please come in here to me with the cash-book?"

"Yes, Mr. Fleury. I'll tell Valentine at once."

Isaac Fleury closed the door and came back to the creak of his basket-chair. "She will not be long . . . the little one . . . just the time to tell my other assistant to take over in the shop . . . then she will come to us in here."

Anthony thanked the old wig-maker and prepared to wait for the coming of Lucia Saranita.

3

Lucia Saranita of the pale face and sweet mouth entered quietly and closed the door behind her soundlessly. It seemed to Anthony as he watched her enter that she must do everything like that quite quietly and peacefully, softly—silently—and with an entire absence of fuss or fluster. Anthony rose and offered her his chair. But Isaac Fleury waved him back.

"No, Mr. Bathurst. That is quite all right. Lucia can sit on the arm of my old chair—she often does—there is much room on it for her—it is far too big for me."

Lucia Saranita went to the old-fashioned chair and managed to support herself as her employer had indicated. The cash-book was on her lap.

"I can manage quite well—thank you," she said with a frank and simple directness."

Anthony sat down again. "Now you ask Lucia just what you want to ask her," said the old wizard benevolently, "and ask her in your own way. I will not mention to her a single word of what you have already told me." Fleury looked benevolently paternal in the direction of his assistant.

"Thank you, Mr. Fleury," said Anthony again. "I will do as you suggest. If it's necessary, we can always come back to our previous conversation." He looked across at Lucia Saranita. "I take it you have the cash-book there, Miss Saranita?...."

"Yes." The answer came in the same cultured voice and with the same poised dignity.

"That's the idea. Now would you mind turning up a cash debit entry in the amount of twenty pounds on the first of November? It was a Tuesday—if that fact would be of any help to you."

Lucia Saranita turned the pages of the cash-book with deft and skilful fingers. "What would be the name of the debtor?" she asked; "it may be that there is more than one entry on that day for that particular amount? You see—it's a sort of general deposit figure in respect of two wigs."

"Whitburn," replied Anthony, "Mrs. Laura Whitburn. With an address at the Red Deer hotel, Quinster, Downshire."

"Oh, yes—there's no need to remind me of that." Miss Saranita's face cleared and brightened. "I know the case well. I dealt with it all the way through." She paused for a second and then continued. "Yes. Here is the entry. I knew there would be no difficulty. The account was settled by cheque."

Anthony felt a tingle of excitement at what he had just heard. "Miss Saranita, you're a girl after my own heart. I'm going to sit back comfortably now and listen to the answers you're going to give me to the questions I'm going to put to you."

The girl looked from Anthony to Isaac Fleury. She looked a wee bit scared. The look was inquiring also—the eyes a-flutter.

"It is all right, Lucia." Isaac Fleury leaned over in the communal chair and gently and benevolently patted her hand. "You answer everything like the good girl you always are, Lucia. Just as though you and I were alone and you were telling me something. People must always tell the truth, Lucia—especially people like us."

"Very well, Mr. Fleury." Lucia Saranita sat demurely and waited for the questions of Anthony.

4

"I understood you to say, Miss Saranita, that you dealt with the Whitburn order *all the way through*. I fancy that was the phrase that you used. Now, will you be good enough to tell me, Miss Saranita, how the order came to you in the first instance? In fact, tell me everything about it that you are able to remember."

Lucia Saranita closed the Fleury cash-book and placed it carefully on the carpet at the side of the basket-chair. "I will endeavour," she said quietly, "to do as you ask, that is to tell you all I can remember." She paused—to collect mentally the details which she realised Anthony needed. Speaking slowly she said:

"It all started at about five minutes past two on that same Tuesday afternoon. That was Tuesday, the first of November. I had just returned here—after my lunch. I invariably get back here at about that time. The telephone rang just as I was taking off my hat and coat. I answered it. It was a request for two wigs to be delivered, if possible, that same afternoon. I was then told that they were required for an amateur show of *Caste* at Quinster by the Quinster Dramatic Club. One of the wigs was wanted for a man for the part of 'Eccles', and the other for a lady, for the character of the 'Marquise'. The respective head measurements were supplied there and then and I replied by telling the caller the financial terms on which we allowed wigs to go out from here on hire. That we should require a deposit of ten pounds on each wig, which would be returnable when the wigs were sent back here less, of course, the actual hiring fee. Wigs made like ours, sir, are extremely valuable properties these days, as Mr. Fleury here will tell you—and Mr. Fleury is compelled to protect himself against any possible loss by reason of their not being returned or alternatively, by their being sent back in an inferior condition. The caller, and I'm not sure from the voice whether it was a man or a woman, said that was quite understood and that a cheque for the necessary amount would be paid over in exchange for the wigs when delivered. I then asked, naturally, for the name and address to which the wigs were to be forwarded."

Miss Saranita paused for a few seconds and breath. Anthony, however, made no interruption. Anything he had to say could very well wait. When she resumed speaking, he noticed that she spoke at an even slower rate than previously.

"I was then told that the name and address of the hirer was Mrs. Laura Whitburn whose address was given to me as the Red Deer Hotel, Quinster, Downshire—that was the place to which the account was eventually to be sent—but that the lady would arrange for the required articles to be picked up that same afternoon—if I would state a time when they would be ready—at the Muliera Club, 22 Ben Trovato Street. That's just off Piccadilly—I don't know whether you know it or not. Could we send a messenger to the club with the wigs? Would that be possible and in order? If we could—and would—the cheque for the deposit would be exchanged for the two wigs. Mrs. Whitburn, so I was given to understand on the telephone, would be at the Muliera Club until somewhere about five o'clock."

Lucia Saranita looked at Anthony intently—as though the questions *must* come—but Anthony still refrained from interrupting her. She continued therefore, once again, and said: "Well—there isn't a great deal more to tell you. I think I've covered practically all the important points. I got the wigs all ready, put them in their two boxes and instructed our messenger to take them to the Muliera Club in Ben Trovato Street. Oh—I forgot to tell you—I'm putting the cart before the horse before I rang off I told the caller it would be quite all right and that the wigs would be delivered at the club at four o'clock. Well our messenger went to the Muliera Club in Ben Trovato Street, delivered the wigs as had been arranged and came back here with Mrs. Whitburn's cheque. I paid it into the bank on the following morning—and sent the receipted account to the lady concerned at the Red Deer Hotel, Quinster. There you are, sir. That's the detailed history of the entire transaction. I think that I've told you everything."

Lucia Saranita folded her hands in her lap—and waited.

5

During the time that Lucia Saranita had been telling her story, Anthony's spirits had fallen considerably. She had told him in detail as she herself had just stated—the full circumstances attendant upon the wig-hire transaction—and it had turned out to be everything *he hadn't wanted to* hear. There was no excluding Mrs. Whitburn from the affair it seemed. She had been responsible for those two wigs it appeared, from start to finish. There was no third man here—no third woman—even in the background somewhere. If anything, the pattern of the crimes grew crazier. It had been Laura Whitburn all the way through and all the time.

He offered his two companions his cigarette-case and then lit a cigarette for himself. For some little time he put no question. To either Lucia or Isaac Fleury. He had to think things over very carefully. He knew with a kind of sickening chill, that unless he trod his way with the utmost care and discretion, the inevitable blank wall would loom up in front of him before many minutes had passed. Eventually, after careful consideration, he formulated his first question.

"This may sound a rather extraordinary query, Miss Saranita, but have you any idea as to what actually took place at the Muliera Club when your messenger delivered the wigs? I refer, again, of course, to details."

The question provoked a half-smile from the girl. "I'm afraid I haven't. But could you be a trifle more explicit?"

Anthony smiled back at her. The effort was not entirely in harmony with his feelings.

"Well—what I actually meant was this. What really did occur? You see—I must probe and delve—here—there—and everywhere—it's murder I'm up against—and it's the apparently insignificant gossamer-like trifles that sometimes mean so much. For instance, did your messenger say anything to you with regard to his tour of duty when he returned from the Muliera Club? Did he make any reference to it?"

Lucia nodded. "Yes. I can tell you exactly what he said. He said, 'Wigs O.K.—cheque ditto.' Then he handed the cheque to me in the shop out there."

"Nothing more than that?"

"Nothing more." Miss Saranita smoothed out her skirt as she made the statement.

"Absolutely positive?"

"Absolutely."

Anthony fell on silence again. There was no shaking this girl with the braided hair and the prim manner. She was confident, competent and cute.

"I wonder," said Anthony slowly, "whether I could have a few words with your messenger? The messenger to Ben Trovato Street? Would that be convenient at the moment, Mr. Fleury?" The old man looked at Lucia. The look held enquiry. "Is Stan about do you know, my dear?"

"He should be in the other workroom," replied Miss Saranita.

Anthony smiled. "In that case, then, Mr. Fleury, would you mind asking him to step this way?"

"But certainly," replied Isaac Fleury. "I'll go and find him."

CHAPTER 14

1

The old wig-maker piloted the junior member of his staff into the room which Anthony occupied with Lucia Saranita. Anthony saw a tall, thin boy, about seventeen years of age with a pert, humorous face, quick-moving intelligent eyes, long arms and big feet. A perpetual grimace played round his mouth and Anthony assessed him immediately as a Cockney, born and bred.

"Come in here, Stan," said old Fleury. "There's a gentleman inside wishes to ask you a few questions which I should like you to answer. Nothing to worry about, my boy. Just tell the truth—that's all that's required of you."

Anthony's quick glance at the Fleury messenger assured him that Stan and personal worry were as far apart as the poles. The lad stood at the side of Lucia and cocked a perky glance towards Anthony.

Fleury said, "This gentleman, Stan, is from Scotland Yard."

Stan said, "Blimey," and drew the back of his hand across his mouth. Then he looked at Anthony again and said with a touch of gamin-like impudence: "What can I do you for, sir?"

"I'll tell you," replied Anthony, "and please listen to me carefully. On the afternoon of Tuesday, the first of November, you delivered on the instructions of Miss Saranita here, two wigs to the Muliera Club in Ben Trovato Street. I've been informed that you delivered them at approximately four o'clock. In exchange for the wigs you accepted a cheque in the value of twenty pounds. This cheque was drawn by a Mrs. Whitburn and made payable to Isaac Fleury. All of which was entirely in order. Is that all true?"

Stan grinned happily. He knew where he was now—knew where his feet were. These two conditions, following a period of doubt, invariably added to Stan's fund of natural confidence. "Well, sir," he replied, "it's true enough—what you said—in a manner o' speakin'."

"And what exactly," Anthony flashed back at him, "do you mean by that?"

Stan's grin broadened. "Well, sir, I delivered the goods at the club. As per instructions from our little piece of 'omework 'ere and I come away with the doin's. Also—as per instructions. I was actually back 'ere in the shop by half-four."

"I see. Now tell me this. Did Mrs. Whitburn make any remark to you when you handed her the wigs?" For a fleeting second, Stan changed countenance. The fact was noticeable to all in the room.

"No, sir," he answered, after the momentary hesitation; "but that was becos' I didn't actually see the lady 'erself." Anthony stared at him rather uncomprehendingly. "How do you mean you didn't actually see her?"

Stan was obviously less comfortable than he had been. His eyes flickered unsteadily from their contemplation of Anthony over to Isaac Fleury. But they received no help. Instead—the old man said quietly: "Tell this gentleman just what happened, Stan. That's all that he wants you to do. Just tell the truth."

Stan's mouth quirked into one of its habitual grimaces and he shrugged his shoulders a little ungraciously.

"Well, sir," he said quickly, almost impetuously, as though he were embarking on a job that he wanted over and done with as speedily as possible, "I never see the lady—Mrs. Whitburn—as I just said. She didn't make no appearance—as you might say. What 'appened was this. My orders was to be at the Muliera Club by four o'clock. Well—I was. Although I says it myself I kep' me time to the minute almost. Which wasn't so bad when you consider what transport's like in the city these days. At the door of the club was the commissionaire bloke. Very 'poshed' up—I can tell you. You know—'at and uniform, and creased trousers! When 'e sees me, 'is face sort of lights up. He says to me, 'is that the parcel for Mrs. Whitburn?' I natcher-ally says, 'Yes, me lord.' He says, 'That's O.K. then. 'And it to me, me lad, and I'll take it in for 'er. She's upstairs playin' Bridge at the moment. Before she went up she arst me to look out for you at 4 pip emma. Said she didn't want to be disturbed.' I said, 'Ang up a minute. What about the dough?' He says back to me. 'Hall in good time, young feller me-lad. 'Ere's the cheque as what she told me

I was to give yer. Plus 'arf an Oxford for your trouble.' I 'ands over the wigs, 'e 'ands over the che-kew and the 'arf Oxford. I scrams and comes back 'ere to duty. Now tell me any of yer—for I'd like to know—what was wrong with any o' that?"

Stan's tone was argumentatively defensive. Anthony felt the thrill of excitement *sharpened by satisfaction.* The break had come at last! Or had it? Even now it might be that . . .

2

"So the commissionaire at the Muliera Club took the wigs and not Mrs. Whitburn herself?"

"That's it. Just as you say, Guv'nor."

"Did you stop outside long enough to see what he did with them?"

"I did! Disappeared inside the club with the two boxes in 'is 'ands. You couldn't see his—er . . . I mean 'e went inside like greased lightning."

Anthony pressed him for further details. "You're absolutely sure he went inside? Definitely inside?"

"Absolutely, sir. No doubt about it whatever. I see 'im as plain as a pike-staff."

Stan paused for a moment, only to continue. "Don't think I've been playin' a funny sort o' game. I never mentioned nothink about this when I got back 'ere—for the simple reason that I didn't think as 'ow it signified. I just nipped in, 'anded the cheque over to Loose 'ere"—he gestured in the direction of Miss Saranita "and went back on me job. If I did it all wrong —sorry and all that."

It was at this moment that Isaac Fleury intervened. "I think, Stan," he said quietly and with a certain natural dignity, "that you can do the same now. Now that you have told us your story. Get back on your job. Unless, of course, Mr. Bathurst—"

Anthony saw what Fleury meant.

"That's all right with me, Mr. Fleury. Your assistant can do as you say. Thank you—both of you—all of you—very much indeed. You have been of inestimable help to me." He rose from his chair.

Isaac Fleury said, "It gratifies me exceedingly to hear you say that. I hope that you catch your criminal. It is not good for evil people to be at large."

He held out his hand to Anthony. Anthony took it and repeated the shaking of hands with Lucia Saranita.

"Thank you both once again," he said. "As I said just now, your assistance has been most valuable."

Miss Saranita smiled graciously at him and went back to her place behind the glass cases.

3

Anthony waited for a cruising taxi with its 'stalk' right and drove swiftly to Ben Trovato Street. He paid off the taxi-driver some twenty yards from the entrance to the Muliera Club and walked the remainder of the way with many matters jostling in his mind.

Contrary to all his expectations there was—as far as he could see no commissionaire anywhere near the vestibule. Anthony entered the club premises, cooled his heels for a few moments in the particularly draughty hall, evoked no attention, interest, or attendance from anybody—and then proceeded to move on his own to repair these deficiencies.

Making his way down a corridor to the right of the entrance, he encountered a page-boy in a uniform of near-chocolate hue. The page-boy was whistling as he walked. He had evidently recently patronised the cinema, to witness *The Third Man*. It was clear to Anthony's ear that the music of the film tantalised his memory. Anthony pulled him up from a rather headlong method of perambulation.

"Just a minute, if you don't mind I'd like to see the secretary," said Anthony, "and I shall take a dim view of any unnecessary delay. See to it for me, will you please?" The page-boy turned—impudence in his eyes and impertinence almost on his lips.

Anthony spoke again. "Take that to her, sonny, and I'll follow on a few paces behind you."

Anthony gave the page-boy one of his official cards. The boy goggled at what he saw and read.

"Certainly, Sexton," he replied impishly; "watch me—and you won't take the wrong turning. How's Dr. Watson these days? Bearin' up under the old wound?"

Anthony grinned. "You're getting tangled up, sonny. You'd better stick to Charlie Chan. Get up them stairs."

"How did you guess?" came back the page-boy. He turned quickly and pointed to a flight of stone steps at the end of the corridor.

"I never guess," countered Anthony.

"String along with me, Sherlock," the page-boy called back over his shoulder.

4

Anthony followed the boy up the flight of steps and along another corridor. They passed several closed doors on their way. From behind most of these doors could be heard the high-pitched tones of women's voices. None seemed to be in lineal descent from *Lear's* Cordelia. At the last door, the page-boy paused and knocked. The knock preceded by a second of time only, his actual entry into the room.

"Patience, Philo." Anthony heard the whisper quite plainly as the boy edged past him and grinned for the second time. Anthony was compelled to wait in the corridor for perhaps five minutes. He tried to hear if there were any conversational efforts taking place behind the closed door.

But eventually, the chocolate uniform appeared again and one of its fingers beckoned to him. "She's all yours, Paul Temple. I've prepared 'er for a fate worse than death. Enter and do your stuff," said the wearer of the uniform, as he opened the door wider to admit Anthony to the room.

5

The secretary proved to be a remarkably efficient, presentable and business-like young woman. Her first reactions to the force of law and order were on the frigid side, perhaps, but when she saw and heard Anthony, the winter of her disapproval was made much more like glorious summer.

"My name is Merton," she declared, "Angela Merton. I am the secretary of the Muliera Club. Now, to what do I owe the pleasure of your company, Mr . . . . er . . ." she looked again at Anthony's card on the desk in front of her . . . "Bathurst."

"Just a mere matter of murder, Miss Merton. Neither more nor less. Surely you don't need me to remind you of the death of Mrs. Whitburn? *Your* Mrs. Whitburn?"

The secretary's interest was reflected in her face. "Oh dear—that ghastly affair! I suppose I ought to have guessed your business at once. I should have connected you with that dreadful affair directly you came in. All the same—I don't think I quite understand. Unless I'm very much mistaken the poor lady was murdered near her home at Quinster. Miles from here. So what can it possibly have to do with the Muliera Club?" Anthony told Angela Merton some details of the Fleury wigs and of the circumstances connected with their delivery to the Muliera Club by the Fleury messenger. For the better part of the time, Miss Merton listened to him with keen interest. Towards the conclusion of his narrative, however, a puzzled, bewildered look took possession of her features and as he began to finish up, she was much more puzzled than merely interested.

"So you see, Miss Merton," concluded Anthony, "what I feel I simply must have, are five minutes with your commissionaire. If you employ two—and they divide their duties—then with the commissionaire who was acting at the club here at four o'clock on the afternoon of Tuesday, the Ist of November last."

To his surprise, Angela Merton began shaking her head. "But you can't," she said, almost as though he was in a precarious sort of plight that had provoked her pity.

"I can't?"

"No—you can't. What you ask me is an absolute impossibility, Mr. Bathurst. Indeed I can't understand why you've asked me. We don't possess such an august creature as a commissionaire and, what is more, we never have possessed one. The page-boy you saw just now is the absolute limit that we can go to especially in these hard times."

Anthony read the writing on the wall. The letters were large, plain, disconcertingly and amazingly legible.

"I see," he said quietly—almost as though he were talking to himself. "I begin to see. So that's how the job was done."

Miss Merton leant over to him exuding sympathy. "This, I suppose, is a terrific disappointment to you? It means you've been barking up the wrong tree. Is that it?"

Anthony smiled at the lady. "Not altogether. Call it the wrong side of the tree—that would be nearer perhaps than saying the tree itself."

The secretary waited for him to go on. After a few seconds Anthony said, "This man whom I'm endeavouring to trace posed as your commissionaire and was on the steps of this club at the time I mentioned. Very possibly, also, at some time or the other, he ventured inside the vestibule and stood on the club premises. Which adds up to this—he may have been seen by somebody other than Fleury's messenger. Any comment on that, Miss Merton?" Miss Merton considered the question before slowly shaking her head.

"I don't think that he could have been seen by anybody. That is if you mean by members of the staff here. Anybody seeing him would have known at once that the man was an impostor. To anybody familiar with our club he would have looked so . . . so out of place."

"Yes. I was afraid you'd say that. Now that we know what we do know. Sticks out rather, doesn't it? But who *might* have seen him? Reasonably? Through being—say—in a likely spot to see him?"

Again Miss Merton shook her head. "Well—that's not exactly an easy question to answer, is it? 'Might' is a word with such tremendous possibilities. But in the ordinary course of things, I should say only Derek Skinner. He would be the only one."

"The page-boy?"

"Yes the boy in uniform who brought you up here to see me. He's about the only person I can think who'd have been in the region of the front doors of the club at that time on a Tuesday afternoon. He buzzes round the place, you see—doing all kinds of jobs for the better part of the day. If anybody saw your man—it's ten to one it would have been Derek. And if he *had* spotted him—I tell you frankly I don't think the man would have got away with it, whoever he may have been."

"You mean Derek would have reported it? To you?" Angela Merton smiled at the question. "He'd have done something. He's pretty bright, you know. But anyhow, I'll have him in and we'll ask him. That'll settle it conclusively, won't it?"

"I agree," returned Anthony; "have him in at once and let's hear what he has to say when he's questioned."

Angela Merton extended a well-shaped hand and pressed a buzzer. "That'll fetch him," she said smilingly to Anthony, "and in the meantime you and I can sit back and wait."

"Thank you, Miss Merton," said Anthony.

6

A few moments later Derek Skinner, the page-boy, entered the room at Miss Merton's bidding. As he stood in front of the secretary's table, he nodded impudently and gracelessly towards Anthony.

"Derek," said Miss Merton, "carry your mind back, if you can, to the afternoon of Tuesday, the first of November." Derek turned his head rather theatrically. "Yes, Miss Merton—Tuesday the first of November. I can remember the day quite well."

"Good. Now try to remember something else. Where were you—mainly during that afternoon?"

The page-boy furrowed his brows. "Dodgin' about, miss, much the same as usual. 'Ere and there—and to and fro."

"Were you on the front of the club at all. Or near the vestibule?"

More brow-furrowing. And then a nod of assent. "Yes, miss. In the early part of the afternoon. I was dodgin' about a bit in the front. Three or four of the ladies came in taxis for the Bridge session and I saw 'em on to the premises."

Anthony leant forward at this juncture to interrogate the boy.

"Was Mrs. Whitburn one of those ladies, Skinner? Whom you attended in that manner?"

"No. Mrs. Whitburn was here for lunch. She was already in the club. I know that for certain—because I saw her come in somewhere around twelve o'clock."

The boy paused—his eyes round and rather scared-looking. The name he had just heard had rung a bell. He had realised for the first time that this was no trivial round or common task on the contrary—Sexton Blake was on a murder case and nothing less! Why hadn't he thought of the Whitburn connexion when he had first encountered Anthony half an hour previously? Must be losing his grip!

Anthony motioned to Miss Merton to proceed with the interrogation.

"You were on the front, you say, Derek, *early* in that afternoon? What time *exactly* do you mean when you say that?"

Time! The time factor! Alibis! Yes, that's what they were after. The page-boy's self-esteem burgeoned at the question. On his statement a man's life might well depend. He must endeavour to be uncannily accurate.

"I should say, miss," he replied slowly, "it would have been from about half-past two—until about . . . well . . . say three o'clock."

"I see. Where were you at four o'clock, Derek? Can you tell me that?"

The page-boy scratched his head. "At four o'clock, miss? Let me see now." Suddenly his face cleared into understanding. "I was movin' the card tables, miss, in the Chandos room. After the ladies' Bridge had finished. They packed up about five to four and I went up there to clear the top half off the room. Don't you remember givin' me the wire to do it?"

Angela Merton nodded brightly. "That's quite right. I remember. And you were there, I suppose, till—till when, Derek?"

"I worked on the card-tables for a good half hour, miss. Quite that."

The secretary turned to Anthony. "That's all in order, Mr. Bathurst. I remember it all, well! I can confirm what Derek has said—so you see—"

She gestured with her hands significantly. Anthony resolved to take one last chance. He put the question straight to the page-boy.

"Tell me, Skinner, and think carefully, please, before you answer."

"Yes, sir; I will, sir."

"Did you at any time on that afternoon of Tuesday, the Ist of November, see any man near the entrance to this club who resembled in any way a commissionaire? I'll attempt to give you some sort of description of him. He would have been wearing a uniform of some kind and a peaked cap."

The page-boy's reply was short and sharp and was given without the slightest hint of hesitation. "No, sir. Definitely not, sir. Never clapped eyes on such a bloke."

"You're sure of that?"

"Absolutely positive, sir. Word of honour."

"Now tell me this, then. Could such a person, dressed as I've just described, come into the club, stay inside for a few moments say and then go out again without being spotted by somebody here?"

The page-boy looked at the secretary. It seemed to Anthony that he sought guidance.

"You answer that, Derek," said the latter, "you're much more qualified to answer it than I am. You're often near the entrance—I seldom am. I'm almost always up here somewhere."

Derek nodded his head. "Well then—I should say 'yes', sir. It *could* be brought off that way. If the chap didn't stay inside the premises too long. Sometimes, especially in the afternoon, there mightn't be anybody knockin' about at the front. Nearly all the ladies who are members come straight in—and unless I've been told in advance the actual time a lady might be arrivin' and arrange to meet her car and show her in—I might be dodgin' about anywhere. Yes, sir—what you've asked about certainly *could* 'appen. It 'ud be dead easy."

"Thank you, said Anthony "that's clear then—it was a point I wasn't quite certain about."

"Will you be requiring Derek any more?" asked Miss Merton sweetly.

"I think not," returned Anthony.

"You may go, Derek," said the secretary of the Muliera Club.

The page-boy gave one last lingering look at Anthony and took his departure. "For cryin' out loud," he said as he sped downstairs, "I'm 'in' on murder! Murder and the 'Yard'. Blimey—what perishin' luck."

7

Anthony left the precincts of the Muliera Club and repeated his exercise with a cruising taxi. When he was lucky to find one with the 'stalk' up, he sped straight back to Fleury's and Long Acre. Unless his senses deceived him when he entered, there was something like a welcoming light in the eyes of Lucia Saranita as she saw and recognised him.

"You are back?" she said (rather foolishly for her).

"Yes. I'm back, Miss Saranita. With my tail between my legs and more trouble in my pocket than was there when you last saw me."

"Why—what has happened?" asked Lucia.

"The commissionaire was bogus. There's nobody of that kind employed by the club. Never has been. Whoever it was planted himself there for the sole purpose of relieving your messenger of the wigs. Is he about? Stan—I mean? Because if he is, I'd like another word with him."

Lucia Saranita nodded. "Yes. He is not out—he is here. In one of the workrooms. I will get him for you."

She walked to the end of the shop and Anthony could hear her calling. Immediately she raised her voice, old man Fleury appeared at the back of the shop. He saw Anthony and came towards him.

"You are here again, then, Mr. Bathurst? What is it that we can do for you this time?"

Anthony explained the situation in a few crisp words. Just as he reached his conclusion, Stan materialised from somewhere like the nether regions.

"Ah," exclaimed Anthony, "just the man I want. Give me the fullest description of the commissionaire who relieved you of the Whitburn wigs, will you, Stan? And that means don't leave out anything—do you hear, Stan?"

Stan coughed twice—once behind his hand, the second time *coram publico*. Anthony prodded him with unusual gentleness.

"Come on, Stan—time's highly valuable—believe me. The sooner I hear from you, the better I shall be pleased."

Stan, thus prodded, began to speak slowly. "A full description you want—eh? You're askin' somethin'. I wasn't with 'is nibs very long, you know. Still—'ere goes. Medjum 'eight. Thin, wispy grey moustache—almost white—come to that. Eyes—can't recall his eyes at all—and that's a blinkin' fact. Didn't see 'em long enough, I suppose. Not too stout in build. Thinnish rather than stout. Looked a bit lean and 'ungry—if you know what I mean. Brown uniform with brown peaked cap. Brown shoes. Smartly creased trousers. Oh—I know—I meant to 'ave told you this when you were 'ere before—the bloke 'ad only one arm. You know—empty sleeve business—the badge of the 'ero. 'Ome from the wars."

"One arm?" repeated Anthony in tones of surprise.

"That's it, sir. One flipper only."

"Which one was missing?"

Stan considered the question for the flash of a second. "The left, Guv'nor. The bloke took the wig boxes with his right. My right 'and to 'is right 'and."

Anthony cut in. "Certain of that?"

Stan nodded. "Yes—you can bank on that, Guv'nor. The left was the missin' flipper."

Anthony thought hard. "Now, Stan—another question—and take your time about answering it. What age do you give this chap? Take your time now and think carefully—as I said."

Stan grimaced towards Miss Saranita. "Age—eh? Bit of a poser that. Out of my line somewhat. Let me see now." He looked at Isaac Fleury and then at Anthony as though estimating and assessing differences of appearance in relation to age.

"Well," he declared at length, "I should say he was pretty old—as ages go. Older, in my opinion than he really looked. His skin and the flesh of his face looked sort of 'dried up'—if you know what I mean. And his moustache—well you could call it white—and that 'ud be the nearest you'd get. Well I'll 'ave a bash. Say, seventy, guv'nor—or close on that way."

Stan folded up suddenly. As though he had said enough—or even more than enough. Seventy—eh, thought Anthony—which is no earthly use to me. How many men of that age are there who impinge on the case? But then the idea struck him that the one-armed man was almost certainly an agent—and not a principal. If he could be traced, it might be possible to—

Anthony's thoughts went to the uniform the man had worn. Was it false? Like the man himself? Was it real? Borrowed or hired? Suppose the commissionaire *were* genuine enough in himself—but acting away from his authentic territory? Such a thing might have taken place—if the inducement to act so had been made sufficiently attractive to him.

Anthony turned away from the Fleury group gathered round him, with a shrug of the shoulder The realization that there were many more avenues to be explored had suddenly become appallingly acute. And delay at this stage would be doubly dangerous. No benefit would accrue to him by staying where he was any longer.

"Good-bye," he said with a wave of the hand, "and once again many thanks to all of you."

As Anthony closed the Fleury door, there was disappointment in the eyes of La Saranita.

PART FIVE

THE THREADS ARE DISENTANGLED

CHAPTER 1

1

Anthony talked to Andrew MacMorran at great length. As he proceeded, the graver and more troubled MacMorran became. When Anthony reached his finish, MacMorran said, simply, "And what's the motive, Mr. Bathurst? Can you tell me that? All this cunning network of false clues and sinister subtleties—and two ladies murdered—and can you tell me why? Because I'm damned if I can see a reason. Or even half a reason."

Anthony replied quietly. "No—Andrew—as far as the question of motive is concerned, my darkness is as black as yours. I can't see a ray of light anywhere. My one and only hope is that something will turn up from somewhere before many more days are past and give the motive to us on a plate. It all depends on the amount of *knowledge* you happen to possess. Knowledge which enables you to *recognise* true values and authentic meanings. One minute you're groping in the dark as we are now —the next minute you collect a tiny fragment of additional knowledge and hey presto—there's your motive in front of you as clear as day."

"That's all very well," grumbled MacMorran, "providing you *do* collect it. If you don't, though—if that tiny fragment of additional knowledge as you call it, *doesn't* come your way—you've had it, chum. Take it from me. I know what I'm talking about."

"Yes—you have to keep your eyes open for it. No doubt about that. And that's what *we* have to do, Andrew. Actually—when I look back on today's work, I feel it was worth while and that I haven't wasted my time. We certainly know a great deal more than we did. For instance, we have the whole history of the wigs. We know they're 'authentic' from beginning to end."

"So we may," interrupted MacMorran, "but there's still no rhyme or reason in them. So what good does it do us? From the point of view of the crimes they're just as plumb crazy as they were before."

"True. But yet—conceding all that, they may eventually lead us somewhere, Andrew. And 'somewhere's' to the murderer. Via a one-armed commissionaire of about seventy years of age who receives wigs on the steps of ladies' clubs. There's work for you there, Andrew. See if it's possible to trace the fellow. I'll let you have a full description of him. It's just on the cards that he may be the genuine article somewhere else and was specially hired for the job—see what I mean?"

MacMorran seemed to brighten somewhat at the suggestion. "Yes—that's an idea. I'll have that put in hand at once. There might be something there. Because of the uniform angle." The inspector produced pencil and paper. "Give me those details again, will you please?"

Anthony detailed the points one by one: "Man of medium height. Ordinary build. Thin—rather than anything else. Wispy grey moustache—almost white. Aged about seventy. Lean and hungry look. Left arm missing—empty sleeve worn that side. Wore brown uniform and brown peaked cap. With smartly creased trousers. There you are, Andrew—you could almost draw the figure of the man from the details I've given you. See if any of your chaps can get a line on him. Try Chatterton."

MacMorran noted down the particulars and rose from the chair in which he had been sitting. "I'll get this through to the Yard at once. Muliera Club, No. 22 Ben Trovato Street—Tuesday November the 1st—4 p.m. That's so, isn't it?"

"That's the ticket, Andrew. And do you mind making it a priority?"

"No. Not a bit. As a matter of fact I was going to." MacMorran made his way to the telephone.

2

Directly MacMorran went out, Anthony thought of something else. He suddenly remembered an omission on his own part and an omission which so far he had failed to rectify. The omission had occurred in this way and Anthony had taken himself severely to task for his culpability.

In the first place, Lucia Saranita had stated that the order for the two *Caste* wigs had reached Isaac Fleury's establishment on that November afternoon by way of the telephone. The time had been 2.05 p.m. Lucia remembered it clearly because she had just returned to Fleury's from lunch. That was point number one. In the second place, the dead Laura Whitburn had arrived at the Muliera Club *before* that time. In this connection there was the statement of Derek Skinner, the chocolate-uniformed page-boy. Anthony endeavoured to recall his precise words.

"Mrs. Whitburn was here for lunch because I saw her come in somewhere round twelve o'clock."

Ergo—if Mrs. Whitburn *had* made the telephone-call for the wigs to Fleury's—and Anthony didn't yet rule it out entirely—there might be a record of it somewhere in the documentary files of the Muliera Club. That was what he should have checked when he had been on the premises. Before he had come away and gone back to Fleury's. When Andrew MacMorran had finished with the telephone, he'd go along there and get through to Angela Merton.

3

The resolve had scarcely registered when the door opened. to admit MacMorran again.

"That's all O.K.," he said briskly; "Chatterton's got it. I told him why that was—that you were singling him out." Anthony detected a note in the voice-tone and looked up quickly.

"How did he take it? Was he bucked?"

"His language was terrible," replied the inspector dryly. "So he must have been."

Anthony grinned at the thrust. "All right, Andrew—I can take it. Is the box clear? Because I've a spot of 'phoning to do myself."

"Oh—where to this time?"

"Ben Trovato Street again. The venue of the Muliera Club. There's a question I should have asked the secretary while I was with her and didn't. Culpable negligence on my part. I purpose repairing the omission before I forget it again."

"Nice girl?"

"Very. Definitely charming."

"Thought so. *And* I might have known! The box *is* clear. Or it was when you started your flippancies." Anthony rose and smiled. "Let's hope it's still clear, Andrew, for a continuation of the same." He walked to the door of the lounge, paused and turned with finger uplifted. "I'll let you know what she tells me, Andrew. S'truth, I will. See my finger wet?"

"Very decent of you," answered MacMorran.

4

"Mr. Anthony Bathurst," came the voice of Angela Merton at the other end, "why, of course! Only too pleased. Of course I remember you. What is it I can do for you this time?"

Anthony explained his requirements in two short, sharp sentences. He waited expectantly for Miss Merton's further reply. When it came, it held two qualities for him.

"Well, Mr. Bathurst," said the voice of the secretary, "I think I can tell you whether Mrs. Whitburn used our 'phone that afternoon. I should certainly be able to tell you that. On the other hand, though, I may not be in a position to inform you as to whom the call was made. We only get special 'chits' made out when the call's more than the ordinary charge. Will you please hold on and I'll see what I can do for you."

Anthony intimated to her that he would hold on with pleasure which activity he embraced for what seemed to him an extraordinarily long time. Eventually, Miss Merton came back to the telephone and he heard her voice again.

"Are you there, Mr. Bathurst?"

Anthony conveyed the impression that almost incredibly—he was. "Well," continued Angela Merton in an annoyingly hopeful tone of voice, "sorry to keep you waiting so long but I'm afraid you're going to be disappointed. I've had a word with our people concerned and it's worked out more or less as I said. Mrs. Whitburn *did* use the telephone on that particular afternoon, but there's no record on our premises here as to whom she contacted or at what time she made the call. That means almost certainly that it was somebody moderately close at hand. It can't have been a person anything like a distance away. You can rest assured on that."

Anthony heard and digested the Merton information. It might mean anything—it might mean nothing. Then he thanked the lady, hung up and came out of the cabinet. Deep in thought he made his way back to MacMorran. Should he follow up the Whitburn telephoning with the P.M.G.—or should he? As he saw things now, the problem was beginning to take just a little shape—it was, he thought, becoming definitely less amorphous than it had been.

CHAPTER 2

1

It was now Guthrie who talked with Andrew MacMorran at some length. "I've seen to twenty-four hours' routine stuff," he stated, "had three men on it practically all that time. In accordance with our arrangement and your later instructions. Mainly with regard to the five people—outside the staff and the permanent residents—who slept in the hotel on the Thursday evening of the crime. You agree with me that the murders must have been committed somewhere between 8 p.m. and midnight?"

"Ay," replied MacMorran, "that time's consistent with the train of events as we know them and also with your Dr. Manner's medical opinion."

"Well," proceeded the Quinster inspector, "I fancy you'll be rather interested in something that we've managed to pick up."

Guthrie waited to see the effect of his remark upon MacMorran. "Let's have it, Inspector, and I'll be the judge. The commercial traveller contingent were all absolutely vouched for by Melville. That's so, isn't it?"

"That is undoubtedly so," replied Guthrie; "but you listen to what I'm about to tell you."

MacMorran nodded. "O.K. Go ahead."

"We've made personal contact with each of the four travellers in turn. You may or may not remember their names. They are Walter Chester, employed by the Novis Bread Company, Gavin Crawford of the Rose Petal Soap Associated Companies, Ltd., Arthur Stewart, representing the Derwent Motor Company and James Ashdown of the Green Star Meat people."

MacMorran nodded again. "Yes—I recall all the details."

"Chester was the most informative of the four men," continued Guthrie, "as was to be expected. He's the senior of the men from most angles and has been associated with the Red Deer for some years. Much longer than any of the others. What he was able to tell us in connection with the two dead ladies concerning that last meal of theirs, bore out in every way what we already know. That is to say from Melville, Bassett the waiter, and the other occupants of the dining-room that evening whose statements have already been taken. I allude to the Grahames and the Danburys. I can honestly say—if it'll give you any satisfaction—that Chester's story absolutely tallies with everything else. Ashdown, Stewart and Crawford—the three other 'commercials'—had much less to say—as I said just now—Chester's the daddy of the crowd from nearly all points of view—but what they have found time to tell us—and of course all of the men were contacted separately—once again linked up with Chester's statement and with all the other statements."

MacMorran looked at him curiously. "Well—there's nothing much there, is there?"

"Nothing at all," returned Guthrie equably; "but I haven't finished yet. I haven't covered all the ground. There's still the matter of what you yourself once called the solitary stranger. Remember him? The man who came into the Red Deer some time on the Thursday evening, dined there on his own, and stayed the night? He paid his account and went away early on the following morning."

"That's right. Lilley was the name. J. H. Lilley, I fancy—giving him his initials."

"That's right," repeated Guthrie; "that's the man I've been after. Well—he gave an address to the Red Deer people, according to the girl Skeggs, the receptionist, which was 17, Wiltshire Crescent, London, S.W.2." Guthrie took a note-book from his pocket. "Here it is. I made a note of it when the girl gave it to me, 17, Wiltshire Crescent, S.W.2. Well—and this is the point which I thought might interest you—enquiries have been made and there's nobody of his name known at that address."

MacMorran looked a trifle annoyed. "Is that a fact, Inspector?"

"That is. And that's why I've shoved it in front of you without delay. It's significant—to say the least of it."

"Did you get a description of him?"

"Well—so-so."

"Whom did you take it from?"

"Bassett. I thought he'd be the best man. Although he didn't actually wait on Lilley's table, he must have seen something of him during that evening."

Macmorran nodded his approval. "Good. You've done well, Inspector. Anything startling in the description Bassett gave you? Anything to stick out?"

Guthrie shook his head rather ruefully. "Afraid not. It's the usual sort of description that's more nondescript than anything else. And the one that you invariably seem to get. Here it is. Look at it for yourself."

Guthrie handed over the Lilley details. MacMorran gave it a quick glance but no spoken comment. It was, he saw, entirely on the lines that Guthrie had indicated.

"I'll get this through to the 'Yard' at once. They may get a line on the fellow from somewhere. We'll hope for the best. Anything else before I buzz off?"

"I don't think so—oh yes, there is—I was forgetting—the finger-prints reports. I don't think I've told you—I intended to this morning. The original findings have been confirmed. The prints that were taken from Lady Blanchflower's room gave two sets only."

"Hers and Mrs. Whitburn's?"

Guthrie nodded. "As you say, sir. Hers and Mrs. Whitburn's. So we're still more or less stymied in that direction. Our dabs wallah had strong hopes that he might have got on to something—but they've come unstuck."

"H'm. Pity! See you later."

MacMorran made his exit. To the telephone—and after that—to find Anthony.

2

"I've just seen Guthrie," MacMorran said to Anthony. "Spent some time with him."

"Oh—anything exciting?"

"Not exactly. What he really wanted to tell me was this. He's vetted the four 'commercials' who were here on the Thursday evening—and they all seem to toe the line satisfactorily."

"I expected they would—didn't you? For this reason. They were all *where* they were, *when* they were, out of their normal and lawful occasions. Earning their daily bread plus anything else they can snatch to put on it. Table delicacies such as snoek or whalemeat for example. Can't see the murders down any of their streets. Don't you agree?"

"In the main—I suppose I do. There's just this, though, while we're on them. Chester, the senior man of the four, had been a 'regular' here for years. For that reason, he knew both Lady Blanchflower and Mrs. Whitburn fairly well. There is, perhaps, half a line there. I haven't eliminated him altogether. Have you?"

Anthony grinned at the question. "My dear Andrew—you use the word eliminate. I never eliminate anybody until I have *all* the reasons. But go on. You hadn't finished what you were saying, had you?"

"No. There is just one other matter that I must mention. You recall the fellow whom we called the solitary stranger? The chap who dined here on that Thursday evening at a table by himself?"

"Lilley," replied Anthony—"J. H. Lilley. With an address in Wiltshire Crescent, S.W.2. Paid his account and left the hotel some time on the Friday morning."

"That's the man. Well—Guthrie tried to do a 'vet' on him at the London address that he gave—and he can't be found."

"Do you mean that Guthrie says 'there ain't no sich person'?"

"That's how it looks. And it's what Guthrie thinks. I've just sent a description of the chap to the 'Yard'. It certainly would appear, to say the least of it, that he gave either a false name or a false address."

Anthony pulled at his top lip. "H'm. Lilley—eh? Determined to blush unseen since his visit to Quinster. To say nothing of the destination of his personal fragrance or otherwise. Well, Andrew, it's another point that will bear looking into, and another candidate for your elimination stakes. Or the other thing! I must think about this, Andrew. This disappearing and fading Lilley."

Before MacMorran could comment, Anthony had gone on: "Let me know if the 'Yard' come through with anything concerning friend Lilley, Andrew—will you? As soon as you get it—do you mind?"

"You shall have it at once," replied MacMorran, "if there is anything."

"And yet, Andrew," said Anthony musingly, "if our name for him be substantially correct, I can't see how this Lilley fellow can possibly be the killer of Lady Blanchflower and Mrs. Whitburn. It would be too altogether contradictory."

MacMorran stared. "*Our* name for him? J. H. Lilley, do you mean?"

"No, you old ruffian. *Our* name for him! J. H. Lilley's one of his own labels. One of the many—more than likely. Bearing in mind what Guthrie has reported. Our name was the solitary stranger. I rather fancy you christened him that yourself."

MacMorran nodded his agreement. "Yes. You're right, of course. I was wool-gathering. No stranger would have been aware of the Blanchflower—Whitburn dinner arrangements. No stranger could have acted with such certainty. Yes—you're right. All the same—I can't help feeling that it's rather suspicious that the address he gave to the Red Deer doesn't reveal him."

Anthony still appeared to muse. After an appreciable interval he said: "But, of course, Andrew, all that depends on the soundness of our judgment when we fastened the name on him. I'd forgotten that. It's on the cards *we* may have erred. Supposing our stranger was no more a stranger to Quinster and the Red Deer than apple-pie and custard? In that case—'pon my soul, Andrew, I think friend Lilley's worth following up after all. I do indeed."

"Don't worry," remarked MacMorran dryly, "my chaps will follow him up all right. The ball's rolling even now. I saw to that about half an hour ago."

He turned to look at Anthony. But the latter was miles away. His eyes held that distant look which MacMorran had seen so many times in the past.

"Lilley—" MacMorran heard him say. "Lilley—well I'm blessed—now I wonder if . . . ."

3

Anthony looked through the glass panel of the receptionist's office and saw that La Skeggs was seated at the receipt of custom. He caught the Skeggs eye (glad) eventually and their smiles were synchronous. There was a difference, however, in their quality. Anthony's was mercenary. Valerie Skeggs's smile was cunningly fertile in calculating femininity. Anthony gestured to the door of the Skeggs office.

"May I come in for a moment?" he enquired engagingly. A second Skeggs smile was radiant with agreement and approval. Anthony walked round to the front and quietly entered the office.

"Good morning, Miss Skeggs," he observed lightly. "You've plenty to do, I see? Quite the busy bee—eh?"

"Yes, Mr. Bethurst. Ai've generally got me hends pretty full. But this is an unexpected pleasure I must seeay." Valerie turned on the full candle-power of the Skeggs simper.

Anthony smiled.

"I'm glad you regard it as a pleasure, Miss Skeggs, and not as an annoying interruption. Some people, I'm afraid, wouldn't treat me as generously as you do."

"Oh, Mr. Bethurst—don't say that. Yew are a one. Ai'me sure you're flattering me. But, please tell me, can I be of any service to yew?"

"Ah," smiled Anthony, "now we're getting places. That's what I've been waiting for you to say. I've an idea that you can."

"Tell me how—please."

"Quite a simple matter—really. No trouble at all. All I want is this. To glance, for a moment, at your visitors' book. Register of admissions. You know what I mean."

"No sooner said than done," replied Valerie Skeggs, with an undoubtedly spurious exhilaration. "You want the best registers—we heve them."

She reached for a book which was lying open on the counter at the front of the office and pushed it over to Anthony. "There yew are," she added coquettishly. "Service—help yourself."

Anthony opened the register and saw at once the particular entry with which he was concerned. There it was—right in front of him and plain to see. The page upon which it had been inscribed was still current. Anthony read the entry carefully.

J. H. Lilley, 17, Wiltshire Crescent, London, S.W.2. British.

The last word, naturally, was in relation to nationality. And then Anthony looked at the entry again. More closely this time as though he were seeing something which he hadn't seen before. A second later he shut the register. Handing it to Miss Skeggs with a smile, he said brightly:

"Thank you very much, Miss Skeggs. Your register is returned. Very charming of you."

"The pleasure's maine," responded Valerie. "I'd do anything for yew, Mr. Bethurst."

"Interesting name—Lilley," murmured Anthony, "might stand for so many things when you begin to think about it."

4

Anthony alighted from the train at Paddington, collected a taxi and intimated Wiltshire Crescent to the knob-nosed driver—who looked at him as though he (the driver) had just glimpsed the gallows for the first time and realised how near they were to his late cell.

"Stop on the corner," added Anthony; "that'll be near enough for me."

"Right-o, chum," replied the old Wykehamist at the wheel—"you're lucky you picked on me—I knows a short cut."

"If you didn't, you soon would," returned Anthony. He made a quick sign, which to the descendant of Nimshi could mean but one thing.

"For cryin' out loud," the driver muttered to himself as he swung the cab round the first corner. " 'Endon—I suppose. Perishin' 'Endon! It's always 'Endon these days. I never seem able to miss those blighters—and I can't never remember breakin' no mirror neither. Wonder why it is!"

5

At an appropriate corner, Anthony paid off the merchant with the Hibernian nasal organ, added a generous pourboire, and began to walk down Wiltshire Crescent. He saw at once, from the numbers he was passing that from the Lilley angle he had come to the wrong end. He was on the odd number side—that part of it was all right—but still some distance from the Crescent's beginning.

When he reached the house numbered 17, he passed it and walked on briskly. When he came to number 7, he opened the iron gate, walked up the steps and rang a bell which obviously from both its position and size invited ringing. An elderly woman came to the door clad in a dress of dingy black.

"Yes?" she enquired, rather forbiddingly, "wot is it?" Anthony raised his hat to her. "Good-afternoon, madam," he said in his most debonair manner, "would it be convenient for me to have a word with Mr. Blanchflower?"

CHAPTER 3

1

The elderly woman stood there and looked at him blankly—at the same time taking a firmer grip of the front door. "What name did you say?" she demanded. "Blanchflower," repeated Anthony. He commenced to spell it. "B—L—A—N—"

The woman in black cut into the effort. "You've come to the wrong 'ouse, young man," she said rather spitefully. "There's nobody lives here who goes by that name. I don't take foreigners."

To Anthony, her statement had the effect, almost, of a *coup de grâce*. His spine wriggled in cascades of icy cold water. "Are you sure of that?" he asked again.

"Well," said the woman rather discourteously, "who should know if I don't? Seeing as 'ow I'm the landlady of the 'ouse? I tell you I don't know the name—I've never 'eard the name—and nobody of that name 'as ever lived in this 'ouse while I've been 'ere. Is that plain enough?"

Anthony's spine-ice turned from semi-liquid to berg. Surely his hunch that the presumed 17 in the Red Deer register was actually a crudely formed 7 hadn't been wrong after all? And yet—this woman had no sense of compromise about her whatever and there was no shadow of doubt that she had meant every word she had said. Suddenly, Anthony thought he saw light petering through the darkness and the spine-berg seemed a trifle less weighty.

"Perhaps," he said tentatively, "you know him better as Mr. Lilley? Mr. J. H. Lilley?"

Directly Anthony mentioned this second name, the woman's face changed. It became less hostile and less suspicious.

"I did 'ave a gentleman named Lilley 'ere. But 'e's not 'ere now. As a matter of fact 'e left on the afternoon of the 5th of November. A Saturday, it was. I can remember the date because of the blarsted noise the kids was makin' with their fireworks. To say nothin' of the row the dogs made at the same time. 'Ours of it we 'ad. 'Ours and 'ours. Nearly drove me crackers—and I ain't bein' funny neither."

All the pack-ice that had clasped and chilled Anthony's spine broke up suddenly and began to float away. "I wonder if you would be able to give me Mr. Lilley's new address?" he asked, hopefully.

The elderly woman shook her head. "No—I'm afraid I can't. When 'e packed up from 'ere 'e didn't tell me where 'e was goin' —and I never asked 'im. Wasn't none of my business. 'E paid me my rightful dues—as 'e always did. 'E'd bin with me over three years and then 'e cleared off."

Anthony exhibited signs of sympathy. "Looks as though he doesn't intend to come back here, doesn't it?"

The question evoked the desired answer. "Come back? 'E won't come back 'ere—you can bank on that, mister. Took all 'is things with 'im. Clothes and belongings—and everythink."

"Left nothing behind—eh?"

"Not a stitch, mister. And now if you'll excuse me—I'll get back to my work. I don't 'ave no time to waste—I can tell yer. A woman needs six pairs of 'ands, and eyes in 'er be'ind to keep a 'ouse like this tidy. They didn't put labour-savin' gadgets in when this 'ouse was 'shoved up,' believe me."

Before Anthony could make any move to prevent it, the front door of Number 7 Wiltshire Crescent moved quickly forward and was closed against him. He walked thoughtfully down the white steps, along the path and out by the iron gate. On the whole, he thought, honours might be regarded as easy. He had been right about the number in the Red Deer register—Lilley's number—but all the same he had missed his man. And if the man you miss is fast and resolute and runs straight, he usually stands a great chance of crossing your line. Even though it may be near the corner flag.

Anthony thought things over carefully. As he walked away from Wiltshire Crescent he was undecided as to his next step. He had the choice of two immediate actions. Should he telephone to MacMorran at Quinster, or should he ring the Yard? If he did the latter, it was possible that he might get Hemingway or Chatterton—or even Evershed. On the other hand, however, there was an equal chance that he might not. After some moments of conflicting thought, he decided to 'phone MacMorran at Quinster. After that MacMorran could take over. Anyhow, whichever way you looked at it—the sooner the Yard caught up with Lilley—the better!

2

Anthony telephoned to MacMorran at Quinster from the first telephone-box to which he came. Luckily, he found the inspector in. In a few brief sentences, he told MacMorran the new position. MacMorran, at first breath, was inclined to chuckle.

"Wiping Guthrie's vigilant eye—eh? I suppose it was a '7' —now you've told me all about it. Always pays to look closely at a thing like that. Ah well—it'll learn him."

Anthony cut in, with no mention however of the direction Blanchflower. That, he thought, could very well wait. MacMorran couldn't expect to have the whole cake at once.

"Now there's this about it. As a matter of fact, I was half a mind to 'phone the Yard direct. But I wasn't sure whom I should get hold of. I might have clicked; on the other hand, I might not. But—*Lilley has scrammed*! For the second time, mark you. He scrammed from Quinster—back to Wiltshire Crescent. Then he scrams again. Unknown destination this time. And according to the hard-faced old hag at the house, he'd been there with her between three and four years. What do you think of it? Significant—eh?"

MacMorran replied in like terms.

"Right," replied Anthony. "I'll leave all that in your hands, then. What? Yes . . . yes . . . all the big towns and cities . . . . I agree . . . ports and airports. O.K. Oh yes, of course . . . at once mustn't risk delay. Who? Chatterton? Just as well, I should think, taking the business all round. If he's available. What's that? Yes . . . you must guard against that, of course. Right-o, then—that's settled—and I'll proceed again in the direction of Paddington and a train for Quinster. When? Oh—I don't know. Depends on the afternoon service. Expect me round dinner-time. And—Andrew—before you ring off—be prepared for something in the nature of a surprise. What? No—not exactly a hundred per cent certain—not just yet—say just 'confident'. What's that? Lord—no! Hell of a way to go yet. Not even in the straight. Cheerio!"

Anthony hung up and edged himself out of the kiosk. He began to think. If Lilley were Blanchflower and Blanchflower Lilley—there would be a Lilley that would—! His thoughts ran at random. But they persisted in returning to this man who had left Quinster suddenly . . . and then after that . . . his long-familiar room in Wiltshire Crescent. Where was he now? Would the Yard find him in time?

3

Anthony had calculated well and arrived back in Quinster just about the time he had anticipated—in time for dinner. When he ran into MacMorran in the vestibule of the hotel he saw at once that the latter was in relatively good spirits.

"I've passed your news on to Guthrie," said MacMorran with a chuckle. "He almost foamed at the mouth when he realised that little twist which had occurred with the numbers. About eight o'clock this evening I should say, he'll be taking a running jump at himself—judged by the language I heard trembling on his lips when I broke the news to him.' Anthony grinned.

"I don't know, Andrew. You can't very well blame him over that number. You can't really wonder at him doing what he did. I was just lucky to spot it—that's all. If you don't mind I'll just pop upstairs for a wash and brush-up—then I'll join you at dinner. Just about got time, haven't I?"

MacMorran looked at his watch. "Just about," replied he.

4

When Anthony joined MacMorran at the dinner-table the inspector had a question for him immediately.

"What's this surprise I'm to be prepared for? What you told me on the 'phone this afternoon. What is it?"

Anthony smiled in return. "Wait and see, Andrew. Learn to curb that impatience of yours—it gets worse instead of better."

MacMorran persisted—he was not to be put off. "Something to do with this man Lilley? Is that the idea?"

"It might be."

Anthony changed his tone. "You shoved it all through to the Yard, didn't you? As I asked you to?"

MacMorran looked solemn. "I acted at once. Within a quarter of an hour of your 'phoning me—the boys had the whole basinful. You've no cause to worry on that score."

Anthony began to assess and calculate chances. "They should pick him up all right. And before very long at that. At the same time, though, Andrew, he has the advantage of several days' start. We mustn't forget that. He scrammed from Wiltshire Crescent on the 5th."

"What about the second wig? The one from the bonfire? If he scrammed on the 5th from Wiltshire Crescent we know that he scrammed from Quinster on the 4th. Early on the Friday morning. At least—so we've been informed. The wig was in the bonfire."

"That's all right, Andrew. That ties up. Don't forget that the bonfire was already assembled. He could have poked the wig into the bonfire *before* the night of the 5th. All the same—" Anthony paused suddenly.

"All the same—what?" prompted MacMorran with interest. "There are any number of things need explaining. I can't get away from that fact. I may be beginning to get faint traces of a pattern—but it's no more than that. Still—we must wait and be patient—and see what this Lilley business turns up. It may well be the turning-point."

As Anthony finished speaking, he saw Bassett coming down the dining-room and approaching the table. The head-waiter made straight for MacMorran. He bent to speak.

"If you'll excuse me, sir," said Bassett to the Yard inspector, "Mr. Melville asked me to tell you you're wanted on the telephone—very urgent, sir."

MacMorran rose quickly. "This may be it," he said to Anthony; and then to the waiter, "Thank you, Bassett." Anthony watched MacMorran leave the dining-room and felt a thrill of excitement run through him. What was coming now? Were Lilley Blanchflower—and Blanchflower Lilley . . . .

5

Five minutes later MacMorran walked slowly back to the table. He seemed unusually grave and preoccupied. Anthony's heart sank when he saw the inspector's face.

"We've boobed," said MacMorran, from the side of his mouth, as he resumed his seat.

"How do you mean, Andrew, and what do you mean?" Anthony's tone was anxious as he put the two questions.

"That was the Yard," said MacMorran quietly, "and they've just had Birmingham on. And what do you think Birmingham had to say? Lilley actually walked into the police-station at Aston this morning and reported himself. He'd seen the Press notice that the police would like a word with him arising out of my first message to the Yard following on what Guthrie had told me. Well—to cut a long story short-Birmingham report that Lilley's O.K. He's the genuine article. The Birmingham police have frisked him generally—and he's O.K. He's a printer—and he's just landed a good job in the Birmingham area. They've checked him up hill and down dale. Been in touch with his previous employers and his antecedents generally—his parents—his bank—and he comes out white as the driven snow."

MacMorran sat back in his chair. For some seconds Anthony was silent. "There's no doubt about all this, I suppose, Andrew?"

"None at all, I should say."

"Why was he in Quinster that week-end? What was his story?"

"Week-end?"

"Well on the Thursday and Friday—that's near enough to the week-end."

"He'd come after a position with Waterfall's that they were advertising—the big printing firm—and which he failed to obtain. That's been confirmed as well."

Again Anthony came to silence. MacMorran waited for him. Eventually, Anthony said, "You say the Birmingham people have been in touch with Mr. and Mrs. Lilley Senior? You did say that, didn't you?"

MacMorran nodded. "Yes. That's so. As it happened, it was a comparatively simple matter for them. Lilley's parents live at Kidderminster. Lived there for over thirty years. Lilley himself was born and bred there. On the Birmingham doorstep almost."

Anthony nodded gloomily. "Right-o, Andrew. That settles it pretty conclusively. I'm perfectly satisfied with what you've told me. I've had it! Sorry to let you down. If ever you think my head shows signs of developing in size—just whisper the word 'Lilley' to me. It'll have a salutary effect. Do you mind?"

MacMorran grinned. "That's O.K. by me. I'll be delighted. But where do we go from here? That's my headache."

Anthony shook his head. "Don't know, Andrew. Don't even know that. But between now and midnight I must make an intensive effort to pull myself together."

CHAPTER 4

1

Anthony lit a cigarette from a filled case and began to pace his bedroom. He knew this evening, without the shadow of a doubt that the time had come for him to concentrate on this amazing problem—the case of the two murdered ladies of Quinster. He was more annoyed with himself than he had ever been before. Why hadn't he zealously obeyed the immutable laws of the science of deduction? Twice already, since the investigation began, he had missed the boat. And missed it badly. Firstly with regard to the search for the body in the bonfire—he had been hopelessly out there—and now, secondly, he had been badly out in his calculations in relation to this man Lilley. The name had inveigled him—'Lilley' could so easily have been a pseudonym for 'Blanchflower'. For there had been a son in the Blanchflower family—he knew that. A son, too, who according to rumour, had been something of a ne'er-do-well.

He *must* concentrate! He lit a second cigarette from his case as he prepared himself for one of his exercises in intensive thought—this time it would come perilously close to mental castigation. What vital factor was he missing? He knew what he must do. First of all he must probe for *motive*. He must ask himself the same question he had asked himself before, and he must find the answer to that question. Before he chased more stray hares. Motive!

Was the primary motive for the crimes, the murder of Lady Blanchflower or was it the killing of Laura Whitburn? An old problem with him. And one which he had never satisfactorily settled. Or could it conceivably be the elimination of *both* ladies? Each contingency was a distinct possibility. If the motive lay against Lady Blanchflower—did it go back in any way to her earlier life? To her life with her husband? Perhaps before they came to reside in Quinster? Or even to an association prior to that? When she had cut a distinguished figure in Edwardian England?

If any of these possibilities were sound, the magnitude of his task became even greater. He felt assured that he must—in a fashion—retrace his mental steps. That is to say—go back to his original theory that the killer had acted as he had in order to throw suspicion of the murder on to Mrs. Whitburn. The murderer had banked on the possibility that the body would lie undiscovered for an appreciable time. When Anthony had solved the problem of the lady's disappearance, he had cut some of the ground at least from the killer's feet.

Mrs. Whitburn! Suppose the motive had lain against her—and not against Lady Blanchflower? Anthony marshalled his thoughts—logically—and in an attempt to obtain some sort of sequence and order. Why had he allowed himself to be lured away to chase false gods?

Take the clues to start with. (1) The wigs. (2) The account for the wigs. (3) The cheque in payment for the wigs. (4) The silk stocking. (5) The bogus commissionaire on the steps of the Muliera Club. (6) The slip of paper between the stubs of Laura Whitburn's cheque-book. 'Lil says come quickly—mistress away.' Six in all. He could think of no more.

Just a moment, though—there *was* one other point he had considered looking into. What was it now? He cudgelled his brains for the appropriate remembrance. Something to do with that cheque-book of Mrs. Whitburn's. Ah—he had it. The cheque-payment to the firm by the name of Page, Ingram and Co. Nothing in it in all probability—but he'd follow it up—you never knew. Call that point clue number seven. Now where was he? He'd take the clues again one by one—in the order in which he had just listed them.

The wigs. Well—he'd been to Fleury's and gone into the matter most thoroughly. The order (from somebody—either Mrs. Whitburn or another person) had been authentic. No shadow of doubt about that. The account. The account was absolutely genuine, too. Lucia Saranita's evidence backed by Isaac Fleury had assured him of that.

The cheque. Nothing wrong with regard to the cheque. Nothing whatever. He'd seen it—seen all its details—seen too, the cancellation of the paying bank. Drawn by Laura Whitburn on the 20th of October—the wigs ordered on the Ist of November—Anthony stopped short. He'd been blind—culpably blind. There was something significant here. Why the blazes hadn't he seen it before? He must get it straight. Take it in the proper order and examine it with the utmost care.

The cheque in favour of Isaac Fleury had been drawn by Laura Whitburn on the 20th of October. But the wigs hadn't been ordered from Fleury until the 1st of November. The murders had been committed on the night of the 3rd. Never mind about that last point, though! The other point was the crucial one. The interval between the drawing of the cheque and the ordering of the wigs. How was it that Laura Whitburn had drawn a cheque to Fleury in the correct amount of twenty pounds when it wasn't until twelve days later that she knew the figure which Fleury would require as the deposit? What satisfactory explanation could there be for this? Anthony thought hard. It could have been, he considered after due reflection, that Mrs. Whitburn had filled in the date on the counterfoil, preparatory to drawing a cheque, had changed her mind for some reason or other *at the time* and decided *not* to draw it. And at the same time had not troubled to *alter* the date. Had left it. And then, when the time had come to draw the next cheque which she required, had *still* left the original date of October the 20th, standing.

Possibly, Anthony thought, but definitely *unlikely*. Because this would mean, that she inserted the *old date* also on the cheque itself. Yes—that was possible too—in order that the counterfoil date and the cheque date should be in agreement. But again, Anthony thought, definitely improbable. Where was he getting to? Anthony shook his head. There was something wrong here, he felt confident. Something that he must come back to even though he passed on for the time being.

The next clue he had listed was the silk stocking. Without doubt, the property of Laura Whitburn. Stolen from her by the murderer or purchased from the same source as hers had come. Anthony thought that he was at last beginning to see a little light.

The bogus commissionaire! Yes—all part and parcel of the plan— played right through by the same person—the guilty person.

The slip of paper between the stubs. Anthony could make nothing of that. Beyond the fact that in some fashion it was linked up with Lady Blanchflower and Laura Whitburn. In some fashion! He could get no farther than that. This brought him to the last point he had assembled. The cheque payment to Page, Ingram and Co. As far as Anthony was able to remember, there had been no trace amongst Mrs. Whitburn's papers of the receipted account in relation to this cheque. Which fact had caused him to segregate the payment, as it were, from the others. There might be nothing in the point, of course, and Mrs. Whitburn might very well have mislaid the account. On the other hand, he felt strongly inclined to follow up the matter by calling at the establishment of this firm, wherever it might happen to be.

Stay a moment, though. Supposing it was a couple of hundred miles away? In Lancashire, Yorkshire or even Devon? Each of these was a possibility—Mrs. Whitburn might have transacted an order through the channels of the post. In that case it would mean a telephone enquiry.

At that moment, however, he thought of something. A reminiscence clicked somewhere within his brain. He felt moderately certain that Page, Ingram and Co. were a local firm with an address either in Quinster itself or within the Quinster district. He had noticed the name somewhere. Somewhere recently too. His brain fought hard for the association and a matter of seconds brought it back to him. He had seen their advertisement in the local paper which he had picked up one evening in the lounge after dinner.

2

Anthony looked at the time by his wrist-watch. It wanted a few minutes to ten o'clock. Not too late—although close on closing-time. Leaving his bedroom, he went quickly downstairs to the receptionist's office. There was no Skeggs to be seen—she had departed for home long since—so he decided to scout round the lounge himself. There might be a copy of this week's local paper on one of the tables. More than likely in fact. As he made his way to the lounge, he ran into John Melville coming out of his office.

"Good evening, Mr. Bathurst. Now I didn't expect to see you about. Your colleague told me you'd gone up to your room early this evening. He was wrong, evidently. Were you looking for anybody?"

Anthony smiled at the proprietor. "Not a person, Mr. Melville. Actually, I was looking for a copy of your local Quinster paper. Do you happen to have it handy?"

Melville nodded. "There should be one in the lounge, I think you mean the *Quinster Herald.*"

"That's the chap I'm after. Many thanks."

"I'll find it for you," continued Melville good-naturedly. "Come with me."

Anthony followed Melville into the lounge. MacMorran had evidently gone to bed—as the only people present were the Danburys and Edith Grahame. Melville walked straight to a table in the far corner. There were both newspapers and periodicals on it. Anthony waited while Melville rummaged through them.

"Not here," he said after a few moments' searching. "Now that's funny—I could have sworn I saw a copy there earlier on. I know it's been here—because I put it here myself yesterday morning."

Melville looked round—puzzled. Then he caught sight of the other people present. Melville walked over to them.

"Do you happen to have a copy of the *Quinster Herald* amongst you, ladies and gentlemen? Mr. Bathurst here wanted to glance at the current issue and I promised to get it for him. But I can't find it on the newspaper-table."

Each of the Danburys shook a head negatively and Edith Grahame looked up from a book which she was reading. "What was that you said, Mr. Melville? I'm afraid I was thousands of miles away."

Melville repeated his request. Edith Grahame said, "Now where did I see a copy of the *Quinster Herald*? Not long ago. And not far away from here. That's funny—I saw somebody reading it. Oh—my memory's positively awful these days—I know—Stephen had it. My husband. Didn't he put it back on the table?"

"Apparently not, Mrs. Grahame," replied Melville. "Any idea where Mr. Grahame is, so that I can supply Mr. Bathurst with his wants?"

Edith Grahame looked at Melville wearily. "Don't you think, Mr. Melville," she said with an equal quality of weariness in her voice, "that he's almost certainly in the bar? I should be extremely surprised if he were not."

Melville bowed. "I'll go and have a look, Mrs. Grahame."

Anthony smiled at the proprietor. "I'm sorry to have become such a nuisance. Can't I see it through for myself? Save you the trouble?"

"Certainly," said Melville; "if you would rather."

"O.K.," replied Anthony; "I'll pop into the bar and see if I can spot Grahame."

"You'll have no difficulty, Mr. Bathurst," replied Melville; "you'll see him in one of the alcove-seats underneath the big set of chain harness."

Anthony made for the bar—but there was no sign of Stephen Grahame there either in the alcove seat or out of it. Anthony looked all round in order to make sure. No—the position was clear—Stephen Grahame was not making his usual contribution to the receipts and revenue of the Red Deer that evening.

Anthony went back to the lounge. Edith Grahame said: "Did you get your paper, Mr. Bathurst?"

Anthony told her what had happened. "Not in the bar?" she said incredulously; "then there's but one answer to that. He can't be feeling well. I knew he wasn't too good at tea-time. All his horses lost today. That always upsets him. Perhaps he's gone to bed. Oh dear, I suppose I'd better go up and see. I'm afraid he must be very ill indeed. Please excuse me, Mr. Bathurst. You will, I feel sure. "

Edith Grahame gathered up her book and various other impedimenta, said a hasty good night to Anthony and the Danburys and hurried upstairs.

3

Anthony stayed by the fire in the lounge for some little time. The Danburys were inclined towards conversation so Anthony rang the bell and ordered a round of drinks. One of the waitresses brought the drinks and was on the point of placing the tray on a table when the door of the lounge opened again to admit Mrs. Grahame. In her hands she carried a copy of the current issue of the *Quinster Herald*.

"My husband's not in bed," she informed the company, "so I presume he's refreshing himself elsewhere. Gone out with somebody I expect. Very likely to the Thatched House. It does happen sometimes. But here's the paper you wanted, Mr. Bathurst. It was in our bedroom. Stephen must have taken it up there after dinner—and then forgotten all about it. Don't you think it nice of me to bring it down for you?"

She handed Anthony the newspaper. "I do indeed, Mrs. Grahame. Very nice of you, indeed. Very charming. I just wanted to glance at something before I turned in tonight. Will you please excuse me for a few minutes?"

"You'll have another drink before we part," said Frank Danbury.

Anthony shook his head. "If you don't mind, Mr. Danbury, leave me out this time. There's something I must do before I go to bed."

"But, my dear chap, I can't accept your hospitality and then—"

Anthony smiled and waved him down. "I'll take the will for the deed, Mr. Danbury—no more for me if you don't mind. Some other time. I don't suppose the opportunity will be lacking."

"Oh—well—if you insist. Tomorrow evening, then. Let's make it a date."

"O.K. Mr. Danbury. That's on then. Good night—good night ladies."

Anthony waved the newspaper and made a bee-line for the small lounge. As he expected it was empty. MacMorran must have gone to bed.

4

Anthony settled himself in the arm-chair and opened the *Quinster Herald*. He harboured a strong idea in his mind that the advertisement with which he was concerned had showed itself on the inside of the back sheet. Most of the columns there had been devoted to 'classified advertisements', but the last column, if his memory were to be relied on, had featured trading announcements by various firms—mainly local.

He hurried at once to the page that was in his mind. And saw at once that he had been right in his surmise. There were six columns of 'classified advertisements'—but the last column on the page-the seventh-was given up entirely to local firms, and local interests.

Anthony ran his eyes down it quickly. "British Railways: Engine-Cleaners required at Swindon"; "The Quinster Sanitary Steam Laundry, Ltd.: Women and Girls wanted for Laundry Work"; "Crosbie Sportswear, Ltd.: Skirt Machinists wanted for Modern Factory"; "James and Geo. H. Lucas: Seed Potatoes, Vegetable, Flower and Lawn Grass Seeds"; "Winslow Furs: 53 Castle Street, Quinster"; "Messrs. Potter and Schofield, Maidenhair Rd., Quinster: High Class Groceries of all descriptions"—yes—here it was—he had been right after all "Page, Ingram and Company—22 Castle Street, Quinster: For Radio and Television. All models in stock. Demonstrations on request. Arrangements made for extended payments."

'H'm,' thought Anthony, 'nothing sinister about that.' All the same he was glad he'd satisfied himself. You never knew what you might turn up on an investigation of this kind. And yet—funny thing—why should Mrs. Whitburn have bothered about radio matters or television? There had been nothing of either kind in her room. And the radiogram in the major lounge would undoubtedly be the concern of the hotel. Should he follow it up? 22 Castle Street, the address, wasn't more than five minutes' walk from the Red Deer.

After a few more minutes of cogitation, Anthony came to the decision that he would. As it turned out eventually, the decision proved to be momentous. Great events from little causes spring.

He began to fold up the edition of the *Quinster Herald*. As he did so, his eye caught the foot of the advertisement column in which had appeared the Page, Ingram announcement. There was a gap right at the bottom of the advertisements. Somebody, evidently, had used the scissors to make a cutting. Anthony's questing mind wondered 'who' and 'why'. As he prepared for bed, the wonder began to grow. Before he found sleep, his mind had become definitely disturbed. Something told him, clearly and unmistakably that the scissored gap concerned the crime. And yet—why should it? Or even *how* could it?

CHAPTER 5

1

Immediately after breakfast on the following morning, Anthony found himself faced with the necessity of making yet another decision. He had two things to do. The problem was which of the two should he do first? There was the call to be made on the establishment of Page, Ingram and Co.—and there was the follow up with regard to the missing advertisement. Inasmuch as the former consideration was, in all probability the easier, he decided to walk along to the radio and television experts.

When he came to 22 Castle Street, he found that the shop was eminently typical of the usual radio shop to be found in the streets of almost every country and provincial town. Anthony entered and a young man appeared quickly to deal with him. Anthony produced his talisman-card. The young man read it and raised his eyebrows.

"If possible," remarked Anthony, "I'd like a word with the person in charge. Would it be Mr. Page?"

The young man shook his head. "No—it's Mrs. Page," he replied. "Mrs. Page is actually the owner of the business."

"Is she on the premises?"

"I think so. I'll find out for you. Would you mind waiting here for a moment or so?"

The young man disappeared somewhere at the back of the shop. When he reappeared he was smiling and came up the shop quite briskly.

"Will you come this way, please? Mrs. Page will see you in here."

Anthony found himself in a small room. A middle-aged woman, in blue overalls, with a rather florid, much-lined face and large old-fashioned spectacles greeted him. The young man closed the door and went away.

"Good morning," said Mrs. Page, "I haven't the least idea what it is you've come about. Perhaps you'll be good enough to inform me."

"I'm here," said Anthony quietly, "in the matter of the late Mrs. Whitburn."

Mrs. Page looked scared out of her life. Anthony went on. "Please don't be alarmed at my visit. There's nothing for you to worry about, I assure you." Mrs. Page's colour came back. "I believe I'm right in saying, Mrs. Page, that Mrs. Whitburn was a customer of yours? That is so, isn't it?"

"Well," replied Mrs. Page, "she had been. That's perfectly true—and not so very long ago, either. But what was your point with regard to that?"

"Just this, Mrs. Page. We noticed that the lady had drawn a cheque in your favour fairly recently and we could find no account amongst her papers in relation to that payment. That's all my enquiry's about. Just to sort things out. We like to tie things up as much as we possibly can, you know. So that's why I've come along to see you this morning. Can you tell me please, what it was, actually, that Mrs. Whitburn paid you the cheque for?"

"Oh yes. Of course I can." Mrs. Page made the statement with the utmost confidence. She even smiled at Anthony as she made it. "I can do so, too, without any reference to my books. I remember it quite well, you see. Because I put it through myself. About two months ago, I should think it was. Perhaps a little bit more. Mrs. Whitburn bought a portable radio-set off me. She came into the shop here and chose it herself. And a very charming old lady she was. It was a pleasure to serve her. I think it's a terrible thing what's happened to her and that poor old Lady Blanchflower as well! It doesn't bear thinking about—I said as much to my son only last evening."

Anthony nodded. "As you say, Mrs. Page—a shocking business altogether. We'll hope that justice overtakes the criminal. Can you remember—did you deliver the radio to the Red Deer Hotel?"

"Oh—no." Mrs. Page shook her head decisively. "It wasn't for Mrs. Whitburn herself. Don't think that. She didn't buy it for her own use. It was a present that she gave to somebody. Somebody, I fancy, who'd once been in her service. It was delivered from here—straight to that person's address. I can't remember off-hand where it was—but I can easily find out for you. It would be no trouble at all." Mrs. Page paused. "Would you like me to?"

"If it would be no trouble, Mrs. Page."

"I won't keep you more than a few minutes."

Mrs. Page disappeared into the shop-proper. Anthony waited expectantly for her return. The wait was not long. Mrs. Page returned, carrying a slip of paper. She handed it to him. "There you are, sir—there's the name and the address that you were requiring. I've written them on there for you." Anthony looked at the slip. "Mrs. H. B. Milton, 19 Virginia Terrace, Thornton Heath, Surrey."

"You can keep that," added Mrs. Page. "Thank you," returned Anthony, "and thank you, too, Mrs. Page for your help and kindness. This name and address explains everything."

"Only too pleased, sir," said Mrs. Page.

"Good morning," said Anthony.

He left the shop and started to walk back down Castle Street. Another blank! Well and truly drawn. No more, or no less, however than he had really expected when he had set out. He fell to musing. Not a bad sort— Mrs. Page! Unusual for a woman to be the head of a radio business. Didn't run to that sort of stuff as a rule. The husband, in all probability, was dead. His wife had been left behind to shoulder the responsibilities of the business. Good for her! Good for Mistress Page!

And at that precise second, as the thought came to his brain Anthony caught his breath! For he had thought of something else—something in close and definite association. Good lord—why on earth hasn't he thought of it before?

2

Within a few minutes he had returned to the Red Deer in a state of controlled excitement. But once again, as things had turned out, there were two hares for him to chase. On this occasion, though, they were brothers of the same form with a definite link of relationship between. It seemed to him scarcely to matter which of the hares he should pursue first. For the reason that in the chase of the one, it might well be that he would catch the other also.

As he entered the Red Deer and came past the receptionist's office, he saw the Skeggs in her customary lair. Anthony leant across the ledge and spoke to her.

"Good morning, Miss Skeggs. By Jove—you must have been born on the Sabbath Day. You're just the person I wanted to see."

Miss Skeggs simpered. "Oh, Mr. Bethurst, fancy yew saying that. Yew are a one, yew know."

"Now, now," said Anthony, "don't try to turn my head. I'm here on strict business. In other words, I want you to do something else for me. I know from experience that you're absolutely reliable."

The Skeggs simper sunned itself visibly. "What is it yew want this time, Mr. Bethurst?"

"First of all—may I come in?" asked Anthony, "and speak to you confidentially? It's just a little on the public side out here."

"Of course you mee. Jest fency asking me laike that. Why—I'll ecktually meek room for yew."

Valerie Skeggs made great play of shifting her chair some inches. Anthony slid round the door into the receptionist's office and then carefully closed the door behind him.

"Is it the books again?" asked Miss Skeggs.

Anthony shook his head at her. "No. Not this time. Something very different. Something more personal altogether—something absolutely between you and me. Something I want you to get for me.' "

The Skeggs eyes fluttered at Anthony. "And where em ay to get it, Mr. Bethurst?"

"Close at hand, Miss Skeggs," replied Anthony; "indeed I doubt if anything could be any closer. But let me tell you what it is then you can judge for yourself."

"Oh, Mr. Bethurst—the things yew, say—I do declare."

"What I want, Miss Skeggs," continued Anthony, "is a copy of *last* week's *Quinster Herald*. Not this week's, mind you. I've seen this week's. Saw it last evening in the lounge. Am I too late for last week's issue?"

Valerie Skeggs fell to calculation. "Let me see now—no—ay don't think so. If yew know where to look for it. It should be still about somewhere. Ay'll see if ay cen find it for yew."

Anthony steeled himself to pat the back of the Skeggs hand. "Thank you very much, Miss Skeggs," and then from the side of his mouth, "and if you don't mind make it an absolute confidence between us two. Don't let anybody else know what you're after. That's very important. O.K.?"

Valerie Skeggs nodded. "O. Key, Mr. Bethurst. Come back here say—at ten minutes to twelve."

"At your service, Miss Skeggs," returned Anthony. "For the time being I'll efface myself."

3

Punctually at ten minutes to twelve, Anthony was back in the Skeggs sanctum. The Skeggs herself had the air of an amateur Lady Macbeth.

"I've got it for yew," she said almost triumphantly. "Ay told yew it was a cese of knowing where to look, didn't ey? Well—look under thet book there."

Anthony moved one of the account-books, as indicated by Valerie Skeggs and revealed a copy of the *Quinster Herald*. A quick glance at the date assured him that it was the one he wanted. He nodded with satisfaction in the Skeggs direction.

"Good work, Miss Skeggs. You're a treasure if ever there was one. What shall I do with it when I've finished with it?"

"Bring it beck here, Mr. Bethurst when yew've done with it, and slide it under thet same book."

Valerie gestured to the book which had covered the newspaper previously. "Do thet," she went on, "if there's anybody about even though Ay mee be in here. Then nothing will be suspected. See?"

Anthony said that he saw and moved for the door again. "Here's where I efface myself again," he whispered. "I'll be seeing you."

4

With the week-old copy of the *Quinster Herald* tucked away in his pocket, Anthony played for safety. He made his way quickly up the main staircase—straight to the privacy of his bedroom. Once there, he immediately unfolded the Skeggs newspaper on the dressing-table. This time his mind harboured no doubts at all. He knew the page he desired to look at and also the column—to say nothing of the actual place within the column.

His hands found the page and his eyes found the place. But that was all they found. This copy of the *Quinster Herald* was in exactly the same condition as the copy which had succeeded it! The last paragraph of the column had been cut out!

Anthony began to pace the room.

"This," he muttered to himself, "is the most unkindest cut of all."

CHAPTER 6

1

There was only one thing to be done. That was obvious. He must obtain a perfect edition of the *Quinster Herald* in the town somewhere and see what advertisement it was which had been cut out each week by somebody either in the Red Deer or a constant visitor to it.

Of course, Anthony argued to himself—there might well be nothing at all in it. The advertisement which had become a scissors victim, might conceivably be as harmless and as innocent as curds and whey. It might have no connection with the murders. It might even be an agricultural firm dangling an attractive bait before an enthusiastic gardener. All the same—the matter must be put to the test. Anthony knew the necessity for that. And with as little delay as possible. Anthony looked at the time. No time very well before lunch. He'd make it his priority job directly afterwards.

Anthony went downstairs again. At the foot of the main staircase looking up the flight—was Kenneth Whitburn. His face registered pleasure when he caught sight of Anthony. He came forward at once and shook hands.

"I had to come along today, Bathurst. Felt that I simply must. Is there any news?"

Anthony shook his head. "Not a lot. We're still more or less groping in the dark. But come to our table and have lunch with MacMorran and me. It's quite on the cards that you may be able to cross a few 't's' for us."

"If I couldn't before, Bathurst—I don't suppose that I can now. All the same, I'll come along and see MacMorran."

Kenneth Whitburn followed Anthony into the dining-room. Anthony looked for Andrew MacMorran but Bassett crossed his line of vision. When Bassett saw Kenneth Whitburn, his face dropped appreciably.

2

Whitburn sat opposite to MacMorran and Anthony. He seemed, Anthony thought, in rather better spirits. He discussed the case with MacMorran very fully and with scrupulous attention to detail. Suddenly, he turned away from MacMorran and looked directly at Anthony.

"Now tell me, Bathurst," he said, "what particular 't's' are there that you suggest I may be able to cross for you? That remark of yours before lunch has caused me to think furiously."

Anthony helped himself to sugar. "Well, chiefly," he answered, "this!" He paused and Kenneth Whitburn waited for it. "This point has been worrying me for days. Until I find a satisfactory answer to it—it will continue to worry me—and the worry will grow in direct proportion to the period of delay. If your mother, Mr. Whitburn—and you notice that I use the word 'if'—required wigs for the 9th of November, wasn't it—and ordered them on the 1st—why did she draw the cheque in payment of them on the 20th day of October? Can you answer me that one?"

Whitburn frowned. "I've told you before. My mother didn't order those ridiculous wigs. That's where the 'frame-up' has been."

"All right," replied Anthony with sweet insistence, "granted that the fact still remains that she drew the cheque to Isaac Fleury, the wig-maker on October the 20th. Which is what I *can't* understand! *Why* did she do that?"

Kenneth Whitburn remained silent under the question. "You see," said Anthony, "you can't dispose of that cheque in the same manner as you disposed of the wigs. There's nothing dud about the cheque at all. Your mother drew it, signed it and the bankers honoured it. You see that, don't you, Mr. Whitburn?"

"Yes I see all those things," replied Kenneth Whitburn steadily "but it's a 't' which I can't cross for you. Are there any others I can try for you?"

"Ask the inspector," said Anthony.

Whitburn looked askance at MacMorran. He repeated his question. "I don't think so," replied the 'Yard' inspector.

"O.K. then," said Anthony; "here's another one for you from me. Can you give me a line on a Mrs. H. B. Milton residing at Thornton Heath, Surrey? Does the name ring a bell anywhere?"

For once Kenneth Whitburn's face cleared. "It does and I can. Mrs. Milton is by way of being an old family retainer of mother's. Worked for her for years. I had no idea, though, that she had gone to Thornton Heath. Still—there's nothing in that I haven't heard of her for a long time. But what on earth are you bringing *her* up for? Surely, there's been no—"

Anthony explained the Milton angle and Whitburn nodded. "That was just like my dear old mother. Always doing somebody or other a damn good turn."

When Anthony left the table, Whitburn and MacMorran were still talking.

3

As he walked quickly up Castle Street, Anthony tried to remember the situation of the nearest newsagent's. Funny thing he couldn't remember one in Castle Street itself so where had he best—of course, he thought—Smith's—the book-stall on the platform of Quinster station. But a few yards from the River Street entrance of the Red Deer itself. He'd been slow there. He should have made for there in the first place.

Anthony doubled back in his tracks, came along Castle Street, turned down River Street, as far as the station entrance and dashed in. The railway station at Quinster is by no means small as railway stations go. Doubtless due to the ducal influence and prestige. It possesses three platforms and Anthony thought, as he entered, that the bookstall was on the middle platform. Events proved him right. No porter or ticket-collector challenged him on to the platform, and he was able to walk down the main platform and buy a current copy of the *Quinster Herald* without difficulty.

He unfolded it as he made the roadway again. The excitement of the chase tingled in his veins. For he knew that this copy was complete—different from the copy he had replaced that day in the office of the receptionist, in the appropriate manner as requested by Valerie Skeggs. Now what the devil was this advertisement which interested somebody so much? Interested him or her to the extent that the scissors were used on it week after week to keep it from specially prying eyes? When he saw the name of the advertiser, the sight almost brought Anthony's eyes from his head! The purpose had been there behind the scissors all right and in a flash he almost saw the complete pattern of the crimes. For these were the terms of the advertisement which Anthony read at the foot of that last column on the inside of the back sheet of the *Quinster Herald*. The advertisement which somebody had seen fit to keep deliberately out of his way.

Great News for Downshire and all Downshire Sportsmen. T. Fleury. Turf Accountant of Old Bond St. W.1 and Argyle Chambers, Adelaide Rd., Reading. Telephone Reading 12369 (6 lines) No Limit (And when we say no limit—we mean it) Horses or Greyhounds—S.P.— Ante-Post—All Principal Racing Events Accounts opened within 24 hours.

This plus Mistress Page and all that—good Lord—what a blind bat he had been! A pit pony could have done the job better.

CHAPTER 7

1

Anthony knew very well what he had to do now. Two more things—and very possibly two more things only. If matters went as they should. He must telephone to the offices of one of the more important sporting newspapers—the *Sporting Life* he considered would be the best—and he must also communicate in some way with the Turf Accountant whose advertisement he had just been privileged to read in the columns of the *Quinster Herald*.

Which should he do first? The two hares had left the slips once again. On the whole, he thought, the *Sporting Life* enquiry should take precedence. If he could only 'link' up, by means of that, he would be all the more fortified for his visit to Adelaide Road, Reading. Yes—that was the course he *must* pursue—ring up the offices of the *Sporting Life* directly he got back to the Red Deer—satisfy himself eventually, that his pattern of the crimes was correct in every detail—and then clinch the matter with an interview at Reading with Fleury Number Two.

Anthony permitted himself to rub his hands. A neat job—after all. An exceedingly neat job! Despite the many and culpable mistakes he had made—he would land his fish after all. Land a savage, lean-jawed pike! Cunning and resentful! Under a mask of suavity and pretence which deceived everybody! And it *had* been Lady Blanchflower after all! 'Lil says.' When she had said to Laura Whitburn what she *had* said, she had signed her death-warrant and the death-warrant too, of the charming little woman to whom she had spoken.

Anthony thought hard—and as he thought—he knew once again that it never pays dividend to disregard the commonplace.

2

As chance had it on that particular afternoon, Anthony entered the Red Deer, by the main entrance in Castle Street—since he had been staying in the hotel he had almost invariably used the River Street door.

Standing in the wide hall as he went in, was no less a person than Inspector Guthrie. Guthrie greeted him.

"I'm waiting for the Chief," he explained; "I'm told he's about somewhere."

"Any news?" said Anthony.

Guthrie shook his head. "Nothing much—I'm afraid. Nothing that seems to be leading anywhere. How are things with the Chief?"

Anthony shrugged his shoulders non-committally. As he did. so, he half-turned and caught sight of a photograph on the wall just behind where Guthrie was standing. It had been hung at an altitude which caused it to be almost in shadow. As it caught Anthony's eye on this particular occasion he realised that it was something he had never actually looked at properly before. If he had indeed ever seen it, he had certainly never troubled to look at it.

But this afternoon he had caught sight of something in the photograph which had excited his keenest interest. He moved straight over behind Guthrie. It was a large photograph of the Red Deer, taken during Ascot week of the year 1939. It showed a group of people assembled together outside the hotel. The group was not large—there were but eight figures showing.

Anthony judged that the party was doubtless on its way to the royal heath. One of the men shown in the group was evidently the proprietor of the hotel (the man, in all probability who had been Melville's predecessor) and one of the ladies in Anthony's opinion was undoubtedly the late Lady Blanchflower. The features were unmistakable.

It was, however, neither of these two people, that attracted Anthony's greatest attention. All his eyes were for a man standing at the extreme edge of the group and somewhat to the back. Anthony examined the photograph of this third person with mounting and excited curiosity. To think that this item of evidence had actually been hanging on this portion of wall all the time that he and MacMorran had been staying at the Red Deer.

How comparatively simple it is, he mused, always to overlook or to neglect, the matter which lies closest to hand. If he had only happened to see this photograph a week ago! It would have made an enormous difference to him on the score of time.

Guthrie came closer. "Seems like another world, doesn't it? Looking at that, these days? Look at the dresses! What would the ladies think of 'em today? Still—they were good times. Better than now. I'll say they were. I don't suppose we shall ever see the like of them again."

Anthony nodded. "I couldn't agree with you more, inspector. You've seen this before, of course?"

Guthrie smiled indulgently. "Many times. It used to hang in the dining-room. One of the show pieces of the hotel. Actually it's a very distinguished group. That's why Chaplin had it taken."

"Chaplin?"

"Chaplin was the man who had the place before the present man Melville. He's at the back there with his hands on his lapels. There's Sir Hugo and Lady Blanchflower standing together in the front and, next to them, Lord and Lady Fulton. They used to live in the neighbourhood. Old Lord Fulton would always insist on driving to Ascot in style—as his father and grandfather had always done—would never go by car—and Chaplin used to fix the job up for him with one of the local jobmasters. They used to start from here. Or at any rate close by. He was a quaint old bird—old Lord Fulton. Proper old character in his way. Of course you know who the other—"

At that precise moment, MacMorran appeared. Guthrie turned to him. "You asked me to come along, Chief—here I am. At your service. But now that I'm here I don't know that I've got much for you."

MacMorran looked grim and unresponsive. Before he could reply to Guthrie, Anthony cut in.

"Come over here, Chief—will you? Something I want to show you. Come and take a look at this photograph. You won't be wasting your time, I assure you."

MacMorran moved forward and ranged himself at Anthony's side. "How the gentry went to Ascot in pre-war days. It's an interesting old picture. Take a good look at it." Anthony spoke pointedly. "See anybody you know?" he asked MacMorran.

The latter looked carefully at the photograph. "Why—yes. There's the late Lady Blanchflower there. No mistaking her. You'd know that nose anywhere."

"You certainly would, Andrew. Fine old girl. The man at the back with his hands on the lapels of his coat is the previous proprietor—the man who had this place before Melville. I'm indebted to Inspector Guthrie here for that piece of information. Any other recognitions?"

MacMorran peered closely at the faces of the other people in the photograph.

"No—o," he said after a time, "no—I don't think so."

"1939, you know," urged Anthony; "don't forget that—other times— other manners. Put on your best thinking-cap, Andrew."

MacMorran quizzed the group again—but ended with a shake of the head. "No. Can't get it. Tell me—who is it I should recognise?"

Anthony smiled. "I'll give you another chance, Andrew—later on. In the meantime, you have that word or two you wanted with Inspector Guthrie. I'll be seeing you."

3

Anthony went straight to the public telephone-kiosk in Castle Street—a few yards beyond Quinster railway station—and dialled 'Temple Bar, 1200', the offices of the *Sporting Life*.

The call went through smoothly and he was soon able to explain his needs.

"I should like it forwarded," he said in conclusion, "to Anthony Bathurst, Red Deer Hotel, Castle Street, Quinster, Downshire. And as a great favour, I'd like it delivered by the first post to-morrow morning. Did you get that?"

"I'm afraid—" came from the other end—Anthony cut in again. The personal details that he presented to his hearer were both formidable and convincing.

"In that case, Mr. Bathurst," came the ready reply, "I'll certainly do my very best to meet your requirements and send them off some time this afternoon. You understand, of course, that the information you receive will not go beyond the Thursday of that last week?"

"That will be entirely in order," returned Anthony, "and my very best thanks to you."

He rang off. As he walked back to the Red Deer there was a gleam in his grey eyes.

CHAPTER 8

1

Anthony's post on the following morning was in no sense a disappointment to him. The representative of the premier sporting paper to whom he had spoken on the telephone had fulfilled his promise and Anthony found himself in possession of the full details of the Flat Racing results from the period commencing Thursday, October the 2nd until Wednesday, November 6th.

MacMorran saw the four editions on the breakfast table when Anthony had opened the enclosing envelope. He raised his eyebrows.

"What's the idea?" he enquired.

Anthony grinned.

"I'm in the mood, Andrew, for a little research. A spot of delicate delving into the archives of the Turf. Just what you might describe as a rough guide." Anthony grinned. "Sorry, Andrew."

"Is it necessary?"

"Definitely, Andrew. I've an idea it will lead us to our criminal."

MacMorran stared incredulously. "Now don't try to pull my—"

Anthony looked round the room. "I see all our permanent residents are in their customary places."

"What's behind that?"

"Oh—nothing much. Except that I like to see things trim—and orderly."

MacMorran glared and grunted.

"There's one thing, Andrew, that you and I must never permit ourselves to forget."

"What's that?"

"That the late Mrs. Whitburn would put the cat in the oven and the apple-pie outside the back door. Don't you remember that Mrs. Danbury told us that? And that Kenneth Whitburn more or less confirmed it?"

Anthony picked up the copies of the *Sporting Life* Weekly Edition and made for the door. MacMorran jumped up and joined him.

"On to something?" he whispered.

"Yes," replied Anthony in a low voice—"I think so. In fact, Andrew, I'm *almost* certain. Get Guthrie to polish up a pair of bracelets, will you?"

"As near as that?"

Anthony nodded. "Should be—if I am where I think I am."

"When?" whispered MacMorran.

"This evening, Andrew—with anything like a scrap of luck."

2

Anthony went into the small lounge of the Red Deer and began to put his sporting papers in order. For what he wanted to check, they must be arranged in chronological order. Anthony found the weeks by their various publication dates. October 14th, October 21st, October 28th and November 4th. A thrill of excitement took possession of him—he was on the point of testing his theory. If he were wrong—well then the case was crazy and would die on him. Because, however, he was largely in the dark—he was by no means sure either when or where to begin. So he concentrated for a few moments on the science of deduction.

There was *murder* in this case he was investigating. And double murder! And murder isn't wrought for a helping of fish and chips in a newspaper. For some little time, Anthony thought hard with an intense power of concentration. Eventually he came to a conclusion. First of all, he would try the second October meeting at Newmarket. He fancied that was the meeting at which the Cesarewitch Stakes had been run. One of the biggest betting races of the Jockey Club season and the first leg of the immensely popular Autumn Double.

According to his reckoning it would have been run on Wednesday, October the 19th. Taking all the circumstances into consideration, it seemed to Anthony the most likely jumping-off point. Right, said Anthony to himself, I'll put it to the test. He took the second copy of the *Sporting Life* Weekly Edition and turned up the racing results for Wednesday, October the 19th. His heart beat with a wild triumphant excitement. For this is what he read.

"2.45 Cesarewitch Stakes Handicap £3,368-5-0. 2¼ m. Come Away, 3-7-13 (E. Britt) 1; Veranda, 3-7-10 (D. Smith) 2; Honi Soit Qui Mal Y Pense, 6-8-8 (G. Richards) 3." The starting prices of the three placed horses were 33/1, 100/9 and 10/1 respectively.

3

"Dare I," whispered Anthony to the small lounge. "Dare I turn straight to the returns of the Newmarket Houghton meeting? To the result of the Cambridgeshire? The second leg of the great autumn double? And yet I think I must."

Anthony turned to the volume dated November 4th. To Wednesday, November the 2nd. To read, with a triumphant surge:

"2.45 Cambridgeshire Stakes Handicap. £3,038-5-0. 1 m. 1 f. Mistress Quickly, 3-6-4 (C. Outram) 1; Royal Consort, 5-9-0 (C. Smirke) 2; Escutcheon, 7-8-10 (E. C. Elliott) 3." The starting prices of the three placed horses were 40/1, 100/8, and 40/1 respectively.

A very nice, comfortable, and appetizing 'double' thought Anthony. And the reason—he knew this without the vestige of a doubt—why Lady Blanchflower and Laura Whitburn had each been strangled by a silk stocking. The motive had been foul and sordid—trivial and commonplace. Money! The age-old lust for money. There it had been underneath their noses all the time and neither he nor MacMorran had had the sense or the intelligence to recognise it. They had searched for a grander passion, an ancient shadow, a private secret—none of which they had found. For the best of all reasons—there had been none to find.

4

Anthony walked quietly back to Valerie Skeggs and tapped on the glass panel of the receptionist's office. Miss Skeggs looked up.

"Oh, Mr. Bethurst—yew again?"

"Too true, Miss Skeggs—may I come in?"

"So early in the morning? Yew must have positively *swallowed* your breakfast."

"I do as a general rule," replied Anthony. "I've an idea it does me most good that way. You should try it yourself. I said—'may I come in?'"

Miss Skeggs produced her best line in simpers. "Ai've told you before—yew never need ask. Ai'm always pleased to see yew."

Anthony sidled into the office. "Very nice of you. I shan't disturb you for long. May I glance at an A.B.C.?"

"Help yourself," said Valerie Skeggs—"on the shelf there on the right. And it's a new one. The service yew do get here—Ay do declare."

Anthony saw the shelf, found the book and flicked the pages. "Leaving us?" asked Valerie coquettishly.

"Only to return, lady. Should I look so happy—if I were leaving you for ever?"

Anthony found his page. To his intense gratification the service between Quinster and Reading was excellent. Comparatively fast trains were reasonably frequent. There was a train at 10.22. Anthony closed the A.B.C. and looked at his wrist-watch. He'd have time to find Andrew and make for the railway station.

CHAPTER 9

1

Anthony found MacMorran in the small lounge. "Andrew," he said, "put on your hat and coat, old man, I'm going to take you for a ride. We won't bother with the car. I'll give you five minutes."

"Where are we bound for?" queried the inspector.

"First the railway station, and then for the thriving and prosperous town of Reading in the county of Berkshire."

"How come?" said a surprised MacMorran.

"All details in the train, me lad—there's no time for them at the moment. I'll meet you at the River Street entrance in five minutes from now. On my way I'll tell the Skeggs woman that we shan't be in for lunch. And for your strictly private ear, Andrew, we're nearly home and dry. How does that sound to you? Glad tidings—eh?"

"Cert?" questioned the inspector.

"As good as," returned Anthony, "unless I'm very hopelessly mistaken."

"In that case—I'll get my hat and coat," said Andrew MacMorran.

"And I'll go Skeggswards," responded Anthony; "if we're lucky we'll have a snack in Reading. Reading ales are justly famous."

MacMorran grinned. "I haven't seen Guthrie yet. To pass on your instructions."

"We'll do without the polish. Our friend will have to put up with the common touch."

2

The 10.22 from Quinster was a few minutes late—the morning had turned misty with the inevitable railway consequences. "Tell me," said

MacMorran, as they entered a vacant compartment, "then I shall feel I'm not being rushed quite so much. To say nothing of passing judgment on this certainty of yours."

Anthony began his story. MacMorran listened to the reconstruction of the Blanchflower and Whitburn murders with scrupulous attention. Anthony built his edifice stone by stone, brick by brick. When he had finished MacMorran whistled softly. "What's involved would you say? Financially?"

Anthony shrugged his shoulders. "Something like £25,000 in my opinion. You can't tell, of course. That's judging by the S.P. Near enough."

MacMorran whistled again. "And you're certain of your man?"

Anthony nodded. "Who else, Andrew? Think of the photograph taken in the year of Our Lord 1939. I was rather puzzled you didn't spot it yesterday."

"But it's incredible," remonstrated MacMorran.

"I don't think so. The puzzle, with all its bits and pieces, falls beautifully into the appropriate pattern. Everything that so far bewildered us, now explains itself."

MacMorran nodded. "I know what you mean. All the same it's—"

Anthony's enthusiasm knew no bounds. "Don't you see, Andrew, that the beauty of the case—from the criminal's point of view was the fact that there was nothing, nothing whatever—to connect him with it. The only trail running through the affair was the Laura Whitburn trail. The murderer's position was the right position from his standpoint—he came into the picture quite naturally. I'll lay a wager, Andrew, that you yourself have never viewed him with the slightest suspicion. Am I right in that belief?"

MacMorran assented—albeit rather grudgingly. "Well—I suppose you are. If you put it like that. I had no occasion to. How long have you—come to that?"

Anthony grinned as he lit a cigarette. "*Touché*, Andrew. Only the last day or so. It was the photograph which really set me thinking. And to think it had hung there all the time—and I'd never troubled to look at it. Only shows you, Andrew, how we fail to recognise the merits of the near-at-hand and the simple. 'Are not Abana and Pharpar, rivers of Damascus, better than all the waters of Israel?' Thus it was, Andrew—and thus it is."

Anthony pointed out of the window. "There you are—there's the Kennet. Not far to go now—and then for the second Fleury. Or his accredited representative. Wonder how he'll look when I shove my list in front of him."

"List?" queried MacMorran.

"List of names. Possible starters. I've prepared a few. He'll probably take it better that way."

"Show me the list," said MacMorran.

Anthony fished in his overcoat pocket and produced the list. MacMorran scrutinised it—and raised his eyebrows. "Bit of a social scramble, isn't it?"

Anthony smiled. "I said 'possible', Andrew—I didn't say 'probable'. There's a difference, you know." Just as he finished speaking the train ran into Reading station.

3

MacMorran harangued a newspaper-seller outside the station. "Argyle Chambers, Adelaide Road—which way—can you tell me, please?"

"I can, chum!" The man pointed down the street. "Third right—then second left. Then cross to the big advertisement-hoarding and Bob's your uncle. Can't miss it."

"How long?"

"Quarter of an hour. To a smart fellow like you."

"Thanks," said MacMorran.

Twelve minutes later they saw the Fleury advertisement. "You take over to begin with," said Anthony—"and I'll come in when you pass it back to me. I expect you'll find that the going'll be a bit on the sticky side—to start with at least."

"Cagey, you mean?"

"That rather was my idea."

"I'll soon put a stop to that," declared MacMorran with grim determination. "Well—here goes."

4

They were shown into a well-appointed office. The young lady in residence about to explain certain rules and restrictions appertaining to the Fleury method of business, was put completely out of her stride by MacMorran's prompt revelation of his official status.

"In that case, then," she said in a changed voice, "I'd better have a word with Mr. Thorneycroft. Will you please wait here?" When Thorneycroft saw fit to receive them some minutes later, MacMorran was at once reminded of Anthony's recent prophecy. Thorneycroft was rather more hostile than even merely cagey.

"I'm afraid," he said with an irritating pomposity, "that without explicit instructions from my head office I cannot possibly see my way to—"

MacMorran leant over towards him and tapped the table. "Look here, young man," he said, "I don't think you've got this quite right. You saw my card. You know whom I represent. And what! I'm investigating a case of murder—not the disappearance of a bag of peanuts. Do these facts mean anything to you? Because I give you my word that if you withhold vital information at this juncture—",

Thorneycroft capitulated. "I admit," he said mincingly, "that puts a somewhat different complexion on the matter. If you will kindly outline the information that you require of me, I'll do my best to supply it."

"That's a great deal better," said MacMorran; "if you're prepared to act reasonably towards me, you'll find that I shall reciprocate. Half a dozen answers to half a dozen questions—possibly not so many as that. That's the sum of my requirements."

"Very good," returned Thorneycroft stiffly. "What is it you desire to know?"

MacMorran turned to Anthony. "Will you carry on from there, Mr. Bathurst?"

"Very good, Chief." Anthony looked at the representative of T. Fleury.

"I notice, Mr. Thorneycroft, from the terms of your published advertisements, both in the Press and also elsewhere that you claim to pay winning investments at 'no limit' conditions."

"That is so. We have *certain* limits—but taking our business by and large, I can honestly affirm that we are a 'no limit' firm of Turf accountants. But what exactly is your point?"

"I'm coming to it," said Anthony. "I take it," he continued, "that with regard to winning bets on say, the big autumn double, concerning the two handicaps the Cesarewitch and the Cambridgeshire, you would pay the full multiplied odds in accordance with prices shown in your published lists?"

"That is so," said Thorneycroft again; "under, of course, normal ante-post betting conditions."

"I see. I imagined that would be so. What did the actual winning double come to?"

"That would depend, of course, on when the bet was laid. Our prices have varied considerably since we opened our book, as you may well guess. The prices of some horses shorten—while others, of course, go out in the betting. The actual S.P. double would have worked out at . . . let me see now . . . thirteen hundred and twenty to one. What I might describe as an average ante-post double would have come to about . . . shall we say . . . fifteen or sixteen hundred. The winner of the Cesarewitch came in a bit on the day of the race . . . the price shortened, I mean. There was a time when we were laying forties."

Anthony leant over towards Thorneycroft and looked him squarely in the eyes. "And how many of your clients, Mr Thorneycroft, were successful in finding the double? Very few I should imagine."

"One—and one only—I'm pleased to say. An extremely fortunate man. He must have had exceedingly inspired information. I should say from the stables concerned. I'm more than gratified from the point of view of the business I represent that he didn't spread it round the district. As it was—it meant paying him over £30,000. £32,000 to be exact. We laid him '40's' each of the horses. Actually, only about a day before the Cesarewitch was run. A straight win double—he didn't even bother to have an each way bet. And to a very much larger stake . . . than he . . . er . . . normally invested. That's what I call confidence."

Thorneycroft smiled and showed his teeth. Anthony followed up at once.

"Am I correct in assuming, Mr. Thorneycroft, that that successful backer you mentioned is resident in the town of Quinster?"

Thorneycroft hesitated for the fraction of a second before replying. Then he evidently thought better of his hesitation and said quietly: "Er . . . yes . . . you are entirely correct in that assumption."

"Thank you," said Anthony. His hand went to his pocket. He took out the paper he had previously shown to MacMorran. "I have a list of names here, Mr. Thorneycroft. That list has been prepared by Chief Det. Inspector MacMorran and me. We know a great deal—but we don't know all—yet. We are convinced, however, that the name of that highly successful backer you've just been telling us about is included somewhere *on that list*. Will you be good enough, therefore, to place a small pencil tick against the name, assuming that the name is there? If I'm correct in all my theories, I rather fancy that your tick will appear against the third name on the list." Anthony handed the paper to Thorneycroft.

5

Thorneycroft frowned as his fingers closed over Anthony's slip of paper. Then he placed it in front of him and smoothed it out. Anthony saw him run his eyes down the list of names. For a split second Anthony had a sharp shock of misgiving. Thorneycroft's face was impassive—it betrayed nothing. But he suddenly his face still impassive—leant forward and picked up a pencil from the tray in front of him. Anthony and MacMorran saw the pencil make the tick against one of the names. Then he pushed the paper back to Anthony.

"The third name?" questioned Anthony quietly. Thorneycroft gave a little half-bow.

"The third name," he answered gravely.

There was a silence. Thorneycroft looked up. "And if I may say so—putting two and two together from what you gentlemen have been good enough to tell me—a very great shock to me."

There came another period of silence.

6

"Another question—if I may," said Anthony. "The answer may help to elucidate certain aspects of the case. Prior to the success of this double—what was the account like? The account of the person in question? In the general way?"

Thorneycroft smiled. "As it happens I can answer that without reference to the Personal Account Ledgers. I looked it up myself before the big cheque was paid. It was regularly in the red. There had been a steady loss all the year."

"All the year?" queried MacMorran. "Since March. Since the Flat opened."

"Amounting to much?"

"Some hundreds," replied Thorneycroft; "more, I should say, than was well—how can I put it—are there any rich men, these days? You gentlemen know what things are like as well as I do—"

Anthony nodded. "An edge to the motive—no doubt."

"Afraid you're right," agreed the inspector. He rose from his chair. "Well, Mr. Thorneycroft—that's about the lot I think. Many thanks. We'll write direct to your head offices. Old Bond Street, aren't they? Then they can pass the instructions on to you."

"Instructions?" repeated Thorneycroft questioningly.

"Afraid so," returned MacMorran; "you'll have the honour of being one of the chief witnesses for the Crown. Most juries, you know, like a nice satisfying motive put in front of them. It lubricates the wheels of Justice."

CHAPTER 10

1

"Satisfied?" queried Anthony on the return journey. "Yes," replied MacMorran; "I've no doubts at all. Thorneycroft tied it up properly—as far as I was concerned. But despite what I said to him just before we came away from Argyle Chambers—I'm not 'the twelve good men and true'. Have we enough, do you think? Or should we wait?"

Anthony considered the inspector's question. "We've no proof at all—that the bet wasn't his own. You know it wasn't—I know it wasn't—but can we convince a jury? We're distinctly weak there. Seems to me it's the Fleury set-up that's our strongest card. I mean the Long Acre Fleury. The Fleury at the other end. There's the cheque—we might put in the handwriting expert on that. And there's the cunningly-woven plot of the wigs. The whole structure of the plot in all its details. And there's the other matter as well. We *may* score heavily with that."

"What other matter are you referring to?"

"Come, come, Andrew. The photograph-man. That evidence was eloquent, wasn't it? If we can only manage to get hold of—"

MacMorran shook his head. "I know what you mean now. But I should be very much inclined to doubt it. And even if we *are* lucky—it merely strengthens our case—it doesn't anything like clinch it."

Anthony still pondered. "It's like this with me. I doubt if we can afford to wait, Andrew. I doubt it very much indeed."

"Why not? I can't see why not."

Anthony shrugged his shoulders. "Mainly I think because I never like delays. Never have. When you dither I always think you stick your neck out."

"I think the case in point is rather different from the ordinary run."

"In what way, Andrew?"

"Well, in this way, for one. Our fellow thinks he's safe. His general position for one thing. I doubt whether he's ever thought that he might have incurred even the slightest suspicion. Which makes me pretty certain he'll stay put. Which means that we needn't be hasty. You can't visualise him scramming—can you? I certainly can't."

Anthony made no immediate answer. When he eventually spoke, he said: "I think we've got a case, Andrew. With a rather more than even money chance of bringing it home. But I make a proviso."

"What's that?"

"That's it's got to be properly handled on the day. We certainly shan't pull it off if the Crown man goes at it like a bull at a gate. Which I've seen happen in the past more than once. There's another point, too. One that we haven't yet considered. Do you know what I mean?"

"You tell me," said the inspector.

"Well—what may happen if we do go for the gloves and you make the arrest? The cunning may crumble. The craft may collapse. I should say that Life has been full of wear and tear for our friend during this last week or so—and the arrest—coming right out of the blue as you might say—*may* produce an extraordinary reaction. I'm not banking on such a thing, of course on the other hand I don't altogether rule it out." This time MacMorran remained silent.

"When will you decide?" asked Anthony.

"I'm not sure. I'll let you know. I should like to think it over first. I may be some time thinking it over."

"Don't forget the evidence in the photograph, Andrew. Couldn't we have a shot in that particular direction some time this evening?"

"It would help," murmured MacMorran, almost under his breath, "if the evidence is still there—which I doubt."

"If we could only bring it off. It would be by no means in the way," smiled Anthony, "and also—as a project—it shouldn't be too difficult."

He paused for a moment and then went on: "And at any rate, Andrew, we've nothing to lose by trying."

2

As Anthony came downstairs to dinner, MacMorran met him at the foot of the staircase. Anthony thought that the inspector looked extremely worried. MacMorran beckoned to him as he reached the bottom stair.

"Rather remarkable," said MacMorran, "but the Chief Constable wants another conference. This evening."

"Where?"

"He suggests here. I'm pretty certain Melville will keep the small lounge reserved for us. He's been very decent about it in the past so he's not likely to kick this evening."

"What did you say?"

"I'm afraid I was a little difficult. Intentionally, of course. So much so that he's ringing up again at seven o'clock or thereabouts to confirm or otherwise. What do I do?"

"Who's attending the conference—if it comes off? Same as before?"

MacMorran smiled. "So I believe. I understand His Grace desires to be present again. As I asked you before—what do I do?"

Anthony shook his head uncertainly—but he made no reply. MacMorran, after a wait, put the question again.

"On the whole, Andrew," said Anthony slowly, "I think if I were you, I'd side-step in some way. Duck! Can't you be out when the second call comes through? I'll take it for you if you like and explain matters."

"Out? How come? Where can I be?"

"You could be," said Anthony even more slowly, "arresting your man. Seems a way out to me. Perhaps the best." MacMorran was silent.

Anthony waited for a reply that did not come. "Or," he began again, "if you like the idea better, you could attend the conference . . . and while the conference is on . . . and all our friends busily engaged . . . I *might* be able to get busy elsewhere and put my hand on something . . . which, if it didn't clinch the case would, to use your own words of this afternoon . . . strengthen it considerably. I think you can guess to what I'm referring."

MacMorran looked at him intently. "Wait a minute. How should I know? Whether you . . . had been successful?"

"Before I answer that, Andrew—tell me this. Let's see exactly where we are. If I were successful—would you act?"

"In the circumstances—and knowing what I know now—I think I would."

"Right. Listen then. If I come to the small lounge this evening while you're all in there, and I'm smoking a cigarette, you'll know that I've clicked. On the other hand—no cigarette —nothing doing."

MacMorran listened but made no reply. People were beginning to pass them now, as they stood there at the foot of the main staircase and suddenly there came the beat of the dinner gong. Anthony still waited for MacMorran's decision. Suddenly, the latter turned.

"O.K. As you say! You've never let me down yet. I'll watch for the cigarette."

"How will you play it? The tailpiece, I mean? There mustn't be the slightest hint given. He may not suspect anything even now, but all the same we mustn't give him the chance to think even—in that direction."

"Well," said MacMorran, "I thought about planning something on these lines. Tell me your views on it."

MacMorran spoke at some length. Anthony listened to the suggestions and expressed approval.

"Tell you what you could do, Andrew. You could get Melville in the room first, that wouldn't be at all a bad idea . . . it would make the coast clear as it were . . . and then you could send the message out from the lounge. Once the message is delivered . . . to strengthen it you could say it was an order from Mr. Melville . . . seems to me the trap should spring all right."

MacMorran rubbed his hands as he and Anthony moved off to the dining-room. "By George," he said, "I've caught some of your confidence. I believe we shall pull it off after all."

CHAPTER 11

1

The conference called by the Chief Constable started at a quarter past eight. MacMorran had an early word with Melville and explained to him what had occurred and what would be required. Melville was entirely co-operative and the small lounge was once again placed at the inspector's disposal.

Guthrie was the first to arrive, but was quickly followed by Sir George himself and the Duke of Quinster. Contrary rather to MacMorran's anticipations, the Chief Constable on this occasion showed a more reasonable approach to most matters than he had hitherto displayed. Guthrie was extremely quiet and for a long time the Duke did most of the talking. MacMorran himself was on mental tenter-hooks. To make matters worse for him he was actually aware of it. One part of his brain was occupied with what was going on around him and the other part (the more active) was concerned with the arrangement he had made with Anthony just before dinner.

Much of the discussion was desultory and as point by point was reached and then discarded, MacMorran's glances at his watch became more and more frequent. Suddenly he realised that the Chief Constable had addressed a question to him which he had not answered—or even acknowledged. Sir George Nightingale repeated the question.

"I'm sorry, sir," said MacMorran, "my apologies. My thoughts, I'm afraid, were straying rather. But in reply to your question, I would go so far as to say that we have made very definite progress. In fact we have made so much progress during the last few days that I am very hopeful of making an arrest within a very short time. Certain information reached me late this afternoon which after examination has proved to be most important. It reached me so late that I have not yet had the opportunity of discussing it with anybody. I hope you understand and accept that, sir—and also Inspector Guthrie. It is not anything like conclusive—nothing like as conclusive as I should wish it to be—but nevertheless I cannot blind myself to its distinct importance."

Sir George looked up with a certain amount of surprise showing on his face. "This is gratifying. Very gratifying indeed. To say nothing of being somewhat of a surprise to me. May I ask you the nature of this—"

MacMorran knew that the question was coming which at the moment he had no desire to answer. Would it be possible for him to fend Sir George off in some way?

At that precise moment, the door of the small lounge opened and Anthony entered. MacMorran looked anxiously towards him. The smoke from Anthony's cigarette curled slowly upwards.

2

Anthony entered the room quietly, apologised to the company for his late arrival and took a vacant chair. It was the chair nearest to the door. On his way he had passed through the main lounge and noted that the Grahames and the Danburys were seated therein. MacMorran braced himself for what he knew was coming.

He looked enquiringly towards the Chief Constable who appeared to understand and nodded to him to go on. Up to a point, MacMorran embarked upon a short but succinct explanation. When he reached a certain stage of that explanation he rather surprised the company by saying, "Now that is roughly where we were before Mr. Bathurst's recent arrival. Now that he has joined us, I am able to say that the case for the Crown has been strengthened. Well, gentlemen, I'm going to ask you to leave the matter in my hands—for say the next quarter of an hour."

A surge of sensation passed over the assembled company. "Very well, Inspector," said the Chief Constable, "if you feel as confident about things, as you say you do."

"Thank you," said MacMorran quietly. He went over to the corner by the fireplace and pressed the bell. The company waited—tense and expectant. Not a word was spoken by anybody. The Duke of Quinster fidgeted in his chair. Guthrie stared straight into the fire. Sir George blew out his cheeks in an excellent impersonation of a walrus. MacMorran looked straight ahead of him. Anthony tossed away the stub of the cigarette he had been smoking when he entered and prepared to light another. There came a tap on the door—a light, rather nervous tap.

"Come in," cried the Yard inspector.

To Anthony's surprise, Mrs. Barlow, the housekeeper entered. "One of you gentlemen rang?" she asked with a smile.

"Yes," replied MacMorran. "I did."

"Mr. Melville thought it would be better if I came," explained Mrs. Barlow, "in preference to one of the girls."

MacMorran nodded. "Thank you, Mrs. Barlow. Actually, it's Mr. Melville himself whom we wanted to see. Will you ask him please, if he can spare a minute to step in here?"

"Certainly, sir," replied Mrs. Barlow. "I'll convey your message to him immediately."

Mrs. Barlow turned, smiled again to the people in general and made her exit. The silence that had prevailed previously came back to the room . . . and the company waited.

3

In less than a couple of minutes Melville tapped on the door and then entered to MacMorran's invitation. Anthony thought he looked drawn and tired. Not to be wondered at, thought Anthony again.

"Thanks for coming so promptly, Mr. Melville," said MacMorran, "but we think—all of us—and that includes the Duke of Quinster *and* the Chief Constable, Sir George Nightingale—that it's only fair to you, as proprietor of the hotel here, to be present for the next stage in the proceedings. After all—the staff were engaged by you, presumably, and are actually in your service and the guests are in your care. But the truth of the matter is—I won't beat about the bush—we hope to make an arrest."

"Do you mean, Inspector MacMorran," asked Melville, "an arrest for the murders?"

MacMorran nodded. "That's just what I do mean." Melville mumbled something else which Anthony failed to hear. Evidently MacMorran was in like position. Anthony saw him lean forward and heard him say:

"I didn't catch what you said, Mr. Melville."

Melville said, turning to the others in the room, "What I said, Inspector MacMorran, was that I thought it was going to prove a pretty dreadful business for my hotel. What's already taken place has been bad enough. What you propose to do will just about put the lid on it. I'm sorry—but I must look at things from a business point of view. And I don't like to see my business going west without doing something about it."

MacMorran replied a trifle grimly, "I see your angle, Mr. Melville, but I'm afraid that what's about to happen is inevitable. It's just an unlucky break for you. We all get 'em at times and we must all learn to take the rough with the smooth."

Melville forced a smile to his lips. "Very good, Inspector. Cold comfort eh? I must grin and bear it, I suppose. Very naturally, my interests can't be yours. Anyhow, I've made my protest and it appears that I can do no more than that. Now—what is it that you require me to do?"

MacMorran pointed to an empty seat. "Sit down there, Mr. Melville. I want you to help us. When the time comes I shall ask you and you'll know what to do. In the first place, Mr. Bathurst will give an order to one of your staff—with your permission, of course. And which will appear to emanate from you. If he requires any help, he may be called upon to rope in somebody else. That statement will give you just a roughish idea of the next move we purpose making. Is that O.K.?"

"Quite," replied John Melville; "I'm in your hands, Inspector."

MacMorran spoke across to Anthony. "Do you mind, Mr. Bathurst?"

Anthony slipped quietly out of the room.

4

Melville strained his ears to hear what was going on. Surely nobody on his staff was due to be arrested for murder? Such a happening would be absurd. Too absurd even to be contemplated. And yet MacMorran's recent statements had certainly suggested that something of that kind was on the way. An order to one of his staff. That's what the inspector had just said. The other fellow Bathurst—had gone out to give that order. And it was an order which would appear to the person to whom it was given as having emanated from Melville himself. What on earth were the police thinking of? These Scotland Yard fellows, Inspector Guthrie, the Chief Constable . . .

Melville looked round the room at them. None of them was talking . . . they were just sitting there . . . waiting . . . what the heck were they waiting for? And whom—in the name of conscience? One of the staff? At the Red Deer? The idea was preposterous. But stay a moment—hadn't MacMorran hinted at somebody else? What were the exact words he had used? John Melville began to fidget at his brain. "Rope in!" That was the expression which had been MacMorran's. Somebody else was concerned then—but . . . what was that noise he could hear?

5

When Anthony slipped out of the small lounge at MacMorran's bidding, he made straight for that part of the entrance hall where hung the picture of the 1939 Ascot group taken outside the Red Deer.

He looked up at the picture, as though he were calculating the precise height at which it was hung. The frame was pretty solid and taking its size and shape generally, Anthony could see that his original assessment of them was not very far out. He turned and walked towards the dining-room. He could see the two waitresses busy with various types of glass but he was unable to see the man whom he wanted. Anthony therefore walked through the dining-room, into the corridor, past the Skeggs reception-office and then, close to the River Street door, he spotted the thin, almost shadowy figure of the head-waiter. Anthony went quickly up to him. Bassett turned suddenly and impulsively—almost as though he had been taken by surprise against his will. Anthony touched him on the sleeve.

"Can you spare me a minute, Bassett? Mr. Melville told me to find you. There's something he'd like you to do for me."

"What is it?" inquired Bassett suspiciously.

"If you come this way," replied Anthony, "I'll show you."

6

Bassett accompanied Anthony to the entrance-hall. From his manner, Anthony could tell that he was suspicious and apprehensive. When they came to the place Anthony had in mind, the latter stopped and pointed up to the Ascot picture.

"It's that picture up there, Bassett. Featuring the late Lady Blanchflower amongst others, of course. Mr. Melville wants you to lift it down and take it along to him. He's in the small lounge at the moment."

Bassett grunted. Anthony watched his face carefully. "It's a bit on the 'eavy side, sir," remonstrated the head-waiter.

"More than you can manage—you mean?"

Bassett shrugged his shoulders. "Well—I ain't exactly a superman—am I? Not quite in the 'eavy-weight class."

"You'd like some help with it? Is that the idea?"

"That's it, sir. Then I can take one side—and somebody else the other."

"I can't do it myself," Anthony excused himself, "as I've something else to do almost at once—but I'll see if I can get hold of somebody to give you a hand. Wait here, will you—and I'll be back in a jiffy."

Anthony dashed off in the direction of the main lounge. As he opened the door, he prayed that the luck would hold until the final curtain. The Danburys and the Grahames were still seated round the fire, just as he had seen them earlier in the evening.

"Oh I say," said Anthony apparently to the world at large. "I'm frightfully sorry to disturb you—you look delightfully comfortable—but would one of you chaps give me a hand with something outside? It means helping to move a picture—which is rather on the big side."

Anthony turned suddenly and looked at Stephen Grahame. "Perhaps you wouldn't mind, Mr. Grahame?"

Stephen Grahame blinked his eyes and stood up. "It won't take more than a couple of minutes," said Anthony, "it's awfully decent of you."

Grahame blinked again. "Where do we go from here?" he asked easily.

"Come with me," said Anthony, "and very many thanks."

The two men moved off together.

7

They found Bassett waiting where Anthony had left him. The head-waiter's face wore a puzzled look. He eyed Anthony as though he didn't know what to make of him.

"Here you are, Bassett," said Anthony, "Mr. Grahame has kindly offered to lend me a hand. If you take one side on the lines you suggested, he'll take the other."

Grahame looked up at the picture. "Funny thing—I've never really looked at that picture. Every time I glance at it—I seem to be looking the other way—if you know what I mean. Who wants it now?"

"Mr. Melville," replied Anthony; "there are at least two interesting points about it."

"I don't think I see," said Stephen Grahame, "and yet I suppose I do—in a way."

Bassett found two chairs. He placed one against the wall for himself the other for Stephen Grahame.

"There are two 'angers," said Bassett—"I'll lift mine off first—the one on my side—then you lift off the other one. O.K.?"

"I think I know what you mean," said Grahame. "I pick up ideas pretty quickly. Tell me when you're ready and I'll let you know when I'm not. That's the way it'll probably work out."

Bassett was already on his chair. Grahame stepped up on to his.

"Let's 'ope the cord ain't rotten," said Bassett. "I've known that to 'appen before this."

Anthony watched them. All went well. The picture was lifted from the rail and the two men stepped down. "Thank you very much, gentlemen," said Anthony. "Perhaps Bassett will give it a dusting—and then, if you don't mind, will you please carry it into the small lounge?"

Bassett procured a cloth from one of the waitresses and dusted the picture. He and Grahame then lifted it and carried it into the room of its destination.

8

Anthony tapped on the door of the small lounge and then opened it for Bassett and Grahame to carry the picture in. "Ah," said MacMorran, "that's what I wanted. Thank you, Mr. Bathurst and thank you, gentlemen. Stand it down there against that chair—do you mind? That's right—the very idea—thank you."

As Grahame and Bassett stooped down to put the heavy frame in place, Anthony moved quickly to the door again and stood there with his back against it.

"This picture," said MacMorran, "has become unusually important. As you see, it was taken in 1939. I don't know the name of the proprietor of this hotel at that time. Doubtless Mr. Melville could tell us. But it doesn't matter. The point about the picture is this. What I will describe as the really interesting feature. It is this figure. The one on the other side of the late Lady Blanchflower—whom, no doubt, some of you have already recognised. If you look closely at the figure to which I refer, you will notice—"

MacMorran paused deliberately. Anthony looked round the room at the various faces. As he looked—he knew that there was no doubt. The guilty man's face was eloquent of his knowledge that the game was up!

MacMorran turned quickly from the picture and said: "John Melville . . . I arrest you . . ."

It is doubtful whether any more of the charge was audible, for Melville, his face ashen-grey, slid from his chair to the floor in a dead faint.

CHAPTER 12

1

A nthony handed drinks to MacMorran and Kenneth Whitburn in the dining-room of his flat.

"I appreciate your invitation," said the latter to Anthony, "I appreciate it intensely. Although it may be sad hearing for me, I feel that I'd like to hear the details all the same. I suppose you made me wait until after dinner purposely?"

Anthony smiled. "I did! I always think that sort of thing comes better after you've fed. Draw your chair up to the fire. You as well, Andrew. And I'll take my own chair here in the middle. That's the idea. And now, I'll see if I can oblige Whitburn with the details he's asked me for. Cigarette? Pipe for you, Andrew? Thought so. Right."

Anthony reclined in his chair and thrust out his long legs. "It all began, of course, when Lady Blanchflower wrote to Nigel Carruthers, the trainer. Stables at Queen's Pyland. Carruthers was a second cousin or something of Lady B's—on her mother's side. He's told us all this himself in his letter. She'd noticed, she told him, that one of his horses was engaged in the 'Cambridgeshire' and was actually listed in the bookmakers' Press advertisements. She asked him point blank if she should back it as she was by no means too well-off and could do with a good investment. Carruthers wrote back and told her that his horse had a great chance at the weights and also—if she fancied a 'double' that he'd heard from the best of all sources —the stable concerned—that 'Come Away' was a really sound bet for the 'Cesarewitch'. He told her, too, to keep the information *strictly to herself* and that if she did actually back the horses, she was to give the impression they were merely the 'fancies' of an old lady and in no way inspired. There," said Anthony, as he lifted his glass to drink, "you have what I'll term the 'Prologue'. Lady

Blanchflower in the possession of two items of information each from the absolutely right source—and wondering as to the best way in which she might be enabled to use them to her personal profit."

Whitburn nodded. "And that, of course, is where my poor old lady came in."

"Yes. It brings us to Scene One. The *only* person in whom Lady Blanchflower confided was her friend at the Red Deer, who took her to dinner each evening and who brought her back. And, of course, the question then immediately arose—who would make the bet for them? They would each invest ten pounds but neither of them, naturally, had an account with a bookmaker and they probably chatted their little problem over together more than once. With the result, I think, that it was decided that Mrs. Whitburn, as a permanent resident at the Red Deer, should ask Mr. Melville. He might know somebody who would take the bet and, in the event of it being successful, pay up with promptitude. And when our two ladies made that decision, gentlemen, Fate crooked one of her black fingers at them. For Melville was the wrong man to whom they should have gone. For the reason that he had been losing consistently —and not lightly either—all through the flat-racing season. Fleury's, the bookmakers, had had considerable sums of money from him and there was a great deal more owing. Melville didn't bet in half-crowns."

Kenneth Whitburn leant forward towards the fire. "Yes. I heard the evidence of their Reading manager on Tuesday. Melville had lost consistently ever since March—or as good as."

Anthony continued: "Well, of course, Melville didn't mind obliging his old resident, Mrs. Whitburn. It meant little trouble to him. Just a few minutes' telephoning—no more."

MacMorran interrupted for the first time. "You heard his denials? And you heard his defence? What do you think Mrs. Whitburn actually said to him?"

"Something like this, Andrew. And I'm certain that what I say is right. 'Mr. Melville—I want you to oblige me over something. You know— do me a personal favour. Lady Blanchflower and I are going to have a little bit of fun together. Why shouldn't we? We're going to have a bet—what they call a 'double' for the two big races—the 'Cesarewitch' and the 'Cambridgeshire'. You mustn't tell anybody—because it's an absolute secret between her and me (that was the sop to Carruthers). Lady Blanchflower's picked out a name *she* likes—and I've done the same. We want £10 each—to win—that's £20—now can *you* put it on for us?"

Before Anthony could go on any further, Whitburn nodded again and said: "No doubt about it, Bathurst. I can almost hear the old lady saying it. And, of course, Melville promised to oblige."

"Exactly. With all the contempt that the regular backer of horses invariably feels for the woman who picks her choices out by whim, fantasy, folly and frolic and doesn't appear to know that such things as 'form' exist. Just think of it! The ladies had such sublime confidence in Carruthers's information that they didn't even trouble to make the bet 'each way'. Still—there you are—Scene Two—Melville promises to oblige and 'phones the bet at ante-post conditions to Fleury's, his own Reading bookmakers—little realizing that he is dabbling with some real hot, live information."

Anthony paused—to proceed again within a few seconds—more slowly and more deliberately:

"And here we come, gentlemen, to one of those trifling little incidents—which eventually take on terrific eloquence. It's inception took place, I fancy, something on these lines. I'll make it a dialogue.

> "Mrs. W.   'Now what about the money? Shall I pay you now?' "
> "M.   'No—that's all right, Mrs. W. No need to do that. I'll let   you know when I require it.' "
> "Mrs. W.   'Thank you, Mr. M.' "

Again Anthony paused. Neither of his hearers commented. He therefore proceeded: "I'll return to that incident later. You'll realise its importance much more when I do."

Anthony took one of Kenneth Whitburn's cigarettes and waited for Whitburn to use the lighter.

"Well," he went on, "we can go from there, I think, to the first of the two races. To the Wednesday when the Cesarewitch was run and won by 'Come Away' and the two ladies (and the man who had placed the bet for them) knew that the first leg of the 'double' was home and dry. This was the evening no doubt when Bassett first noticed their condition of excitement. Very natural in the circumstances. But it was the evening, also, when something else was born. I allude, gentlemen, to the idea of murder in the heart of the embryo-murderer."

"Rather early, wasn't it?" queried the inspector.

There was no hesitation in Anthony's answer. "Yes. But let us collect all the data and have a look at them. Melville was none too sound financially. And like a large percentage of inveterate gamblers, he was avaricious. In his hands—from the executive point of view—was the possibility of a wonderful 'double' coming home. Something in the thirty-thousand quid line. He began to think things. And a clever, cunningly-contrived scheme began to dance in his brain. As far as he could see, in these early stages, he could pull it off, if the chance did come, at the paltry expenditure of twenty pounds. And with care and calculated cunning, he could divert any suspicion that might raise its head, to an innocent party. The beauty of the scheme lay in this. *There would be nothing whatever to connect him with the crime he had begun to contemplate.* Although he would act as *diabolus ex machina* his name would never show in the affair at all. For here is how he planned.

"(A) If the 'double' did come off, the money would be paid to him without question by the bookmaker. It was his account that had been used, he had placed the bet—the two ladies were dead all through the act. So far so good. (B) He would ask Mrs. Whitburn at once for her cheque in payment of the stake involved and instruct her as to the name of the payee—which would be that of his bookmaker. This request he actually put into effect on the following morning, October the 20th. Whichever way he ultimately jumped—no harm would accrue by reason of his holding the Whitburn cheque. (C) He would then implicate Mrs. Whitburn to the hilt. He'd think of something in the interval between then and say, the next of the races. And what he would think of, would pivot mainly on the Fleury cheque that by that time would be in his pocket. He *would be prepared—in good time—*in case!" Anthony stopped again. He saw that the glasses were empty and rose to replenish them. "You're following me, I take it? Or is there anything that I—"

The two men to whom he spoke assured him of their understanding. Anthony filled the three glasses again and returned to his chair.

"We'll call that," he said, "the end of Scene Three."

2

There came a short period of silence. MacMorran drank. The best way that he knew of drowning both care and silence. Anthony began again.

"As Melville coquetted with his idea of double murder, he concentrated mainly on the idea of the implication of the innocent Mrs. Whitburn. He reasoned in this fashion. If Lady Blanchflower were found dead, strangled . . . shall we say . . . by one of Mrs. Whitburn's silk stockings . . . and something else were found by the body . . . which could be definitely traced to Mrs. Whitburn . . . and Mrs. Whitburn herself suddenly disappeared . . . and remained missing for some considerable time . . . he failed to see how suspicion could ever reasonably be laid at his own door. Why should it be? *There wouldn't be the faintest suggestion of a motive*—the bet transaction need never be known to anybody beyond the principals—himself and Fleury—if it were, there wasn't anything to connect it with the two women . . . nobody would ever dream of such a thing . . . two old ladies like that . . . indeed it was *against* his interest to lose Mrs. Whitburn as a resident in his hotel . . . in a lesser degree, this argument also applied to Lady Blanchflower . . . thus his brain worked. And from that point it moved to the matter of the cheque in his pocket. Made out to T. Fleury, his bookmaker. You see the trend, don't you?"

His two hearers assented. "You mean," said Kenneth Whitburn, "that T. Fleury was the one person in the world to whom that cheque mustn't be paid. Otherwise it would establish the connection between—"

Anthony cut in eagerly. "Exactly. Melville saw at once what his next step must be. He searched the London Telephone directory for another Fleury. And for one who possessed a not too inconvenient initial or initials. You know whom he found. Isaac Fleury of Long Acre, the perruquier and wig-maker. How simple to put a stroke at the foot of Mrs. Whitburn's 'T' to turn it into an 'I'. Still—wigs! Wigs weren't perhaps, the best of commodities from his point of view. Could they be used to implicate Mrs. Whitburn? It wanted thinking out."

"I suppose that's Scene Four—eh?" grinned MacMorran.

"Just about, Andrew. But the figure of Melville has emerged clearly. The plot is in his mind. He knows what he will do if he ultimately decides to do it. The days go by. Until . . . shall we say . . . somewhere about the week-end which preceded the race for the 'Cambridgeshire'. The date would be, say, round about the last days of October. Melville is waiting . . . wondering . . . weighing chances and, on the Monday following, perhaps, he determines *to complete the preparations* on the following day. He put an anonymous telephone-call through to Isaac Fleury as to their terms and he found that by a stroke of almost incredibly good fortune, their deposit terms for the hire of two wigs came to exactly twenty pounds. The exact figure of the Whitburn cheque he held in his possession. Thus does Fate beckon to and inveigle those victims upon whose destruction she is bent."

"Why was that," questioned Whitburn, "seeing that the race wasn't until the Wednesday?"

"A good question," rejoined Anthony, "and one that I more than once asked myself. I think the reason was this. Your mother always went to her club on a Tuesday. Melville knew that better than anybody. She had done so for years. If the wigs of the Fleury substitution plot were ordered the day she was in Town to be delivered to her at the Muliera Club, he had taken a fair stride towards his 'suspicion-casting' idea. So it had to be Tuesday from his angle—again whether he ultimately went the whole hog or not."

Whitburn nodded. "I see. You're right, of course."

"Thank you," said Anthony; "we know what he did—and how he contrived to get hold of the wigs himself. Which is another point to which I'll return later."

"What made him choose *Caste*?" asked Andrew MacMorran; "bit dated, wasn't it?"

"Probably, I think, Andrew, for two reasons. It was a play he knew and had in all likelihood seen years ago somewhere, and in it there was a wig required for an elderly lady. Which, if found by the police in certain circumstances would, so he argued, probably clutter up the minds of the authorities and be yet another factor in the general scheme of diverting suspicion."

MacMorran shook his head. Anthony noticed the gesture. "What's the trouble, Andrew? Not in agreement?"

"In agreement—generally. But not in particular relation to the female wig. I don't know if wigs have a sex—but you know what I mean. It was that particular wig he didn't use. He used the man's wig. The other was hidden in the bonfire."

Anthony nodded. "I know. He changed his mind, I suggest. The male wig—under Lady Blanchflower's body—was used, I fancy, to bolster up the *possible* idea of a night-marauder. The question was bound to be asked. Had a man been in the Blanchflower apartments? On the other hand, Andrew, and I don't entirely rule out the possibility, Melville *may have picked up the wrong box* on the evening of Thursday, November 3rd."

"We've almost reached that, haven't we?" queried Kenneth Whitburn.

"Not quite. We mustn't skip the 'Cambridge'. Don't forget that. When the result came through early on that Wednesday afternoon that "Mistress Quickly" had gone by, Melville was all set. Eliminate the two old ladies—and there was a little matter of thirty thousand in his pocket. Should he? Or should he not? He hadn't much time for soliloquy—remember. At the end of the week, or early in the next, Mrs. Whitburn would expect payment. Should he? Or should he not? He deliberated all the remainder of the Wednesday, nearly all day Thursday . . . until perhaps . . . say 6 p.m."

Anthony rose to find more cigarettes, MacMorran stared at him.

"How do you mean—6 p.m.? I don't think I get that." Anthony found cigarettes and came back to his chair.

3

He smiled at MacMorran. "A long shot, perhaps, Andrew. But all the same I think I'm right. The radio announcement, Andrew. That thick fog or mist was likely in all river districts and close to large towns. Thick fog! Or mist! And he knew the path into Quinster Castle much better than the next man. He could slip by Catterall in a mist with but little trouble. Money for old rope! If the ladies came to dinner, and unless the fog was too bad, they would, he'd strangle them in Lady Blanchflower's place *when they returned.* It would all depend how the weather went. Gentlemen, for the matter of murder, it went well. A mist round about seven o'clock, the ladies came to the Red Deer for their usual evening meal, and after that it gradually got worse. Melville went to Mrs. Whitburn's room for the stocking—don't forget that if necessary he had a master-key of all rooms in the hotel—and was then ready for the deed. Now might he do it pat! He followed the two ladies out, slipped by Catterall, slipped into the apartment behind them—"

Anthony broke off and shrugged his shoulders. Whitburn was visibly affected. Anthony waited for him to pull himself together."

"The unspeakable swine," said Whitburn. "I hope he'll enjoy what's coming to him. And to hide my mother's body—as he did—and where he did! When I think of it—" He clenched his hands.

"It might have lain there for weeks," said Anthony; "it was right at the bottom. It's astonishing how long the bottom of those affairs can often remain undisturbed. The work is nearly always done from the top. I've noticed it frequently."

He broke off. "Well—there you are, gentlemen—there you have the story of the crime."

4

"Now for the solution," continued Anthony. "I'm afraid that, generally speaking, I cut an inglorious figure. Pretty well all through the piece. I was almost culpably negligent. For the reason that for so long I was blind to the most vital clue of all. I allowed my mind to be side-tracked . . . and this occurred not only once but even three or four times. You know, of course, the clue to which I refer?"

Whitburn said, "The slip of paper in my mother's chequebook?"

"No; I'll deal with that in a few moments. No—not that. What do you say, Andrew?"

"Well the cheque, I suppose. But I don't know that I quite see how you mean—exactly."

"The vital clue," said Anthony, "was the date on the cheque. Why should a person draw a cheque on October the 20th as a deposit for articles not ordered until November the 1st—an interval of twelve days? One or two days, perhaps—but certainly not twelve. I tell you—I puzzled over the conditions of that cheque for nights and days. Until at last I began to toy with the idea of a substitution of some kind. And here again, I'm afraid I was far from bright. I should have deduced the existence of a second Fleury."

Whitburn shook his head. "You blame yourself unduly. I think, taking the case all through, your work was amazingly clever."

"Very nice of you—but you're too kind. Incidentally, it was Melville who led me to the second Fleury. He was hoist with his own petard, as the Victorian novelists used to say—and this is the way it went. I happened to tell him I wanted to glance at the local paper that used to decorate the Red Deer lounge once a week. When the paper reached me, I noticed that an advertisement had been cut out. This aroused my curiosity —so much so that I tested the edition of the paper for the previous week."

Anthony stopped and smiled.

"The previous paper had been treated in similar fashion. Naturally after that—I saw it through. The advertisement that had been removed was T. Fleury's. Melville, you see, had done all he knew in that direction to prevent that name or that firm reaching my eyes or my knowledge—to say nothing of the inspector's. When I found the second Fleury, I was in the straight. I knew 'why' even though I mightn't be sure as to 'whom'."

Anthony rose and stood with his arm on the corner of the mantelpiece.

"The remaining clues—there were two big ones—almost fell into my lap. One—because my brain has a habit of playing funny tricks, usually parented by the association of ideas, and the other because my eyes spotted something very suddenly —which previously they had been content to miss. I'll tell you about the 'brain' clue first. When I was ferreting after the cheque business, I remembered that Mrs. Whitburn had drawn a cheque, fairly recently, to a firm by the name of 'Page, Ingram and Co.' At the time, I was following up anything and everything and I decided, especially as I discovered it was a local firm, to give them a look. To my surprise, I found that the head of the firm was a woman. A widow. A Mrs. Page. As I was leaving the premises I happened to say to myself 'so much for Mistress Page'. You can easily guess the 'sequence' thoughts that immediately followed. They were 'Mistress Ford' and 'Dame Quickly'. The Merry Wives of Quinster—eh?

"Then the rest of the thought-association came. Quickly. Mistress Quickly. Mistress Quickly! Hadn't a horse of that name won a big race recently? My thoughts pranced violently—but I had been in Switzerland in October and hadn't particularly noticed the English sporting results. But the word 'quickly' had been in the message which Lady Blanchflower had passed to Mrs. Whitburn. The latter, as we had discovered, had placed it on record. Amongst other purposes to tell *you*, Whitburn! Then, gentlemen, for the first time, perhaps, I began to feel I was 'getting warm'."

Anthony came away from the mantelpiece and sat down again.

"Cigarette," said Whitburn, case in hand. Anthony took one. "I then began to concentrate," he went on, "on the words that Mrs. Whitburn had written. The words of the real message. 'Lil says "come quickly—mistress away".' Do you remember, either of you, another phrase that she used? In connection with the word 'telegram'?" Anthony waited for an answer.

5

It was Kenneth Whitburn who supplied it. "I think," he said, "that I can answer that. Wasn't it what a telegram they would make? Or near enough?"

Anthony smiled. "It was. And I was unable to understand for a long time why she had used the plural. Why she had written '*they* would make' instead of '*it* would make'. I should have hammered away at that instead of going away from it. She had done so, of course, because she had been referring to two horses. That slip of paper was the one link and the one link only between the two ladies and the two horses, that was on record anywhere. And Melville, of course, was unaware of its existence. When he went to the cheque-book stub afterwards to stroke the base of the "T" he couldn't have noticed it. At the same time," proceeded Anthony, "it was a weak link and its weakness proved our temporary undoing. Mrs. Danbury had told us, Inspector MacMorran and me, that your mother's was a strange, unreliable, mixed-up kind of brain that had a habit of reversing things, of twisting ends till they tangled. You, Whitburn—when I asked you—confirmed Mrs. Danbury's opinion. And that's what had happened. Lady Blanchflower's tips from the famous Carruthers stable had been "Come Away" and "Mistress Quickly." Your mother's genius for getting things of that sort round her neck, had twisted them to 'Come Quickly—Mistress Away'. And that's the way it so often goes. The tiny discrepancy which creates a gulf of meaning."

Anthony paused again and looked whimsically at his two companions. "Now what else is there?"

"The other clue we picked up," said MacMorran, "the one you spotted and brought me into. Mr. Whitburn hasn't heard about that."

"Oh—yes—of course. The clue that really clinched the issue. It was a gift from Olympus. In the entrance-hall of the Red Deer, I noticed a group-photograph. It was pre-war and had been taken just outside the hotel. By a strange coincidence, Lady Blanchflower was in it. Whom else do you think it showed?"

Whitburn shook his head. "I'm afraid I haven't the foggiest notion. And it wouldn't be any good if I started guessing."

"A man," replied Anthony, "in the uniform of a commissionaire—in other words—the commissionaire at that time at the Red Deer. It had been the hotel custom, in pre-war days, so we've learned since, to employ a man in that capacity. When I saw it, my brain went on time and a half. I began to wonder and went on wondering. There were the coat and the peaked cap that fitted the description given to me by Fleury's messenger.

Was the uniform still on the premises and had Melville had access to it? It was certainly a distinct possibility. Later on, when Andrew here called Melville in to a conference, I went exploring in the upper parts of the Red Deer—all round its antlers shall we say. I ran the uniform to earth in one of the gentleman's cupboards. The man who had worn it in 1939 had been called to the Services and had left it behind for the use of his successor. But owing to the war, no successor was ever appointed and the only man to wear it again was Melville himself. He was of normal build for a uniform of that kind and used it for his visit to the Muliera Club. By taking his left arm out of the sleeve he contrived to give the impression that he had lost it. In addition he put up a small moustache which he had obtained previously. Very probably, I think, also from Fleury's. Isaac—this time. Over the counter. But that's immaterial."

Anthony chuckled. "While he was engaged in removing paragraphs from local papers, it would have paid him better dividends to have shifted that picture. When he saw it brought in to the conference—Inspector MacMorran and I decided we'd use it in that way if I found the uniform—he knew the game was up. He just crumpled up and collapsed. And now, I fancy, you've got the full story.'

Anthony rose and stretched his arms. MacMorran looked up at him with an air of profound wisdom.

"It only goes to show you," he said, "all that marvellous 'double' brought was trouble. Trouble! Toil and trouble."

"I rather fancy, Andrew," said Anthony, "that something like that has been said before. By a greater than you, Andrew. 'Double, double toil and trouble; Fire burn…' but why waste our time on witches? Aren't there more attractive possibilities?"

"There should be," said Kenneth Whitburn.

"There are," said Anthony.

THE END

9 781917 382106